HIS DARK MATERIALS

Northern
Lights

Also by Philip Pullman

His Dark Materials
The Subtle Knife
The Amber Spyglass

Lyra's Oxford

The Sally Lockhart Quartet
The Ruby in the Smoke
The Shadow in the North
The Tiger in the Well
The Tin Princess

The New Cut Gang
Thunderbolt's Waxwork
The Gas-Fitters' Ball

Contemporary Novels
The Broken Bridge
The Butterfly Tattoo

Books with Pictures and Fairy Tales
The Scarecrow and his Servant
Spring-Heeled Jack
Count Karlstein
The Firework-Maker's Daughter
I Was A Rat!
Puss in Boots
Mossycoat
Aladdin
Clockwork

Plays
Frankenstein *(adaptation)*
Sherlock Holmes and the Limehouse Horror

HIS DARK MATERIALS

Northern Lights

Philip Pullman

SCHOLASTIC

www.philip-pullman.com

Scholastic Children's Books
An imprint of Scholastic Ltd
Euston House, 24 Eversholt Street, London, NW1 1DB, UK
Registered office: Westfield Road, Southam, Warwickshire, CV47 0RA
SCHOLASTIC and associated logos are trademarks and or registered trademarks of Scholastic Inc.

First published in the UK by Scholastic Ltd, 1995
This edition published by Scholastic Ltd, 2007

10 digit ISBN 1 407 10254 2
13 digit ISBN 978 1 407 10254 2

A CIP catalogue record for this book is available from the British Library

Printed by CPI Mackays of Chatham plc

Papers used by Scholastic Children's Books
are made from wood grown in sustainable forests.

3 5 7 9 10 8 6 4

www.scholastic.co.uk/zone

Into this wild abyss,
The womb of nature and perhaps her grave,
Of neither sea, nor shore, nor air, nor fire,
But all these in their pregnant causes mixed
Confusedly, and which thus must ever fight,
Unless the almighty maker them ordain
His dark materials to create more worlds,
Into this wild abyss the wary fiend
Stood on the brink of hell and looked a while,
Pondering his voyage...

John Milton: *Paradise Lost,* Book II

NORTHERN LIGHTS is the first part of a story in three volumes. The first volume is set in a universe just like ours, but different in many ways. The second volume, THE SUBTLE KNIFE, moves between three universes: the universe of NORTHERN LIGHTS; the universe we know; and a third universe, which differs from ours in many ways again. The final volume of the trilogy, THE AMBER SPYGLASS, moves between several universes.

Note: the word dæmon which appears throughout the book, is to be pronounced like the English word "demon".

Contents

Part Three: *Svalbard*

Part One

Oxford

1

The Decanter of Tokay

*L*yra and her dæmon moved through the darkening Hall, taking care to keep to one side, out of sight of the kitchen. The three great tables that ran the length of the Hall were laid already, the silver and the glass catching what little light there was, and the long benches were pulled out ready for the guests. Portraits of former Masters hung high up in the gloom along the walls. Lyra reached the dais and looked back at the open kitchen door and, seeing no one, stepped up beside the high table. The places here were laid with gold, not silver, and the fourteen seats were not oak benches but mahogany chairs with velvet cushions.

Lyra stopped beside the Master's chair and flicked the biggest glass gently with a fingernail. The sound rang clearly through the Hall.

"You're not taking this seriously," whispered her dæmon. "Behave yourself."

Her dæmon's name was Pantalaimon, and he was currently in the form of a moth, a dark brown one so as not to show up in the darkness of the Hall.

"They're making too much noise to hear from the kitchen," Lyra whispered back. "And the Steward doesn't come in till the first bell. Stop fussing."

But she put her palm over the ringing crystal anyway, and Pantalaimon fluttered ahead and through the slightly open door of the Retiring Room at the other end of the dais. After a moment he appeared again.

"There's no one there," he whispered. "But we must be quick."

Crouching behind the high table, Lyra darted along and through the door into the Retiring Room, where she stood up and looked around. The only light in here came from the fireplace, where a bright blaze of logs settled slightly as she looked, sending a fountain of sparks up into the chimney. She had lived most of her life in the College, but had never seen the Retiring Room before: only Scholars and their guests were allowed in here, and never females. Even the maidservants didn't clean in here. That was the Butler's job alone.

Pantalaimon settled on her shoulder.

"Happy now? Can we go?" he whispered.

"Don't be silly! I want to look around!"

It was a large room, with an oval table of polished rosewood on which stood various decanters and glasses, and a silver smoking-mill with a rack of pipes. On a sideboard nearby there was a little chafing-dish and a basket of poppy-heads.

"They do themselves well, don't they, Pan?" she said under her breath.

She sat in one of the green leather armchairs. It was so deep she found herself nearly lying down, but she sat up again and tucked her legs under her to look at the portraits on the walls. More old Scholars, probably: robed, bearded and gloomy, they stared out of their frames in solemn disapproval.

"What d'you think they talk about?" Lyra said, or began to say, because before she'd finished the question she heard voices outside the door.

"Behind the chair – quick!" whispered Pantalaimon, and in a flash Lyra was out of the armchair and crouching behind it. It wasn't the best one for hiding behind: she'd chosen one in the very centre of the room, and unless she kept very quiet...

The door opened, and the light changed in the room: one of the incomers was carrying a lamp, which he put down on the sideboard. Lyra could see his legs, in their dark green trousers and shiny black shoes. It was a servant.

Then a deep voice said, "Has Lord Asriel arrived yet?"

It was the Master. As Lyra held her breath she saw the servant's dæmon (a dog, like almost all servants' dæmons) trot in and sit quietly at his feet, and then the Master's feet became visible too, in the shabby black shoes he always wore.

"No, Master," said the Butler. "No word from the Aërodock, either."

"I expect he'll be hungry when he arrives. Show him straight into Hall, will you?"

"Very good, Master."

"And you've decanted some of the special Tokay for him?"

"Yes, Master. The 1898, as you ordered. His Lordship is very partial to that, I remember."

"Good. Now leave me, please."

"Do you need the lamp, Master?"

"Yes, leave that too. Look in during dinner to trim it, will you?"

The Butler bowed slightly and turned to leave, his dæmon trotting obediently after him. From her not-much-of-a-hiding place Lyra watched as the Master went to a large oak wardrobe in the corner of the room, took his gown from a hanger, and pulled it laboriously on. The Master had been a powerful man, but he was well over seventy now, and his movements were stiff and slow. The Master's dæmon had the form of a raven, and as soon as his robe was on, she jumped down from the wardrobe and settled in her accustomed place on his right shoulder.

Lyra could feel Pantalaimon bristling with anxiety, though he made no sound. For herself, she was pleasantly excited. The visitor mentioned by the Master, Lord Asriel, was her uncle, a man whom she admired and feared greatly. He was said to be involved in high politics, in secret exploration, in distant warfare, and she never knew when he was going to appear. He was fierce: if he caught her in here she'd be severely punished, but she could put up with that.

What she saw next, however, changed things completely.

The Master took from his pocket a folded paper and laid it on the table. He took the stopper out of the mouth of a decanter containing a rich golden wine, unfolded the paper, and poured a thin stream of white powder into the decanter before crumpling the paper and throwing it into the fire. Then he took a pencil from his pocket and stirred the wine until the powder had dissolved, and replaced the stopper.

His dæmon gave a soft brief squawk. The Master replied in an undertone, and looked around with his hooded, clouded eyes before leaving through the door he'd come in by.

Lyra whispered, "Did you see that, Pan?"

"Of course I did! Now hurry out, before the Steward comes!"

But as he spoke, there came the sound of a bell ringing once from the far end of the Hall.

"That's the Steward's bell!" said Lyra. "I thought we had more time than that."

Pantalaimon fluttered swiftly to the Hall door, and swiftly back.

"The Steward's there already," he said. "And you can't get out of the other door…"

The other door, the one the Master had entered and left by, opened on to the busy corridor between the Library and the Scholars' Common Room. At this time of day it was thronged with men pulling on their gowns for dinner, or hurrying to leave papers or briefcases in the Common Room before moving into the Hall. Lyra had planned to leave the way she'd come, banking on another few minutes before the Steward's bell rang.

And if she hadn't seen the Master tipping that powder into the wine she might have risked the Steward's anger, or hoped to avoid being noticed in the busy corridor. But she was confused, and that made her hesitate.

Then she heard heavy footsteps on the dais. The Steward was coming to make sure the Retiring Room was ready for the Scholars' poppy and wine after dinner. Lyra darted to the oak wardrobe, opened it, and hid inside, pulling the door shut just as the Steward entered. She had no fear for Pantalaimon: the room was sombre-coloured, and he could always creep under a chair.

She heard the Steward's heavy wheezing, and through the crack where the door hadn't quite shut she saw him adjust the pipes in the rack by the smoking-mill and cast a glance over the decanters and glasses. Then he smoothed the hair over his ears with both palms and said something to his dæmon. He was a servant, so she was a dog; but a superior servant, so a superior dog. In fact, she had the form of a red setter. The dæmon seemed suspicious, and cast around as if she'd sensed an intruder, but didn't make for the wardrobe, to Lyra's intense relief. Lyra was afraid of the Steward, who had twice beaten her.

Lyra heard a tiny whisper; obviously Pantalaimon had squeezed in beside her.

"We're going to have to stay here now. Why don't you listen to me?"

She didn't reply until the Steward had left. It was his job to supervise the waiting at the high table; she could hear the Scholars coming into the Hall, the murmur of voices, the shuffle of feet.

"It's a good thing I didn't," she whispered back. "We wouldn't have seen the Master put poison in the wine otherwise. Pan, that was the Tokay he asked the Butler about! They're going to kill Lord Asriel!"

"You don't know it's poison."

"Oh, of course it is. Don't you remember, he made the Butler leave the room before he did it? If it was innocent it wouldn't have mattered the Butler seeing. And I *know* there's something going on – something political. The servants have been talking about it for days. Pan, we could prevent a murder!"

"I've never heard such nonsense," he said shortly. "How do you think you're going to keep still for four hours in this poky wardrobe? Let me go and look in the corridor. I'll tell you when it's clear."

He fluttered from her shoulder, and she saw his little shadow appear in the crack of light.

"It's no good, Pan, I'm staying," she said. "There's another robe or something here. I'll put that on the floor and make myself comfortable. I've just *got* to see what they do."

She had been crouching. She carefully stood up, feeling around for the clothes-hangers in order not to make a noise, and found that the wardrobe was bigger than she'd thought. There were several academic robes and hoods, some with fur around them, most faced with silk.

"I wonder if these are all the Master's?" she whispered. "When he gets honorary degrees from other places, perhaps they give him fancy robes and he keeps them here for dressing up… Pan, do you really think it's not poison in that wine?"

"No," he said. "I think it is, like you do. And I think it's none of our business. And I think it would be the silliest thing you've ever done in a lifetime of silly things to interfere. It's nothing to do with us."

"Don't be stupid," Lyra said. "I can't sit in here and watch them give him poison!"

"Come somewhere else, then."

"You're a coward, Pan."

"Certainly I am. May I ask what you intend to do? Are you going to leap out and snatch the glass from his trembling fingers? What did you have in mind?"

"I didn't have anything in mind, and well you know it," she snapped quietly. "But now I've seen what the Master did, I haven't got any choice. You're supposed to know about conscience, aren't you? How can I just go and sit in the Library or somewhere and twiddle my thumbs, knowing what's going to happen? I don't intend to do *that*, I promise you."

"This is what you wanted all the time," he said after a moment. "You wanted to hide in here and watch. Why didn't I realize that before?"

"All right, I do," she said. "Everyone knows they get up to something secret. They have a ritual or something. And I just wanted to know what it was."

"It's none of our business! If they want to enjoy their little secrets you should just feel superior and let them get on with it. Hiding and spying is for silly children."

"Exactly what I knew you'd say. Now stop nagging."

The two of them sat in silence for a while, Lyra uncomfortable on the hard floor of the wardrobe and Pantalaimon self-righteously twitching his temporary antennae on one of the robes. Lyra felt a mixture of thoughts contending in her head, and she would have liked nothing better than to share them with her dæmon, but she was proud too. Perhaps she should try to clear them up without his help.

Her main thought was anxiety, and it wasn't for herself. She'd been in trouble often enough to be used to it. This time she was anxious about Lord Asriel, and about what this all meant. It wasn't often that he visited the College, and the fact that this was a time of high political tension meant that he hadn't come simply to eat and drink and smoke with a few old friends. She knew that both Lord Asriel and the Master were members of the Cabinet Council, the Prime Minister's special advisory body, so it might have been something to do with that; but meetings of the Cabinet Council were held in the Palace, not in the Retiring Room of Jordan College.

Then there was the rumour that had been keeping the College servants whispering for days. It was said that the Tartars had invaded Muscovy, and were surging north to St Petersburg, from where they would be able to dominate the Baltic Sea and eventually overcome the entire west of Europe. And Lord Asriel had been in the far North: when she'd seen him last, he was preparing an expedition to Lapland...

"Pan," she whispered.

"Yes?"

"Do *you* think there'll be a war?"

"Not yet. Lord Asriel wouldn't be dining here if it was going to break out in the next week or so."

"That's what I thought. But later?"

"Sssh! Someone's coming."

She sat up and put her eye to the crack of the door. It was the Butler, coming to trim the lamp as the Master had ordered him to. The Common Room and the Library were lit by anbaric light, but the Scholars preferred the older, softer naphtha lamps in the Retiring

Room. They wouldn't change that in the Master's lifetime.

The Butler trimmed the wick, and put another log on the fire as well, and then listened carefully at the Hall door before helping himself to a handful of leaf from the smoking-mill.

He had hardly replaced the lid when the handle of the other door turned, making him jump nervously. Lyra tried not to laugh. The Butler hastily stuffed the leaf into his pocket and turned to face the incomer.

"Lord Asriel!" he said, and a shiver of cold surprise ran down Lyra's back. She couldn't see him from where she was, and she tried to smother the urge to move and look.

"Good evening, Wren," said Lord Asriel. Lyra always heard that harsh voice with a mixture of pleasure and apprehension. "I arrived too late to dine. I'll wait in here."

The Butler looked uncomfortable. Guests entered the Retiring Room at the Master's invitation only, and Lord Asriel knew that; but the Butler also saw Lord Asriel looking pointedly at the bulge in his pocket, and decided not to protest.

"Shall I let the Master know you've arrived, my lord?"

"No harm in that. You might bring me some coffee."

"Very good, my lord."

The Butler bowed and hastened out, his dæmon trotting submissively at his heels. Lyra's uncle moved across to the fire and stretched his arms high above his head, yawning like a lion. He was wearing travelling clothes. Lyra was reminded, as she always was when she saw him again, of how much he frightened her. There was no question now of creeping out unnoticed: she'd have to sit tight and hope.

Lord Asriel's dæmon, a snow leopard, stood behind him.

"Are you going to show the projections in here?" she said quietly.

"Yes. It'll create less fuss than moving to the Lecture Theatre. They'll want to see the specimens, too; I'll send for the Porter in a minute. This is a bad time, Stelmaria."

"You should rest."

He stretched out in one of the armchairs, so that Lyra could no longer see his face.

"Yes, yes. I should also change my clothes. There's probably some ancient etiquette that allows them to fine me a dozen bottles for coming in here dressed improperly. I should sleep for three days. The fact remains that —"

There was a knock, and the Butler came in with a silver tray bearing a coffee-pot and a cup.

"Thank you, Wren," said Lord Asriel. "Is that the Tokay I can see on the table?"

"The Master ordered it decanted especially for you, my lord," said the Butler. "There are only three dozen bottles left of the '98."

"All good things pass away. Leave the tray here beside me. Oh, ask the Porter to send up the two cases I left in the Lodge, would you?"

"Here, my lord?"

"Yes, here, man. And I shall need a screen and a projecting lantern, also here, also now."

The Butler could hardly prevent himself from opening his mouth in surprise, but managed to suppress the question, or the protest.

"Wren, you're forgetting your place," said Lord Asriel. "Don't question me; just do as I tell you."

"Very good, my lord," said the Butler. "If I may suggest it, I should perhaps let Mr Cawson know what you're planning, my lord, or else he'll be somewhat taken aback, if you see what I mean."

"Yes. Tell him, then."

Mr Cawson was the Steward. There was an old and well-established rivalry between him and the Butler. The Steward was the superior, but the Butler had more opportunities to ingratiate himself with the Scholars, and made full use of them. He would be delighted to have this chance of showing the Steward that he knew more about what was going on in the Retiring Room.

He bowed and left. Lyra watched as her uncle poured a cup of coffee, drained it at once, and poured another before sipping more slowly. She was agog: cases of specimens? A projecting lantern? What did he have to show the Scholars that was so urgent and important?

Then Lord Asriel stood up and turned away from the fire. She saw him fully, and marvelled at the contrast he made with the plump Butler, the stooped and languid Scholars. Lord Asriel was a tall man with powerful shoulders, a fierce dark face, and eyes that seemed to flash and glitter with savage laughter. It was a face to be dominated by, or to fight: never a face to patronize or pity. All his movements were large and perfectly balanced, like those of a wild animal, and when he appeared in a room like this, he seemed a wild animal held in a cage too small for it.

At the moment his expression was distant and preoccupied. His dæmon came close and leant her head on his waist, and he looked down at her unfathomably before turning away and walking to the table. Lyra suddenly felt her stomach lurch, for Lord Asriel had taken the stopper from the decanter of Tokay, and was pouring a glass.

"No!"

The quiet cry came before she could hold it back. Lord Asriel heard and turned at once.

"Who's there?"

She couldn't help herself. She tumbled out of the wardrobe and scrambled up to snatch the glass from his hand. The wine flew out, splashing on the edge of the table and the carpet, and then the glass fell and smashed. He seized her wrist and twisted hard.

"Lyra! What the hell are you doing?"

"Let go of me and I'll tell you!"

"I'll break your arm first. How dare you come in here?"

"I've just saved your life!"

They were still for a moment, the girl twisted in pain but grimacing to prevent herself from crying out louder, the man bent over her frowning like thunder.

"What did you say?" he said more quietly.

"That wine is poisoned," she muttered between clenched teeth. "I saw the Master put some powder in it."

He let go. She sank to the floor, and Pantalaimon fluttered anxiously to her shoulder. Her uncle looked down with a restrained fury, and she didn't dare meet his eyes.

"I came in just to see what the room was like," she said. "I know I shouldn't have. But I was going to go out before anyone came in, except that I heard the Master coming and got trapped. The wardrobe was the only place to hide. And I saw him put the powder in the wine. If I hadn't –"

There was a knock on the door.

"That'll be the Porter," said Lord Asriel. "Back in the wardrobe. If I hear the slightest noise I'll make you wish you were dead."

She darted back there at once, and no sooner had she pulled the door shut than Lord Asriel called, "Come in."

As he'd said, it was the Porter.

"In here, my lord?"

Lyra saw the old man standing doubtfully in the doorway, and behind him, the corner of a large wooden box.

12

"That's right, Shuter," said Lord Asriel. "Bring them both in and put them down by the table."

Lyra relaxed a little, and allowed herself to feel the pain in her shoulder and wrist. It might have been enough to make her cry, if she was the sort of girl who cried. Instead she gritted her teeth and moved the arm gently until it felt looser.

Then came a crash of glass and the glug of spilled liquid.

"Damn you, Shuter, you careless old fool! Look what you've done!"

Lyra could see, just. Her uncle had managed to knock the decanter of Tokay off the table, and made it look as if the Porter had done it. The old man put the box down carefully and began to apologize.

"I'm truly sorry, my lord – I must have been closer than I thought –"

"Get something to clear this mess up. Go on, before it soaks into the carpet!"

The Porter and his young assistant hurried out. Lord Asriel moved closer to the wardrobe and spoke in an undertone.

"Since you're in there, you can make yourself useful. Watch the Master closely when he comes in. If you tell me something interesting about him, I'll keep you from getting further into the trouble you're already in. Understand?"

"Yes, Uncle."

"Make a noise in there and I won't help you. You're on your own."

He moved away and stood with his back to the fire again as the Porter came back with a brush and dustpan for the glass and a bowl and cloth.

"I can only say once again, my lord, I do most earnestly beg your pardon; I don't know what –"

"Just clear up the mess."

As the Porter began to mop the wine from the carpet, the Butler knocked and came in with Lord Asriel's manservant, a man called

Thorold. They were carrying between them a heavy case of polished wood with brass handles. They saw what the Porter was doing and stopped dead.

"Yes, it was the Tokay," said Lord Asriel. "Too bad. Is that the lantern? Set it up by the wardrobe, Thorold, if you would. I'll have the screen up at the other end."

Lyra realized that she would be able to see the screen and whatever was on it through the crack in the door, and wondered whether her uncle had arranged it like that for the purpose. Under the noise the manservant made unrolling the stiff linen and setting it up on its frame, she whispered:

"See? It was worth coming, wasn't it?"

"It might be," Pantalaimon said austerely, in his tiny moth-voice. "And it might not."

Lord Asriel stood by the fire sipping the last of the coffee and watching darkly as Thorold opened the case of the projecting lantern and uncapped the lens before checking the oil-tank.

"There's plenty of oil, my lord," he said. "Shall I send for a technician to operate it?"

"No. I'll do it myself. Thank you, Thorold. Have they finished dinner yet, Wren?"

"Very nearly, I think, my lord," replied the Butler. "If I understand Mr Cawson aright, the Master and his guests won't be disposed to linger once they know you're here. Shall I take the coffee-tray?"

"Take it and go."

"Very good, my lord."

With a slight bow, the Butler took the tray and left, and Thorold went with him. As soon as the door closed, Lord Asriel looked across the room directly at the wardrobe, and Lyra felt the force of his glance almost as if it had physical form, as if it were an arrow or a spear. Then he looked away and spoke softly to his dæmon.

She came to sit calmly at his side, alert and elegant and dangerous, her green eyes surveying the room before turning, like his black ones, to the door from the Hall as the handle turned. Lyra couldn't see the door, but she heard an intake of breath as the first man came in.

"Master," said Lord Asriel. "Yes, I'm back. Do bring in your guests; I've got something very interesting to show you."

2

The Idea of North

"Lord Asriel," said the Master heavily, and came forward to shake his hand. From her hiding-place Lyra watched the Master's eyes, and indeed, they flicked towards the table for a second, where the Tokay had been.

"Master," said Lord Asriel. "I came too late to disturb your dinner, so I made myself at home in here. Hello, Sub-Rector. Glad to see you looking so well. Excuse my rough appearance; I've only just landed. Yes, Master, the Tokay's gone. I think you're standing in it. The Porter knocked it off the table, but it was my fault. Hello, Chaplain. I read your latest paper with great interest…"

He moved away with the Chaplain, leaving Lyra with a clear view of the Master's face. It was impassive, but the dæmon on his shoulder was shuffling her feathers and moving restlessly from foot to foot. Lord Asriel was already dominating the room, and although he was careful to be courteous to the Master in the Master's own territory, it was clear where the power lay.

The Scholars greeted the visitor and moved into the room, some sitting around the table, some in the armchairs, and soon a buzz of conversation filled the air. Lyra could see that they were powerfully intrigued by the wooden case, the screen and the lantern. She knew the Scholars well: the Librarian, the Sub-Rector, the Enquirer and the rest; they were men who had been around her all her life, taught her, chastised her, consoled her, given her little presents, chased her away from the fruit trees in the Garden; they were all she had for a family. They might even have felt like a family if she knew what a family was, though if she did, she'd have been more likely to feel that about the College servants. The Scholars had more important things to do than attend to the affections of a half-wild, half-civilized girl, left among them by chance.

The Master lit the spirit-lamp under the little silver chafing-dish and heated some butter before cutting half a dozen poppy-heads open and tossing them in. Poppy was always served after a Feast: it clarified the mind and stimulated the tongue, and made for rich conversation. It was traditional for the Master to cook it himself.

Under the sizzle of the frying butter and the hum of talk, Lyra shifted around to find a more comfortable position for herself. With enormous care she took one of the robes – a full-length fur – off its hanger and laid it on the floor of the wardrobe.

"You should have used a scratchy old one," whispered Pantalaimon. "If you get too comfortable you'll go to sleep."

"If I do, it's your job to wake me up," she replied.

She sat and listened to the talk. Mighty dull talk it was, too; almost all of it politics, and London politics at that, nothing exciting about Tartars. The smells of frying poppy and smoke-leaf drifted pleasantly in through the wardrobe door, and more than once Lyra found herself nodding. But finally she heard someone rap the table. The voices fell silent, and then the Master spoke.

"Gentlemen," he said. "I feel sure I speak for all of us when I bid

Lord Asriel welcome. His visits are rare but always immensely valuable, and I understand he has something of particular interest to show us tonight. This is a time of high political tension, as we are all aware; Lord Asriel's presence is required early tomorrow morning in White Hall, and a train is waiting with steam up ready to carry him to London as soon as we have finished our conversation here; so we must use our time wisely. When he has finished speaking to us, I imagine there will be some questions. Please keep them brief and to the point. Lord Asriel, would you like to begin?"

"Thank you, Master," said Lord Asriel. "To start with, I have a few slides to show you. Sub-Rector, you can see best from here, I think. Perhaps the Master would like to take the chair near the wardrobe?"

The old Sub-Rector was nearly blind, so it was courteous to make room for him nearer the screen, and his moving forward meant that the Master would be sitting next to the Librarian, only a matter of a yard or so from where Lyra was crouched in the wardrobe. As the Master settled in the armchair, Lyra heard him murmur:

"The devil! He *knew* about the wine, I'm sure of it."

The Librarian murmured back, "He's going to ask for funds. If he forces a vote –"

"If he does that, we must just argue against, with all the eloquence we have."

The lantern began to hiss as Lord Asriel pumped it hard. Lyra moved slightly so that she could see the screen, where a brilliant white circle had begun to glow. Lord Asriel called, "Could someone turn the lamp down?"

One of the Scholars got up to do that, and the room darkened.

Lord Asriel began:

"As some of you know, I set out for the North twelve months ago on a diplomatic mission to the King of Lapland. At least, that's what I pretended to be doing. In fact my real aim was to go further north still, right on to the ice, to try and discover what had happened to the Grumman expedition. One of Grumman's last messages to the Academy in Berlin spoke of a certain natural phenomenon only seen in the lands of the North. I was determined to investigate that as well as find out what I could about Grumman. But the first picture I'm going to show you isn't directly about either of those things."

And he put the first slide into the frame and slid it behind the lens. A circular photogram in sharp black and white appeared on the screen. It had been taken at night under a full moon, and it showed a wooden hut in the middle distance, its walls dark against the snow that surrounded it and lay thickly on the roof. Beside the hut stood an array of philosophical instruments, which looked to Lyra's eye like something from the Anbaric Park on the road to Yarnton: aerials, wires, porcelain insulators, all glittering in the moonlight and thickly covered in frost. A man in furs, his face hardly visible in the deep hood of his garment, stood in the foreground, with his hand raised as if in greeting. To one side of him stood a smaller figure. The moonlight bathed everything in the same pallid gleam.

"That photogram was taken with a standard silver nitrate emulsion," Lord Asriel said. "I'd like you to look at another one, taken from the same spot only a minute later, with a new specially prepared emulsion."

He lifted out the first slide and dropped another into the frame. This was much darker; it was as if the moonlight had been filtered out. The horizon was still visible, with the dark shape of the hut and its light snow-covered roof standing out, but the complexity of the instruments was hidden in darkness. But the man had altogether changed: he was bathed in light, and a fountain of glowing particles seemed to be streaming from his upraised hand.

"That light," said the Chaplain, "is it going up or coming down?"

"It's coming down," said Lord Asriel, "but it isn't light. It's Dust."

Something in the way he said it made Lyra imagine *Dust* with a capital letter, as if this wasn't ordinary dust. The reaction of the Scholars confirmed her feeling, because Lord Asriel's words caused a sudden collective silence, followed by gasps of incredulity.

"But how –"

"Surely –"

"It can't –"

"Gentlemen!" came the voice of the Chaplain. "Let Lord Asriel explain."

"It's Dust," Lord Asriel repeated. "It registered as light on the plate because particles of Dust affect this emulsion as photons affect silver nitrate emulsion. It was partly to test it that my expedition went North in the first place. As you see, the figure of the man is perfectly visible. Now I'd like you to look at the shape to his left."

He indicated the blurred shape of the smaller figure.

"I thought that was the man's dæmon," said the Enquirer.

"No. His dæmon was at the time coiled around his neck in the form of a snake. That shape you can dimly see is a child."

"A severed child – ?" said someone, and the way he stopped showed that he knew this was something that shouldn't have been voiced.

There was an intense silence.

Then Lord Asriel said calmly, "An entire child. Which, given the nature of Dust, is precisely the point, is it not?"

No one spoke for several seconds. Then came the voice of the Chaplain.

"Ah," he said, like a thirsty man who, having just drunk deeply, puts down the glass to let out the breath he has held while drinking. "And the streams of Dust…"

"– Come from the sky, and bathe him in what looks like light. You may examine this picture as closely as you wish: I'll leave it behind when I go. I'm showing it to you now to demonstrate the effect of this new emulsion. Now I'd like to show you another picture."

He changed the slide. The next picture was also taken at night, but this time without moonlight. It showed a small group of tents in the foreground, dimly outlined against the low horizon, and beside them an untidy heap of wooden boxes and a sledge. But the main interest of the picture lay in the sky. Streams and veils of light hung like curtains, looped and festooned on invisible hooks hundreds of miles high or blowing out sideways in the stream of some unimaginable wind.

"What is that?" said the voice of the Sub-Rector.

"It's a picture of the Aurora."

"It's a very fine photogram," said the Palmerian Professor. "One of the best I've seen."

"Forgive my ignorance," said the shaky voice of the old Precentor, "but if I ever knew what the Aurora was, I have forgotten. Is it what they call the Northern Lights?"

"Yes. It has many names. It's composed of storms of charged particles and solar rays of intense and extraordinary strength – invisible in themselves, but causing this luminous radiation when they interact with the atmosphere. If there'd been time I would have had this slide tinted to show you the colours; pale green and rose, for the most part, with a tinge of crimson along the lower edge of that curtain-like formation. This is taken with ordinary emulsion. Now I'd like you to look at a picture taken with the special emulsion."

He took out the slide. Lyra heard the Master say quietly, "If he forces a vote, we could try to invoke the residence clause. He hasn't been resident in the College for thirty weeks out of the last fifty-two."

"He's already got the Chaplain on his side…" the Librarian murmured in reply.

Lord Asriel put a new slide in the lantern frame. It showed the same scene. As with the previous pair of pictures, many of the features visible by ordinary light were much dimmer in this one, and so were the curtains of radiance in the sky.

But in the middle of the Aurora, high above the bleak landscape, Lyra could see something solid. She pressed her face to the crack to see more clearly, and she could see Scholars near the screen leaning forward, too. As she gazed, her wonder grew, because there in the sky was the unmistakable outline of a city: towers, domes, walls … buildings and streets, suspended in the air! She nearly gasped with wonder.

The Cassington Scholar said, "That looks like … a city."

"Exactly so," said Lord Asriel.

"A city in another world, no doubt?" said the Dean, with contempt in his voice.

Lord Asriel ignored him. There was a stir of excitement among some of the Scholars, as if, having written treatises on the existence of the unicorn without ever having seen one, they'd been presented with a living example newly captured.

"Is this the Barnard–Stokes business?" said the Palmerian Professor. "It is, isn't it?"

"That's what I want to find out," said Lord Asriel.

He stood to one side of the illuminated screen. Lyra could see his dark eyes searching among the Scholars as they peered up at the slide of the Aurora, and the green glow of his dæmon's eyes beside him. All the venerable heads were craning forward, their spectacles glinting; only the Master and the Librarian leant back in their chairs, with their heads close together.

The Chaplain was saying, "You said you were searching for news of the Grumman expedition, Lord Asriel. Was Dr Grumman investigating this phenomenon too?"

"I believe he was, and I believe he had a good deal of information about it. But he won't be able to tell us what it was, because he's dead."

"No!" said the Chaplain.

"I'm afraid so, and I have the proof here."

A ripple of excited apprehension ran round the Retiring Room as, under Lord Asriel's direction, two or three of the younger Scholars carried the wooden box to the front of the room. Lord Asriel took out the last slide but left the lantern on, and in the dramatic glare of the circle of light he bent to lever open the box. Lyra heard the screech of nails coming out of damp wood. The Master stood up to look, blocking Lyra's view. Her uncle spoke again:

"If you remember, Grumman's expedition vanished eighteen months ago. The German Academy sent him up there to go as far north as the magnetic pole and make various celestial observations. It was in the course of that journey that he observed the curious phenomenon we've already seen. Shortly after that, he vanished. It's been assumed that he had an accident and that his body's been lying in a crevasse all this time. In fact there was no accident."

"What have you got there?" said the Dean. "Is that a vacuum container?"

Lord Asriel didn't answer at first. Lyra heard the snap of metal clips and a hiss as air rushed into a vessel, and then there was a silence. But the silence didn't last long. After a moment or two Lyra heard a confused babble break out: cries of horror, loud protests, voices raised in anger and fear.

"But what –"

"– hardly human –"

"– it's been –"

"– what's *happened* to it?"

The Master's voice cut through them all.

"Lord Asriel, what in God's name have you got there?"

"This is the head of Stanislaus Grumman," said Lord Asriel's voice.

Over the jumble of voices Lyra heard someone stumble to the door and out, making incoherent sounds of distress. She wished she could see what they were seeing.

Lord Asriel said, "I found his body preserved in the ice off Svalbard. The head was treated in this way by his killers. You'll notice the characteristic scalping pattern. I think you might be familiar with it, Sub-Rector."

The old man's voice was steady as he said, "I have seen the Tartars do this. It's a technique you find among the aboriginals of Siberia and the Tungusk. From there, of course, it spread into the lands of the Skraelings, though I understand that it is now banned in New Denmark. May I examine it more closely, Lord Asriel?"

After a short silence he spoke again.

"My eyes are not very clear, and the ice is dirty, but it seems to me that there is a hole in the top of the skull. Am I right?"

"You are."

"Trepanning?"

"Exactly."

That caused a murmur of excitement. The Master moved out of the way and Lyra could see again. The old Sub-Rector, in the circle of light

24

thrown by the lantern, was holding a heavy block of ice up close to his eyes, and Lyra could see the object inside it: a bloody lump barely recognizable as a human head. Pantalaimon fluttered around Lyra, his distress affecting her.

"Hush," she whispered. "Listen."

"Dr Grumman was once a Scholar of this College," said the Dean hotly.

"To fall into the hands of the Tartars –"

"But that far north?"

"They must have penetrated further than anyone imagined!"

"Did I hear you say you found it near Svalbard?" said the Dean.

"That's right."

"Are we to understand that the *panserbjørne* had anything to do with this?"

Lyra didn't recognize that word, but clearly the Scholars did.

"Impossible," said the Cassington Scholar firmly. "They'd never behave in that manner."

"Then you don't know Iofur Raknison," said the Palmerian Professor, who had made several expeditions himself to the Arctic regions. "It wouldn't surprise me at all to learn that he had taken to scalping people in the Tartar fashion."

Lyra looked again at her uncle, who was watching the Scholars with a glitter of sardonic amusement, and saying nothing.

"Who is Iofur Raknison?" said someone.

"The king of Svalbard," said the Palmerian Professor. "Yes, that's right, one of the *panserbjørne*. He's a usurper, of sorts; tricked his way on to the throne, or so I understand; but a powerful figure, by no means a fool, in spite of his ludicrous affectations – having a palace built of imported marble – setting up what he calls a university –"

"For whom? For the *bears*?" said someone else, and everyone laughed.

But the Palmerian Professor went on, "For all that, I tell you that Iofur Raknison would be capable of doing this to Grumman. At the same time, he could be flattered into behaving quite differently, if the need arose."

"And you know how, do you, Trelawney?" said the Dean sneeringly.

"Indeed I do. Do you know what he wants above all else? Even more than an honorary degree? He wants a dæmon! Find a way to give him a dæmon, and he'd do anything for you."

The Scholars laughed heartily.

Lyra was following this with puzzlement: what the Palmerian Professor said made no sense at all. Besides, she was impatient to hear more about scalping and the Northern Lights and that mysterious Dust. But she was disappointed, for Lord Asriel had finished show-ing his relics and pictures, and the talk soon turned into a college wrangle about whether or not they should give him some money to fit out another expedition. Back and forth the arguments ranged, and Lyra felt her eyes closing. Soon she was fast asleep, with Pantalaimon curled around her neck in his favourite sleeping-form as an ermine.

She woke up with a start when someone shook her shoulder.

"Quiet," said her uncle. The wardrobe door was open, and he was crouched there against the light. "They've all gone, but there are still some servants around. Go to your bedroom now, and take care that you say nothing about this."

"Did they vote to give you the money?" she said sleepily.

"Yes."

"What's Dust?" she said, struggling to stand up after having been cramped for so long.

"Nothing to do with you."

"It *is* to do with me," she said. "If you wanted me to be a spy in the wardrobe you ought to tell me what I'm spying about. Can I see the man's head?"

Pantalaimon's white ermine-fur bristled: she felt it tickling her neck. Lord Asriel laughed shortly.

"Don't be disgusting," he said, and began to pack his slides and specimen-box. "Did you watch the Master?"

"Yes, and he looked for the wine before he did anything else."

"Good. But I've scotched him for now. Do as you're told and go to bed."

"But where are *you* going?"

"Back to the North. I'm leaving in ten minutes."

"Can I come?"

He stopped what he was doing, and looked at her as if for the first time. His dæmon turned her great green leopard-eyes on her too, and under the concentrated gaze of both of them, Lyra blushed. But she gazed back fiercely.

"Your place is here," said her uncle finally.

"But why? Why is my place here? Why can't I come to the North with you? I want to see the Northern Lights and bears and icebergs and everything. I want to know about Dust. And that city in the air. Is it another world?"

"You're not coming, child. Put it out of your head; the times are too dangerous. Do as you're told and go to bed, and if you're a good girl, I'll bring you back a walrus tusk with some Eskimo carving on it. Don't argue any more or I shall be angry."

And his dæmon growled with a deep savage rumble that made Lyra suddenly aware of what it would be like to have teeth meeting in her throat.

Lyra compressed her lips and frowned hard at her uncle. He was pumping the air from the vacuum flask, and took no notice; it was as if he'd already forgotten her. Without a word, but with lips tight and narrowed eyes, the girl and her dæmon left and went to bed.

The Master and the Librarian were old friends and allies, and it was their habit, after a difficult episode, to take a glass of brantwijn and console each other. So after they'd seen Lord Asriel away, they strolled to the Master's Lodging and settled in his study with the curtains drawn and the fire refreshed, their dæmons in their familiar places on knee or shoulder, and prepared to think through what had just happened.

"Do you really believe he knew about the wine?" said the Librarian.

"Of course he did. I have no idea how, but he knew, and he spilled the decanter himself. Of course he did."

"Forgive me, Master, but I can't help being relieved. I was never happy about the idea of…"

"Of poisoning him?"

"Yes. Of murder."

"Hardly anyone would be happy at that idea, Charles. The question was whether doing that would be worse than the consequences of not doing it. Well, some Providence has intervened, and it hasn't happened. I'm only sorry I burdened you with the knowledge of it."

"No, no," protested the Librarian. "But I wish you had told me more."

The Master was silent for a while before saying, "Yes, perhaps I should have done. The alethiometer warns of appalling consequences if

Lord Asriel pursues this research. Apart from anything else, the child will be drawn in, and I want to keep her safe as long as possible."

"Is Lord Asriel's business anything to do with this new initiative of the Consistorial Court of Discipline? The what-do-they-call-it: the Oblation Board?"

"Lord Asriel – no, no. Quite the reverse. The Oblation Board isn't entirely answerable to the Consistorial Court, either. It's a semi-private initiative; it's being run by someone who has no love of Lord Asriel. Between them both, Charles, I tremble."

The Librarian was silent in his turn. Ever since Pope John Calvin had moved the seat of the Papacy to Geneva and set up the Consistorial Court of Discipline, the Church's power over every aspect of life had been absolute. The Papacy itself had been abolished after Calvin's death, and a tangle of courts, colleges, and councils, collectively known as the Magisterium, had grown up in its place. These agencies were not always united; sometimes a bitter rivalry grew up between them. For a large part of the previous century, the most powerful had been the College of Bishops, but in recent years the Consistorial Court of Discipline had taken its place as the most active and the most feared of all the Church's bodies.

But it was always possible for independent agencies to grow up under the protection of another part of the Magisterium, and the Oblation Board, which the Librarian had referred to, was one of these. The Librarian didn't know much about it, but he disliked and feared what he'd heard, and he completely understood the Master's anxiety.

"The Palmerian Professor mentioned a name," he said after a minute or so. "Barnard-Stokes? What is the Barnard-Stokes business?"

"Ah, it's not our field, Charles. As I understand it, the Holy Church teaches that there are two worlds: the world of everything we can see and hear and touch, and another world, the spiritual world of heaven and hell. Barnard and Stokes were two – how shall I put it – *renegade* theologians who postulated the existence of numerous other worlds like this one, neither heaven nor hell, but material and sinful. They are there, close by, but invisible and unreachable. The Holy Church naturally disapproved of this abominable heresy, and Barnard and Stokes were silenced.

"But unfortunately for the Magisterium there seem to be sound mathematical arguments for this other-world theory. I have never followed them myself, but the Cassington Scholar tells me that they are sound."

"And now Lord Asriel has taken a picture of one of these other worlds," the Librarian said. "And we have funded him to go and look for it. I see."

"Quite. It'll seem to the Oblation Board, and to its powerful protectors, that Jordan College is a hotbed of support for heresy. And between the Consistorial Court and the Oblation Board, Charles, I have to keep a balance; and meanwhile the child is growing. They won't have forgotten her. Sooner or later she would have become involved, but she'll be drawn in now whether I want to protect her or not."

"But how do you know that, for God's sake? The alethiometer again?"

"Yes. Lyra has a part to play in all this, and a major one. The irony is that she must do it all without realizing what she's doing. She can be helped, though, and if my plan with the Tokay had succeeded, she would have been safe for a little longer. I would have liked to spare her a journey to the North. I wish above all things that I were able to explain it to her…"

"She wouldn't listen," the Librarian said. "I know her ways only too well. Try to tell her anything serious and she'll half-listen for five minutes and then start fidgeting. And quiz her about it next time and she'll have completely forgotten."

"If I talked to her about Dust? You don't think she'd listen to that?"

The Librarian made a noise to indicate how unlikely he thought that was.

"Why on earth should she?" he said. "Why should a distant theological riddle interest a healthy thoughtless child?"

"Because of what she must experience. Part of that includes a great betrayal…"

"Who's going to betray her?"

"No, no, that's the saddest thing: *she* will be the betrayer, and the experience will be terrible. She mustn't know that, of course, but there's no reason for her not to know about the problem of Dust. And you might be wrong, Charles; she might well take an interest in it, if it were explained in a simple way. And it might help her later on. It would certainly help me to be less anxious about her."

"That's the duty of the old," said the Librarian, "to be anxious on behalf of the young. And the duty of the young is to scorn the anxiety of the old."

They sat for a while longer, and then parted, for it was late, and they were old and anxious.

3

Lyra's Jordan

ordan College was the grandest and richest of all the colleges in Oxford. It was probably the largest, too, though no one knew for certain. The buildings, which were grouped around three irregular quadrangles, dated from every period from the early Middle Ages to the mid-eighteenth century. It had never been planned; it had grown piecemeal, with past and present overlapping at every spot, and the final effect was one of jumbled and squalid grandeur. Some part was always about to fall down, and for five generations the same family, the Parslows, had been employed full-time by the College as masons and scaffolders. The present Mr Parslow was teaching his son the craft; the two of them and their three workmen would scramble like industrious termites over the scaffolding they'd erected at the corner of the Library, or over the roof of the Chapel, and haul up bright new blocks of stone or rolls of shiny lead or baulks of timber.

The College owned farms and estates all over Brytain. It was said that you could walk from Oxford to Bristol in one direction and to London in the other, and never leave Jordan land. In every part of the kingdom there were dye-works and brick-kilns, forests and atomcraft-works that paid rent to Jordan, and every Quarter-Day the Bursar and his clerks would tot it all up, announce the total to Concilium, and order a pair of swans for the Feast. Some of the money was put by for re-investment – Concilium had just approved the purchase of an office-block in Manchester – and the rest was used to pay the Scholars' modest stipends and the wages of the servants (and the Parslows, and the other dozen or so families of craftsmen and traders who served the College), to keep the wine-cellar richly filled, to buy books and anbarographs for the immense Library that filled one side of the Melrose Quadrangle and extended, burrow-like, for several floors beneath the ground; and, not least, to buy the latest philosophical apparatus to equip the Chapel.

It was important to keep the Chapel up to date, because Jordan College had no rival, either in Europe or in New France, as a centre of experimental theology. Lyra knew that much, at least. She was proud of her College's eminence, and liked to boast of it to the various urchins and ragamuffins she played with by the Canal or the Claybeds; and she regarded visiting scholars and eminent professors from elsewhere with pitying scorn, because they didn't belong to Jordan and so must know less, poor things, than the humblest of Jordan's Under-Scholars.

As for what experimental theology was, Lyra had no more idea than the urchins. She had formed the notion that it was concerned with magic, with the movements of the stars and planets, with tiny particles of matter, but that was guesswork, really. Probably the stars had dæmons just as humans did, and experimental theology involved talking to them. Lyra imagined the Chaplain speaking loftily, listening to the star-dæmons' remarks, and then nodding judiciously or shaking his head in regret. But what might be passing between them, she couldn't conceive.

Nor was she particularly interested. In many ways Lyra was a barbarian. What she liked best was clambering over the College roofs with Roger, the Kitchen boy who was her particular friend, to spit plum-stones on the heads of passing Scholars or to hoot like owls outside a window where a tutorial was going on; or racing through the narrow streets, or stealing apples from the market, or waging war. Just as she was unaware of the hidden currents of politics running below the surface of College affairs, so the Scholars, for their part, would have been unable to see the rich seething stew of alliances and enmities and feuds and treaties which was a child's life in Oxford. Children playing together: how pleasant to see! What could be more innocent and charming?

In fact, of course, Lyra and her peers were engaged in deadly warfare. First, the children (young servants, and the children of servants, and Lyra) of one college waged war on those of another. But this enmity was swept aside when the town children attacked a colleger: then all the colleges banded together and went into battle against the townies. This rivalry was hundreds of years old, and very deep and satisfying.

But even this was forgotten when the other enemies threatened. One enemy was perennial: the brick-burners' children, who lived by the Claybeds and were despised by collegers and townies alike. Last year Lyra and some townies had made a temporary truce and raided the Claybeds, pelting the brick-burners' children with lumps of heavy clay and tipping over the soggy castle they'd built, before rolling them over and over in the clinging substance they lived by until victors and vanquished alike resembled a flock of shrieking golems.

The other regular enemy was seasonal. The gyptian families, who lived in canal-boats, came and went with the spring and autumn fairs, and were always good for a fight. There was one family of gyptians in particular, who regularly returned to their mooring in that part of the city known as Jericho, with whom she'd been feuding ever since she could first throw a stone. When they were last in Oxford, she and Roger and some of the other kitchen-boys from Jordan and St Michael's College had laid an ambush for them, throwing mud at their brightly painted narrow-boat until the whole family came out to chase them away – at which point the reserve squad under Lyra raided the boat and cast it off from the bank, to float down the canal getting in the way of all the other water-traffic while Lyra's raiders searched the boat from end to end, looking for the bung. Lyra firmly believed in this bung. If they pulled it out, she assured her troop, the boat would sink at once; but they didn't find it, and had to abandon ship when the gyptians caught them up, to flee dripping and crowing with triumph through the narrow lanes of Jericho.

That was Lyra's world and her delight. She was a coarse and greedy little savage, for the most part. But she always had a dim sense that it wasn't her whole world; that part of her also belonged in the grandeur and ritual of Jordan College; and that somewhere in her life there was a connection with the high world of politics represented by Lord Asriel. All she did with that knowledge was to give herself airs and lord it over the other urchins. It had never occurred to her to find out more.

So she had passed her childhood, like a half-wild cat. The only variation in her days came on those irregular occasions when Lord Asriel visited the College. A rich and powerful uncle was all very well to boast about, but the price of boasting was having to be caught by the most agile Scholar and brought to the Housekeeper to be washed and dressed in a clean frock, following which she was escorted (with many threats) to the Senior Common Room to have tea with Lord Asriel. A group of senior Scholars would be invited as well. Lyra would slump mutinously in an armchair until the Master told her sharply to sit up, and then she'd glower at them all till even the Chaplain had to laugh.

What happened on those awkward, formal visits never varied. After the tea, the Master and the other few Scholars who'd been invited left Lyra and her uncle together, and he called her to stand in front of him and tell him what she'd learned since his last visit. And she would mutter whatever she could dredge up about geometry or Arabic or history or anbarology, and he would sit back with one ankle resting on the other knee and watch her inscrutably until her words failed.

Last year, before his expedition to the North, he'd gone on to say, "And how do you spend your time when you're not diligently studying?"

And she mumbled, "I just play. Sort of around the College. Just … play, really."

And he said, "Let me see your hands, child."

She held out her hands for inspection, and he took them and turned them over to look at her fingernails. Beside him, his dæmon lay Sphinx-like on the carpet, swishing her tail occasionally and gazing unblinkingly at Lyra.

"Dirty," said Lord Asriel, pushing her hands away. "Don't they make you wash in this place?"

"Yes," she said. "But the Chaplain's fingernails are always dirty. They're even dirtier than mine."

"He's a learned man. What's your excuse?"

"I must've got them dirty after I washed."

"Where do you play to get so dirty?"

She looked at him suspiciously. She had the feeling that being on the roof was forbidden, though no one had actually said so. "In some of the old rooms," she said finally.

"And where else?"

"In the Claybeds, sometimes."

"And?"

"Jericho and Port Meadow."

"Nowhere else?"

"No."

"You're a liar. I saw you on the roof only yesterday."

She bit her lip and said nothing. He was watching her sardonically.

"So, you play on the roof as well," he went on. "Do you ever go into the Library?"

"No. I found a rook on the Library roof, though," she went on.

"Did you? Did you catch it?"

"It had a hurt foot. I was going to kill it and roast it but Roger said we should help it get better. So we gave it scraps of food and some wine and then it got better and flew away."

"Who's Roger?"

"My friend. The Kitchen boy."

"I see. So you've been all over the roof –"

"Not all over. You can't get on to the Sheldon Building because you have to jump up from Pilgrim's Tower across a gap. There's a skylight that opens on to it, but I'm not tall enough to reach it."

"You've been all over the roof except the Sheldon Building. What about underground?"

"Underground?"

"There's as much College below ground as there is above it. I'm surprised you haven't found that out. Well, I'm going in a minute. You look healthy enough. Here."

He fished in his pocket and drew out a handful of coins, from which he gave her five gold dollars.

"Haven't they taught you to say thank you?" he said.

"Thank you," she mumbled.

"Do you obey the Master?"

"Oh, yes."

"And respect the Scholars?"

"Yes."

Lord Asriel's dæmon laughed softly. It was the first sound she'd made, and Lyra blushed.

"Go and play then," said Lord Asriel.

Lyra turned and darted to the door with relief, remembering to turn and blurt out a "Goodbye."

So Lyra's life had been, before the day when she decided to hide in the Retiring Room, and first heard about Dust.

And of course the Librarian was wrong in saying to the Master that she wouldn't have been interested. She would have listened eagerly now to anyone who could tell her about Dust. She was to hear a great deal more about it in the months to come, and eventually she would know more about Dust than anyone in the world; but in the meantime, there was all the rich life of Jordan still being lived around her.

And in any case there was something else to think about. A rumour had been filtering through the streets for some weeks: a rumour that made some people laugh and others grow silent, as some people scoff at ghosts and others fear them. For no reason that anyone could imagine, children were beginning to disappear.

It would happen like this.

East along the great highway of the River Isis, thronged with slow-moving brick-barges and asphalt-boats and corn-tankers, way down past Henley and Maidenhead to Teddington, where the tide from the German Ocean reaches, and further down still: to Mortlake, past the house of the great magician Dr Dee; past Falkeshall, where the pleasure-gardens spread out bright with fountains and banners by day, with tree-lamps and fireworks by night; past White Hall Palace, where the King holds his weekly Council of State; past the Shot Tower, dropping its endless drizzle of molten lead into vats of murky water; further down still, to where the river, wide and filthy now, swings in a great curve to the south.

This is Limehouse, and here is the child who is going to disappear.

He is called Tony Makarios. His mother thinks he's nine years old, but she has a poor memory that the drink has rotted; he might be eight, or ten. His surname is Greek, but like his age, that is a guess on his mother's part, because he looks more Chinese than Greek, and there's Irish and Skraeling and Lascar in him from his mother's side, too. Tony's not very bright, but he has a sort of clumsy tenderness that sometimes prompts him to give his mother a rough hug and plant a sticky kiss on her cheeks. The poor woman is usually too fuddled to start such a procedure herself; but she responds warmly enough, once she realizes what's happening.

At the moment Tony is hanging about the market in Pie Street. He's hungry. It's early evening, and he won't get fed at home. He's got a shilling in his pocket that a soldier gave him for taking a message to his best girl, but Tony's not going to waste that on food, when you can pick up so much for nothing.

So he wanders through the market, between the old-clothes stalls and the fortune-paper stalls, the fruit-mongers and the fried-fish seller, with his little dæmon on his shoulder, a sparrow, watching this way and that; and when a stall-holder and her dæmon are both looking elsewhere, a brisk chirp sounds, and Tony's hand shoots out and returns to his loose shirt with an apple or a couple of nuts, and finally with a hot pie.

The stall-holder sees that, and shouts, and her cat-dæmon leaps, but Tony's sparrow is aloft and Tony himself halfway down the street already. Curses and abuse go with him, but not far. He stops running at the steps of St Catherine's Oratory, where he sits down and takes out his steaming, battered prize, leaving a trail of gravy on his shirt.

And he's being watched. A lady in a long yellow-red fox-fur coat, a beautiful young lady whose dark hair falls shining delicately under the shadow of her fur-lined hood, is standing in the doorway of the Oratory, half a dozen steps above him. It might be that a service is finishing, for light comes from the doorway behind her, an organ is playing inside, and the lady is holding a jewelled breviary.

Tony knows nothing of this. His face contentedly deep in the pie, his toes curled inwards and his bare soles together, he sits and chews and swallows while his dæmon becomes a mouse and grooms her whiskers.

The young lady's dæmon is moving out from beside the fox-fur coat. He is in the form of a monkey, but no ordinary monkey: his fur is long and silky and of the most deep and lustrous gold. With sinuous movements he inches down the steps towards the boy, and sits a step above him.

Then the mouse senses something, and becomes a sparrow again, cocking her head a fraction sideways, and hops along the stone a step or two.

The monkey watches the sparrow; the sparrow watches the monkey.

The monkey reaches out slowly. His little hand is black, his nails perfect horny claws, his movements gentle and inviting. The sparrow can't resist. She hops further, and further, and then, with a little flutter, up on to the monkey's hand.

The monkey lifts her up, and gazes closely at her before standing and swinging back to his human, taking the sparrow-dæmon with him. The lady bends her scented head to whisper.

And then Tony turns. He can't help it.

"Ratter!" he says, half in alarm, his mouth full.

The sparrow chirps. It must be safe. Tony swallows his mouthful and stares.

"Hello," says the beautiful lady. "What's your name?"

"Tony."

"Where do you live, Tony?"

"Clarice Walk."

"What's in that pie?"

"Beefsteak."

"Do you like chocolatl?"

"Yeah!"

"As it happens, I've got more chocolatl than I can drink myself. Will you come and help me drink it?"

He's lost already. He was lost the moment his slow-witted dæmon hopped on to the monkey's hand. He follows the beautiful young lady and the golden monkey down Denmark Street and along to Hangman's Wharf, and down King George's Steps to a little green door in the side of a tall warehouse. She knocks, the door is opened; they go in, the door is closed. Tony will never come out – at least, by that entrance; and he'll never see his mother again. She, poor drunken thing, will think he's run away, and when she remembers him, she'll think it was her fault, and sob her sorry heart out.

Little Tony Makarios wasn't the only child to be caught by the lady with the golden monkey. He found a dozen others in the cellar of the warehouse, boys and girls, none older than twelve or so; though since all of them had histories like his, none could be sure of their age. What Tony didn't notice, of course, was the factor that they all had in common. None of the children in that warm and steamy cellar had reached the age of puberty.

The kind lady saw him settled on a bench against the wall, and provided by a silent serving-woman with a mug of chocolatl from the saucepan on the iron stove. Tony ate the rest of his pie and drank the sweet hot liquor without taking much notice of his surroundings, and the surroundings took little notice of him: he was too small to be a threat, and too stolid to promise much satisfaction as a victim.

It was another boy who asked the obvious question.

"Hey, lady! What you got us all here for?"

He was a tough-looking wretch with dark chocolatl on his top lip and a gaunt black rat for a dæmon. The lady was standing near the door, talking to a stout man with the air of a sea-captain, and as she turned to answer, she looked so angelic in the hissing naphtha light that all the children fell silent.

"We want your help," she said. "You don't mind helping us, do you?"

No one could say a word. They all gazed, suddenly shy. They had never seen a lady like this; she was so gracious and sweet and kind that they felt they hardly deserved their good luck, and whatever she asked, they'd give it gladly so as to stay in her presence a little longer.

She told them that they were going on a voyage. They would be well fed and warmly clothed, and those who wanted to could send messages back to their families to let them know they were safe. Captain Magnusson would take them on board his ship very soon, and then when the tide was right they'd sail out to sea and set a course for the North.

Soon those few who did want to send a message to whatever home they had were sitting around the beautiful lady as she wrote a few lines at their dictation and, having let them scratch a clumsy X at the foot of the page, folded it into a scented envelope and wrote the address they told her. Tony would have liked to send something to his mother, but he had a realistic idea of her ability to read it. He plucked at the lady's fox-fur sleeve and whispered that he'd like her to tell his mum where he was going, and all, and she bent her gracious head close enough to his malodorous little body to hear, and stroked his head and promised to pass the message on.

Then the children clustered around to say goodbye. The golden monkey stroked all their dæmons, and they all touched the fox-fur for luck, or as if they were drawing some strength or hope or goodness out of the lady, and she bade them all farewell and saw them in the care of the bold captain on board a steam launch at the jetty. The sky was dark now, the river a mass of bobbing lights. The lady stood on the jetty and waved till she could see their faces no more.

Then she turned back inside, with the golden monkey nestled in her breast, and threw the little bundle of letters into the furnace before leaving the way she had come.

Children from the slums were easy enough to entice away, but eventually people noticed, and the police were stirred into reluctant action. For a while there were no more bewitchings. But a rumour had been born, and little by little it changed and grew and spread, and when after a while a few children disappeared in Norwich, and then Sheffield, and then Manchester, the people in those places who'd heard of the disappearances elsewhere added the new vanishings to the story and gave it new strength.

And so the legend grew of a mysterious group of enchanters who spirited children away. Some said their leader was a beautiful lady, others said a tall man with red eyes, while a third story told of a youth who laughed and sang to his victims so that they followed him like sheep.

As for where they took these lost children, no two stories agreed. Some said it was to Hell, under the ground, to Fairyland. Others said to a farm where the children were kept and fattened for the table. Others said that the children were kept and sold as slaves to rich Tartars... And so on.

But one thing on which everyone agreed was the name of these invisible kidnappers. They had to have a name, or not be referred to at all, and talking about them – especially if you were safe and snug at home, or in Jordan College – was delicious. And the name that seemed to settle on them, without anyone's knowing why, was the Gobblers.

"Don't stay out late, or the Gobblers'll get you!"

"My cousin in Northampton, she knows a woman whose little boy was took by the Gobblers..."

"The Gobblers've been in Stratford. They say they're coming south!"

And, inevitably:

"Let's play kids and Gobblers!"

So said Lyra to Roger the Kitchen boy from Jordan College. He would have followed her to the ends of the earth.

"How d'you play that?"

"You hide and I find you and slice you open, right, like the Gobblers do."

"You don't know what they do. They might not do that at all."

"You're afraid of 'em," she said. "I can tell."

"I en't. I don't believe in 'em, anyway."

"I do," she said decisively. "But I en't afraid either. I'd just do what my uncle done last time he came to Jordan. I seen him. He was in the Retiring Room and there was this guest who weren't polite, and my uncle just give him a hard look and the man fell dead on the spot, with all foam and froth round his mouth."

"He never," said Roger doubtfully. "They never said anything about that in the Kitchen. Anyway, you en't allowed in the Retiring Room."

"Course not. They wouldn't tell servants about a thing like that. And I *have* been in the Retiring Room, so there. Anyway, my uncle's always doing that. He done it to some Tartars when they caught him once. They tied him up and they was going to cut his guts out, but when the first man come up with the knife my uncle just looked at him, and he fell dead, so another one come up and he done the same to him, and finally there was only one left. My uncle said he'd leave him alive if he untied him, so he did, and then my uncle killed him anyway just to teach him a lesson."

Roger was less sure about that than about Gobblers, but the story was too good to waste, so they took it in turns to be Lord Asriel and the expiring Tartars, using sherbet dip for the foam.

However, that was a distraction; Lyra was still intent on playing Gobblers, and she inveigled Roger down into the wine cellars, which they entered by means of the Butler's spare set of keys. Together they crept through the great vaults where the College's Tokay and Canary, its Burgundy and brantwijn were lying under the cobwebs of ages. Ancient stone arches rose above them supported by pillars as thick as ten trees, irregular flagstones lay underfoot, and on all sides were ranged rack upon rack, tier upon tier, of bottles and barrels. It was fascinating. With Gobblers forgotten again, the two children tiptoed from end to end holding a candle in trembling fingers, peering into every dark corner, with a single question growing more urgent in Lyra's mind every moment: what did the wine taste like?

There was an easy way of answering that. Lyra – over Roger's fervent protests – picked out the oldest, twistiest, greenest bottle she could find, and, not having anything to extract the cork with, broke it off at the neck. Huddled in the furthest corner, they sipped at the heady crimson liquor, wondering when they'd become drunk, and how they'd tell when they were. Lyra didn't like the taste much, but she had to admit how grand and complicated it was. The funniest thing was watching their two dæmons, who seemed to be getting more and more muddled: falling over, giggling senselessly, and changing shape to look like gargoyles, each trying to be uglier than the other.

Finally, and almost simultaneously, the children discovered what it was like to be drunk.

"Do they *like* doing this?" gasped Roger, after vomiting copiously.

"Yes," said Lyra, in the same condition. "And so do I," she added stubbornly.

Lyra learned nothing from that episode except that playing Gobblers led to interesting places. She remembered her uncle's words in their last interview, and began to explore underground, for what was above ground was only a small fraction of the whole. Like some enormous fungus whose root-system extended over acres, Jordan (finding itself jostling for space above ground with St Michael's College on one side, Gabriel College on the other, and the University Library behind) had begun, sometime in the Middle Age, to spread below the surface. Tunnels, shafts, vaults, cellars, staircases had so hollowed out the earth below Jordan and for several hundred yards around it that there was almost as much air below ground as above; Jordan College stood on a sort of froth of stone.

And now that Lyra had the taste for exploring it, she abandoned her usual haunt, the irregular Alps of the College roofs, and plunged with Roger into this netherworld. From playing at Gobblers she had turned to hunting them, for what could be more likely than that they were lurking out of sight below the ground?

So one day she and Roger made their way into the crypt below the Oratory. This was where generations of Masters had been buried, each in his lead-lined oak coffin in niches along the stone walls. A stone tablet below each space gave their names:

Simon Le Clerc, Master 1765–1789 Cerebaton
Requiescant in pace

"What's that mean?" said Roger.

"The first part's his name, and the last bit's Roman. And there's the dates in the middle when he was Master. And the other name must be his dæmon."

They moved along the silent vault, tracing the letters of more inscriptions:

Francis Lyall, Master 1748–1765 Zohariel
Requiescant in pace

Ignatius Cole, Master 1745–1748 Musca
Requiescant in pace

On each coffin, Lyra was interested to see, a brass plaque bore a picture of a different being: this one a basilisk, this a fair woman, this a serpent, this a monkey. She realized that they were images of the dead men's dæmons. As people became adult, their dæmons lost the power to change and assumed one shape, keeping it permanently.

"These coffins've got skeletons in 'em!" whispered Roger.

"Mouldering flesh," whispered Lyra. "And worms and maggots all twisting about in their eye sockets."

"Must be ghosts down here," said Roger, shivering pleasantly.

Beyond the first crypt they found a passage lined with stone shelves. Each shelf was partitioned off into square sections, and in each section rested a skull.

Roger's dæmon, tail tucked firmly between her legs, shivered against him and gave a little quiet howl.

"Hush," he said.

Lyra couldn't see Pantalaimon, but she knew his moth-form was resting on her shoulder and probably shivering too.

She reached up and lifted the nearest skull gently out of its resting place.

"What you doing?" said Roger. "You en't supposed to touch 'em!"

She turned it over and over, taking no notice. Something suddenly fell out of the hole at the base of the skull – fell through her fingers and rang as it hit the floor, and she nearly dropped the skull in alarm.

"It's a coin!" said Roger, feeling for it. "Might be treasure!"

He held it up to the candle and they both gazed wide-eyed. It was not a coin, but a little disc of bronze with a crudely engraved inscription showing a cat.

"It's like the ones on the coffins," said Lyra. "It's his dæmon. Must be."

"Better put it back," said Roger uneasily, and Lyra upturned the skull and dropped the disc back into its immemorial resting-place before returning the skull to the shelf. Each of the other skulls, they found, had its own dæmon-coin, showing its owner's lifetime companion still close to him in death.

"Who d'you think these were when they were alive?" said Lyra. "Probably Scholars, I reckon. Only the Masters get coffins. There's probably been so many Scholars all down the centuries that there wouldn't be room to bury the whole of 'em, so they just cut their heads off and keep them. That's the most important part of 'em anyway."

They found no Gobblers, but the catacombs under the Oratory kept Lyra and Roger busy for days. Once she tried to play a trick on some of the dead Scholars, by switching around the coins in their skulls so they were with the wrong dæmons. Pantalaimon became so agitated at this that he changed into a bat and flew up and down uttering shrill cries and flapping his wings in her face, but she took no notice: it was too good a joke to waste. She paid for it later, though. In bed in her narrow room at the top of Staircase Twelve she was visited by a night-ghast, and woke up screaming at the three robed figures who stood at the bedside pointing their bony fingers before throwing back their cowls to show bleeding stumps where their heads should have been. Only when Pantalaimon became a lion and roared at them did they retreat, backing away into the substance of the wall until all that was visible was their arms, then their horny yellow-grey hands, then their twitching fingers, then nothing. First thing in the morning she hastened down to the catacombs and restored the dæmon-coins to their rightful places, and whispered "Sorry! Sorry!" to the skulls.

The catacombs were much larger than the wine-cellars, but they too had a limit. When Lyra and Roger had explored every corner of them and were sure there were no Gobblers to be found there, they turned their attention elsewhere – but not before they were spotted leaving the crypt by the Intercessor, who called them back into the Oratory.

The Intercessor was a plump, elderly man known as Father Heyst. It was his job to lead all the College services, to preach and pray and hear confessions. When Lyra was younger he had taken an interest in her spiritual welfare, only to be confounded by her sly indifference and insincere repentances. She was not spiritually promising, he had decided.

When they heard him call, Lyra and Roger turned reluctantly and walked, dragging their feet, into the great musty-smelling dimness of the Oratory. Candles flickered here and there in front of images of the saints; a faint and distant clatter came from the organ-loft, where some repairs were going on; a servant was polishing the brass lectern. Father Heyst beckoned from the vestry door.

"Where have you been?" he said to them. "I've seen you come in here two or three times now. What are you up to?"

His tone was not accusatory. He sounded as if he were genuinely interested. His dæmon flicked a lizard-tongue at them from her perch on his shoulder.

Lyra said, "We wanted to look down in the crypt."

"Whatever for?"

"The ... the coffins. We wanted to see all the coffins," she said.

"But why?"

She shrugged. It was her constant response when she was pressed.

"And you," he went on, turning to Roger. Roger's dæmon anxiously wagged her terrier-tail to propitiate him. "What's your name?"

"Roger, Father."

"If you're a servant, where do you work?"

"In the Kitchen, Father."

"Should you be there now?"

"Yes, Father."

"Then be off with you."

Roger turned and ran. Lyra dragged her foot from side to side on the floor.

"As for you, Lyra," said Father Heyst, "I'm pleased to see you taking an interest in what lies in the Oratory. You are a lucky child, to have all this history around you."

"Mm," said Lyra.

"But I wonder about your choice of companions. Are you a lonely child?"

"No," she said.

"Do you... Do you miss the society of other children?"

"No."

"I don't mean Roger the Kitchen boy. I mean children such as yourself. Nobly born children. Would you like to have some companions of that sort?"

"No."

"But other girls, perhaps..."

"No."

"You see, none of us would want you to miss all the usual childhood pleasures and pastimes. I sometimes think it must be a lonely life for you here among a company of elderly Scholars, Lyra. Do you feel that?"

"No."

He tapped his thumbs together over his interlaced fingers, unable to think of anything else to ask this stubborn child.

"If there is anything troubling you," he said finally, "you know you can come and tell me about it. I hope you feel you can always do that."

"Yes," she said.

"Do you say your prayers?"

"Yes."

"Good girl. Well, run along."

With a barely concealed sigh of relief, she turned and left. Having failed to find Gobblers below ground, Lyra took to the streets again. She was at home there.

Then, almost when she'd lost interest in them, the Gobblers appeared in Oxford.

The first Lyra heard of it was when a young boy went missing from a gyptian family she knew.

It was about the time of the Horse Fair, and the canal basin was crowded with narrow boats and butty boats, with traders and travellers, and the wharves along the waterfront in Jericho were bright with gleaming harness and loud with the clop of hooves and the clamour of bargaining. Lyra always enjoyed the Horse Fair; as well as the chance of stealing a ride on a less-than-well-attended horse, there were endless opportunities for provoking warfare.

And this year she had a grand plan. Inspired by the capture of the narrow boat the year before, she intended this time to make a proper voyage before being turned out. If she and her cronies from the college kitchens could get as far as Abingdon they could play havoc with the weir...

But this year there was to be no war. As she sauntered along the edge of the boatyard in Port Meadow in the morning sun with a couple of urchins, passing a stolen cigarette from one to another and blowing out the smoke ostentatiously, she heard a cry in a voice she recognized.

"Well, what have you *done* with him, you half-arsed pillock?"

It was a mighty voice, a woman's voice, but a woman with lungs of brass and leather. Lyra looked around for her at once, because this was

Ma Costa, who had clouted Lyra dizzy on two occasions but given her hot gingerbread on three, and whose family was noted for the grandeur and sumptuousness of their boat. They were princes among gyptians, and Lyra admired Ma Costa greatly, but she intended to be wary of her for some time yet, for theirs was the boat she had hijacked.

One of Lyra's brat-companions picked up a stone automatically when he heard the commotion, but Lyra said, "Put it down. She's in a temper. She could snap your backbone like a twig."

In fact, Ma Costa looked more anxious than angry. The man she was addressing, a horse-trader, was shrugging and spreading his hands.

"Well, I dunno," he was saying. "He was here one minute and gone the next. I never saw where he went…"

"He was helping you! He was holding your bloody horses for you!"

"Well, he should've stayed there, shouldn't he? Runs off in the middle of a job –"

He got no further, because Ma Costa suddenly dealt him a mighty blow on the side of the head, and followed it up with such a volley of curses and slaps that he yelled and turned to flee. The other horse-traders nearby jeered, and a flighty colt reared up in alarm.

"What's going on?" said Lyra to a gyptian child who'd been watching open-mouthed. "What's she angry about?"

"It's her kid," said the child. "It's Billy. She prob'ly reckons the Gobblers got him. They might've done, too. I ain't seen him meself since—"

"The Gobblers? Has they come to Oxford, then?"

The gyptian boy turned away to call to his friends, who were all watching Ma Costa.

"She don't know what's going on! She don't know the Gobblers is here!"

Half a dozen brats turned with expressions of derision, and Lyra threw her cigarette down, recognizing the cue for a fight. Everyone's dæmon instantly became warlike: each child was accompanied by fangs, or claws, or bristling fur, and Pantalaimon, contemptuous of the limited imaginations of these gyptian dæmons, became a dragon the size of a deer-hound.

But before they could all join battle, Ma Costa herself waded in, smacking two of the gyptians aside and confronting Lyra like a prize-fighter.

"You seen him?" she demanded of Lyra. "You seen Billy?"

"No," Lyra said. "We just got here. I en't seen Billy for months."

Ma Costa's dæmon was wheeling in the bright air above her head, a hawk, fierce yellow eyes snapping this way and that, unblinking. Lyra was frightened. No one worried about a child gone missing for a few hours, certainly not a gyptian: in the tight-knit gyptian boat-world, all children were precious and extravagantly loved, and a mother knew that if a child was out of *her* sight, it wouldn't be far from someone else's who would protect it instinctively.

But here was Ma Costa, a queen among the gyptians, in a terror for a missing child. What was going on?

Ma Costa looked half-blindly over the little group of children and turned away to stumble through the crowd on the wharf, bellowing for her child. At once the children turned back to one another, their feud abandoned in the face of her grief.

"What *is* them Gobblers?" said Simon Parslow, one of Lyra's companions.

The first gyptian boy said, "*You* know. They been stealing kids all over the country. They're pirates –"

"They en't pirates," corrected another gyptian. "They're cannaboles.

That's why they call 'em Gobblers."

"They *eat* kids?" said Lyra's other crony Hugh Lovat, a kitchen boy from St Michael's.

"No one knows," said the first gyptian. "They take 'em away and they en't never seen again."

"We all know that," said Lyra. "We been playing kids and Gobblers for months, before you were, I bet. But I bet no one's seen 'em."

"They have," said one boy.

"Who, then?" persisted Lyra. "Have *you* seen 'em? How d'you know it en't just one person?"

"Charlie seen 'em in Banbury," said a gyptian girl. "They come and talked to this lady while another man took her little boy out the garden."

"Yeah," piped up Charlie, a gyptian boy. "I seen 'em do it!"

"What did they look like?" said Lyra.

"Well ... I never properly saw 'em," Charlie said. "I saw their truck, though," he added. "They come in a white truck. They put the little boy in the truck and drove off quick."

"But why do they call 'em Gobblers?" Lyra asked.

"'Cause they eat 'em," said the first gyptian boy. "Someone told us in Northampton. They been up there and all. This girl in Northampton, her brother was took, and she said the men as took him told her they was going to eat him. Everyone knows that. They gobble 'em up."

A gyptian girl standing nearby began to cry loudly.

"That's Billy's cousin," said Charlie.

Lyra said, "Who saw Billy last?"

"Me," said half a dozen voices. "I seen him holding Johnny Fiorelli's old horse – I seen him by the toffee-apple seller – I seen him swinging on the crane –"

When Lyra had sorted it out, she gathered that Billy had been seen for certain not less than two hours previously.

"So," she said, "some time in the last two hours there must've been Gobblers here…"

They all looked around, shivering in spite of the warm sun, the crowded wharf, the familiar smells of tar and horses and smoking-leaf. The trouble was that because no one knew what these Gobblers looked like, anyone might be a Gobbler, as Lyra pointed out to the appalled gang, who were now all under her sway, collegers and gyptians alike.

"They're *bound* to look like ordinary people, else they'd be seen at once," she explained. "If they only came at night, they could look like anything. But if they come in the daylight they got to look ordinary. So any of these people might be Gobblers…"

"They en't," said a gyptian uncertainly. "I know 'em all."

"All right, not *these*, but anyone else," said Lyra. "Let's go and look for 'em! And their white truck!"

And that precipitated a swarm. Other searchers soon joined the first ones, and before long, thirty or more gyptian children were racing from end to end of the wharves, running in and out of stables, scrambling over the cranes and derricks in the boatyard, leaping over the fence into the wide meadow, swinging fifteen at a time on the old swing bridge over the green water, and running full pelt through the narrow streets of Jericho, between the little brick terraced houses and into the great square-towered oratory of St Barnabas the Chymist. Half of them didn't know what they were looking for, and thought it was just a lark, but those closest to Lyra felt a real fear and apprehension every time they glimpsed a solitary figure down an alley or in the dimness of the Oratory: was it a Gobbler?

But of course they weren't. Eventually, with no success, and with the shadow of Billy's real disappearance hanging over them all, the fun faded away. As Lyra and the two college boys left Jericho when supper-time neared, they saw the gyptians gathering on the wharf next to where the Costas' boat was moored. Some of the women were crying loudly, and the men were standing in angry groups, with all their dæmons agitated and rising in nervous flight or snarling at shadows.

"I bet them Gobblers wouldn't dare come in here," said Lyra to Simon Parslow, as the two of them stepped over the threshold into the great lodge of Jordan.

"No," he said uncertainly. "But I know there's a kid missing from the Market."

"Who?" Lyra said. She knew most of the Market children, but she hadn't heard of this.

"Jessie Reynolds, out the saddler's. She weren't there at shutting-up time yesterday, and she'd only gone for a bit of fish for her dad's tea. She never come back and no one'd seen her. They searched all through the Market and everywhere."

"I never heard about that!" said Lyra, indignant. She considered it a deplorable lapse on the part of her subjects not to tell her everything and at once.

"Well, it was only yesterday. She might've turned up now."

"I'm going to ask," said Lyra, and turned to leave the Lodge.

But she hadn't got out of the gate before the Porter called her.

"Here, Lyra! You're not to go out again this evening. Master's orders."

"Why not?"

"I told you, Master's orders. He says if you come in, you stay in."

"You catch me," she said, and darted out before the old man could leave his doorway.

She ran across the narrow street and down into the alley where the vans unloaded goods for the Covered Market. This being shutting-up time, there were few vans there now, but a knot of youths stood smoking and talking by the central gate opposite the high stone wall of St Michael's College. Lyra knew one of them, a sixteen-year-old she admired because he could spit further than anyone else she'd ever heard of, and she went and waited humbly for him to notice her.

"Yeah? What do you want?" he said finally.

"Is Jessie Reynolds disappeared?"

"Yeah. Why?"

" 'Cause a gyptian kid disappeared today and all."

"They're always disappearing, gyptians. After every Horse Fair they disappear."

"So do horses," said one of his friends.

"This is different," said Lyra. "This is a kid. We was looking for him all afternoon and the other kids said the Gobblers got him."

"The what?"

"The Gobblers," she said. "En't you heard of the Gobblers?"

It was news to the other boys as well, and apart from a few coarse comments they listened closely to what she told them.

"Gobblers," said Lyra's acquaintance, whose name was Dick. "It's stupid. These gyptians, they pick up all kinds of stupid ideas."

"They said there was Gobblers in Banbury a couple of weeks ago," Lyra insisted, "and there was five kids taken. They probably come to Oxford now to get kids from us. It must've been them what got Jessie."

"There was a kid lost over Cowley way," said one of the other boys. "I remember now. My auntie, she was there yesterday, 'cause she sells fish and chips out a van, and she heard about it… Some little boy, that's it… I dunno about the Gobblers, though. They en't real, Gobblers. Just a story."

"They are!" Lyra said. "The gyptians seen 'em. They reckon they eat the kids they catch, and…"

She stopped in mid-sentence, because something had suddenly come into her mind. During that strange evening she'd spent hidden in the Retiring Room, Lord Asriel had shown a lantern slide of a man holding up a wand with streams of light pouring into it; and there'd been a small figure beside him, with less light around it; and he'd said it was a child; and someone had asked if it was a severed child, and her uncle had said no, that was the point. Lyra remembered that severed meant cut.

And then something else hit her heart: where was Roger?

She hadn't seen him since the morning…

Suddenly she felt afraid. Pantalaimon, as a miniature lion, sprang into her arms and growled. She said goodbye to the youths by the gate and walked quietly back into Turl Street, and then ran full pelt for Jordan Lodge, tumbling in through the door a second before the now cheetah-shaped dæmon.

The Porter was sanctimonious.

"I had to ring the Master and tell him," he said. "He en't pleased at all. I wouldn't be in your shoes, not for money I wouldn't."

"Where's Roger?" she demanded.

"I en't seen him. He'll be for it, too. Ooh, when Mr Cawston catches him –"

Lyra ran to the Kitchen and thrust her way into the hot, clangorous, steaming bustle.

"Where's Roger?" she shouted.

"Clear off, Lyra! We're busy here!"

"But where is he? Has he turned up or not?"

No one seemed interested.

"But where is he? You *must've* heard!" Lyra shouted at the chef, who boxed her ears and sent her storming away.

Bernie the pastrycook tried to calm her down, but she wouldn't be consoled.

"They got him! Them bloody Gobblers, they oughter catch 'em and bloody kill 'em! I hate 'em! You don't care about Roger –"

"Lyra, we all care about Roger –"

"You don't, else you'd all stop work and go and look for him right now! I hate you!"

"There could be a dozen reasons why Roger en't turned up. Listen to sense. We got dinner to prepare and serve in less than an hour; the Master's got guests in the Lodging, and he'll be eating over there, and that means Chef'll have to attend to getting the food there quick so it don't go cold; and what with one thing and another, Lyra, life's got to go on. I'm sure Roger'll turn up..."

Lyra turned and ran out of the Kitchen, knocking over a stack of silver dish-covers and ignoring the roar of anger that arose. She sped down the steps and across the quadrangle, between the Chapel and Palmer's Tower and into the Yaxley Quad, where the oldest buildings of the College stood.

Pantalaimon scampered before her like a miniature cheetah, flowing up the stairs to the very top, where Lyra's bedroom was. Lyra barged open the door, dragged her rickety chair to the window, flung wide the casement and scrambled out. There was a lead-lined stone gutter a foot wide just below the window, and once she was standing in that, she turned and clambered up over the rough tiles until she stood on the topmost ridge of the roof. There she opened her mouth and screamed. Pantalaimon, who always became a bird once on the roof, flew round and round shrieking rook-shrieks with her.

The evening sky was awash with peach, apricot, cream: tender little ice-cream clouds in a wide orange sky. The spires and towers of Oxford stood around them, level but no higher; the green woods of Château-Vert and White Ham rose on either side to the east and the west. Rooks were cawing somewhere, and bells were ringing, and from the Oxpens the steady beat of a gas engine announced the ascent of the evening Royal Mail zeppelin for London. Lyra watched it climb away beyond the spire of St Michael's Chapel, as big at first as the tip of her little finger when she held it at arm's length, and then steadily smaller until it was a dot in the pearly sky.

She turned and looked down into the shadowed quadrangle, where the black-gowned figures of the Scholars were already beginning to drift in ones and twos towards the Buttery, their dæmons strutting or fluttering alongside or perching calmly on their shoulders. The lights were going on in the Hall; she could see the stained-glass windows gradually beginning to glow as a servant moved up the tables lighting the naphtha lamps. The Steward's bell began to toll, announcing half an hour before dinner.

This was her world. She wanted it to stay the same for ever and ever, but it was changing around her, for someone out there was stealing children. She sat on the roof-ridge, chin in hands.

"We better rescue him, Pantalaimon," she said.

He answered in his rook-voice from the chimney.

"It'll be dangerous," he said.

"Course! I know that."

"Remember what they said in the Retiring Room."

"What?"

"Something about a child up in the Arctic. The one that wasn't attracting the Dust."

"They said it was an entire child… What about it?"

"That might be what they're going to do to Roger and the gyptians and the other kids."

"What?"

"Well, what does *entire* mean?"

"Dunno. They cut 'em in half, probably. I reckon they make slaves out of 'em. That'd be more use. They probably got mines up there. Uranium mines for atomcraft. I bet that's what it is. And if they sent grown-ups down the mine they'd be dead, so they use kids instead because they cost less. That's what they've done with him."

"I think –"

But what Pantalaimon thought had to wait, because someone began to shout from below.

"Lyra! Lyra! You come in this instant!"

There was a banging on the window-frame. Lyra knew the voice and the impatience: it was Mrs Lonsdale the Housekeeper. There was no hiding from her.

Tight-faced, Lyra slid down the roof and into the gutter, and then climbed in through the window again. Mrs Lonsdale was running some water into the little chipped basin, to the accompaniment of a great groaning and hammering from the pipes.

"The number of times you been told about going out there… Look at you! Just look at your skirt – it's filthy! Take it off at once and wash yourself while I look for something decent that en't torn. Why you can't keep yourself clean and tidy…"

Lyra was too sulky even to ask why she was having to wash and dress, and no grown-up ever gave reasons of their own accord. She dragged the dress over her head and dropped it on the narrow bed, and began to wash desultorily while Pantalaimon, a canary now, hopped closer and closer to Mrs Lonsdale's dæmon, a stolid retriever, trying in vain to annoy him.

"Look at the state of this wardrobe! You en't hung nothing up for weeks! Look at the creases in this –"

Look at this, look at that … Lyra didn't want to look. She shut her eyes as she rubbed at her face with the thin towel.

"You'll just have to wear it as it is. There en't time to take an iron to it. God bless me, girl, your *knees* – look at the state of them…"

"Don't want to look at nothing," Lyra muttered.

Mrs Lonsdale smacked her leg. "Wash," she said ferociously. "You get all that dirt off."

"Why?" Lyra said at last. "I never wash my knees usually. No one's going to look at my knees. What've I got to do all this for? You don't care about Roger neither, any more than Chef does. I'm the only one that –"

Another smack, on the other leg.

"None of that nonsense. I'm a Parslow, same as Roger's father. He's my second cousin. I bet you didn't know that, 'cause I bet you never asked, Miss Lyra. I bet it never occurred to you. Don't you chide me with not caring about the boy. God knows, I even care about you, and you give me little enough reason and no thanks."

She seized the flannel and rubbed Lyra's knees so hard she left the skin bright pink and sore, but clean.

"The reason for this is you're going to have dinner with the Master and his guests. I hope to God you behave. Speak when you're spoken to, be quiet and polite, smile nicely and don't you ever say *Dunno* when someone asks you a question."

She dragged the best dress on to Lyra's skinny frame, tugged it straight, fished a bit of red ribbon out of the tangle in a drawer, and brushed Lyra's hair with a coarse brush.

"If they'd let me know earlier I could've given your hair a proper wash. Well, that's too bad. As long as they don't look too close… There.

Now stand up straight. Where's those best patent-leather shoes?"

Five minutes later Lyra was knocking on the door of the Master's Lodging, the grand and slightly gloomy house that opened into the Yaxley Quadrangle and backed on to the Library Garden. Pantalaimon, an ermine now for politeness, rubbed himself against her leg. The door was opened by the Master's manservant Cousins, an old enemy of Lyra's; but both knew that this was a state of truce.

"Mrs Lonsdale said I was to come," said Lyra.

"Yes," said Cousins, stepping aside. "The Master's in the Drawing Room."

He showed her into the large room that overlooked the Library Garden. The last of the sun shone into it, through the gap between the Library and Palmer's Tower, and lit up the heavy pictures and the glum silver the Master collected. It also lit up the guests, and Lyra realized why they weren't going to dine in Hall: three of the guests were women.

"Ah, Lyra," said the Master. "I'm so glad you could come. Cousins, could you find some sort of soft drink? Dame Hannah, I don't think you've met Lyra … Lord Asriel's niece, you know."

Dame Hannah Relf was the Head of one of the women's colleges, an elderly grey-haired lady whose dæmon was a marmoset. Lyra shook hands as politely as she could, and was then introduced to the other guests, who were, like Dame Hannah, scholars from other Colleges and quite uninteresting. Then the Master came to the final guest.

"Mrs Coulter," he said, "this is our Lyra. Lyra, come and say hello to Mrs Coulter."

"Hello, Lyra," said Mrs Coulter.

She was beautiful and young. Her sleek black hair framed her cheeks, and her dæmon was a golden monkey.

4

The Alethiometer

"I hope you'll sit next to me at dinner," said Mrs Coulter, making room for Lyra on the sofa. "I'm not used to the grandeur of a Master's Lodging. You'll have to show me which knife and fork to use."

"Are you a female Scholar?" said Lyra. She regarded female Scholars with a proper Jordan disdain: there *were* such people but, poor things, they could never be taken more seriously than animals dressed up and acting a play. Mrs Coulter, on the other hand, was not like any female Scholar Lyra had seen, and certainly not like the two serious elderly ladies who were the other female guests. Lyra had asked the question expecting the answer no, in fact, for Mrs Coulter had such an air of glamour that Lyra was entranced. She could hardly take her eyes off her.

"Not really," Mrs Coulter said. "I'm a member of Dame Hannah's college, but most of my work takes place outside Oxford... Tell me about yourself, Lyra. Have you always lived at Jordan College?"

Within five minutes Lyra had told her everything about her half-wild life: her favourite routes over the roof-tops, the battle of the

Claybeds, the time she and Roger had caught and roasted a rook, her intention to capture a narrow-boat from the gyptians and sail it to Abingdon, and so on. She even (looking around and lowering her voice) told her about the trick she and Roger had played on the skulls in the crypt.

"And these ghosts came, right, they came to my bedroom without their heads! They couldn't talk except for making sort of gurgling noises, but I knew what they wanted all right. So I went down next day and put their coins back. They'd probably have killed me else."

"You're not afraid of danger, then?" said Mrs Coulter admiringly. They were at dinner by this time, and as Mrs Coulter had hoped, sitting next to each other. Lyra ignored completely the Librarian on her other side and spent the whole meal talking to Mrs Coulter.

When the ladies withdrew for coffee, Dame Hannah said, "Tell me, Lyra – are they going to send you to school?"

Lyra looked blank. "I dun – I don't know," she said. "Probably not," she added for safety. "I wouldn't want to put them to any trouble," she went on piously. "Or expense. It's probably better if I just go on living at Jordan and getting educated by the Scholars here when they've got a bit of spare time. Being as they're here already, they're probably free."

"And does your uncle Lord Asriel have any plans for you?" said the other lady, who was a Scholar at the other women's college.

"Yes," said Lyra. "I expect so. Not school, though. He's going to take me to the North next time he goes."

"I remember him telling me," said Mrs Coulter.

Lyra blinked. The two female Scholars sat up very slightly, though their dæmons, either well-behaved or torpid, did no more than flick their eyes at each other.

"I met him at the Royal Arctic Institute," Mrs Coulter went on. "As a matter of fact it's partly because of that meeting that I'm here today."

"Are you an explorer too?" said Lyra.

"In a kind of way. I've been to the North several times. Last year I spent three months in Greenland making observations of the Aurora."

That was it; nothing and no one else existed now for Lyra. She gazed at Mrs Coulter with awe, and listened rapt and silent to her tales of igloo-building, of seal-hunting, of negotiating with the Lapland witches. The two female Scholars had nothing so exciting to tell, and sat in silence until the men came in.

Later, when the guests were preparing to leave, the Master said, "Stay behind, Lyra. I'd like to talk to you for a minute or two. Go to my study, child; sit down there and wait for me."

Puzzled, tired, exhilarated, Lyra did as he told her. Cousins the manservant showed her in, and pointedly left the door open so that he could see what she was up to from the hall, where he was helping people on with their coats. Lyra watched for Mrs Coulter, but she didn't see her, and then the Master came into the study and shut the door.

He sat down heavily in the armchair by the fireplace. His dæmon flapped up to the chair-back and sat by his head, her old hooded eyes on Lyra. The lamp hissed gently as the Master said:

"So, Lyra. You've been talking to Mrs Coulter. Did you enjoy hearing what she said?"

"Yes!"

"She is a remarkable lady."

"She's wonderful. She's the most wonderful person I've ever met."

The Master sighed. In his black suit and black tie he looked as much like his dæmon as anyone could, and suddenly Lyra thought that one day, quite soon, he would be buried in the crypt under the Oratory, and an artist would engrave a picture of his dæmon on the brass plate for his coffin, and her name would share the space with his.

"I should have made time before now for a talk with you, Lyra," he said after a few moments. "I was intending to do so in any case, but it seems that time is further on than I thought. You have been safe here in Jordan, my dear. I think you've been happy. You haven't found it easy to obey us, but we are very fond of you, and you've never been a bad child. There's a lot of goodness and sweetness in your nature, and a lot of determination. You're going to need all of that. Things are going on in the wide world I would have liked to protect you from – by keeping you here in Jordan, I mean – but that's no longer possible."

She merely stared. Were they going to send her away?

"You knew that sometime you'd have to go to school," the Master went on. "We have taught you some things here, but not well or systematically. Our knowledge is of a different kind. You need to know things that elderly men are not able to teach you, especially at the age you are now. You must have been aware of that. You're not a servant's child either; we couldn't put you out to be fostered by a town family. They might have cared for you in some ways, but your needs are different. You see, what I'm saying to you, Lyra, is that the part of your life that belongs to Jordan College is coming to an end."

"No," she said, "no, I don't want to leave Jordan. I like it here. I want to stay here for ever."

"When you're young, you do think that things last for ever. Unfortunately, they don't. Lyra, it won't be long – a couple of years at most – before you will be a young woman, and not a child any more. A young lady. And believe me, you'll find Jordan College a far from easy place to live in then."

"But it's my home!"

"It has been your home. But now you need something else."

"Not school. I'm not going to school."

"You need female company. Female guidance."

The word *female* only suggested female Scholars to Lyra, and she involuntarily made a face. To be exiled from the grandeur of Jordan, the splendour and fame of its scholarship, to a dingy brick-built boarding-house of a college at the northern end of Oxford, with dowdy female Scholars who smelt of cabbage and mothballs like those two at dinner!

The Master saw her expression, and saw Pantalaimon's polecat-eyes flash red.

He said, "But suppose it were Mrs Coulter?"

Instantly Pantalaimon's fur changed from coarse brown to downy white. Lyra's eyes widened.

"Really?"

"She is by way of being acquainted with Lord Asriel. Your uncle, of course, is very concerned with your welfare, and when Mrs Coulter heard about you, she offered at once to help. There is no Mr Coulter, by the way; she is a widow; her husband died very sadly in an accident some years ago; so you might bear that in mind before you ask."

Lyra nodded eagerly, and said, "And she's really going to ... look after me?"

"Would you like that?"

"Yes!"

She could hardly sit still. The Master smiled. He smiled so rarely that he was out of practice, and anyone watching (Lyra wasn't in a state to notice) would have said it was a grimace of sadness.

"Well, we had better ask her in to talk about it," he said.

He left the room, and when he came back a minute later with Mrs Coulter, Lyra was on her feet, too excited to sit. Mrs Coulter smiled, and her dæmon bared his white teeth in a grin of imp–like pleasure. As she passed her on the way to the armchair, Mrs Coulter touched Lyra's hair briefly, and Lyra felt a current of warmth flow into her, and blushed.

When the Master had poured some brantwijn for her, Mrs Coulter said, "So, Lyra, I'm to have an assistant, am I?"

"Yes," said Lyra simply. She would have said yes to anything.

"There's a lot of work I need help with."

"I can work!"

"And we might have to travel."

"I don't mind. I'd go anywhere."

"But it might be dangerous. We might have to go to the North."

Lyra was speechless. Then she found her voice: "Soon?"

Mrs Coulter laughed, and said, "Possibly. But you know you'll have to work very hard. You'll have to learn mathematics, and navigation, and celestial geography."

"Will *you* teach me?"

"Yes. And you'll have to help me by making notes and putting my papers in order and doing various pieces of basic calculation, and so on. And because we'll be visiting some important people, we'll have to find you some pretty clothes. There's a lot to learn, Lyra."

"I don't mind. I want to learn it all."

"I'm sure you will. When you come back to Jordan College you'll be a famous traveller. Now we're going to leave very early in the morning, by the dawn zeppelin, so you'd better run along and go straight to bed. I'll see you at breakfast. Good night!"

"Good night," said Lyra and, remembering the few manners she had, turned at the door and said, "Good night, Master."

He nodded. "Sleep well," he said.

"And thanks," Lyra added to Mrs Coulter.

She did sleep, finally, though Pantalaimon wouldn't settle until she snapped at him, when he became a hedgehog out of pique. It was still dark when someone shook her awake.

"Lyra – hush – don't start – wake up, child."

It was Mrs Lonsdale. She was holding a candle, and she bent over and spoke quietly, holding Lyra still with her free hand.

"Listen. The Master wants to see you before you join Mrs Coulter for breakfast. Get up quickly and run across to the Lodging now. Go into the garden and tap at the French window of the study. You understand?"

Fully awake and on fire with puzzlement, Lyra nodded and slipped her bare feet into the shoes Mrs Lonsdale put down for her.

"Never mind washing – that'll do later. Go straight down and come straight back. I'll start your packing and have something for you to wear. Hurry now."

The dark quadrangle was still full of the chill night air. Overhead the last stars were still visible, but the light from the east was gradually soaking into the sky above the Hall. Lyra ran into the Library Garden, and stood for a moment in the immense hush, looking up at the stone pinnacles of the Chapel, the pearl-green cupola of the Sheldon Building, the white-painted lantern of the Library. Now she was going to leave these sights, she wondered how much she'd miss them.

Something stirred in the study window and a glow of light shone out for a moment. She remembered what she had to do and tapped on the glass door. It opened almost at once.

"Good girl. Come in quickly. We haven't got long," said the Master, and drew the curtain back across the door as soon as she had entered.

He was fully dressed in his usual black.

"Aren't I going after all?" Lyra asked.

"Yes; I can't prevent it," said the Master, and Lyra didn't notice at the time what an odd thing that was to say. "Lyra, I'm going to give you something, and you must promise to keep it private. Will you swear to that?"

"Yes," Lyra said.

He crossed to the desk and took from a drawer a small package wrapped in black velvet. When he unfolded the cloth, Lyra saw something like a large watch or a small clock: a thick disc of brass and crystal. It might have been a compass or something of the sort.

"What is it?" she said.

"It's an alethiometer. It's one of only six that were ever made. Lyra, I urge you again: keep it private. It would be better if Mrs Coulter didn't know about it. Your uncle –"

"But what does it do?"

"It tells you the truth. As for how to read it, you'll have to learn by yourself. Now go – it's getting lighter – hurry back to your room before anyone sees you."

He folded the velvet over the instrument and thrust it into her hands. It was surprisingly heavy. Then he put his own hands on either side of her head and held her gently for a moment.

She tried to look up at him, and said, "What were you going to say about Uncle Asriel?"

"Your uncle presented it to Jordan College some years ago. He might –"

Before he could finish, there came a soft urgent knock on the door. She could feel his hands give an involuntary tremor.

"Quick now, child," he said quietly. "The powers of this world are very strong. Men and women are moved by tides much fiercer than you can imagine, and they sweep us all up into the current. Go well, Lyra; bless you, child; bless you. Keep your own counsel."

"Thank you, Master," she said dutifully.

Clutching the bundle to her breast, she left the study by the garden door, looking back briefly once to see the Master's dæmon watching her from the windowsill. The sky was lighter already; there was a faint fresh stir in the air.

"What's that you've got?" said Mrs Lonsdale, closing the battered little suitcase with a snap.

"The Master gave it me. Can't it go in the suitcase?"

"Too late. I'm not opening it now. It'll have to go in your coat pocket, whatever it is. Hurry on down to the Buttery; don't keep them waiting…"

It was only after she'd said goodbye to the few servants who were up, and to Mrs Lonsdale, that she remembered Roger; and then she felt guilty for not having thought of him once since meeting Mrs Coulter. How quickly it had all happened!

And now she was on her way to London: sitting next to the window in a zeppelin, no less, with Pantalaimon's sharp little ermine-paws digging into her thigh while his front paws rested against the glass he gazed through. On Lyra's other side Mrs Coulter sat working through some papers, but she soon put them away and talked. Such brilliant talk! Lyra was intoxicated; not about the North this time, but about London, and the restaurants and ballrooms, the soirées at Embassies or Ministries, the intrigues between White Hall and Westminster. Lyra was almost more fascinated by this than by the changing landscape below the airship. What Mrs Coulter was saying seemed to be accompanied by a scent of grown-upness, something disturbing but enticing at the same time: it was the smell of glamour.

The landing in Falkeshall Gardens, the boat ride across the wide brown river, the grand mansion-block on the Embankment where a stout commissionaire (a sort of porter with medals) saluted Mrs Coulter and winked at Lyra, who sized him up expressionlessly...

And then the flat...

Lyra could only gasp.

She had seen a great deal of beauty in her short life, but it was Jordan College beauty, Oxford beauty – grand and stony and masculine. In Jordan College, much was magnificent, but nothing was pretty. In Mrs Coulter's flat, everything was pretty. It was full of light, for the wide windows faced south, and the walls were covered in a delicate gold-and-white striped wallpaper. Charming pictures in gilt frames, an antique looking-glass, fanciful sconces bearing anbaric lamps with frilled shades; and frills on the cushions too, and flowery valances over the curtain-rail, and a soft green leaf-pattern carpet underfoot; and every surface was covered, it seemed to Lyra's innocent eye, with pretty little china boxes and shepherdesses and harlequins of porcelain.

Mrs Coulter smiled at her admiration.

"Yes, Lyra," she said, "there's such a lot to show you! Take your coat off and I'll take you to the bathroom. You can have a wash, and then we'll have some lunch and go shopping..."

The bathroom was another wonder. Lyra was used to washing with hard yellow soap in a chipped basin, where the water that struggled out of the taps was warm at best, and often flecked with rust. But here the water was hot, the soap rose-pink and fragrant, the towels thick and cloudy-soft. And around the edge of the tinted mirror there were little pink lights, so that when Lyra looked into it she saw a softly illuminated figure quite unlike the Lyra she knew.

Pantalaimon, who was imitating the form of Mrs Coulter's dæmon, crouched on the edge of the basin making faces at her. She pushed him into the soapy water and suddenly remembered the alethiometer in her coat pocket. She'd left the coat on a chair in the other room. She'd promised the Master to keep it secret from Mrs Coulter...

Oh, this *was* confusing. Mrs Coulter was so kind and wise, whereas Lyra had actually seen the Master trying to poison Uncle Asriel. Which of them did she owe most obedience to?

She rubbed herself dry hastily and hurried back to the sitting room, where her coat still lay untouched, of course.

"Ready?" said Mrs Coulter. "I thought we'd go to the Royal Arctic Institute for lunch. I'm one of the very few female members, so I might as well use the privileges I have."

Twenty minutes' walk took them to a grand stone-fronted building where they sat in a wide dining-room with snowy cloths and bright silver on the tables, and ate calves' liver and bacon.

"Calves' liver is all right," Mrs Coulter told her, "and so is seal liver, but if you're stuck for food in the Arctic, you mustn't eat bear liver. That's full of a poison that'll kill you in minutes."

As they ate, Mrs Coulter pointed out some of the members at the other tables.

"D'you see the elderly gentleman with the red tie? That's Colonel Carborn. He made the first balloon flight over the North Pole. And the tall man by the window who's just got up is Dr Broken Arrow."

"Is he a Skraeling?"

"Yes. He was the man who mapped the ocean currents in the Great Northern Ocean..."

Lyra looked at them all, these great men, with curiosity and awe. They were scholars, no doubt about that, but they were explorers too. Dr Broken Arrow would know about bear livers; she doubted whether the Librarian of Jordan College would.

After lunch Mrs Coulter showed her some of the precious Arctic relics in the Institute Library – the harpoon with which the great whale Grimssdur had been killed; the stone carved with an inscription in an unknown language which was found in the hand of the explorer Lord Rukh, frozen to death in his lonely tent; a fire-striker used by Captain Hudson on his famous voyage to Van Tieren's Land. She told the story of each one, and Lyra felt her heart stir with admiration of these great, brave, distant heroes.

And then they went shopping. Everything on this extraordinary day was a new experience for Lyra, but shopping was the most dizzying. To go into a vast building full of beautiful clothes, where people let you try them on, where you looked at yourself in mirrors... And the clothes were so *pretty*... Lyra's clothes had come to her through Mrs Lonsdale, and a lot of them had been handed down and much mended. She had seldom had anything new, and when she had, it had been picked for wear and not for looks; and she had never chosen anything for herself. And now to find Mrs Coulter suggesting this, and praising that, and paying for it all, and more...

By the time they'd finished, Lyra was flushed and bright-eyed with tiredness. Mrs Coulter ordered most of the clothes packed up and delivered, and took one or two things with her when she and Lyra walked back to the flat.

Then a bath, with thick scented foam. Mrs Coulter came into the bathroom to wash Lyra's hair, and she didn't rub and scrape like Mrs Lonsdale either. She was gentle. Pantalaimon watched with powerful curiosity until Mrs Coulter looked at him, and he knew what she meant and turned away, averting his eyes modestly from these feminine mysteries as the golden monkey was doing. He had never had to look away from Lyra before.

Then, after the bath, a warm drink with milk and herbs; and a new flannel nightdress with printed flowers and a scalloped hem, and sheepskin slippers dyed soft blue; and then bed.

So soft, this bed! So gentle, the anbaric light on the bedside table! And the bedroom so cosy with little cupboards and a dressing-table and a chest of drawers where her new clothes would go, and a carpet from one wall to the other, and pretty curtains covered in stars and moons and planets! Lyra lay stiffly, too tired to sleep, too enchanted to question anything.

When Mrs Coulter had wished her a soft good night and gone out, Pantalaimon plucked at her hair. She brushed him away, but he whispered, "Where's the thing?"

She knew at once what he meant. Her old shabby overcoat hung in the wardrobe; a few seconds later, she was back in bed, sitting up cross-legged in the lamplight, with Pantalaimon watching closely as she unfolded the black velvet and looked at what it was the Master had given her.

"What did he call it?" she whispered.

"An alethiometer."

There was no point in asking what that meant. It lay heavily in her hands, the crystal face gleaming, the brass body exquisitely machined. It was very like a clock, or a compass, for there were hands pointing to places around the dial, but instead of the hours or the points of the compass there were several little pictures, each of them painted with extraordinary precision, as if on ivory with the finest and slenderest sable brush. She turned the dial around to look at them all. There was an anchor; an hourglass surmounted by a skull; a bull, a beehive... Thirty-six altogether, and she couldn't even guess what they meant.

"There's a wheel, look," said Pantalaimon. "See if you can wind it up."

There were three little knurled winding-wheels, in fact, and each of them turned one of the three shorter hands, which moved around the dial in a series of smooth satisfying clicks. You could arrange them to point at any of the pictures, and once they had clicked into position, pointing exactly at the centre of each one, they would not move.

The fourth hand was longer and more slender, and seemed to be made of a duller metal than the other three. Lyra couldn't control its movement at all; it swung where it wanted to, like a compass-needle, except that it didn't settle.

"Meter means measure," said Pantalaimon. "Like thermometer. The Chaplain told us that."

"Yes, but that's the easy bit," she whispered back. "What d'you think it's *for*?"

Neither of them could guess. Lyra spent a long time turning the hands to point at one symbol or another (angel, helmet, dolphin; globe, lute, compasses; candle, thunderbolt, horse) and watching the long needle swing on its never-ceasing errant way, and although she understood nothing, she was intrigued and delighted by the complexity and the detail. Pantalaimon became a mouse to get closer to it, and rested his tiny paws on the edge, his button eyes bright black with curiosity as he watched the needle swing.

"What do you think the Master meant about Uncle Asriel?" she said.

"Perhaps we've got to keep it safe and give it to him."

"But the Master was going to poison him! Perhaps it's the opposite.

Perhaps he was going to say, don't give it to him."

"No," Pantalaimon said, "it was *her* we had to keep it safe from –"

There was a soft knock on the door.

Mrs Coulter said, "Lyra, I should put the light out if I were you. You're tired, and we'll be busy tomorrow."

Lyra had thrust the alethiometer swiftly under the blankets.

"All right, Mrs Coulter," she said.

"Good night now."

"Good night."

She snuggled down and switched off the light. Before she fell asleep, she tucked the alethiometer under the pillow, just in case.

5

The Cocktail Party

 *I*n the days that followed, Lyra went every-
where with Mrs Coulter, almost as if she
were a dæmon herself. Mrs Coulter knew a
great many people, and they met in all kinds of
different places. In the morning there might
be a meeting of geographers at the Royal
Arctic Institute, and Lyra would sit by and lis-
ten; and then Mrs Coulter might meet a politician or a cleric for lunch
in a smart restaurant, and they would be very taken with Lyra and order
special dishes for her, and she would learn how to eat asparagus or what
sweetbreads tasted like. And then in the afternoon there might be more
shopping, for Mrs Coulter was preparing her expedition, and there
were furs and oilskins and waterproof boots to buy, as well as sleeping-
bags and knives and drawing instruments that delighted Lyra's heart.
After that they might go to tea and meet some ladies, as well-dressed as
Mrs Coulter if not so beautiful or accomplished: women so unlike
female scholars or gyptian boat-mothers or college servants as almost to
be a new sex altogether, one with dangerous powers and qualities such
as elegance, charm, and grace. Lyra would be dressed up prettily for
these occasions, and the ladies would pamper her and include her in

their graceful delicate talk, which was all about people: this artist, or that politician, or those lovers.

And when the evening came, Mrs Coulter might take Lyra to the theatre, and again there would be lots of glamorous people to talk to and be admired by, for it seemed that Mrs Coulter knew everyone important in London.

In the intervals between all these other activities Mrs Coulter would teach her the rudiments of geography and mathematics. Lyra's knowledge had great gaps in it, like a map of the world largely eaten by mice, for at Jordan they had taught her in a piecemeal and disconnected way: a Junior Scholar would be detailed to catch her and instruct her in such-and-such, and the lessons would continue for a sullen week or so until she "forgot" to turn up, to the Scholar's relief. Or else a Scholar would forget what he was supposed to teach her, and drill her at great length about the subject of his current research, whatever that happened to be. It was no wonder her knowledge was patchy. She knew about atoms and elementary particles, and anbaromagnetic charges and the four fundamental forces and other bits and pieces of experimental theology, but nothing about the solar system. In fact, when Mrs Coulter realized this and explained how the earth and the other five planets revolved around the sun, Lyra laughed loudly at the joke.

However, she was keen to show that she did know some things, and when Mrs Coulter was telling her about electrons, she said expertly, "Yes, they're negatively charged particles. Sort of like Dust, except that Dust isn't charged."

As soon as she said that, Mrs Coulter's dæmon snapped his head up to look at her, and all the golden fur on his little body stood up, bristling, as if it were charged itself. Mrs Coulter laid a hand on his back.

"Dust?" she said.

"Yeah. You know, from space, that Dust."

"What do you know about Dust, Lyra?"

"Oh, that it comes out of space, and it lights people up, if you have a special sort of camera to see it by. Except not children. It doesn't affect children."

"Where did you learn that from?"

By now Lyra was aware that there was a powerful tension in the room, because Pantalaimon had crept ermine-like on to her lap and was trembling violently.

"Just someone in Jordan," Lyra said vaguely. "I forget who. I think it was one of the Scholars."

"Was it in one of your lessons?"

"Yes, it might have been. Or else it might've been just in passing. Yes. I think that was it. This Scholar, I think he was from New Denmark, he was talking to the Chaplain about Dust and I was just passing and it sounded interesting so I couldn't help stopping to listen. That's what it was."

"I see," said Mrs Coulter.

"Is it right, what he told me? Did I get it wrong?"

"Well, I don't know. I'm sure you know much more than I do. Let's get back to those electrons…"

Later, Pantalaimon said, "You know when all the fur stood up on her dæmon? Well, I was behind him, and she grabbed his fur so tight her knuckles went white. You couldn't see. It was a long time till his fur went down. I thought he was going to leap at you."

That was strange, no doubt; but neither of them knew what to make of it.

And finally, there were other kinds of lesson so gently and subtly given that they didn't feel like lessons at all. How to wash one's own hair; how to judge which colours suited one; how to say no in such a charming way that no offence was given; how to put on lipstick, powder, scent. To be sure, Mrs Coulter didn't teach Lyra the latter arts directly, but she knew Lyra was watching when she made herself up, and she took care to let Lyra see where she kept the cosmetics, and to allow her time on her own to explore and try them out for herself.

Time passed, and autumn began to change into winter. From time to time Lyra thought of Jordan College, but it seemed small and quiet compared to the busy life she led now. Every so often she thought of Roger, too, and felt uneasy, but there was an opera to go to, or a new dress to wear, or the Royal Arctic Institute to visit, and then she forgot him again.

When Lyra had been living there for six weeks or so, Mrs Coulter decided to hold a cocktail party. Lyra had the impression that there was something to celebrate, though Mrs Coulter never said what it was. She ordered flowers, she discussed canapés and drinks with the caterer, and she spent a whole evening with Lyra deciding whom to invite.

"We must have the Archbishop. I couldn't afford to leave him out, though he's the most hateful old snob. Lord Boreal is in town: he'll be fun. And the Princess Postnikova. Do you think it would be right to invite Erik Andersson? I wonder if it's about time to take him up…"

Erik Andersson was the latest fashionable dancer. Lyra had no idea what "take him up" meant, but she enjoyed giving her opinion none the less. She dutifully wrote down all the names Mrs Coulter suggested, spelling them atrociously and then crossing them out when Mrs Coulter decided against them after all.

When Lyra went to bed, Pantalaimon whispered from the pillow:

"She's never going to the North! She's going to keep us here for ever. When are we going to run away?"

"She is," Lyra whispered back. "You just don't like her. Well, that's hard luck. I like her. And why would she be teaching us navigation and all that if she wasn't going to take us North?"

"To stop you getting impatient, that's why. You don't really want to stand around at the cocktail party being all sweet and pretty. She's just making a pet out of you."

Lyra turned her back and closed her eyes. But what Pantalaimon said was true. She had been feeling confined and cramped by this polite life, however luxurious it was. She would have given anything for a day with her Oxford ragamuffin friends, with a battle in the Claybeds and a race along the canal. The one thing that kept her polite and attentive to Mrs Coulter was that tantalizing hope of going North. Perhaps they would meet Lord Asriel. Perhaps he and Mrs Coulter would fall in love, and they would get married and adopt Lyra, and go and rescue Roger from the Gobblers.

On the afternoon of the cocktail party Mrs Coulter took Lyra to a fashionable hairdresser's, where her stiff dark blonde hair was softened and waved, and her nails were filed and polished, and where they even applied a little make-up to her eyes and lips to show her how to do it. Then they went to collect the new dress Mrs Coulter had ordered for her, and to buy some patent-leather shoes, and then it was time to go back to the flat and check the flowers and get dressed.

"Not the shoulder-bag, dear," said Mrs Coulter as Lyra came out of her bedroom, glowing with a sense of her own prettiness.

Lyra had taken to wearing a little white leather shoulder-bag everywhere, so as to keep the alethiometer close at hand. Mrs Coulter, loosening the cramped way some roses had been bunched into a vase, saw that Lyra wasn't moving and glanced pointedly at the door.

"Oh, please, Mrs Coulter, I do love this bag!"

"Not indoors, Lyra. It looks absurd to be carrying a shoulder-bag in your own home. Take it off at once, and come and help check these glasses…"

It wasn't so much her snappish tone as the words "in your own home" that made Lyra resist stubbornly. Pantalaimon flew to the floor and instantly became a polecat, arching his back against her little white ankle-socks. Encouraged by this, Lyra said:

"But it won't be in the way. And it's the only thing I really like wearing. I think it really suits –"

She didn't finish the sentence, because Mrs Coulter's dæmon sprang off the sofa in a blur of golden fur and pinned Pantalaimon to the carpet before he could move. Lyra cried out in alarm, and then in fear and pain, as Pantalaimon twisted this way and that, shrieking and snarling, unable to loosen the golden monkey's grip. Only a few seconds, and the monkey had overmastered him: with one fierce black paw around his throat and his back paws gripping the polecat's lower limbs, he took one of Pantalaimon's ears in his other paw and pulled as if he intended to tear it off. Not angrily, either, but with a cold curious force that was horrifying to see and even worse to feel.

Lyra sobbed in terror.

"Don't! Please! Stop hurting us!"

Mrs Coulter looked up from her flowers.

"Do as I tell you, then," she said.

"I promise!"

The golden monkey stepped away from Pantalaimon as if he were suddenly bored. Pantalaimon fled to Lyra at once, and she scooped him up to her face to kiss and gentle.

"Now, Lyra," said Mrs Coulter.

Lyra turned her back abruptly and slammed into her bedroom, but no sooner had she banged the door shut behind her than it opened again. Mrs Coulter was standing there only a foot or two away.

"Lyra, if you behave in this coarse and vulgar way we shall have a confrontation, which I will win. Take off that bag this instant. Control that unpleasant frown. Never slam a door again in my hearing or out of it. Now the first guests will be arriving in a few minutes, and they are going to find you perfectly behaved, sweet, charming, innocent, attentive, delightful in every way. I particularly wish for that, Lyra, do you understand me?"

"Yes, Mrs Coulter."

"Then kiss me."

She bent a little and offered her cheek. Lyra had to stand on tiptoe to kiss it. She noticed how smooth it was, and the slight perplexing smell of Mrs Coulter's flesh: scented, but somehow metallic. She drew away and laid the shoulder-bag on her dressing-table before following Mrs Coulter back to the drawing-room.

"What do you think of the flowers, dear?" said Mrs Coulter as sweetly as if nothing had happened. "I suppose one can't go wrong with roses, but you can have too much of a good thing... Have the caterers brought enough ice? Be a dear and go and ask. Warm drinks are *horrid*..."

Lyra found it was quite easy to pretend to be light-hearted and charming, though she was conscious every second of Pantalaimon's disgust, and of his hatred for the golden monkey. Presently the doorbell rang, and soon the room was filling up with fashionably-dressed ladies and handsome or distinguished men. Lyra moved among them offering canapés or smiling sweetly and making pretty answers when they spoke to her. She felt like a universal pet, and the second she voiced that thought to herself, Pantalaimon stretched his goldfinch-wings and chirruped loudly.

She sensed his glee at having proved her right, and became a little more retiring.

"And where do you go to school, my dear?" said an elderly lady, inspecting Lyra through a lorgnette.

"I don't go to school," Lyra told her.

"Really? I thought your mother would have sent you to her old school. A *very* good place…"

Lyra was mystified until she realized the old lady's mistake.

"Oh! She's not my mother! I'm just here helping her. I'm her personal assistant," she said importantly.

"I see. And who *are* your people?"

Again Lyra had to wonder what she meant before replying.

"They were a count and countess," she said. "They both died in an aëronautical accident in the North."

"Which count?"

"Count Belacqua. He was Lord Asriel's brother."

The old lady's dæmon, a scarlet macaw, shifted as if in irritation from one foot to another. The old lady was beginning to frown with curiosity, so Lyra smiled sweetly and moved on.

She was going past a group of men and one young woman near the large sofa when she heard the word *Dust*. She had seen enough of society now to understand when men and women were flirting, and she watched the process with fascination, though she was more fascinated by the mention of Dust, and she hung back to listen. The men seemed to be scholars; from the way the young woman was questioning them, Lyra took her to be a student of some kind.

"It was discovered by a Muscovite – stop me if you know this already —" a middle-aged man was saying, as the young woman gazed at him in admiration — "a man called Rusakov, and they're usually called Rusakov Particles after him. Elementary particles that don't interact in any way with others — very hard to detect, but the extraordinary thing is that they seem to be attracted to human beings."

"Really?" said the young woman, wide-eyed.

"And even more extraordinary," he went on, "some human beings more than others. Adults attract them, but not children. At least, not much, and not until adolescence. In fact, that's the very reason —" his voice dropped, and he moved closer to the young woman, putting his hand confidentially on her shoulder — "that's the very reason the Oblation Board was set up. As our good hostess here could tell you."

"Really? Is she involved with the Oblation Board?"

"My dear, she *is* the Oblation Board. It's entirely her own project —"

The man was about to tell her more when he caught sight of Lyra. She stared back at him unblinkingly, and perhaps he had had a little too much to drink, or perhaps he was keen to impress the young woman, for he said:

"This little lady knows all about it, I'll be bound. You're safe from the Oblation Board, aren't you, my dear?"

"Oh, yes," said Lyra. "I'm safe from everyone here. Where I used to live, in Oxford, there was all kinds of dangerous things. There was gyptians — they take kids and sell 'em to the Turks for slaves. And on Port Meadow at the full moon there's a werewolf that comes out from the old nunnery at Godstow. I heard him howling once. And there's the Gobblers..."

"That's what I mean," the man said. "That's what they call the Oblation Board, don't they?"

Lyra felt Pantalaimon tremble suddenly, but he was on his best behaviour. The dæmons of the two grown-ups, a cat and a butterfly, didn't seem to notice.

"Gobblers?" said the young woman. "What a peculiar name! Why do they call them Gobblers?"

Lyra was about to tell her one of the blood-curdling stories she'd made up to frighten the Oxford kids with, but the man was already speaking.

"From the initials, d'you see? General Oblation Board. Very old idea, as a matter of fact. In the Middle Ages, parents would give their children to the church to be monks or nuns. And the unfortunate brats were known as oblates. Means a sacrifice, an offering, something of that sort. So the same idea was taken up when they were looking into the Dust business... As our little friend probably knows. Why don't you go and talk to Lord Boreal?" he added to Lyra directly. "I'm sure he'd like to meet Mrs Coulter's protégée... That's him, the man with grey hair and the serpent-dæmon."

He wanted to get rid of Lyra so that he could talk more privately with the young woman; Lyra could tell that easily. But the young woman, it seemed, was still interested in Lyra, and slipped away from the man to talk to her.

"Stop a minute... What's your name?"

"Lyra."

"I'm Adèle Starminster. I'm a journalist. Could I have a quiet word?"

Thinking it only natural that people should wish to talk to her, Lyra said simply, "Yes."

The woman's butterfly-dæmon rose into the air, casting about to left and right, and fluttered down to whisper something, at which Adèle Starminster said, "Come to the window seat."

This was a favourite spot of Lyra's; it overlooked the river, and at this time of night, the lights across on the south bank were glittering brilliantly over their reflections in the black water of the high tide. A line of barges hauled by a tug moved upriver. Adèle Starminster sat down and moved along the cushioned seat to make room.

"Did Professor Docker say that you had some connection with Mrs Coulter?"

"Yes."

"What is it? You're not her daughter, or something? I suppose I should know –"

"No!" said Lyra. "Course not. I'm her personal assistant."

"Her personal assistant? You're a bit young, aren't you? I thought you were related to her or something. What's she like?"

"She's very clever," said Lyra. Before this evening she would have said much more, but things were changing.

"Yes, but personally," Adèle Starminster insisted. "I mean, is she friendly or impatient or what? Do you live here with her? What's she like in private?"

"She's very nice," said Lyra stolidly.

"What sort of things do you do? How do you help her?"

"I do calculations and all that. Like for navigation."

"Ah, I see... And where do you come from? What was your name again?"

"Lyra. I come from Oxford."

"Why did Mrs Coulter pick you to –"

She stopped very suddenly, because Mrs Coulter herself had appeared close by. From the way Adèle Starminster looked up at her, and the agitated way her dæmon was fluttering around her head, Lyra could tell that the young woman wasn't supposed to be at the party at all.

"I don't know your name," said Mrs Coulter very quietly, "but I shall find it out within five minutes, and then you will never work as a journalist again. Now get up very quietly, without making a fuss, and leave. I might add that whoever brought you here will also suffer."

Mrs Coulter seemed to be charged with some kind of anbaric force. She even smelled different: a hot smell, like heated metal, came off her body. Lyra had felt something of it earlier, but now she was seeing it directed at someone else, and poor Adèle Starminster had no force to resist. Her dæmon fell limp on her shoulder and flapped his gorgeous wings once or twice before fainting, and the woman herself seemed to be unable to stand fully upright. Moving in a slight awkward crouch, she made her way through the press of loudly talking guests and out of the drawing-room door. She had one hand clutched to her shoulder, holding the swooning dæmon in place.

"Well?" said Mrs Coulter to Lyra.

"I never told her anything important," Lyra said.

"What was she asking?"

"Just about what I was doing and who I was, and stuff like that."

As she said that, Lyra noticed that Mrs Coulter was alone, without her dæmon. How could that be? But a moment later the golden monkey appeared at her side, and, reaching down, she took his hand and swung him up lightly to her shoulder. At once she seemed at ease again.

"If you come across anyone else who obviously hasn't been invited, dear, do come and find me, won't you?"

The hot metallic smell was vanishing. Perhaps Lyra had only imagined it. She could smell Mrs Coulter's scent again, and the roses, and the cigarillo-smoke, and the scent of other women. Mrs Coulter smiled at Lyra in a way that seemed to say, "You and I understand these things, don't we?" and moved on to greet some other guests.

Pantalaimon was whispering in Lyra's ear.

"While she was here, her dæmon was coming out of our bedroom. He's been spying. He knows about the alethiometer!"

Lyra felt that that was probably true, but there was nothing she could do about it. What had that Professor been saying about the Gobblers? She looked around to find him again, but no sooner had she seen him than the commissionaire (in servant's dress for the evening) and another man tapped the Professor on the shoulder and spoke quietly to him, at which he turned pale and followed them out. That took no more than a couple of seconds, and it was so discreetly done that hardly anyone noticed. But it left Lyra feeling anxious and exposed.

She wandered through the two big rooms where the party was taking place, half-listening to the conversations around her, half-interested in the taste of the cocktails she wasn't allowed to try, and increasingly fretful. She wasn't aware that anyone was watching her until the commissionaire appeared at her side and bent to say:

"Miss Lyra, the gentleman by the fireplace would like to speak to you. He's Lord Boreal, if you didn't know."

Lyra looked up across the room. The powerful-looking grey-haired man was looking directly at her, and as their eyes met he nodded and beckoned.

Unwilling, but more interested now, she went across.

"Good evening, child," he said. His voice was smooth and commanding. His serpent-dæmon's mailed head and emerald eyes glittered in the light from the cut-glass lamp on the wall nearby.

"Good evening," said Lyra.

"How is my old friend the Master of Jordan?"

"Very well, thank you."

"I expect they were all sorry to say goodbye to you."

"Yes, they were."

"And is Mrs Coulter keeping you busy? What is she teaching you?"

Because Lyra was feeling rebellious and uneasy, she didn't answer this patronizing question with the truth, or with one of her usual flights of fancy. Instead she said, "I'm learning about Rusakov Particles, and about the Oblation Board."

He seemed to become focused at once, in the same way that you could focus the beam of an anbaric lantern. All his attention streamed at her fiercely.

"Suppose you tell me what you know," he said.

"They're doing experiments in the North," Lyra said. She was feeling reckless now. "Like Dr Grumman."

"Go on."

"They've got this special kind of photogram where you can see Dust, and when you see a man there's like all light coming to him, and there's none on a child. At least not so much."

"Did Mrs Coulter show you a picture like that?"

Lyra hesitated, for this was not lying but something else, and she wasn't practised at it.

"No," she said after a moment. "I saw that one at Jordan College."

"Who showed it to you?"

"He wasn't really showing it to *me*," Lyra admitted. "I was just passing and I saw it. And then my friend Roger was taken by the Oblation Board. But –"

"Who showed you that picture?"

"My Uncle Asriel."

"When?"

"When he was in Jordan College last time."

"I see. And what else have you been learning about? Did I hear you mention the Oblation Board?"

"Yes. But I didn't hear about that from him, I heard it here."

Which was exactly true, she thought.

He was looking at her narrowly. She gazed back with all the innocence she had. Finally he nodded.

"Then Mrs Coulter must have decided you were ready to help her in that work. Interesting. Have you taken part yet?"

"No," said Lyra. What was he talking about? Pantalaimon was cleverly in his most inexpressive shape, a moth, and couldn't betray her feelings; and she was sure she could keep her own face innocent.

"And has she told you what happens to the children?"

"No, she hasn't told me that. I only just know that it's about Dust, and they're like a kind of sacrifice."

Again, that wasn't exactly a lie, she thought; she had never said that Mrs Coulter herself had told her.

"*Sacrifice* is rather a dramatic way of putting it. What's done is for their good as well as ours. And of course they all come to Mrs Coulter willingly. That's why she's so valuable. They must want to take part, and what child could resist her? And if she's going to use you as well to bring them in, so much the better. I'm very pleased."

He smiled at her in the way Mrs Coulter had: as if they were both in on a secret. She smiled politely back and he turned away to talk to someone else.

She and Pantalaimon could sense each other's horror. She wanted to go away by herself and talk to him; she wanted to leave the flat; she wanted to go back to Jordan College and her little shabby bedroom on Staircase Twelve; she wanted to find Lord Asriel –

And as if in answer to that last wish, she heard his name mentioned, and wandered closer to the group talking nearby with the pretext of helping herself to a canapé from the plate on the table.

94

A man in a bishop's purple was saying:

"… No, I don't think Lord Asriel will be troubling us for quite some time."

"And where did you say he was being held?"

"In the fortress of Svalbard, I'm told. Guarded by *panserbjørne*, you know, armoured bears. Formidable creatures! He won't escape from them if he lives to be a thousand. The fact is that I really think the way is clear, very nearly clear –"

"The last experiments have confirmed what I always believed – that Dust is an emanation from the dark principle itself, and –"

"Do I detect the Zoroastrian heresy?"

"What *used* to be a heresy –"

"And if we could isolate the dark principle –"

"Svalbard, did you say?"

"Armoured bears –"

"The Oblation Board –"

"The children don't suffer, I'm sure of it –"

"Lord Asriel imprisoned –"

Lyra had heard enough. She turned away, and moving as quietly as the moth-Pantalaimon, she went into her bedroom and closed the door. The noise of the party was muffled at once.

"Well?" she whispered, and he became a goldfinch on her shoulder.

"Are we going to run away?" he whispered back.

"Course. If we do it now with all these people about she might not notice for a while."

"*He* will."

Pantalaimon meant Mrs Coulter's dæmon. When Lyra thought of his lithe golden shape she felt ill with fear.

"I'll fight him this time," Pantalaimon said boldly. "I can change and he can't. I'll change so quickly he won't be able to keep hold. This time I'll win, you'll see."

Lyra nodded distractedly. What should she wear? How could she get out without being seen?

"You'll have to go and spy," she whispered. "As soon as it's clear we'll have to run. Be a moth," she added. "Remember, the *second* there's no one looking…"

She opened the door a crack and he crawled out, dark against the warm pink light in the corridor.

Meanwhile, she hastily flung on the warmest clothes she had and stuffed some more into one of the coal-silk bags from the fashionable shop they'd visited that very afternoon. Mrs Coulter had given her money like sweets, and although she had spent it lavishly, there were still several sovereigns left, which she put in the pocket of the dark wolfskin coat.

Last of all she packed the alethiometer in its black velvet cloth. Had that abominable monkey found it? He must have done; he must have told her; oh, if she'd only hidden it better!

She tiptoed to the door. Her room opened into the end of the corridor nearest the hall, luckily, and most of the guests were in the two big rooms further along. There was the sound of voices talking loudly, laughter, the quiet flushing of a lavatory, the tinkle of glasses; and then a tiny moth-voice at her ear said:

"Now! Quick!"

She slipped through the door and into the hall, and in less than three seconds she was opening the front door of the flat. A moment after that she was through and pulling it quietly shut, and with Pantalaimon a goldfinch again, she ran for the stairs and fled.

6

The Throwing-Nets

She walked quickly away from the river, because the Embankment was wide and well-lit. There was a tangle of narrow streets between there and the Royal Arctic Institute, which was the only place Lyra was sure of being able to find, and into that dark maze she hurried now.

If only she knew London as well as she knew Oxford! Then she would have known which streets to avoid; or where she could scrounge some food; or, best of all, which doors to knock on and find shelter. In that cold night, the dark alleys all around were alive with movement and secret life, and she knew none of it.

Pantalaimon became a wildcat and scanned the dark all around with his night-piercing eyes. Every so often he'd stop, bristling, and she would turn aside from the entrance she'd been about to go down. The night was full of noises: bursts of drunken laughter, two raucous voices raised in song, the clatter and whine of some badly-oiled machine in a basement. Lyra walked delicately through it all, her senses magnified and mingled with Pantalaimon's, keeping to the shadows and the narrow alleys.

From time to time she had to cross a wider, well-lit street, where the tramcars hummed and sparked under their anbaric wires. There were rules for crossing London streets, but she took no notice, and when anyone shouted, she fled.

It was a fine thing to be free again. She knew that Pantalaimon, padding on wildcat-paws beside her, felt the same joy as she did to be in the open air, even if it was murky London air laden with fumes and soot and clangorous with noise. Some time soon they'd have to think over the meaning of what they'd heard in Mrs Coulter's flat, but not yet. And some time eventually they'd have to find a place to sleep.

At a crossroads near the corner of a big department store, whose windows shone brilliantly over the wet pavement, there was a coffee stall: a little hut on wheels with a counter under the wooden flap that swung up like an awning. Yellow light glowed inside, and the fragrance of coffee drifted out. The white-coated owner was leaning on the counter talking to the two or three customers.

It was tempting. Lyra had been walking for an hour now, and it was cold and damp. With Pantalaimon a sparrow, she went up to the counter and reached up to gain the owner's attention.

"Cup of coffee and a ham sandwich, please," she said.

"You're out late, my dear," said a gentleman in a top hat and white silk muffler.

"Yeah," she said, turning away from him to scan the busy intersection. A theatre nearby was just emptying, and crowds milled around the lighted foyer, calling for cabs, wrapping coats around their shoulders. In the other direction was the entrance of a Chthonic Railway Station, with more crowds pouring up and down the steps.

"Here you are, love," said the coffee-stall man. "Two shillings."

"Let me pay for this," said the man in the top hat.

Lyra thought, why not? I can run faster than him, and I might need all my money later. The top-hatted man dropped a coin on the counter and smiled down at her. His dæmon was a lemur. It clung to his lapel, staring round-eyed at Lyra.

She bit into her sandwich and kept her eyes on the busy street. She had no idea where she was, because she had never seen a map of London, and she didn't even know how big it was or how far she'd have to walk to find the country.

"What's your name?" said the man.

"Alice."

"That's a pretty name. Let me put a drop of this into your coffee … warm you up…"

He was unscrewing the top of a silver flask.

"I don't like that," said Lyra. "I just like coffee."

"I bet you've never had brandy like this before."

"I have. I was sick all over the place. I had a whole bottle, or nearly."

"Just as you like," said the man, tilting the flask into his own cup. "Where are you going, all alone like this?"

"Going to meet my father."

"And who's he?"

"He's a murderer."

"He's what?"

"I told you, he's a murderer. It's his profession. He's doing a job tonight. I got his clean clothes in here, 'cause he's usually all covered in blood when he's finished a job."

"Ah! You're joking."

"I en't."

The lemur uttered a soft mewing sound and clambered slowly up behind the man's head, to peer out at her. She drank her coffee stolidly and ate the last of her sandwich.

"Good night," she said. "I can see my father coming now. He looks a bit angry."

The top-hat man glanced around, and Lyra set off towards the theatre crowd. Much as she would have liked to see the Chthonic Railway (Mrs Coulter had said it was not really intended for people of their class) she was wary of being trapped underground; better to be out in the open, where she could run, if she had to.

On and on she walked, and the streets became darker and emptier. It was drizzling, but even if there'd been no clouds the city sky was too tainted with light to show the stars. Pantalaimon thought they were going north, but who could tell?

Endless streets of little identical brick houses, with gardens only big enough for a dustbin; great gaunt factories behind wire fences, with one anbaric light glowing bleakly high up on a wall and a night-watchman snoozing by his brazier; occasionally a dismal oratory, only distinguished from a warehouse by the crucifix outside. Once she tried the door of one of these places, only to hear a groan from the bench a foot away in the darkness. She realized that the porch was full of sleeping figures, and fled.

"Where we going to sleep, Pan?" she said as they trudged down a street of closed and shuttered shops.

"A doorway somewhere."

"Don't want to be seen, though. They're all so open."

"There's a canal down there…"

He was looking down a side-road to the left. Sure enough, a patch of dark glimmer showed open water, and when they cautiously went to look, they found a canal basin where a dozen or so barges were tied up at the wharves, some high in the water, some low and laden under the gallows-like cranes. A dim light shone in one window of a wooden hut, and a thread of smoke rose from the metal chimney; otherwise the only lights were high up on the wall of the warehouse or the gantry of a crane, leaving the ground in gloom. The wharves were piled with barrels of coal-spirit, with stacks of great round logs, with rolls of cahuchuc-covered cable.

Lyra tiptoed up to the hut and peeped in at the window. An old man was laboriously reading a picture-story paper and smoking a pipe, with his spaniel-dæmon curled up asleep on the table. As she looked, the man got up and brought a blackened kettle from the iron stove and poured some hot water into a cracked mug before settling back with his paper.

"Should we ask him to let us in, Pan?" she whispered, but he was distracted; he was a bat, an owl, a wildcat again; she looked all round, catching his panic, and then saw them at the same time as he did: two men running at her, one from each side, the nearer holding a throwing-net.

Pantalaimon uttered a harsh scream and launched himself as a leopard at the closer man's dæmon, a savage-looking fox, bowling her backwards so that she tangled with the man's legs. The man cursed and dodged aside, and Lyra darted past him towards the open spaces of the wharf. What she mustn't do was get boxed in a corner.

Pantalaimon, an eagle now, swooped at her and cried, "Left! Left!"

She swerved that way and saw a gap between the coal-spirit barrels and the end of a corrugated iron shed, and darted for it like a bullet.

But those throwing-nets!

She heard a hiss in the air, and past her cheek something lashed and sharply stung, and loathsome tarred strings across her face, her arms,

101

her hands tangled and held her, and she fell, snarling and tearing and struggling in vain.

"Pan! Pan!"

But the fox-dæmon tore at the cat-Pantalaimon, and Lyra felt the pain in her own flesh, and sobbed a great cry as he fell. One man was swiftly lashing cords around her, around her limbs, her throat, body, head, bundling her over and over on the wet ground. She was helpless, exactly like a fly being trussed by a spider. Poor hurt Pan was dragging himself towards her, with the fox-dæmon worrying his back, and he had no strength left to change, even; and the other man was lying in a puddle, with an arrow through his neck –

The whole world grew still as the man tying the net saw it too.

Pantalaimon sat up and blinked, and then there was a soft thud, and the net-man fell choking and gasping right across Lyra, who cried out in horror: that was *blood* gushing out of him!

Running feet, and someone hauled the man away and bent over him; then other hands lifted Lyra, a knife snicked and pulled and the net-strings fell away one by one, and she tore them off, spitting, and hurled herself down to cuddle Pantalaimon.

Kneeling, she twisted to look up at the newcomers. Three dark men, one armed with a bow, the others with knives; and as she turned, the bowman caught his breath.

"That en't Lyra?"

A familiar voice, but she couldn't place it till he stepped forward and the nearest light fell on his face and the hawk-dæmon on his shoulder. Then she had it. A gyptian! A real Oxford gyptian!

"Tony Costa," he said. "Remember? You used to play with my little brother Billy off the boats in Jericho, afore the Gobblers got him."

"Oh, God, Pan, we're safe!" she sobbed, but then a thought rushed into her mind: it was the Costas' boat she'd hijacked that day. Suppose he remembered?

"Better come along with us," he said. "You alone?"

"Yeah. I was running away…"

"All right, don't talk now. Just keep quiet. Jaxer, move them bodies into the shadow. Kerim, look around."

Lyra stood up shakily, holding the wildcat-Pantalaimon to her breast. He was twisting to look at something, and she followed his gaze, understanding and suddenly curious too: what had happened to the dead men's dæmons? They were fading, that was the answer; fading and drifting away like atoms of smoke, for all that they tried to cling to their men. Pantalaimon hid his eyes, and Lyra hurried blindly after Tony Costa.

"What are you doing here?" she said.

"Quiet, gal. There's enough trouble awake without stirring more. We'll talk on the boat."

He led her over a little wooden bridge into the heart of the canal basin. The other two men were padding silently after them. Tony turned along the waterfront and out on to a wooden jetty, from which he stepped on board a narrow-boat and swung open the door to the cabin.

"Get in," he said. "Quick now."

Lyra did so, patting her bag (which she had never let go, even in the net) to make sure the alethiometer was still there. In the long narrow cabin, by the light of a lantern on a hook, she saw a stout powerful woman with grey hair, sitting at a table with a paper. Lyra recognized her as Billy's mother.

"Who's this?" the woman said. "That's never Lyra?"

"That's right. Ma, we got to move. We killed two men out in the basin. We thought they was Gobblers, but I reckon they were Turk traders. They'd caught Lyra. Never mind talk – we'll do that on the move."

"Come here, child," said Ma Costa.

Lyra obeyed, half happy, half apprehensive, for Ma Costa had hands like bludgeons, and now she was sure: it *was* their boat she had captured with Roger and the other collegers. But the boat-mother set her hands on either side of Lyra's face, and her dæmon, the yellow-eyed hawk, crooned a quick welcome to Pantalaimon. Then Ma Costa folded her great arms around Lyra and pressed her to her breast.

"I dunno what you're a-doing here, but you look wore out. You can have Billy's crib, soon's I've got a hot drink in you. Set you down there, child."

It looked as if her piracy was forgiven, or at least forgotten. Lyra slid on to the cushioned bench behind a well-scrubbed pine table-top as the low rumble of the gas-engine shook the boat.

"Where we going?" Lyra asked.

Ma Costa was setting a saucepan of milk on the iron stove and riddling the grate to stir the fire up.

"Away from here. No talking now. We'll talk in the morning."

And she said no more, handing Lyra a cup of milk when it was ready, swinging herself up on deck when the boat began to move, exchanging occasional whispers with the men. Lyra sipped the milk and lifted a corner of the blind to watch the dark wharves move past. A minute or two later she was sound asleep.

She awoke in a narrow bed, with that comforting engine-rumble deep below. She sat up, banged her head, cursed, felt around, and got up more carefully. A thin grey light showed her three other bunks, each empty and neatly made, one below hers and the other two across the tiny cabin. She swung over the side to find herself in her underclothes, and saw the dress and the wolfskin coat folded at the end of her bunk together with her shopping bag. The alethiometer was still there.

She dressed quickly and went through the door at the end to find herself in the cabin with the stove, where it was warm. There was no one there. Through the windows she saw a grey swirl of fog on each side, with occasional dark shapes that might have been buildings or trees.

Before she could go out on deck, the outer door opened and Ma Costa came down, swathed in an old tweed coat on which the damp had settled like a thousand tiny pearls.

"Sleep well?" she said, reaching for a frying pan. "Now sit down out the way and I'll make ye some breakfast. Don't stand about; there en't room."

"Where are we?" said Lyra.

"On the Grand Junction Canal. You keep out of sight, child. I don't want to see you topside. There's trouble."

She sliced a couple of rashers of bacon into the frying pan, and cracked an egg to go with them.

"What sort of trouble?"

"Nothing we can't cope with, if you stay out the way."

And she wouldn't say any more till Lyra had eaten. The boat slowed at one point, and something banged against the side, and she heard men's voices raised in anger; but then someone's joke made them laugh, and the voices drew away and the boat moved on.

Presently Tony Costa swung down into the cabin. Like his mother, he was pearled with damp, and he shook his woollen hat over the stove to make the drops jump and spit.

"What we going to tell her, Ma?"

"Ask first, tell after."

He poured some coffee into a tin cup and sat down. He was a powerful, dark-faced man, and now she could see him in daylight, Lyra saw a sad grimness in his expression.

"Right," he said. "Now you tell us what you was doing in London, Lyra. We had you down as being took by the Gobblers."

"I was living with this lady, right..."

Lyra clumsily collected her story and shook it into order as if she were settling a pack of cards ready for dealing. She told them everything, except about the alethiometer.

"And then last night at this cocktail party I found out what they were really doing. Mrs Coulter was one of the Gobblers herself, and she was going to use me to help her catch more kids. And what they do is —"

Ma Costa left the cabin and went out to the cockpit. Tony waited till the door was shut, and went on:

"We know what they do. Least, we know part of it. We know they don't come back. Them kids is taken up North, far out the way, and they do experiments on 'em. At first we reckoned they tried out different diseases and medicines, but there'd be no reason to start that all of a sudden two or three years back. Then we thought about the Tartars, maybe there's some secret deal they're making up Siberia way; because the Tartars want to move North just as much as the rest, for the coalspirit and the fire-mines, and there's been rumours of war for even longer than the Gobblers been going. And we reckoned the Gobblers were buying off the Tartar chiefs by giving 'em kids, cause the Tartars eat 'em, don't they? They bake children and eat 'em."

"They never!" said Lyra.

"They do. There's plenty of other things to be told, and all. You ever heard of the Nälkäinens?"

Lyra said "No. Not even with Mrs Coulter. What are they?"

"That's a kind of ghost they have up there in those forests. Same size as a child, and they got no heads. They feel their way about at night and if you're a-sleeping out in the forest they get ahold of you and won't nothing make 'em let go. Nälkäinens, that's a Northern word. And the Windsuckers, they're dangerous too. They drift about in the air. You come across clumps of 'em floated together sometimes, or caught snagged on a bramble. As soon as they touch you, all the strength goes out of you. You can't see 'em except as a kind of shimmer in the air. And the Breathless Ones..."

"Who are they?"

"Warriors half-killed. Being alive is one thing, and being dead's another, but being half-killed is worse than either. They just can't die, and living is altogether beyond 'em. They wander about for ever. They're called the Breathless Ones because of what's been done to 'em."

"And what's that?" said Lyra, wide-eyed.

"The North Tartars snap open their ribs and pull out their lungs. There's an art to it. They do it without killing 'em, but their lungs can't work any more without their dæmons pumping 'em by hand, so the result is they're halfway between breath and no breath, life and death, half-killed, you see. And their dæmons got to pump and pump all day and night, or else perish with 'em. You come across a whole platoon of Breathless Ones in the forest sometimes, I've heard. And then there's the *panserbjørne* – you heard of them? That means armoured bears. They're like a kind of Polar bear, except—"

"Yes! I have heard of them! One of the men last night, he said that my uncle, Lord Asriel, he's being imprisoned in a fortress guarded by the armoured bears."

"Is he, now? And what was he doing up there?"

"Exploring. But the way the man was talking I don't think my uncle's on the same side as the Gobblers. I think they were glad he was in prison."

"Well, he won't get out if the armoured bears are guarding him. They're like mercenaries, you know what I mean by that? They sell their strength to whoever pays. They got hands like men, and they learned the trick of working iron way back, meteoric iron mostly, and they make great sheets and plates of it to cover theirselves with. They been raiding the Skraelings for centuries. They're vicious killers, absolutely pitiless. But they keep their word. If you make a bargain with a *panserbjørn*, you can rely on it."

Lyra considered these horrors with awe.

"Ma don't like to hear about the North," Tony said after a few moments, "because of what might've happened to Billy. We know they took him up North, see."

"How d'you know that?"

"We caught one of the Gobblers, and made him talk. That's how we know a little about what they're doing. Them two last night weren't Gobblers; they were too clumsy. If they'd been Gobblers we'd've took 'em alive. See, the gyptian people, we been hit worse than most by these Gobblers, and we're a-coming together to decide what to do about it. That's what we was doing in the basin last night, taking on stores, 'cause we're going to a big muster up in the Fens, what we call a Roping. And what I reckon is we're a-going to send out a rescue party, when we heard what all the other gyptians know, when we put our knowledge together. That's what I'd do, if I was John Faa."

"Who's John Faa?"

"The king of the gyptians."

"And you're really going to rescue the kids? What about Roger?"

"Who's Roger?"

"The Jordan College Kitchen boy. He was took same as Billy the day before I come away with Mrs Coulter. I bet if I was took he'd come and rescue me. If you're going to rescue Billy, I want to come too and rescue Roger."

And Uncle Asriel, she thought; but she didn't mention that.

7

John Faa

 *N*ow that Lyra had a task in mind, she felt much better. Helping Mrs Coulter had been all very well, but Pantalaimon was right: she wasn't really doing any work there, she was just a pretty pet. On the gyptian boat, there was real work to do, and Ma Costa made sure she did it. She cleaned and swept, she peeled potatoes and made tea, she greased the propellor-shaft bearings, she kept the weed-trap clear over the propellor, she washed dishes, she opened lock gates, she tied the boat up at mooring-posts, and within a couple of days she was as much at home with this new life as if she'd been born gyptian.

What she didn't notice was that the Costas were alert every second for unusual signs of interest in Lyra from the waterside people. If she hadn't realized it, she was important, and Mrs Coulter and the Oblation Board were bound to be searching everywhere for her. Indeed, Tony heard from gossip in pubs along the way that the police were making raids on houses and farms and building yards and factories without any explanation, though there was a rumour that they were searching for a missing girl. And that in itself was odd, considering all the kids that had gone missing without being looked for. Gyptians and land folk alike were getting jumpy and nervous.

And there was another reason for the Costas' interest in Lyra; but she wasn't to learn that for a few days yet.

So they took to keeping her below decks when they passed a lock-keeper's cottage or a canal basin, or anywhere there were likely to be idlers hanging about. Once they passed through a town where the police were searching all the boats that came along the waterway, and holding up the traffic in both directions. The Costas were equal to that, though. There was a secret compartment beneath Ma's bunk, where Lyra lay cramped for two hours while the police banged up and down the length of the boat unsuccessfully.

"Why didn't their dæmons find me, though?" she asked afterwards, and Ma showed her the lining of the secret space: cedarwood, which had a soporific effect on dæmons; and it was true that Pantalaimon had spent the whole time happily asleep by Lyra's head.

Slowly, with many halts and detours, the Costas' boat drew nearer the Fens, that wide and never fully mapped wilderness of huge skies and endless marshland in eastern Anglia. The furthest fringe of it mingled indistinguishably with the creeks and tidal inlets of the shallow sea, and the other side of the sea mingled indistinguishably with Holland; and parts of the Fens had been drained and dyked by Hollanders, some of whom had settled there; so the language of the Fens was thick with Dutch. But parts had never been drained or planted or settled at all, and in the wildest central regions, where eels slithered and waterbirds flocked, where eerie marsh-fires flickered and waylurkers tempted careless travellers to their doom in the swamps and bogs, the gyptian people had always found it safe to muster.

And now by a thousand winding channels and creeks and

watercourses, gyptian boats were moving in towards the Byanplats, the only patch of slightly higher ground in the hundreds of square miles of marsh and bog. There was an ancient wooden meeting hall there with a huddle of permanent dwellings around it, and wharves and jetties and an Eelmarket. When a Byanroping was called, a summons or muster of gyptians, so many boats filled the waterways that you could walk for a mile in any direction over their decks; or so it was said. The gyptians ruled in the Fens. No one else dared enter, and while the gyptians kept the peace and traded fairly, the landlopers turned a blind eye to the incessant smuggling and the occasional feuds. If a gyptian body floated ashore down the coast, or got snagged in a fish-net, well – it was only a gyptian.

Lyra listened enthralled to tales of the Fen-dwellers, of the great ghost dog Black Shuck, of the marsh-fires arising from bubbles of witch-oil, and began to think of herself as gyptian even before they reached the Fens. She had soon slipped back into her Oxford voice, and now she was acquiring a gyptian one, complete with Fen-Dutch words. Ma Costa had to remind her of a few things.

"You en't gyptian, Lyra. You might pass for gyptian with practice, but there's more to us than gyptian language. There's deeps in us and strong currents. We're water people all through, and you en't, you're a fire person. What you're most like is marsh-fire, that's the place you have in the gyptian scheme; you got witch-oil in your soul. Deceptive, that's what you are, child."

Lyra was hurt.

"I en't never deceived anyone! You ask…"

There was no one to ask, of course, and Ma Costa laughed, but kindly.

"Can't you see I'm a-paying you a compliment, you gosling?" she said, and Lyra was pacified, though she didn't understand.

When they reached the Byanplats it was evening, and the sun was about to set in a splash of bloody sky. The low island and the Zaal were humped blackly against the light, like the clustered buildings around; threads of smoke rose into the still air, and from the press of boats all around came the smells of frying fish, of smokeleaf, of jenniver-spirit.

They tied up close to the Zaal itself, at a mooring Tony said had been used by their family for generations. Presently Ma Costa had the frying-pan going, with a couple of fat eels hissing and sputtering and the kettle on for potato-powder. Tony and Kerim oiled their hair, put on their finest leather jackets and blue spotted neckerchiefs, loaded their fingers with silver rings, and went to greet some old friends in the neighbouring boats and drink a glass or two in the nearest bar. They came back with important news.

"We got here just in time. The Roping's this very night. And they're a-saying in the town – what d'you think of this? – they're saying that the missing child's on a gyptian boat, and she's a-going to appear tonight at the Roping!"

He laughed loudly and ruffled Lyra's hair. Ever since they'd entered the Fens he had been more and more good-tempered, as if the savage gloom his face showed outside were only a disguise. And Lyra felt an excitement growing in her breast as she ate quickly and washed the dishes before combing her hair, tucking the alethiometer into the wolf-skin coat pocket, and jumping ashore with all the other families making their way up the slope to the Zaal.

She had thought Tony was joking. She soon found that he wasn't, or else that she looked less like a gyptian than she'd thought, for many people stared, and children pointed, and by the time they reached the great doors of the Zaal they were walking alone between a crowd on either side, who had fallen back to stare and give them room.

And then Lyra began to feel truly nervous. She kept close to Ma Costa, and Pantalaimon became as big as he could and took his panther-shape to reassure her. Ma Costa trudged up the steps as if nothing in the world could possibly either stop her or make her go more quickly, and Tony and Kerim walked proudly on either side like princes.

The hall was lit by naphtha lamps, which shone brightly enough on the faces and bodies of the audience, but left the lofty rafters hidden in darkness. The people coming in had to struggle to find room on the floor, where the benches were already crowded; but families squeezed up to make space, children occupying laps and dæmons curling up underfoot or perching out of the way on the rough wooden walls.

At the front of the Zaal there was a platform with eight carved wooden chairs set out. As Lyra and the Costas found space to stand along the edge of the hall (there was nowhere left to sit), eight men appeared from the shadows at the rear of the platform and stood in front of the chairs. A ripple of excitement swept over the audience as they hushed one another and shoved themselves into spaces on the nearest bench. Finally there was silence and seven of the men on the platform sat down.

The one who remained was in his seventies, but tall and bull-necked and powerful. He wore a plain canvas jacket and a checked shirt, like many gyptian men; there was nothing to mark him out but the air of strength and authority he had. Lyra recognized it: Uncle Asriel had it, and so did the Master of Jordan. This man's dæmon was a crow, very like the Master's raven.

"That's John Faa, the lord of the western gyptians," Tony whispered.

John Faa began to speak, in a deep slow voice.

"Gyptians! Welcome to the Roping. We've come to listen and come to decide. You all know why. There are many families here who've lost a child. Some have lost two. Someone is taking them. To be sure, land-lopers are losing children too. We have no quarrel with landlopers over this.

"Now there's been talk about a child and a reward. Here's the truth to stop all gossip. The child's name is Lyra Belacqua, and she's being sought by the landloper police. There is a reward of one thousand sovereigns for giving her up to them. She's a landloper child, and she's in our care, and there she's going to stay. Anyone tempted by those thousand sovereigns had better find a place neither on land nor on water. We en't giving her up."

Lyra felt a blush from the roots of her hair to the soles of her feet; Pantalaimon became a brown moth to hide. Eyes all around were turning to them, and she could only look up at Ma Costa for reassurance.

But John Faa was speaking again:

"Talk all we may, we won't change owt. We must act if we want to change things. Here's another fact for you: the Gobblers, these child-thieves, are a-taking their prisoners to a town in the far North, way up in the land of dark. I don't know what they do with 'em there. Some folk say they kill 'em, other folk say different. We don't know.

"What we do know is that they do it with the help of the landloper police and the clergy. Every power on land is helping 'em. Remember that. They know what's going on and they'll help it whenever they can.

"So what I'm proposing en't easy. And I need your agreement. I'm proposing that we send a band of fighters up North to rescue them kids and bring 'em back alive. I'm proposing that we put our gold into this, and all the craft and courage we can muster. Yes, Raymond van Gerrit?"

A man in the audience had raised his hand, and John Faa sat down to let him speak.

"Beg pardon, Lord Faa. There's landloper kids as well as gyptians been taken captive. Are you saying we should rescue them as well?"

John Faa stood up to answer.

"Raymond, are you saying we should fight our way through every kind of danger to a little group of frightened children, and then say to some of them that they can come home, and to the rest that they have to stay? No, you're a better man than that. Well, do I have your approval, my friends?"

The question caught them by surprise, for there was a moment's hesitation; but then a full-throated roar filled the hall, and hands were clapped in the air, fists shaken, voices raised in excited clamour. The rafters of the Zaal shook, and from their perches up in the dark a score of sleeping birds woke up in fear and flapped their wings, and little showers of dust drifted down.

John Faa let the noise continue for a minute, and then raised his hand for silence again.

"This'll take a while to organize. I want the heads of the families to raise a tax and muster a levy. We'll meet again here in three days' time. In between now and then I'm a-going to talk with the child I mentioned before, and with Farder Coram, and form a plan to put before you when we meet. Good night to ye all."

His massive, plain, blunt presence was enough to calm them. As the audience began to move out of the great doors into the chilly evening, to go to their boats or to the crowded bars of the little settlement, Lyra said to Ma Costa:

"Who are the other men on the platform?"

"The heads of the six families, and the other man is Farder Coram."

It was easy to see who she meant by the other man, because he was the oldest one there. He walked with a stick and all the time he'd been sitting behind John Faa he'd been trembling as if with an ague.

"Come on," said Tony. "I'd best take you up to pay your respects to John Faa. You call him Lord Faa. I don't know what you'll be asked, but mind you tell the truth."

Pantalaimon was a sparrow now, and sat curiously on Lyra's shoulder, his claws deep in the wolfskin coat, as she followed Tony through the crowd up to the platform.

He lifted her up. Knowing that everyone still in the hall was staring at her, and conscious of those thousand sovereigns she was suddenly worth, she blushed and hesitated. Pantalaimon darted to her breast and became a wildcat, sitting up in her arms and hissing softly as he looked around.

Lyra felt a push, and stepped forward to John Faa. He was stern and massive and expressionless, more like a pillar of rock than a man, but he stooped and held out his hand to shake. When she put hers in, it nearly vanished.

"Welcome, Lyra," he said.

Close to, she felt his voice rumbling like the earth itself. She would have been nervous but for Pantalaimon, and the fact that John Faa's stony expression had warmed a little. He was treating her very gently.

"Thank you, Lord Faa," she said.

"Now you come in the parley room and we'll have a talk," said John Faa. "Have they been feeding you proper, the Costas?"

"Oh, yes. We had eels for supper."

"Proper Fen eels, I expect."

The parley room was a comfortable place with a big fire, sideboards laden with silver and porcelain, and a heavy table darkly polished by the years, at which twelve chairs were drawn up.

The other men from the platform had gone elsewhere, but the old shaking man was still with them. John Faa helped him to a seat at the table.

"Now you sit here on my right," John Faa said to Lyra, and took the chair at the head of the table himself. Lyra found herself opposite Farder Coram. She was a little frightened by his skull-like face and his continual trembling. His dæmon was a beautiful autumn-coloured cat, massive in size, who stalked along the table with upraised tail and elegantly inspected Pantalaimon, touching noses briefly before settling on Farder Coram's lap, half-closing her eyes and purring softly.

A woman whom Lyra hadn't noticed came out of the shadows with a tray of glasses, set it down by John Faa, curtseyed and left. John Faa poured little glasses of jenniver from a stone crock for himself and Farder Coram, and wine for Lyra.

"So," John Faa said. "You run away, Lyra."

"Yes."

"And who was the lady you run away from?"

"She was called Mrs Coulter. And I thought she was nice but I found out she was one of the Gobblers. I heard someone say what the Gobblers were, they were called the General Oblation Board, and she was in charge of it, it was all her idea. And they was all working on some plan, I dunno what it was, only they was going to make me help her get kids for 'em. But they never knew…"

"They never knew what?"

"Well, first they never knew that I knew some kids what had been took. My friend Roger the Kitchen boy from Jordan College, and Billy Costa, and a girl out the Covered Market in Oxford. And another thing… My uncle, right, Lord Asriel. I heard them talking about his journeys to the North, and I don't reckon he's got anything to do with the Gobblers. Because I spied on the Master and the Scholars of

Jordan, right, I hid in the Retiring Room where no one's supposed to go except them, and I heard him tell them all about his expedition up North, and the Dust he saw, and he brought back the head of Stanislaus Grumman, what the Tartars had made a hole in. And now the Gobblers've got him locked up somewhere. The armoured bears are guarding him. And I want to rescue him."

She looked fierce and stubborn as she sat there, small against the high carved back of the chair. The two old men couldn't help smiling, but whereas Farder Coram's smile was a hesitant, rich, complicated expression that trembled across his face like sunlight chasing shadows on a windy March day, John Faa's smile was slow, warm, plain and kindly.

"You better tell us what you did hear your uncle say that evening," said John Faa. "Don't leave anything out, mind. Tell us everything."

Lyra did, more slowly than she'd told the Costas but more honestly, too. She was afraid of John Faa, and what she was most afraid of was his kindness. When she'd finished, Farder Coram spoke for the first time. His voice was rich and musical, with as many tones in it as there were colours in his dæmon's fur.

"This Dust," he said. "Did they ever call it anything else, Lyra?"

"No. Just Dust. Mrs Coulter told me what it was, elementary particles, but that's all she called it."

"And they think that by doing something to children, they can find out more about it?"

"Yes. But I don't know what. Except my uncle... There's something I forgot to tell you. When he was showing them lantern slides, there was another one he had. It was the Roarer –"

"The what?" said John Faa.

"The Aurora," said Farder Coram. "Is that right, Lyra?"

"Yeah, that's it. And in the lights of the Roarer there was like a city. All towers and churches and domes and that. It was a bit like Oxford, that's what I thought, anyway. And Uncle Asriel, he was more interested in that, I think, but the Master and the other Scholars were more interested in Dust, like Mrs Coulter and Lord Boreal and them."

"I see," said Farder Coram. "That's very interesting."

"Now, Lyra," said John Faa, "I'm a-going to tell you something. Farder Coram here, he's a wise man. He's a see-er. He's been a-follering all what's been going on with Dust and the Gobblers and Lord Asriel and everything else, and he's been a-follering *you*. Every time the Costas went to Oxford, or half a dozen other families come to that, they brought back a bit of news. About you, child. Did you know that?"

Lyra shook her head. She was beginning to be frightened. Pantalaimon was growling too deep for anyone to hear, but she could feel it in her fingertips down inside his fur.

"Oh, yes," said John Faa, "all your doings, they all get back to Farder Coram here."

Lyra couldn't hold it in.

"We didn't *damage* it! Honest! It was only a bit of mud! And we never got very far –"

"What are you talking about, child?" said John Faa.

Farder Coram laughed. When he did that, his shaking stopped and his face became bright and young.

But Lyra wasn't laughing. With trembling lips she said, "And even if we had found the bung, we'd never've took it out! It was just a joke. We wouldn't've sunk it, never!"

Then John Faa began to laugh too. He slapped a broad hand on the table so hard the glasses rang, and his massive shoulders shook, and he had to wipe away the tears from his eyes. Lyra had never seen such a sight, never heard such a bellow; it was like a mountain laughing.

"Oh, yes," he said when he could speak again, "we heard about that too, little girl! I don't suppose the Costas have set foot anywhere since then without being reminded of it. You better leave a guard on your boat, Tony, people say. Fierce little girls round here! Oh, that story went all over the Fens, child. But we en't going to punish you for it. No, no! Ease your mind."

He looked at Farder Coram, and the two old men laughed again, but more gently. And Lyra felt contented, and safe.

Finally John Faa shook his head and became serious again.

"I were saying, Lyra, as we knew about you from a child. From a baby. You oughter know what we know. I can't guess what they told you at Jordan College about where you came from, but they don't know the whole truth of it. Did they ever tell you who your parents were?"

Now Lyra was completely dazed.

"Yes," she said. "They said I was – they said they – they said Lord Asriel put me there because my mother and father died in an airship accident. That's what they told me."

"Ah, did they? Well now, child, I'm a-going to tell you a story, a true story. I know it's true, because a gyptian woman told me, and they all tell the truth to John Faa and Farder Coram. So this is the truth about yourself, Lyra. Your father never perished in no airship accident, because your father is Lord Asriel."

Lyra could only sit in wonder.

"Here's how it came about," John Faa went on. "When he was a young man, Lord Asriel went exploring all over the North, and came back with a great fortune. And he was a high-spirited man, quick to anger, a passionate man.

"And your mother, she was passionate too. Not so well-born as him, but a clever woman. A scholar, even, and those who saw her said she was very beautiful. She and your father, they fell in love as soon's they met.

"The trouble was, your mother was already married. She'd married a politician. He was a member of the King's party, one of his closest advisers. A rising man.

"Now when your mother found herself with child, she feared to tell her husband the child wasn't his. And when the baby was born – that's you, girl – it was clear from the look of you that you didn't favour her husband, but your true father, and she thought it best to hide you away and give out that you'd died.

"So you was took to Oxfordshire, where your father had estates, and put in the care of a gyptian woman to nurse. But someone whispered to your mother's husband what had happened, and he came a-flying down and ransacked the cottage where the gyptian woman had been, only she'd fled to the great house; and the husband followed after, in a murderous passion.

"Your father was out a-hunting, but they got word to him and he came riding back in time to find your mother's husband at the foot of the great staircase. Another moment and he'd have forced open the closet where the gyptian woman was hiding with you, but Lord Asriel challenged him, and they fought there and then, and Lord Asriel killed him.

"The gyptian woman heard and saw it all, Lyra, and that's how we know.

"The consequence was a great lawsuit. Your father en't the kind of man to deny or conceal the truth, and it left the judges with a problem. He'd killed all right, he'd shed blood, but he was defending his home and his child against an intruder. On t'other hand, the law allows any man to avenge the violation of his wife, and the dead man's lawyers argued that he were doing just that.

"The case lasted for weeks, with volumes of argument back and forth. In the end the judges punished Lord Asriel by confiscating all his property and all his land, and left him a poor man; and he had been richer than a king.

"As for your mother, she wanted nothing to do with it, nor with you. She turned her back. The gyptian nurse told me she'd often been afeared of how your mother would treat you, because she was a proud and scornful woman. So much for her.

"Then there was you. If things had fallen out different, Lyra, you might have been brought up a gyptian, because the nurse begged the court to let her have you; but we gyptians got little standing in the law. The court decided you was to be placed in a Priory, and so you were, with the Sisters of Obedience at Watlington. You won't remember.

"But Lord Asriel wouldn't stand for that. He had a hatred of priors and monks and nuns, and being a high-handed man he just rode in one day and carried you off. Not to look after himself, nor to give to the gyptians; he took you to Jordan College, and dared the law to undo it.

"Well, the law let things be. Lord Asriel went back to his explorations, and you grew up at Jordan College. The one thing he said, your father, the one condition he made, was that your mother shouldn't be let see you. If she ever tried to do that, she was to be prevented, and he was to be told, because all the anger in his nature had turned against her now. The Master promised faithfully to do that; and so time passed.

"Then come all this anxiety about Dust. And all over the country, all over the world, wise men and women too began a-worrying about it. It weren't of any account to us gyptians, until they started taking our kids. That's when we got interested. And we got connections in all sorts of places you wouldn't imagine, including Jordan College. You wouldn't know, but there's been someone a-watching over you and reporting to us ever since you been there. 'Cause we got an interest in you, and that gyptian woman who nursed you, she never stopped being anxious on your behalf."

"Who was it watching over me?" said Lyra. She felt immensely important and strange, that all her doings should be an object of concern so far away.

"It was a Kitchen servant. It was Bernie Johansen, the pastry cook. He's half-gyptian; you never knew that, I'll be bound."

Bernie was a kindly, solitary man, one of those rare people whose dæmon was the same sex as himself. It was Bernie she'd shouted at in her despair when Roger was taken. And Bernie had been telling the gyptians everything! She marvelled.

"So anyway," John Faa went on, "we heard about you going away from Jordan College, and how it came about at a time when Lord Asriel was imprisoned and couldn't prevent it. And we remembered what he'd said to the Master that he must never do, and we remembered that the man your mother had married, the politician Lord Asriel killed, was called Edward Coulter."

"Mrs Coulter?" said Lyra, quite stupefied. "*She* en't my mother?"

"She is. And if your father had been free she wouldn't never have dared to defy him, and you'd still be at Jordan, not knowing a thing. But what the Master was a-doing letting you go is a mystery I can't explain. He was charged with your care. All I can guess is that she had some power over him."

Lyra suddenly understood the Master's curious behaviour on the morning she'd left.

"But he didn't want to…" she said, trying to remember it exactly. "He … I had to go and see him first thing that morning, and I mustn't tell Mrs Coulter... It was like he wanted to protect me from Mrs Coulter..." She stopped, and looked at the two men carefully, and then decided to tell them the whole truth about the Retiring Room. "See, there was something else. That evening I hid in the Retiring Room, I saw the Master try to poison Lord Asriel. I saw him put some powder in the wine and I told my uncle and he knocked the decanter off the table and spilled it. So I saved his life. I could never understand why the Master would want to poison him, because he was always so kind. Then on the morning I left he called me in early to his study, and I had to go secretly so no one would know, and he said..." Lyra racked her brains to try and remember exactly what it was the Master had said. No good; she shook her head. "The only thing I could understand was that he gave me something and I had to keep it secret from her, from Mrs Coulter. I suppose it's all right if I tell you..."

She felt in the pocket of the wolfskin coat and took out the velvet package. She laid it on the table, and she sensed John Faa's massive simple curiosity and Farder Coram's bright flickering intelligence both trained on it like searchlights.

When she laid the alethiometer bare, it was Farder Coram who spoke first.

"I never thought I'd ever set eyes on one of them again. That's a symbol-reader. Did he tell you anything about it, child?"

"No. Only that I'd have to work out how to read it by myself. And he called it an alethiometer."

"What's that mean?" said John Faa, turning to his companion.

"That's a Greek word. I reckon it's from *aletheia*, which means truth. It's a truth-measure. And have you worked out how to use it?" he said to her.

"No. Least, I can make the three short hands point to different pictures, but I can't do anything with the long one. It goes all over. Except sometimes, right, sometimes when I'm sort of concentrating, I can make the long needle go this way or that just by thinking it."

"What's it do, Farder Coram?" said John Faa. "And how do you read it?"

"All these pictures round the rim," said Farder Coram, holding it delicately towards John Faa's blunt strong gaze, "they're symbols, and each one stands for a whole series of things. Take the anchor, there. The first meaning of that is hope, because hope holds you fast like an anchor so you don't give way. The second meaning is steadfastness. The third meaning is snag, or prevention. The fourth meaning is the sea. And so on, down to ten, twelve, maybe a never-ending series of meanings."

"And do you know them all?"

"I know some, but to read it fully I'd need the book. I seen the book and I know where it is, but I en't got it."

"We'll come back to that," said John Faa. "Go on with how you read it."

"You got three hands you can control," Farder Coram explained, "and you use them to ask a question. By pointing to three symbols you can ask any question you can imagine, because you've got so many levels of each one. Once you got your question framed, the other needle swings round and points to more symbols that give you the answer."

"But how does it know what level you're a-thinking of when you set the question?" said John Faa.

"Ah, by itself it don't. It only works if the questioner holds the levels in their mind. You got to know all the meanings, first, and there must be a thousand or more. Then you got to be able to hold 'em in your mind without fretting at it or pushing for an answer, and just watch while the needle wanders. When it's gone round its full range you'll

126

know what the answer is. I know how it works because I seen it done once by a wise man in Uppsala, and that's the only time I ever saw one before. Do you know how rare these are?"

"The Master told me there was only six made," Lyra said.

"Whatever the number, it en't large."

"And you kept this secret from Mrs Coulter, like the Master told you?" said John Faa.

"Yes. But her dæmon, right, he used to go in my room. And I'm sure he found it."

"I see. Well, Lyra, I don't know as we'll ever understand the full truth, but this is my guess, as good as I can make it. The Master was given a charge by Lord Asriel to look after you and keep you safe from your mother. And that was what he did, for ten years or more. Then Mrs Coulter's friends in the Church helped her set up this Oblation Board, for what purpose we don't know, and there she was, as powerful in her way as Lord Asriel was in his. Your parents, both strong in the world, both ambitious, and the Master of Jordan holding you in the balance between them.

"Now the Master's got a hundred things to look after. His first concern is his college and the scholarship there. So if he sees a threat to that, he has to move agin it. And the Church in recent times, Lyra, it's been a-getting more commanding. There's councils for this and councils for that; there's talk of reviving the Office of Inquisition, God forbid. And the Master has to tread warily between all these powers. He has to keep Jordan College on the right side of the Church, or it won't survive.

"And another concern of the Master is you, child. Bernie Johansen was always clear about that. The Master of Jordan and the other Scholars, they loved you like their own child. They'd do anything to keep you safe, not just because they'd promised to Lord Asriel that they would, but for your own sake. So if the Master gave you up to Mrs Coulter when he'd promised Lord Asriel he wouldn't, he must have thought you'd be safer with her than in Jordan College, in spite of all appearances. And when he set out to poison Lord Asriel, he must have thought that what Lord Asriel was a-doing would place all of them in danger, and maybe all of us, too; maybe all the world. I see the Master as a man having terrible choices to make; whatever he chooses will do harm; but maybe if he does the right thing, a little less harm will come about than if he chooses wrong. God preserve me from having to make that sort of choice.

"And when it come to the point where he had to let you go, he gave you the symbol-reader and bade you keep it safe. I wonder what he had in mind for you to do with it; as you couldn't read it, I'm foxed as to what he was a-thinking."

"He said Uncle Asriel presented the alethiometer to Jordan College years before," Lyra said, struggling to remember. "He was going to say something else, and then someone knocked at the door and he had to stop. What I thought was, he might have wanted me to keep it away from Lord Asriel too."

"Or even the opposite," said John Faa.

"What d'you mean, John?" said Farder Coram.

"He might have had it in mind to ask Lyra to return it to Lord Asriel, as a kind of recompense for trying to poison him. He might have thought the danger from Lord Asriel had passed. Or that Lord Asriel could read some wisdom from this instrument and hold back from his purpose. If Lord Asriel's held captive now, it might help set him free. Well, Lyra, you better take this symbol-reader and keep it safe. If you kept it safe so far I en't worried about leaving it with you. But there might come a time when we need to consult it, and I reckon we'll ask for it then."

He folded the velvet over it and slid it back across the table. Lyra wanted to ask all kinds of questions, but suddenly she felt shy of this massive man, with his little eyes so sharp and kindly among their folds and wrinkles.

One thing she had to ask, though.

"Who was the gyptian woman who nursed me?"

"Why, it was Billy Costa's mother, of course. She won't have told you, because I en't let her, but she knows what we're a-talking of here, so it's all out in the open.

"Now you best be getting back to her. You got plenty to be a-thinking of, child. When three days is gone past we'll have another Roping and discuss all there is to do. You be a good girl. Good night, Lyra."

"Good night, Lord Faa. Good night, Farder Coram," she said politely, clutching the alethiometer to her breast with one hand and scooping up Pantalaimon with the other.

Both old men smiled kindly at her. Outside the door of the parley room Ma Costa was waiting and, as if nothing had happened since Lyra was born, the boat-mother gathered her into her great arms and kissed her before bearing her off to bed.

8

Frustration

*L*yra had to adjust to her new sense of her own story, and that couldn't be done in a day. To see Lord Asriel as her father was one thing, but to accept Mrs Coulter as her mother was nowhere near so easy. A couple of months ago she would have rejoiced, of course, and she knew that too, and felt confused.

But, being Lyra, she didn't fret about it for long, for there was the Fen town to explore and many gyptian children to amaze. Before the three days were up she was an expert with a punt (in her eyes, at least) and she'd gathered a gang of urchins about her with tales of her mighty father, so unjustly made captive.

"And then one evening the Turkish Ambassador was a guest at Jordan for dinner. And he was under orders from the Sultan hisself to kill my father, right, and he had a ring on his finger with a hollow stone full of poison. And when the wine come round he made as if to reach across my father's glass, and he sprinkled the poison in. It was done so quick that no one else saw him, but –"

"What sort of poison?" demanded a thin-faced girl.

"Poison out of a special Turkish serpent," Lyra invented, "what they

130

catch by playing a pipe to lure out and then they throw it a sponge soaked in honey and the serpent bites it and can't get his fangs free, and they catch it and milk the venom out of it. Anyway, my father seen what the Turk done, and he says Gentlemen, I want to propose a toast of friendship between Jordan College and the College of Izmir, which was the college the Turkish Ambassador belonged to. And to show our willingness to be friends, he says, we'll swap glasses and drink each other's wine.

"And the Ambassador was in a fix then, 'cause he couldn't refuse to drink without giving deadly insult, and he couldn't drink it because he knew it was poisoned. He went pale and he fainted right away at the table. And when he come round they was all still sitting there, waiting and looking at him. And then he had to either drink the poison or own up."

"So what did he do?"

"He drunk it. It took him five whole minutes to die, and he was in torment all the time."

"Did you see it happen?"

"No, 'cause girls en't allowed at the High Table. But I seen his body afterwards when they laid him out. His skin was all withered like an old apple, and his eyes were starting from his head. In fact they had to push 'em back in the sockets…"

And so on.

Meanwhile, around the edges of the Fen country, the police were knocking at doors, searching attics and outhouses, inspecting papers and interrogating everyone who claimed to have seen a blonde little girl; and in Oxford the search was even fiercer. Jordan College was scoured from the dustiest boxroom to the darkest cellar, and so were Gabriel and St Michael's, till the heads of all the colleges issued a joint protest asserting their ancient rights. The only notion Lyra had of the search for her was the incessant drone of the gas engines of airships criss-crossing the skies. They weren't visible, because the clouds were low and by statute airships had to keep a certain height above Fen country, but who knew what cunning spy-devices they might carry? Best to keep under cover when she heard them, or wear the oilskin sou'wester over her bright distinctive hair.

And she questioned Ma Costa about every detail of the story of her birth. She wove the details into a mental tapestry even clearer and sharper than the stories she made up, and lived over and over again the flight from the cottage, the concealment in the closet, the harsh-voiced challenge, the clash of swords –

"Swords? Great God, girl, you dreaming?" Ma Costa said. "Mr Coulter had a gun, and Lord Asriel knocked it out his hand and struck him down with one blow. Then there was two shots. I wonder you don't remember; you ought to, little as you were. The first shot was Edward Coulter, who reached his gun and fired, and the second was Lord Asriel, who tore it out his grasp a second time and turned it on him. Shot him right between the eyes and dashed his brains out. Then he says, cool as paint, 'Come out, Mrs Costa, and bring the baby,' because you were setting up such a howl, you and that dæmon both; and he took you up and dandled you and sat you on his shoulders, walking up and down in high good humour with the dead man at his feet, and called for wine and bade me swab the floor."

By the end of the fourth repetition of the story Lyra was perfectly convinced she did remember it, and even volunteered details of the colour of Mr Coulter's coat and the cloaks and furs hanging in the closet. Ma Costa laughed.

And whenever she was alone, Lyra took out the alethiometer and pored over it like a lover with a picture of the beloved. So each image had several meanings, did it? Why shouldn't she work them out? Wasn't she Lord Asriel's daughter?

Remembering what Farder Coram had said, she tried to focus her mind on three symbols taken at random, and clicked the hands round to point at them. She found that if she held the alethiometer just so in her palms and gazed at it in a particular lazy way, as she thought of it, the long needle would begin to move more purposefully. Instead of its wayward divagations around the dial it swung smoothly from one picture to another. Sometimes it would pause at three, sometimes two, sometimes five or more, and although she understood nothing of it, she gained a deep calm enjoyment from it, unlike anything she'd known. Pantalaimon would crouch over the dial, sometimes as a cat, sometimes as a mouse, swinging his head round after the needle; and once or twice the two of them shared a glimpse of meaning that felt as if a shaft of sunlight had struck through clouds to light up a majestic line of great hills in the distance – something far beyond, and never suspected. And Lyra thrilled at those times with the same deep thrill she'd felt all her life on hearing the word North.

So the three days passed, with much coming and going between the multitude of boats and the Zaal. And then came the evening of the second Roping. The hall was more crowded than before, if that was possible. Lyra and the Costas got there in time to sit at the front, and as soon as the flickering lights showed that the place was crammed, John Faa and Farder Coram came out on the platform and sat behind the table. John Faa didn't have to make a sign for silence; he just put his great hands flat on the table and looked at the people below, and the hubbub died.

"Well," he said, "you done what I asked. And better than I hoped.

I'm a-going to call on the heads of the six families now to come up here and give over their gold and recount their promises. Nicholas Rokeby, you come first."

A stout black-bearded man climbed on to the platform and laid a heavy leather bag on the table.

"That's our gold," he said. "And we offer thirty-eight men."

"Thank you, Nicholas," said John Faa. Farder Coram was making a note. The first man stood at the back of the platform as John Faa called for the next, and the next; and each came up, laid a bag on the table and announced the number of men he could muster. The Costas were part of the Stefanski family, and naturally Tony had been one of the first to volunteer. Lyra noticed his hawk-dæmon shifting from foot to foot and spreading her wings as the Stefanski money and the promise of twenty-three men were laid before John Faa.

When the six family heads had all come up, Farder Coram showed his piece of paper to John Faa, who stood up to address the audience again.

"Friends, that's a muster of one hundred and seventy men. I thank you proudly. As for the gold, I make no doubt from the weight of it that you've all dug deep in your coffers, and my warm thanks go out for that as well.

"What we're a-going to do next is this. We're a-going to charter a ship and sail North, and find them kids and set 'em free. From what we know, there might be some fighting to do. It won't be the first time, nor it won't be the last, but we never had to fight yet with people who kidnap children, and we shall have to be uncommon cunning. But we en't going to come back without our kids. Yes, Dirk Vries?"

A man stood up and said, "Lord Faa, do you know why they captured them kids?"

"We heard it's a theological matter. They're making an experiment, but what nature it is we don't know. To tell you all the truth, we don't even know whether any harm is a-coming to 'em. But whatever it is, good or bad, they got no right to reach out by night and pluck little children out the hearts of their families. Yes, Raymond van Gerrit?"

The man who'd spoken at the first meeting stood up and said, "That child, Lord Faa, the one you spoke of as being sought, the one as is sitting in the front row now. I heard as all the folk living around the edge of the Fens is having their houses turned upside down on her account. I heard there's a move in Parliament this very day to rescind our ancient privileges on account of this child. Yes, friends," he said, over the babble of shocked whispers, "they're a-going to pass a law doing away with our right to free movement in and out the Fens. Now, Lord Faa, what we want to know is this: who is this child on account of which we might come to such a pass? She en't a gyptian child, not as I heard. How comes it that a landloper child can put us all in danger?"

Lyra looked up at John Faa's massive frame. Her heart was thumping so much she could hardly hear the first words of his reply.

"Now spell it out, Raymond, don't be shy," he said. "You want us to give this child up to them she's a-fleeing from, is that right?"

The man stood obstinately frowning, but said nothing.

"Well, perhaps you would, and perhaps you wouldn't," John Faa continued. "But if any man or woman needs a reason for doing good, ponder on this. That little girl is the daughter of Lord Asriel, no less. For them as has forgotten, it were Lord Asriel who interceded with the Turk for the life of Sam Broekman. It were Lord Asriel who allowed gyptian boats free passage on the canals through his property. It were Lord Asriel who defeated the Watercourse Bill in Parliament, to our great and lasting benefit. And it were Lord Asriel who fought day and night in the floods of '53, and plunged headlong in the water twice to pull out young Ruud and Nellie Koopman. You forgotten that? Shame, shame on you, shame.

"And now that same Lord Asriel is held in the farthest coldest darkest regions of the wild, captive, in the fortress of Svalbard. Do I need to tell you the kind of creatures a-guarding him there? And this is his little daughter in our care, and Raymond van Gerrit would hand her over to the authorities for a bit of peace and quiet. Is that right, Raymond? Stand up and answer, man."

But Raymond van Gerrit had sunk to his seat, and nothing would make him stand. A low hiss of disapproval sounded through the great hall, and Lyra felt the shame he must be feeling, as well as a deep glow of pride in her brave father.

John Faa turned away, and looked at the other men on the platform.

"Nicholas Rokeby, I'm a-putting you in charge of finding a vessel, and commanding her once we sail. Adam Stefanski, I want you to take charge of the arms and munitions, and command the fighting. Roger van Poppel, you look to all the other stores, from food to cold-weather clothing. Simon Hartmann, you be treasurer, and account to us all for a proper apportionment of our gold. Benjamin de Ruyter, I want you to take charge of spying. There's a great deal we ought to find out, and I'm a-giving you the charge of that, and you'll report to Farder Coram. Michael Canzona, you're going to be responsible for co-ordinating the first four leaders' work, and you'll report to me, and if I die, you're my second in command and you'll take over.

"Now I've made my dispositions according to custom, and if any man or woman seeks to disagree, they may do so freely."

After a moment a woman stood up.

"Lord Faa, en't you a-taking any women on this expedition to look after them kids once you found 'em?"

"No, Nell. We shall have little space as it is. Any kids we free will be better off in our care than where they've been."

"But supposing you find out that you can't rescue 'em without some women in disguise as guards or nurses or whatever?"

"Well, I hadn't thought of that," John Faa admitted. "We'll consider that most carefully when we retire into the parley room, you have my promise."

She sat down and a man stood up.

"Lord Faa, I heard you say that Lord Asriel is in captivity. Is it part of your plan to rescue him? Because if it is, and if he's in the power of them bears as I think you said, that's going to need more than a hundred and seventy men. And good friend as Lord Asriel is to us, I don't know as there's any call on us to go as far as that."

"Adriaan Braks, you're not wrong. What I had it in my mind to do was to keep our eyes and ears open and see what knowledge we can glean while we're in the North. It may be that we can do something to help him, and it may not, but you can trust me not to use what you've provided, man and gold, for any purpose outside the stated one of finding our children and bringing 'em home."

Another woman stood up.

"Lord Faa, we don't know what them Gobblers might've been doing to our children. We all heard rumours and stories of fearful things. We hear about children with no heads, or about children cut in half and sewn together, or about things too awful to mention. I'm truly sorry to distress anyone, but we all heard this kind of thing, and I want to get it out in the open. Now in case you find anything of that awful kind, Lord Faa, I hope you're a-going to take powerful revenge. I hope you en't going to let thoughts of mercy and gentleness hold your hand back from striking and striking hard, and delivering a mighty blow to the heart of that infernal wickedness. And I'm sure I speak for any mother as has lost a child to the Gobblers."

There was a loud murmur of agreement as she sat down. Heads were nodding all over the Zaal.

John Faa waited for silence, and said:

"Nothing will hold my hand, Margaret, save only judgement. If I stay my hand in the North, it will only be to strike the harder in the South. To strike a day too soon is as bad as striking a hundred miles off. To be sure, there's a warm passion behind what you say. But if you give in to that passion, friends, you're a-doing what I always warned you agin: you're a-placing the satisfaction of your own feelings above the work you have to do. Our work here is first rescue, then punishment. It en't gratification for upset feelings. Our feelings don't matter. If we rescue the kids but we can't punish the Gobblers, we've done the main task. But if we aim to punish the Gobblers first and by doing so lose the chance of rescuing the kids, we've failed.

"But be assured of this, Margaret. When the time comes to punish, we shall strike such a blow as'll make their hearts faint and fearful. We shall strike the strength out of 'em. We shall leave them ruined and waste, broken and shattered, torn in a thousand pieces and scattered to the four winds. My own hammer is thirsty for blood, friends. She en't tasted blood since I slew the Tartar champion on the steppes of Kazakhstan; she's been a-hanging in my boat and dreaming; but she can smell blood in the wind from the North. She spoke to me last night and told me of her thirst, and I said soon, gal, soon. Margaret, you can worry about a hundred things, but don't you worry that John Faa's heart is too soft to strike a blow when the time comes. And the time will come under judgement. Not under passion.

"Is there anyone else who wants to speak? Speak if you will."

But no one did, and presently John Faa reached for the closing bell and rang it hard and loud, swinging it high and shaking the peals out of it so that they filled the hall and rang the rafters.

John Faa and the other men left the platform for the parley room. Lyra was a little disappointed. Didn't they want her there too? But Tony laughed.

"They got plans to make," he said. "You done your part, Lyra. Now it's for John Faa and the council."

"But I en't done nothing yet!" Lyra protested, as she followed the others reluctantly out of the Hall and down the cobbled road towards the jetty. "All I done was run away from Mrs Coulter! That's just a beginning. I want to go North!"

"Tell you what," said Tony, "I'll bring you back a walrus tooth, that's what I'll do."

Lyra scowled. For his part, Pantalaimon occupied himself by making monkey-faces at Tony's dæmon, who closed her tawny eyes in disdain. Lyra drifted to the jetty and hung about with her new companions, dangling lanterns on strings over the black water to attract the goggle-eyed fishes who swam slowly up to be lunged at with sharp sticks and missed.

But her mind was on John Faa and the parley room, and before long she slipped away up the cobbles again to the Zaal. There was a light in the parley room window. It was too high to look through, but she could hear a low rumble of voices inside.

So she walked up to the door and knocked on it firmly five times. The voices stopped, a chair scraped across the floor, and the door opened, spilling warm naphtha light out on the damp step.

"Yes?" said the man who'd opened it.

Beyond him Lyra could see the other men around the table, with bags of gold stacked neatly, and papers and pens, and glasses and a crock of jenniver.

"I want to come North," Lyra said so they could all hear it. "I want to come and help rescue the kids. That's what I set out to do when I run away from Mrs Coulter. And before that, even, I meant to rescue my friend Roger the Kitchen boy from Jordan who was took. I want to come and help. I can do navigation and I can take anbaromagnetic readings off the Aurora, and I know what parts of a bear you can eat, and all kinds of useful things. You'd be sorry if you got up there and then found you needed me and found you'd left me behind. And like that woman said, you might need women to play a part – well, you might need kids too. You don't know. So you oughter take me, Lord Faa, excuse me for interrupting your talk."

She was inside the room now, and all the men and their dæmons were watching her, some with amusement and some with irritation, but she had eyes only for John Faa. Pantalaimon sat up in her arms, his wildcat eyes blazing green.

John Faa said, "Lyra, there en't no question of taking you into danger, so don't delude yourself, child. Stay here and help Ma Costa and keep safe. That's what you got to do."

"But I'm learning how to read the alethiometer, too. It's coming clearer every day! You're bound to need that – bound to!"

He shook his head.

"No," he said. "I know your heart was set on going North, but it's my belief not even Mrs Coulter was going to take you. If you want to see the North you'll have to wait till all this trouble's over. Now off you go."

Pantalaimon hissed quietly, but John Faa's dæmon took off from the back of his chair and flew at them with black wings, not threateningly, but like a reminder of good manners; and Lyra turned on her heel as the crow glided over her head and wheeled back to John Faa. The door shut behind her with a decisive click.

"We *will* go," she said to Pantalaimon. "Let 'em try to stop us. We *will*!"

9

The Spies

*O*ver the next few days, Lyra concocted a dozen plans and dismissed them impatiently; for they all boiled down to stowing away, and how could you stow away on a narrow-boat? To be sure, the real voyage would involve a proper ship, and she knew enough stories to expect all kinds of hiding-places on a full-sized vessel: the lifeboats, the hold, the bilges, whatever they were; but she'd have to get to the ship first, and leaving the Fens meant travelling the gyptian way.

And even if she got to the coast on her own, she might stow away on the wrong ship. It would be a fine thing to hide in a lifeboat and wake up on the way to High Brazil.

Meanwhile, all around her the tantalizing work of assembling the expedition was going on day and night. She hung around Adam Stefanski, watching as he made his choice of the volunteers for the fighting force. She pestered Roger van Poppel with suggestions about the stores they needed to take: had he remembered snow-goggles? Did he know the best place to get Arctic maps?

The man she most wanted to help was Benjamin de Ruyter, the spy.

But he had slipped away in the early hours of the morning after the second Roping, and naturally no one could say where he'd gone or when he'd return. So in default, Lyra attached herself to Farder Coram.

"I think it'd be best if I helped you, Farder Coram," she said, "because I probably know more about the Gobblers than anyone else, being as I was nearly one of them. Probably you'll need me to help you understand Mr de Ruyter's messages."

He took pity on the fierce, desperate little girl and didn't send her away. Instead he talked to her, and listened to her memories of Oxford and of Mrs Coulter, and watched as she read the alethiometer.

"Where's that book with all the symbols in?" she asked him one day.

"In Heidelberg," he said.

"And is there just the one?"

"There may be others, but that's the one I've seen."

"I bet there's one in Bodley's Library in Oxford," she said.

She could hardly take her eyes off Farder Coram's dæmon, who was the most beautiful dæmon she'd ever seen. When Pantalaimon was a cat he was lean and ragged and harsh, but Sophonax, for that was her name, was golden-eyed and elegant beyond measure, fully twice as large as a real cat and richly furred. When the sunlight touched her, it lit up more shades of tawny-brown-leaf-hazel-corn-gold-autumn-mahogany than Lyra could name. She longed to touch that fur, to rub her cheeks against it, but of course she never did; for it was the grossest breach of etiquette imaginable to touch another person's dæmon. Dæmons might touch each other, of course, or fight; but the prohibition against human-dæmon contact went so deep that even in battle no warrior would touch an enemy's dæmon. It was utterly forbidden. Lyra couldn't remember having to be told that: she just knew it, as instinctively as she felt that nausea was bad and comfort good. So although she admired the fur of

Sophonax and even speculated on what it might feel like, she never made the slightest move to touch her, and never would.

Sophonax was as sleek and healthy and beautiful as Farder Coram was ravaged and weak. He might have been ill, or he might have suffered a crippling blow, but the result was that he could not walk without leaning on two sticks, and he trembled constantly like an aspen leaf. His mind was sharp and clear and powerful, though, and soon Lyra came to love him for his knowledge and for the firm way he directed her.

"What's that hourglass mean, Farder Coram?" she asked, over the alethiometer, one sunny morning in his boat. "It keeps coming back to that."

"There's often a clue there if you look more close. What's that little old thing on top of it?"

She screwed up her eyes and peered.

"That's a skull!"

"So what d'you think that might mean?"

"Death... Is that death?"

"That's right. So in the hourglass range of meanings you get death. In fact after time, which is the first one, death is the second one."

"D'you know what I noticed, Farder Coram? The needle stops there on the second go round! On the first round it kind of twitches, and on the second it stops. Is that saying it's the second meaning, then?"

"Probably. What are you asking it, Lyra?"

"I'm a-thinking..." She stopped, surprised to find that she'd actually been asking a question without realizing it. "I just put three pictures together because ... I was thinking about Mr de Ruyter, see... And I put together the serpent and the crucible and the beehive, to ask how he's a-getting on with his spying, and –"

"Why them three symbols?"

"Because I thought the serpent was cunning, like a spy ought to be, and the crucible could mean like knowledge, what you kind of distil, and the beehive was hard work, like bees are always working hard; so out of the hard work and the cunning comes the knowledge, see, and that's the spy's job; and I pointed to them and I thought the question in my mind, and the needle stopped at death... D'you think that could be really working, Farder Coram?"

"It's working all right, Lyra. What we don't know is whether we're reading it right. That's a subtle art. I wonder if –"

Before he could finish his sentence, there was an urgent knock at the door, and a young gyptian man came in.

"Beg pardon, Farder Coram, there's Jacob Huismans just come back, and he's sore wounded."

"He was with Benjamin de Ruyter," said Farder Coram. "What's happened?"

"He won't speak," said the young man. "You better come, Farder Coram, cause he won't last long, he's a-bleeding inside."

Farder Coram and Lyra exchanged a look of alarm and wonderment, but only for a second, and then Farder Coram was hobbling out on his sticks as fast as he could manage, with his dæmon padding ahead of him. Lyra came too, hopping with impatience.

The young man led them to a boat tied up at the sugar-beet jetty, where a woman in a red flannel apron held open the door for them. Seeing her suspicious glance at Lyra, Farder Coram said, "It's important the girl hears what Jacob's got to say, mistress."

So the woman let them in and stood back, with her squirrel-dæmon perched silent on the wooden clock. On a bunk under a patchwork coverlet lay a man whose white face was damp with sweat and whose eyes were glazed.

"I've sent for the physician, Farder Coram," said the woman shakily. "Please don't agitate him. He's in an agony of pain. He come in off Peter Hawker's boat just a few minutes ago."

"Where's Peter now?"

"He's a-tying up. It was him said I had to send for you."

"Quite right. Now, Jacob, can ye hear me?"

Jacob's eyes rolled to look at Farder Coram sitting on the opposite bunk, a foot or two away.

"Hello, Farder Coram," he murmured.

Lyra looked at his dæmon. She was a ferret, and she lay very still beside his head, curled up but not asleep, for her eyes were open and glazed like his.

"What happened?" said Farder Coram.

"Benjamin's dead," came the answer. "He's dead, and Gerard's captured."

His voice was hoarse and his breath was shallow. When he stopped speaking his dæmon uncurled painfully and licked his cheek, and taking strength from that he went on:

"We was breaking into the Ministry of Theology, because Benjamin had heard from one of the Gobblers we caught that the headquarters was there, that's where all the orders was coming from…"

He stopped again.

"You captured some Gobblers?" said Farder Coram.

Jacob nodded, and cast his eyes at his dæmon. It was unusual for dæmons to speak to other humans than their own, but it happened sometimes, and she spoke now.

"We caught three Gobblers in Clerkenwell and made them tell us who they were working for and where the orders came from and so on. They didn't know where the kids were being taken, except it was

146

North to Lapland..."

She had to stop and pant briefly, her little chest fluttering, before she could go on.

"And so them Gobblers told us about the Ministry of Theology and Lord Boreal. Benjamin said him and Gerard Hook should break into the Ministry and Frans Broekman and Tom Mendham should go and find out about Lord Boreal."

"Did they do that?"

"We don't know. They never came back. Farder Coram, it were like everything we did, they knew about before we did it, and for all we know Frans and Tom were swallowed alive as soon as they got near Lord Boreal."

"Come back to Benjamin," said Farder Coram, hearing Jacob's breathing getting harsher and seeing his eyes close in pain.

Jacob's dæmon gave a little mew of anxiety and love, and the woman took a step or two closer, her hands to her mouth; but she didn't speak, and the dæmon went on faintly:

"Benjamin and Gerard and us went to the Ministry at White Hall and found a little side door, it not being fiercely guarded, and we stayed on watch outside while they unfastened the lock and went in. They hadn't been in but a minute when we heard a cry of fear, and Benjamin's dæmon came a-flying out and beckoned to us for help and flew in again, and we took our knife and ran in after her; only the place was dark, and full of wild forms and sounds that were confusing in their frightful movements; and we cast about, but there was a commotion above, and a fearful cry, and Benjamin and his dæmon fell from a high staircase above us, his dæmon a-tugging and a-fluttering to hold him up, but all in vain, for they crashed on the stone floor and both perished in a moment.

"And we couldn't see anything of Gerard, but there was a howl from above in his voice and we were too terrified and stunned to move, and then an arrow shot down at our shoulder and pierced deep down within…"

The dæmon's voice was fainter, and a groan came from the wounded man. Farder Coram leaned forward and gently pulled back the counterpane, and there protruding from his shoulder was the feathered end of an arrow in a mass of clotted blood. The shaft and the head were so deep in the poor man's chest that only six inches or so remained above the skin. Lyra felt faint.

There was the sound of feet and voices outside on the jetty.

Farder Coram sat up and said, "Here's the physician, Jacob. We'll leave you now. We'll have a longer talk when you're feeling better."

He clasped the woman's shoulder on the way out. Lyra stuck close to him on the jetty, because there was a crowd gathering already, whispering and pointing. Farder Coram gave orders for Peter Hawker to go at once to John Faa, and then said:

"Lyra, as soon as we know whether Jacob's going to live or die, we must have another talk about that alethiometer. You go and occupy yourself elsewhere, child; we'll send for you."

Lyra wandered away on her own, and went to the reedy bank to sit and throw mud into the water. She knew one thing: she was not pleased or proud to be able to read the alethiometer – she was afraid. Whatever power was making that needle swing and stop, it knew things like an intelligent being.

"I reckon it's a spirit," Lyra said, and for a moment she was tempted to throw the little thing into the middle of the fen.

"I'd see a spirit if there was one in there," said Pantalaimon. "Like that old ghost in Godstow. I saw that when you didn't."

"There's more than one kind of spirit," said Lyra reprovingly. "You can't see all of 'em. Anyway, what about those old dead Scholars without their heads? I saw them, remember."

"That was only a night-ghast."

"It was not. They were proper spirits all right, and you know it. But whatever spirit's moving this blooming needle en't that sort of spirit."

"It might not be a spirit," said Pantalaimon stubbornly.

"Well what else could it be?"

"It might be... It might be elementary particles."

She scoffed.

"It could be!" he insisted. "You remember that photo-mill they got at Gabriel? Well then."

At Gabriel College there was a very holy object kept on the high altar of the Oratory, covered (now Lyra thought about it) with a black velvet cloth, like the one around the alethiometer. She had seen it when she accompanied the Librarian of Jordan to a service there. At the height of the invocation the Intercessor lifted the cloth to reveal in the dimness a glass dome inside which there was something too distant to see, until he pulled a string attached to a shutter above, letting a ray of sunlight through to strike the dome exactly. Then it became clear: a little thing like a weathervane, with four sails black on one side and white on the other, that began to whirl around as the light struck it. It illustrated a moral lesson, the Intercessor explained, for the black of ignorance fled from the light, whereas the wisdom of white rushed to embrace it. Lyra took his word for that, but the little whirling vanes were delightful whatever they meant, and all done by the power of photons, said the Librarian as they walked home to Jordan.

So perhaps Pantalaimon was right. If elementary particles could push a photo-mill around, no doubt they could make light work of a needle; but it still troubled her.

"Lyra! Lyra!"

It was Tony Costa, waving to her from the jetty.

"Come over here," he called. "You got to go and see John Faa at the Zaal. Run, gal, it's urgent."

She found John Faa with Farder Coram and the other leaders, looking troubled.

John Faa spoke:

"Lyra, child, Farder Coram has told me about your reading of that instrument. And I'm sorry to say that poor Jacob has just died. I think we're going to have to take you with us after all, against my inclinations. I'm troubled in my mind about it, but there don't seem to be any alternative. As soon as Jacob's buried according to custom we'll take our way. You understand me, Lyra: you're a-coming too, but it en't an occasion for joy or jubilation. There's trouble and danger ahead for all on us.

"I'm a-putting you under Farder Coram's wing. Don't you be a trouble or a hazard to him, or you'll be a-feeling the force of my wrath. Now cut along and explain to Ma Costa, and hold yourself in readiness to leave."

The next two weeks passed more busily than any time of Lyra's life so far. Busily, but not quickly, for there were tedious stretches of waiting, of hiding in damp crabbed closets, of watching a dismal rain-soaked autumn landscape roll past the window, of hiding again, of sleeping near the gas-fumes of the engine and waking with a sick headache, and worst of all, of never once being allowed out into the air to run along the bank or clamber over the deck or haul at the lock gates or catch a mooring-rope thrown from the lockside.

Because of course she had to remain hidden. Tony Costa told her of the gossip in the waterside pubs: that there was a hunt the length of the kingdom for a little fair-haired girl, with a big reward for her discovery and severe punishment for anyone concealing her. There were strange rumours, too: people said she was the only child to have escaped from the Gobblers, and she had terrible secrets in her possession. Another rumour said she wasn't a human child at all but a pair of spirits in the form of child and dæmon, sent to this world by the infernal powers in order to work great ruin; and yet another rumour said it was no child but a fully grown human, shrunk by magic and in the pay of the Tartars, come to spy on good English people and prepare the way for a Tartar invasion.

Lyra heard these tales at first with glee and later with despondency. All those people hating and fearing her! And she longed to be out of this narrow boxy cabin. She longed to be North already, in the wide snows under the blazing Aurora. And sometimes she longed to be back at Jordan College, scrambling over the roofs with Roger with the Steward's Bell tolling half an hour to dinner time and the clatter and sizzle and shouting of the Kitchen... Then she wished passionately that nothing had changed, nothing would ever change, that she could be Lyra of Jordan College for ever and ever.

The one thing that drew her out of her boredom and irritation was the alethiometer. She read it every day, sometimes with Farder Coram and sometimes on her own, and she found that she could sink more and more readily into the calm state in which the symbol-meanings clarified themselves, and those great mountain-ranges touched by sunlight emerged into vision.

She struggled to explain to Farder Coram what it felt like.

"It's almost like talking to someone, only you can't quite hear them, and you feel kind of stupid because they're cleverer than you, only they don't get cross or anything… And they know such a lot, Farder Coram! As if they knew everything, almost! Mrs Coulter was clever, she knew ever such a lot, but this is a different kind of knowing… It's like understanding, I suppose…"

He would ask specific questions, and she would search for answers.

"What's Mrs Coulter doing now?" he'd say, and her hands would move at once, and he'd say, "Tell me what you're doing."

"Well, the Madonna is Mrs Coulter, and I think my *mother* when I put the hand there; and the ant is *busy* – that's easy, that's the top meaning; and the hourglass has got *time* in its meanings, and partway down there's *now*, and I just fix my mind on it."

"And how do you know where these meanings are?"

"I kind of see 'em. Or feel 'em rather, like climbing down a ladder at night, you put your foot down and there's another rung. Well, I put my mind down and there's another meaning, and I kind of sense what it is. Then I put 'em all together. There's a trick in it like focusing your eyes."

"Do that then, and see what it says."

Lyra did. The long needle began to swing at once, and stopped, moved on, stopped again in a precise series of sweeps and pauses. It was a sensation of such grace and power that Lyra, sharing it, felt like a young bird learning to fly. Farder Coram, watching from across the table, noted the places where the needle stopped, and watched the little girl holding her hair back from her face and biting her lower lip just a little, her eyes following the needle at first but then, when its path was settled, looking elsewhere on the dial. Not randomly, though. Farder Coram was a chess player, and he knew how chess players looked at a game in play. An expert player seemed to see lines of force and influence on the board, and looked along the important lines and ignored the weak ones; and Lyra's eyes moved the same way, according to some similar magnetic field that she could see and he couldn't.

The needle stopped at the thunderbolt, the infant, the serpent, the elephant, and at a creature Lyra couldn't find a name for: a sort of lizard with big eyes and a tail curled around the twig it stood on. It repeated the sequence time after time, while Lyra watched.

"What's that lizard mean?" said Farder Coram, breaking into her concentration.

"It don't make sense... I can see what it says, but I must be misreading it. The thunderbolt I think is anger, and the child ... I think it's me ... I was getting a meaning for that lizard thing, but you talked to me, Farder Coram, and I lost it. See, it's just floating any old where."

"Yes, I see that. I'm sorry, Lyra. You tired now? D'you want to stop?"

"No, I don't," she said, but her cheeks were flushed and her eyes bright. She had all the signs of fretful over-excitement, and it was made worse by her long confinement in this stuffy cabin.

He looked out of the window. It was nearly dark, and they were travelling along the last stretch of inland water before reaching the coast. Wide brown scummed expanses of an estuary extended under a dreary sky to a distant group of coal-spirit tanks, rusty and cobwebbed with pipework, beside a refinery where a thick smear of smoke ascended reluctantly to join the clouds.

"Where are we?" said Lyra. "Can I go outside just for a bit, Farder Coram?"

"This is Colby water," he said. "The estuary of the river Cole. When we reach the town we'll tie up by the Smokemarket and go on foot to the docks. We'll be there in an hour or two..."

But it was getting dark, and in the wide desolation of the creek nothing was moving but their own boat and a distant coal-barge labouring towards the refinery; and Lyra was so flushed and tired, and she'd been inside for so long; so Farder Coram went on:

"Well, I don't suppose it'll matter just for a few minutes in the open air. I wouldn't call it fresh; ten't fresh except when it's blowing off the sea; but you can sit out on top and look around till we get closer in."

Lyra leapt up, and Pantalaimon became a seagull at once, eager to stretch his wings in the open. It was cold outside and, although she was well wrapped up, Lyra was soon shivering. Pantalaimon, on the other hand, leapt into the air with a loud caw of delight, and wheeled and skimmed and darted now ahead of the boat, now behind the stern. Lyra exulted in it, feeling with him as he flew, and urging him mentally to provoke the old tillerman's cormorant-dæmon into a race. But she ignored him and settled down sleepily on the handle of the tiller near her man.

There was no life out on this bitter brown expanse, and only the steady chug of the engine and the subdued splashing of the water under the bows broke the wide silence. Heavy clouds hung low without offering rain; the air beneath was grimy with smoke. Only Pantalaimon's flashing elegance had anything in it of life and joy.

As he soared up out of a dive with wide wings white against the grey, something black hurtled at him and struck. He fell sideways in a flutter of shock and pain, and Lyra cried out, feeling it sharply. Another little black thing joined the first; they moved not like birds but like flying beetles, heavy and direct, and with a droning sound.

As Pantalaimon fell, trying to twist away and make for the boat and Lyra's desperate arms, the black things kept driving into him, droning, buzzing, and murderous. Lyra was nearly mad with Pantalaimon's fear and her own, but then something swept past her and upward.

It was the tillerman's dæmon, and clumsy and heavy as she looked, her flight was powerful and swift. Her head snapped this way and that

– there was a flutter of black wings, a shiver of white – and a little black thing fell to the tarred roof of the cabin at Lyra's feet just as Pantalaimon landed on her outstretched hand.

Before she could comfort him, he changed into his wildcat-shape and sprang down on the creature, batting it back from the edge of the roof, where it was crawling swiftly to escape. Pantalaimon held it firmly down with a needle-filled paw and looked up at the darkening sky, where the black wing-flaps of the cormorant were circling higher as she cast around for the other.

Then the cormorant glided swiftly back and croaked something to the tillerman, who said, "It's gone. Don't let that other one escape. Here –" and he flung the dregs out of the tin mug he'd been drinking from, and tossed it to Lyra.

She clapped it over the creature at once. It buzzed and snarled like a little machine.

"Hold it still," said Farder Coram from behind her, and then he was kneeling to slip a piece of card under the mug.

"What is it, Farder Coram?" she said shakily.

"Let's go below and have a look. Take it careful, Lyra. Hold that tight."

She looked at the tillerman's dæmon as she passed, intending to thank her, but her old eyes were closed. She thanked the tillerman instead.

"You oughter stayed below," was all he said.

She took the mug into the cabin, where Farder Coram had found a beer glass. He held the tin mug upside down over it and then slipped the card out from between them, so that the creature fell into the glass. He held it up so they could see the angry little thing clearly.

It was about as long as Lyra's thumb, and dark green, not black. Its

155

wing cases were erect, like a ladybird's about to fly, and the wings inside were beating so furiously that they were only a blur. Its six clawed legs were scrabbling on the smooth glass.

"What is it?" she said.

Pantalaimon, a wildcat still, crouched on the table six inches away, his green eyes following it round and round inside the glass.

"If you was to crack it open," said Farder Coram, "you'd find no living thing in there. No animal nor insect, at any rate. I seen one of these things afore, and I never thought I'd see one again this far north. Afric things. There's a clockwork running in there, and pinned to the spring of it, there's a bad spirit with a spell through its heart."

"But who sent it?"

"You don't even need to read the symbols, Lyra; you can guess as easy as I can."

"Mrs Coulter?"

"Course. She en't only explored up North; there's strange things aplenty in the southern wild. It was Morocco where I saw one of these last. Deadly dangerous; while the spirit's in it, it won't never stop, and when you let the spirit free it's so monstrous angry it'll kill the first thing it gets at."

"But what was it after?"

"Spying. I was a cursed fool to let you up above. And I should have let you think your way through the symbols without interrupting."

"I see it now!" said Lyra, suddenly excited. "It means air, that lizard thing! I saw that, but I couldn't see why, so I tried to work it out and I lost it."

"Ah," said Farder Coram, "then I see it too. It en't a lizard, that's why; it's a chameleon. And it stands for air because they don't eat nor drink, they just live on air."

"And the elephant –"

"Africa," he said, and, "Aha."

They looked at each other. With every revelation of the alethiometer's power, they became more awed by it.

"It was telling us about these things all the time," said Lyra. "We oughter listened. But what can we do about this'un, Farder Coram? Can we kill it or something?"

"I don't know as we can do anything. We shall just have to keep him shut up tight in a box and never let him out. What worries me more is the other one, as got away. He'll be a-flying back to Mrs Coulter now, with the news that he's seen you. Damn me, Lyra, but I'm a fool."

He rattled about in a cupboard and found a smoke-leaf tin about three inches in diameter. It had been used for holding screws, but he tipped those out and wiped the inside with a rag before inverting the glass over it with the card still in place over the mouth.

After a tricky moment when one of the creature's legs escaped and thrust the tin away with surprising strength, they had it captured and the lid screwed down tight.

"As soon's we get about the ship I'll run some solder round the edge to make sure of it," Farder Coram said.

"But don't clockwork run down?"

"Ordinary clockwork, yes. But like I said, this'un's kept tight wound by the spirit pinned to the end. The more he struggles, the tighter it's wound, and the stronger the force is. Now let's put this feller out the way…"

He wrapped the tin in a flannel cloth to stifle the incessant buzzing and droning, and stowed it away under his bunk.

It was dark now, and Lyra watched through the window as the lights of Colby came closer. The heavy air was thickening into mist, and by the time they tied up at the wharves alongside the Smokemarket everything in sight was softened and blurred. The darkness shaded into pearly silver-grey veils laid over the warehouses and the cranes, the wooden market-stalls and the granite many-chimneyed building the market was named after, where day and night fish hung kippering in the fragrant oakwood smoke. The chimneys were contributing their thickness to the clammy air, and the pleasant reek of smoked herring and mackerel and haddock seemed to breathe out of the very cobbles.

Lyra, wrapped up in an oilskin and with a large hood hiding her revealing hair, walked along between Farder Coram and the tillerman. All three dæmons were alert, scouting around corners ahead, watching behind, listening for the slightest footfall.

But they were the only figures to be seen. The citizens of Colby were all indoors, probably sipping jenniver beside roaring stoves. They saw no one until they reached the dock, and the first man they saw there was was Tony Costa, guarding the gates.

"Thank God you got here," he said quietly, letting them through. "We just heard as Jack Verhoeven's bin shot and his boat sunk, and no one'd heard where you was. John Faa's on board already and jumping to go."

The vessel looked immense to Lyra: a wheelhouse and funnel amidships, a high fo'c'sle and a stout derrick over a canvas-covered hatch; yellow light agleam in the portholes and the bridge, and white light at the masthead; and three or four men on deck, working urgently at things she couldn't see.

She hurried up the wooden gangway ahead of Farder Coram, and looked around with excitement. Pantalaimon became a monkey and clambered up the derrick at once, but she called him down again; Farder Coram wanted them indoors, or below, as you called it on board ship.

Down some stairs, or a companionway, there was a small saloon where John Faa was talking quietly with Nicholas Rokeby, the gyptian in charge of the vessel. John Faa did nothing hastily. Lyra was waiting for him to greet her, but he finished his remarks about the tide and pilotage before turning to the incomers.

"Good evening, friends," he said. "Poor Jack Verhoeven's dead, perhaps you've heard. And his boys captured."

"We have bad news too," said Farder Coram, and told of their encounter with the flying spirits.

John Faa shook his great head, but didn't reproach them.

"Where is the creature now?" he said.

Farder Coram took out the leaf-tin and laid it on the table. Such a furious buzzing came from it that the tin itself moved slowly over the wood.

"I've heard of them clockwork devils, but never seen one," John Faa said. "There en't no way of taming it and turning it back, I do know that much. Nor is it any use weighing it down with lead and dropping it in the ocean, because one day it'd rust through and out the devil would come and make for the child wherever she was. No, we'll have to keep it by, and exercise our vigilance."

Lyra being the only female on board (for John Faa had decided against taking women, after much thought), she had a cabin to herself. Not a grand cabin, to be sure; in fact little more than a closet with a bunk and a scuttle, which was the proper name for porthole. She stowed her few things in the drawer below the bunk and ran up excitedly to lean over the rail and watch England vanish behind, only to find that most of England had vanished in the mist before she got there.

But the rush of water below, the movement in the air, the ship's lights glowing bravely in the dark, the rumble of the engine, the smells of salt and fish and coal-spirit, were exciting enough by themselves. It wasn't long before another sensation joined them, as the vessel began to roll in the German Ocean swell. When someone called Lyra down for a bite of supper, she found she was less hungry than she'd thought, and presently she decided it would be a good idea to lie down, for Pantalaimon's sake, because the poor creature was feeling sadly ill at ease.

And so began her journey to the North.

Part Two
Bolvangar

10

The Consul and the Bear

John Faa and the other leaders had decided that they would make for Trollesund, the main port of Lapland. The witches had a consulate in the town, and John Faa knew that without their help, or at least their friendly neutrality, it would be impossible to rescue the captive children.

He explained his idea to Lyra and Farder Coram next day, when Lyra's seasickness had abated slightly. The sun was shining brightly and the green waves were dashing against the bows, bearing white streams of foam as they curved away. Out on the deck, with the breeze blowing and the whole sea a-sparkle with light and movement, she felt little sickness at all; and now that Pantalaimon had discovered the delights of being a seagull and then a stormy petrel and skimming the wave-tops, Lyra was too absorbed by his glee to wallow in landlubberly misery.

John Faa, Farder Coram, and two or three others sat in the stern of the ship, with the sun full on them, talking about what to do next.

"Now Farder Coram knows these Lapland witches," John Faa said. "And if I en't mistaken there's an obligation there."

"That's right, John," said Farder Coram. "It were forty years back, but that's nothing to a witch. Some of 'em live to many times that."

"What happened to bring this obligation about, Farder Coram?" said Adam Stefanski, the man in charge of the fighting troop.

"I saved a witch's life," Farder Coram explained. "She fell out of the air, being pursued by a great red bird like to nothing I'd seen before. She fell injured in the marsh and I set out to find her. She was like to drowning, and I got her on board and shot that bird down, and it fell into a bog, to my regret, for it was as big as a bittern, and flame-red."

"Ah," the other men murmured, captured by Farder Coram's story.

"Now when I got her in the boat," he went on, "I had the most grim shock I'd ever known, because that young woman had no dæmon."

It was as if he'd said, "She had no head." The very thought was repugnant. The men shuddered, their dæmons bristled or shook themselves or cawed harshly, and the men soothed them. Pantalaimon crept into Lyra's breast, their hearts beating together.

"At least," Farder Coram said, "that's what it seemed. Being as she'd fell out of the air, I more than suspected she was a witch. She looked exactly like a young woman, thinner than some and prettier than most, but not seeing that dæmon gave me a hideous turn."

"En't they got dæmons then, the witches?" said the other man, Michael Canzona.

"Their dæmons is invisible, I expect," said Adam Stefanski. "He was there all the time, and Farder Coram never saw him."

"No, you're wrong, Adam," said Farder Coram. "He weren't there at all. The witches have the power to separate theirselves from their dæmons a mighty sight further'n what we can. If need be they can send their dæmons far abroad on the wind or the clouds, or down below the ocean. And this witch I found, she hadn't been resting above an hour when her dæmon came a-flying back, because he'd felt her fear and her injury, of course. And it's my belief, though she never admitted to this, that the great red bird I shot was another witch's dæmon, in pursuit. Lord! That made me shiver, when I thought of that. I'd have stayed my hand; I'd have taken any measures on sea or land; but there it was. Anyway, there was no doubt I'd saved her life, and she gave me a token of it, and said I was to call on her help if ever it was needed. And once she sent me help when the Skraelings shot me with a poison arrow. We had other connections, too... I haven't seen her for many years, but she'll remember."

"And does she live at Trollesund, this witch?"

"No, no. They live in forests and on the tundra, not in a seaport among men and women. Their business is with the wild. But they keep a consul there, and I shall get word to her, make no doubt about that."

Lyra was keen to know more about the witches, but the men had turned their talk to the matter of fuel and stores, and presently she grew impatient to see the rest of the ship. She wandered along the deck towards the bows, and soon made the acquaintance of an Able-Seaman by flicking at him the pips she'd saved from the apple she'd eaten at breakfast. He was a stout and placid man, and when he'd sworn at her and been sworn at in return, they became great friends. He was called Jerry. Under his guidance she found out that having something to do prevented you from feeling seasick, and that even a job like scrubbing a deck could be satisfying, if it was done in a seamanlike way. She was very taken with this notion, and later on she folded the blankets on her bunk in a seamanlike way, and put her possessions in the closet in a seamanlike way, and used "stow" instead of "tidy" for the process of doing so.

After two days at sea, Lyra decided that this was the life for her. She had the run of the ship, from the engine room to the bridge, and she was soon on first-name terms with all the crew. Captain Rokeby let her signal to a Hollands frigate by pulling the handle of the steam-whistle; the cook suffered her help in mixing plum-duff; and only a stern word from John Faa prevented her from climbing the foremast to inspect the horizon from the crow's nest.

All the time they were steaming north, and it grew colder daily. The ship's stores were searched for oilskins that could be cut down for her, and Jerry showed her how to sew, an art she learned willingly from him, though she had scorned it at Jordan and avoided instruction from Mrs Lonsdale. Together they made a waterproof bag for the alethiometer that she could wear around her waist, in case she fell in the sea, she said. With it safely in place she clung to the rail in her oilskins and sou'wester as the stinging spray broke over the bows and surged along the deck. She still felt seasick occasionally, especially when the wind got up and the ship plunged heavily over the crests of the grey-green waves, and then it was Pantalaimon's job to distract her from it by skimming the waves as a stormy petrel, because she could feel his boundless glee in the dash of wind and water, and forget her nausea. From time to time he even tried being a fish, and once joined a school of dolphins, to their surprise and pleasure. Lyra stood shivering in the fo'c'sle and laughed with delight as her beloved Pantalaimon, sleek and powerful, leapt from the water with half a dozen other swift grey shapes. It was pleasure, but not simple pleasure, for there was pain and fear in it too. Suppose he loved being a dolphin more than he loved her?

Her friend the Able-Seaman was nearby, and he paused as he adjusted the canvas cover of the forward hatch to look out at the little girl's dæmon skimming and leaping with the dolphins. His own dæmon, a seagull, had her head tucked under her wing on the capstan. He knew what Lyra was feeling.

"I remember when I first went to sea, my Belisaria hadn't settled on one form, I was that young, and she loved being a porpoise. I was afraid she'd settle like that. There was one old sailorman on my first vessel who could never go ashore at all, because his dæmon had settled as a dolphin, and he could never leave the water. He was a wonderful sailor; best navigator you ever knew; could have made a fortune at the fishing; but he wasn't happy like it. He was never quite happy till he died and he could be buried at sea."

"Why do dæmons have to settle?" Lyra said. "I want Pantalaimon to be able to change for ever. So does he."

"Ah, they always have settled, and they always will. That's part of growing up. There'll come a time when you'll be tired of his changing about, and you'll want a settled kind of form for him."

"I never will!"

"Oh, you will. You'll want to grow up like all the other girls. Anyway, there's compensations for a settled form."

"What are they?"

"Knowing what kind of person you are. Take old Belisaria. She's a seagull, and that means I'm a kind of seagull too. I'm not grand and splendid nor beautiful, but I'm a tough old thing and I can survive anywhere and always find a bit of food and company. That's worth knowing, that is. And when your dæmon settles, you'll know the sort of person you are."

"But suppose your dæmon settles in a shape you don't like?"

"Well, then, you're discontented, en't you? There's plenty of folk as'd like to have a lion as a dæmon and they end up with a poodle. And till they learn to be satisfied with what they are, they're going to be fretful about it. Waste of feeling, that is."

But it didn't seem to Lyra that she would ever grow up.

One morning there was a different smell in the air, and the ship was moving oddly, with a brisker rocking from side to side instead of the plunging and soaring. Lyra was on deck a minute after she woke up, gazing greedily at the land: such a strange sight, after all that water, for though they had only been at sea a few days, Lyra felt as if they'd been on the ocean for months. Directly ahead of the ship a mountain rose, green-flanked and snow-capped, and a little town and harbour lay below it: wooden houses with steep roofs, an oratory spire, cranes in the harbour, and clouds of gulls wheeling and crying. The smell was of fish, but mixed with it came land-smells too: pine-resin and earth and something animal and musky, and something else that was cold and blank and wild: it might have been snow. It was the smell of the North.

Seals frisked around the ship, showing their clown-faces above the water before sinking back without a splash. The wind that lifted spray off the white-capped waves was monstrously cold, and searched out every gap in Lyra's wolfskin, and her hands were soon aching and her face numb. Pantalaimon, in his ermine-shape, warmed her neck for her, but it was too cold to stay outside for long without work to do, even to watch the seals, and Lyra went below to eat her breakfast porridge and look through the porthole in the saloon.

Inside the harbour the water was calm, and as they moved past the massive breakwater Lyra began to feel unsteady from the lack of motion. She and Pantalaimon avidly watched as the ship inched ponderously towards the quayside. During the next hour the sound of the engine died away to a quiet background rumble, voices shouted orders or queries, ropes were thrown, gangways lowered, hatches opened.

"Come on, Lyra," said Farder Coram. "Is everything packed?"

Lyra's possessions, such as they were, had been packed ever since she'd woken up and seen the land. All she had to do was run to the cabin and pick up the shopping bag, and she was ready.

The first thing she and Farder Coram did ashore was to visit the house of the Witch-Consul. It didn't take long to find it; the little town was clustered around the harbour, with the oratory and the Governor's house the only buildings of any size. The Witch-Consul lived in a green-painted wooden house within sight of the sea, and when they rang the bell it jangled loudly in the quiet street.

A servant showed them into a little parlour and brought them coffee. Presently the Consul himself came in to greet them. He was a fat man with a florid face and a sober black suit, whose name was Martin Lanselius. His dæmon was a little serpent, the same intense and brilliant green as his eyes, which were the only witch-like thing about him; though Lyra was not sure what she had been expecting a witch to look like.

"How can I help you, Farder Coram?" he said.

"In two ways, Dr Lanselius. First, I'm anxious to get in touch with a witch-lady I met some years ago, in the Fen country of Eastern Anglia. Her name is Serafina Pekkala."

Dr Lanselius made a note with a silver pencil.

"How long ago was your meeting with her?" he said.

"Must be forty years. But I think she would remember."

"And what is the second way in which you seek my help?"

"I'm representing a number of gyptian families who've lost children. We've got reason to believe there's an organization capturing these children, ours and others, and bringing them to the North for some unknown purpose. I'd like to know whether you or your people have heard of anything like this a-going on."

Dr Lanselius sipped his coffee blandly.

"It's not impossible that notice of some such activity might have come our way," he said. "You realize, the relations between my people and the Northlanders are perfectly cordial. It would be difficult for me to justify disturbing them."

Farder Coram nodded as if he understood very well.

"To be sure," he said. "And it wouldn't be necessary for me to ask you if I could get the information any other way. That was why I asked about the witch-lady first."

Now Dr Lanselius nodded as if *he* understood. Lyra watched this game with puzzlement and respect. There were all kinds of things going on beneath it, and she saw that the Witch-Consul was coming to a decision.

"Very well," he said. "Of course, that's true, and you'll realize that your name is not unknown to us, Farder Coram. Serafina Pekkala is queen of a witch-clan in the region of Lake Enara. As for your other question, it is of course understood that this information is not reaching you through me."

"Quite so."

"Well, in this very town there is a branch of an organization called the Northern Progress Exploration Company, which pretends to be searching for minerals, but which is really controlled by something called the General Oblation Board of London. This organization, I happen to know, imports children. This is not generally known in the town; the Norroway government is not officially aware of it. The children don't remain here long. They are taken some distance inland."

"Do you know where, Dr Lanselius?"

"No. I would tell you if I did."

"And do you know what happens to them there?"

For the first time, Dr Lanselius glanced at Lyra. She looked stolidly back. The little green serpent-dæmon raised her head from the Consul's collar and whispered tongue-flickeringly in his ear.

The Consul said, "I have heard the phrase *the Maystadt Process* in connection with this matter. I think they use that in order to avoid calling what they do by its proper name. I have also heard the word *intercision*, but what it refers to I could not say."

"And are there any children in the town at the moment?" said Farder Coram.

He was stroking his dæmon's fur as she sat alert in his lap. Lyra noticed that she had stopped purring.

"No, I think not," said Dr Lanselius. "A group of about twelve arrived a week ago and moved out the day before yesterday."

"Ah! As recent as that? Then that gives us a bit of hope. How did they travel, Dr Lanselius?"

"By sledge."

"And you have no idea where they went?"

"Very little. It is not a subject we are interested in."

"Quite so. Now, you've answered all my questions very fairly, sir, and here's just one more. If you were me, what question would you ask of the Consul of the Witches?"

For the first time Dr Lanselius smiled.

"I would ask where I could obtain the services of an armoured bear," he said.

Lyra sat up, and felt Pantalaimon's heart leap in her hands.

"I understood the armoured bears to be in the service of the Oblation Board," said Farder Coram in surprise. "I mean, the Northern Progress Company, or whatever they're calling themselves."

"There is at least one who is not. You will find him at the sledge depot at the end of Langlokur Street. He earns a living there at the moment, but such is his temper and the fear he engenders in the dogs, his employment might not last for long."

"Is he a renegade, then?"

"It seems so. His name is Iorek Byrnison. You asked what I would ask, and I told you. Now here is what I would do: I would seize the chance to employ an armoured bear, even if it were far more remote than this."

Lyra could hardly sit still. Farder Coram, however, knew the etiquette for meetings such as this, and took another spiced honey-cake from the plate. While he ate it, Dr Lanselius turned to Lyra.

"I understand that you are in possession of an alethiometer," he said, to her great surprise; for how could he have known that?

"Yes," she said, and then, prompted by a nip from Pantalaimon, added, "Would you like to look at it?"

"I should like that very much."

She fished inelegantly in the oilskin pouch and handed him the velvet package. He unfolded it and held it up with great care, gazing at the face like a scholar gazing at a rare manuscript.

"How exquisite!" he said. "I have seen one other example, but it was not so fine as this. And do you possess the books of readings?"

"No," Lyra began, but before she could say any more, Farder Coram was speaking.

"No, the great pity is that although Lyra owns the alethiometer itself, there's no means of reading it whatsoever," he said. "It's just as much of a mystery as the pools of ink the Hindus use for reading the future. And the nearest book of readings I know of is in the Abbey of St Johann at Heidelberg."

Lyra could see why he was saying this: he didn't want Dr Lanselius to know of Lyra's power. But she could also see something Farder

Coram couldn't, which was the agitation of Dr Lanselius's dæmon, and she knew at once that it was no good to pretend.

So she said, "Actually I *can* read it," speaking half to Dr Lanselius and half to Farder Coram, and it was the Consul who responded.

"That is wise of you," he said. "Where did you obtain this one?"

"The Master of Jordan College in Oxford gave it to me," she said. "Dr Lanselius, do you know who made them?"

"They are said to originate in the city of Prague," said the Consul. "The scholar who invented the first alethiometer was apparently trying to discover a way of measuring the influences of the planets, according to the ideas of astrology. He intended to make a device that would respond to the idea of Mars or Venus as a compass responds to the idea of North. In that he failed, but the mechanism he invented was clearly responding to something, even if no one knew what it was."

"And where did they get the symbols from?"

"Oh, this was in the seventeenth century. Symbols and emblems were everywhere. Buildings and pictures were designed to be read like books. Everything stood for something else; if you had the right dictionary you could read Nature itself. It was hardly surprising to find philosophers using the symbolism of their time to interpret knowledge that came from a mysterious source. But, you know, they haven't been used seriously for two centuries or so."

He handed the instrument back to Lyra, and added:

"May I ask a question? Without the books of symbols, how do you read it?"

"I just make my mind go clear and then it's sort of like looking down into water. You got to let your eyes find the right level, because that's the only one that's in focus. Something like that," she said.

"I wonder if I might ask to see you do it?" he said.

Lyra looked at Farder Coram, wanting to say yes but waiting for his approval. The old man nodded.

"What shall I ask?" said Lyra.

"What are the intentions of the Tartars with regard to Kamchatka?"

That wasn't hard. Lyra turned the hands to the camel, which meant Asia, which meant Tartars; to the cornucopia, for Kamchatka, where there were gold mines; and to the ant, which meant activity, which meant purpose and intention. Then she sat still, letting her mind hold the three levels of meaning together in focus, and relaxed for the answer, which came almost at once. The long needle trembled on the dolphin, the helmet, the baby and the anchor, dancing between them and on to the crucible in a complicated pattern that Lyra's eyes followed without hesitation, but which was incomprehensible to the two men.

When it had completed the movements several times Lyra looked up. She blinked once or twice as if she were coming out of a trance.

"They're going to pretend to attack it, but they're not really going to, because it's too far away and they'd be too stretched out," she said.

"Would you tell me how you read that?"

"The dolphin, one of its deep-down meanings is playing, sort of like being playful," she explained. "I know it's that one because it stopped that number of times and it just got clear at that level but nowhere else. And the helmet means war, and both together they mean pretend to go to war but not be serious. And the baby means – it means difficult – it'd be too hard for them to attack it, and the anchor says why, because they'd be stretched out as tight as an anchor rope. I just see it all like that, you see."

Dr Lanselius nodded.

"Remarkable," he said. "I am very grateful. I shall not forget that."

Then he looked strangely at Farder Coram, and back at Lyra.

"Could I ask you for one more demonstration?" he said. "In the yard behind this house, you will find several sprays of cloud-pine hanging on the wall. One of them has been used by Serafina Pekkala, and the others have not. Could you tell which is hers?"

"Yeah!" said Lyra, always ready to show off, and she took the alethiometer and hurried out. She was eager to see cloud-pine, because the witches used it for flying, and she'd never seen any before.

While she was gone, the Consul said, "Do you realize who this child is?"

"She's the daughter of Lord Asriel," said Farder Coram. "And her mother is Mrs Coulter, of the Oblation Board."

"And apart from that?"

The old gyptian had to shake his head. "No," he said, "I don't know any more. But she's a strange innocent creature, and I wouldn't have her harmed for the world. How she comes to read that instrument I couldn't guess, but I believe her when she talks of it. Why, Dr Lanselius? What do you know about her?"

"The witches have talked about this child for centuries past," said the Consul. "Because they live so close to the place where the veil between the worlds is thin, they hear immortal whispers from time to time, in the voices of those beings who pass between the worlds. And they have spoken of a child such as this, who has a great destiny that can only be fulfilled elsewhere – not in this world, but far beyond. Without this child, we shall all die. So the witches say. But she must fulfil this destiny in ignorance of what she is doing, because only in her ignorance can we be saved. Do you understand that, Farder Coram?"

"No," said Farder Coram, "I'm unable to say that I do."

"What it means is that she must be free to make mistakes. We must hope that she does not, but we can't guide her. I am glad to have seen this child before I die."

"But how did you recognize her as being that particular child? And what did you mean about the beings who pass between the worlds? I'm at a loss to understand you, Dr Lanselius, for all that I judge you're an honest man…"

But before the Consul could answer, the door opened and Lyra came in triumphantly bearing a small spray of pine.

"This is the one!" she said. "I tested 'em all, and this is it, I'm sure."

The Consul looked at it closely, and then nodded.

"Correct," he said. "Well, Lyra, that is remarkable. You are lucky to have an instrument like that, and I wish you well with it. I would like to give you something to take away with you…"

He took the spray and broke off a twig for her.

"Did she fly with this?" Lyra said, awed.

"Yes, she did. I can't give you all of it, because I need it to contact her, but this will be enough. Look after it."

"Yes, I will," she said. "Thank you."

And she tucked it into her purse beside the alethiometer. Farder Coram touched the spray of pine as if for luck, and on his face was an expression Lyra had never seen before: almost a longing. The Consul showed them to the door, where he shook hands with Farder Coram, and shook Lyra's hand too.

"I hope you find success," he said, and stood on his doorstep in the piercing cold to watch them up the little street.

"He knew the answer about the Tartars before I did," Lyra told Farder Coram. "The alethiometer told me, but I never said. It was the crucible."

"I expect he was testing you, child. But you done right to be polite, being as we can't be sure what he knows already. And that was a useful tip about the bear. I don't know how we would a heard otherwise."

They found their way to the depot, which was a couple of concrete warehouses in a scrubby area of waste ground where thin weeds grew between grey rocks and pools of icy mud. A surly man in an office told them that they could find the bear off duty at six, but they'd have to be quick, because he usually went straight to the yard behind Einarsson's Bar, where they gave him drink.

Then Farder Coram took Lyra to the best outfitter's in town and bought her some proper cold-weather clothing. They bought a parka made of reindeer skin, because reindeer hair is hollow and insulates well; and the hood was lined with wolverine fur, because that sheds the ice that forms when you breathe. They bought underclothing and boot liners of reindeer calf skin, and silk gloves to go inside big fur mittens. The boots and mittens were made of skin from the reindeer's forelegs, because that is extra tough, and the boots were soled with the skin of the bearded seal, which is as tough as walrus-hide, but lighter. Finally they bought a waterproof cape that enveloped her completely, made of semi-transparent seal intestine.

With all that on, and a silk muffler around her neck and a woollen cap over her ears and the big hood pulled forward, she was uncomfortably warm; but they were going to much colder regions than this.

John Faa had been supervising the unloading of the ship, and was keen to hear about the Witch-Consul's words, and even keener to learn of the bear.

"We'll go to him this very evening," he said. "Have you ever spoken to such a creature, Farder Coram?"

"Yes, I have; and fought one, too, though not by myself, thank God. We must be ready to treat with him, John. He'll ask a lot, I've no doubt, and be surly and difficult to manage; but we must have him."

"Oh, we must. And what of your witch?"

"Well, she's a long way off, and a clan-queen now," said Farder Coram. "I did hope it might be possible for a message to reach her, but it would take too long to wait for a reply."

"Ah, well. Now let me tell you what *I've* found, old friend."

For John Faa had been fidgeting with impatience to tell them something. He had met a prospector on the quayside, a New Dane by the name of Lee Scoresby, from the country of Texas, and this man had a balloon, of all things. The expedition he'd been hoping to join had failed for lack of funds even before it had left Amsterdam, so he was stranded.

"Think what we might do with the help of an aëronaut, Farder Coram!" said John Faa, rubbing his great hands together. "I've engaged him to sign up with us. Seems to me we struck lucky a-coming here."

"Luckier still if we had a clear idea of where we were going," said Farder Coram, but nothing could damp John Faa's pleasure in being on campaign once more.

After darkness had fallen, and when the stores and equipment had all been safely unloaded and stood in waiting on the quay, Farder Coram and Lyra walked along the waterfront and looked for Einarsson's Bar. They found it easily enough: a crude concrete shed with a red neon sign flashing irregularly over the door and the sound of loud voices through the condensation-frosted windows.

A pitted alley beside it led to a sheet-metal gate into a rear yard, where a lean-to shed stood crazily over a floor of frozen mud. Dim light through the rear window of the bar showed a vast pale form crouching upright and gnawing at a haunch of meat which it held in both hands. Lyra had an impression of blood-stained muzzle and face, small malevolent black eyes, and an immensity of dirty matted yellowish fur. As it gnawed, hideous growling, crunching, sucking noises came from it.

Farder Coram stood by the gate and called:

"Iorek Byrnison!"

The bear stopped eating. As far as they could tell, he was looking at them directly, but it was impossible to read any expression on his face.

"Iorek Byrnison," said Farder Coram again. "May I speak to you?"

Lyra's heart was thumping hard, because something in the bear's presence made her feel close to coldness, danger, brutal power, but a power controlled by intelligence; and not a human intelligence, nothing like a human, because of course bears had no dæmons. This strange hulking presence gnawing its meat was like nothing she had ever imagined, and she felt a profound admiration and pity for the lonely creature.

He dropped the reindeer leg in the dirt and slumped on all fours to the gate. Then he reared up massively, ten feet or more high, as if to show how mighty he was, to remind them how useless the gate would be as a barrier, and he spoke to them from that height.

"Well? Who are you?"

His voice was so deep it seemed to shake the earth. The rank smell that came from his body was almost overpowering.

"I'm Farder Coram, from the gyptian people of Eastern Anglia. And this little girl is Lyra Belacqua."

"What do you want?"

"We want to offer you employment, Iorek Byrnison."

"I am employed."

The bear dropped on all fours again. It was very hard to detect any expressive tones in his voice, whether of irony or anger, because it was so deep and so flat.

"What do you do at the sledge depot?" Farder Coram asked.

"I mend broken machinery and articles of iron. I lift heavy objects."

"What kind of work is that for a *panserbjørn*?"

"Paid work."

Behind the bear, the door of the bar opened a little way and a man put down a large earthenware jar before looking up to peer at them.

"Who's that?"

"Strangers," said the bear.

The bartender looked as if he was going to ask something more, but the bear lurched towards him suddenly and the man shut the door in alarm. The bear hooked a claw through the handle of the jar and lifted it to his mouth. Lyra could smell the tang of the raw spirits that splashed out.

After swallowing several times, the bear put the jar down and turned back to gnaw his haunch of meat, heedless of Farder Coram and Lyra, it seemed; but then he spoke again.

"What work are you offering?"

"Fighting, in all probability," said Farder Coram. "We're moving North until we find a place where they've taken some children captive. When we find it, we'll have to fight to get the children free; and then we'll bring them back."

"And what will you pay?"

"I don't know what to offer you, Iorek Byrnison. If gold is desirable to you, we have gold."

"No good."

"What do they pay you at the sledge depot?"

"My keep here in meat and spirits."

Silence from the bear; and then he dropped the ragged bone and lifted the jar to his muzzle again, drinking the powerful spirits like water.

"Forgive me for asking, Iorek Byrnison," said Farder Coram, "but you could live a free proud life on the ice hunting seals and walruses, or you could go to war and win great prizes. What ties you to Trollesund and Einarsson's Bar?"

Lyra felt her skin shiver all over. She would have thought a question like that, which was almost an insult, would enrage the great creature beyond reason, and she wondered at Farder Coram's courage in asking it. Iorek Byrnison put down his jar and came close to the gate to peer at the old man's face. Farder Coram didn't flinch.

"I know the people you are seeking, the child-cutters," the bear said. "They left town the day before yesterday to go North with more children. No one will tell you about them; they pretend not to see, because the child-cutters bring money and business. Now I don't like the child-cutters, so I shall answer you politely. I stay here and drink spirits because the men here took my armour away, and without that, I can hunt seals but I can't go to war; and I am an armoured bear: war is the sea I swim in and the air I breathe. The men of this town gave me spirits and let me drink till I was asleep, and then they took my armour away from me. If I knew where they keep it, I would tear down the town to get it back. If you want my service, the price is this: get me back my armour. Do that, and I shall serve you in your campaign, either until I am dead or until you have a victory. The price is my armour. I want it back, and then I shall never need spirits again."

11

Armour

When they returned to the ship, Farder Coram and John Faa and the other leaders spent a long time in conference in the saloon, and Lyra went to her cabin to consult the alethiometer. Within five minutes she knew exactly where the bear's armour was, and why it would be difficult to get it back.

She wondered whether to go to the saloon and tell John Faa and the others, but decided that they'd ask her if they wanted to know. Perhaps they knew already.

She lay on her bunk thinking of that savage mighty bear, and the careless way he drank his fiery spirit, and the loneliness of him in his dirty lean-to. How different it was to be human, with one's dæmon always there to talk to! In the silence of the still ship, without the continual creak of metal and timber or the rumble of the engine or the rush of water along the side, Lyra gradually fell asleep, with Pantalaimon on her pillow sleeping too.

She was dreaming of her great imprisoned father when suddenly, for no reason at all, she woke up. She had no idea what time it was. There was a faint light in the cabin that she took for moonlight, and it showed her new cold-weather furs that lay stiffly in the corner of the cabin. No sooner did she see them than she longed to try them on again.

When they were on she had to go out on deck, and a minute later she opened the door at the top of the companionway and stepped out.

At once she saw that something strange was happening in the sky. She thought it was clouds, moving and trembling under a nervous agitation, but Pantalaimon whispered:

"The Aurora!"

Her wonder was so strong that she had to clutch the rail to keep from falling.

The sight filled the northern sky; the immensity of it was scarcely conceivable. As if from Heaven itself, great curtains of delicate light hung and trembled. Pale green and rose-pink, and as transparent as the most fragile fabric, and at the bottom edge a profound and fiery crimson like the fires of Hell, they swung and shimmered loosely with more grace than the most skilful dancer. Lyra thought she could even hear them: a vast distant whispering swish. In the evanescent delicacy she felt something as profound as she'd felt close to the bear. She was moved by it: it was so beautiful it was almost holy; she felt tears prick her eyes, and the tears splintered the light even further into prismatic rainbows. It wasn't long before she found herself entering the same kind of trance as when she consulted the alethiometer. Perhaps, she thought calmly, whatever moves the alethiometer's needle is making the Aurora glow too. It might even be Dust itself. She thought that without noticing that she'd thought it, and she soon forgot it, and only remembered it much later.

And as she gazed, the image of a city seemed to form itself behind the veils and streams of translucent colour: towers and domes, honey-coloured temples and colonnades, broad boulevards and sunlit parkland. Looking at it gave her a sense of vertigo, as if she were looking not up but down, and across a gulf so wide that nothing could ever pass over it. It was a whole universe away.

But something *was* moving across it, and as she tried to focus her eyes on the movement, she felt faint and dizzy, because the little thing moving wasn't part of the Aurora or of the other universe behind it. It was in the sky over the roofs of the town. When she could see it clearly, she had come fully awake and the sky-city was gone.

The flying thing came closer and circled the ship on outspread wings. Then it glided down and landed with brisk sweeps of its powerful pinions, and came to a halt on the wooden deck a few yards from Lyra.

In the Aurora's light she saw a great bird, a beautiful grey goose whose head was crowned with a flash of pure white. And yet it wasn't a bird: it was a dæmon, though there was no one in sight but Lyra herself. The idea filled her with sickly fear.

The bird said:

"Where is Farder Coram?"

And suddenly Lyra realized who it must be. This was the dæmon of Serafina Pekkala, the clan-queen, Farder Coram's witch-friend.

She stammered to reply:

"I – he's – I'll go and get him..."

She turned and scampered down the companionway to the cabin Farder Coram occupied, and opened the door to speak into the darkness:

"Farder Coram! The witch's dæmon's come! He's waiting on the deck! He flew here all by hisself – I seen him coming in the sky –"

The old man said, "Ask him to wait on the after-deck, child."

The goose made his stately way to the stern of the ship, where he looked around, elegant and wild simultaneously, and a cause of fascinated terror to Lyra, who felt as though she were entertaining a ghost.

Then Farder Coram came up, wrapped in his cold-weather gear, closely followed by John Faa. Both old men bowed respectfully, and their dæmons also acknowledged the visitor.

"Greetings," said Farder Coram. "And I'm happy and proud to see you again, Kaisa. Now, would you like to come inside, or would you prefer to stay out here in the open?"

"I would rather stay outside, thank you, Farder Coram. Are you warm enough for a while?"

Witches and their dæmons felt no cold, but they were aware that other humans did.

Farder Coram assured him that they were well wrapped up, and said "How is Serafina Pekkala?"

"She sends her greetings to you, Farder Coram, and she is well and strong. Who are these two people?"

Farder Coram introduced them both. The goose-dæmon looked hard at Lyra.

"I have heard of this child," he said. "She is talked about among witches. So you have come to make war?"

"Not war, Kaisa. We are going to free the children taken from us. And I hope the witches will help."

"Not all of them will. Some clans are working with the Dust-hunters."

"Is that what you call the Oblation Board?"

"I don't know what this Board may be. They are Dust-hunters. They came to our regions ten years ago with philosophical instruments. They paid us to allow them to set up stations in our lands, and they treated us with courtesy."

"What is this Dust?"

"It comes from the sky. Some say it has always been there, some say it is newly falling. What is certain is that when people become aware of it, a great fear comes over them, and they'll stop at nothing to discover what it is. But it is not of any concern to witches."

"And where are they now, these Dust-hunters?"

"Four days north-east of here, at a place called Bolvangar. Our clan made no agreement with them, and because of our ancient obligation to you, Farder Coram, I have come to show you how to find these Dust-hunters."

Farder Coram smiled, and John Faa clapped his great hands together in satisfaction.

"Thank you kindly, sir," he said to the goose. "But tell us this: do you know anything more about these Dust-hunters? What do they do at this Bolvangar?"

"They have put up buildings of metal and concrete, and some underground chambers. They burn coal-spirit, which they bring in at great expense. We don't know what they do, but there is an air of hatred and fear over the place and for miles around. Witches can see these things where other humans can't. Animals keep away too. No birds fly there; lemmings and foxes have fled. Hence the name Bolvangar: the fields of evil. They don't call it that. They call it The Station. But to everyone else it is Bolvangar."

"And how are they defended?"

"They have a company of Northern Tartars armed with rifles. They are good soldiers, but they lack practice, because no one has ever attacked the settlement since it was built. Then there is a wire fence around the compound, which is filled with anbaric force. There may be other means of defence that we don't know about, because as I say they have no interest for us."

Lyra was bursting to ask a question, and the goose-dæmon knew it and looked at her as if giving permission.

"Why do the witches talk about me?" she said.

"Because of your father, and his knowledge of the other worlds," the dæmon replied.

That surprised all three of them. Lyra looked at Farder Coram, who looked back in mild wonder, and at John Faa, whose expression was troubled.

"Other worlds?" he said. "Pardon me, sir, but what worlds would those be? Do you mean the stars?"

"Indeed, no."

"Perhaps the world of spirits?" said Farder Coram.

"Nor that."

"Is it the city in the lights?" said Lyra. "It is, en't it?"

The goose turned his stately head towards her. His eyes were black, surrounded by a thin line of pure sky-blue, and their gaze was intense.

"Yes," he said. "Witches have known of the other worlds for thousands of years. You can see them sometimes in the Northern Lights. They aren't part of this universe at all; even the furthest stars are part of this universe, but the lights show us a different universe entirely. Not further away, but interpenetrating with this one. Here, on this deck, millions of other universes exist, unaware of one another..."

He raised his wings and spread them wide before folding them again.

"There," he said, "I have just brushed ten million other worlds, and they knew nothing of it. We are as close as a heartbeat, but we can never touch or see or hear these other worlds except in the Northern Lights."

"And why there?" said Farder Coram.

"Because the charged particles in the Aurora have the property of making the matter of this world thin, so that we can see through it for a brief time. Witches have always known this, but we seldom speak of it."

"My father believes in it," Lyra said. "I know because I heard him talking and showing pictures of the Aurora."

"Is this anything to do with Dust?" said John Faa.

"Who can say?" said the goose-dæmon. "All I can tell you is that the Dust-hunters are as frightened of it as if it were deadly poison. That is why they imprisoned Lord Asriel."

"But why?" Lyra said.

"They think he intends to use Dust in some way in order to make a bridge between this world and the world beyond the Aurora."

There was a lightness in Lyra's head.

She heard Farder Coram say, "And does he?"

"Yes," said the goose-dæmon. "They don't believe he can, because they think he is mad to believe in the other worlds in the first place. But it is true: that is his intention. And he is so powerful a figure that they feared he would upset their own plans, so they made a pact with the armoured bears to capture him and keep him imprisoned in the fortress of Svalbard, out of the way. Some say they helped the new bear-king to gain his throne, as part of the bargain."

Lyra said, "Do the witches want him to make this bridge? Are they on his side or against him?"

"That is a question with too complicated an answer. Firstly, the witches are not united. There are differences of opinion among us. Secondly, Lord Asriel's bridge will have a bearing on a war being waged at the present between some witches and various other forces, some in the spirit world. Possession of the bridge, if it ever existed, would give a huge advantage to whoever held it. Thirdly, Serafina Pekkala's clan – my clan – is not yet part of any alliance, though great pressure is being put on us to declare for one side or another. You see, these are questions of high politics, and not easily answered."

"What about the bears?" said Lyra. "Whose side are they on?"

"On the side of anyone who pays them. They have no interest whatever in these questions; they have no dæmons; they are unconcerned about human problems. At least, that is how bears used to be, but we have heard that their new king is intent on changing their old ways... At any rate, the Dust-hunters have paid them to imprison Lord Asriel, and they will hold him on Svalbard until the last drop of blood drains from the body of the last bear alive."

"But not all bears!" Lyra said. "There's one who en't on Svalbard at all. He's an outcast bear, and he's going to come with us."

The goose gave Lyra another of his piercing looks. This time she could feel his cold surprise.

Farder Coram shifted uncomfortably, and said, "The fact is, Lyra, I don't think he is. We heard he's serving out a term as an indentured labourer; he en't free, as we thought he might be, he's under sentence. Till he's discharged he won't be free to come, armour or no armour; and he won't never have that back, either."

"But he said they tricked him! They made him drunk and stole it away!"

"We heard a different story," said John Faa. "He's a dangerous rogue, is what we heard."

"If –" Lyra was passionate; she could hardly speak for indignation – "if the alethiometer says something, I know it's true. And I asked it, and it said that he was telling the truth, they did trick him, and they're telling lies and not him. I believe him, Lord Faa! Farder Coram – you saw him too, and you believe him, don't you?"

"I thought I did, child. I en't so certain of things as you are."

"But what are they afraid of? Do they think he's going to go round killing people as soon's he gets his armour on? He could kill dozens of 'em now!"

"He has done," said John Faa. "Well, if not dozens, then some. When they first took his armour away he went a-rampaging round looking for it. He tore open the police house and the bank and I don't know where else, and there's at least two men who died. The only reason they didn't shoot to kill him is because of his wondrous skill with metals; they wanted to use him like a labourer."

"Like a slave!" Lyra said hotly. "They hadn't got the right!"

"Be that as it may, they might have shot him for the killings he done, but they didn't. And they bound him over to labour in the town's interest until he's paid off the damage and the blood-money."

"John," said Farder Coram, "I don't know how you feel, but it's my belief they'll never let him have that armour back. The longer they keep him, the more angry he'll be when he gets it."

"But if *we* get his armour back he'll come with us and never bother 'em again," said Lyra. "I promise, Lord Faa."

"And how are we going to do that?"

"I know where it is!"

There was a silence, in which they all three became aware of the witch's dæmon and his fixed stare at Lyra. All three turned to him, and their own dæmons too, who had until then affected the extreme politeness of keeping their eyes modestly away from this singular creature, here without his body.

"You won't be surprised," said the goose, "to know that the alethiometer is one other reason the witches are interested in you, Lyra. Our consul told us about your visit this morning. I believe it was Dr Lanselius who told you about the bear."

"Yes, it was," said John Faa. "And she and Farder Coram went their-selves and talked to him. I daresay what Lyra says is true, but if we go breaking the law of these people we'll only get involved in a quarrel with them, and what we ought to be doing is pushing on towards this Bolvangar, bear or no bear."

"Ah, but you en't seen him, John," said Farder Coram. "And I do believe Lyra. We could promise on his behalf, maybe. He might make all the difference."

"What do you think, sir?" said John Faa to the witch's dæmon.

"We have few dealings with bears. Their desires are as strange to us as ours are to them. If this bear is an outcast, he might be less reliable than they are said to be. You must decide for yourselves."

"We will," said John Faa firmly. "But now, sir, can you tell us how to get to Bolvangar from here?"

The goose-dæmon began to explain. He spoke of valleys and hills, of the tree-line and the tundra, of star-sightings. Lyra listened a while, and then lay back in the deck-chair with Pantalaimon curled around her neck, and thought of the grand vision the goose-dæmon had brought with him. A bridge between two worlds... This was far more splendid than anything she could have hoped for! And only her great father could have conceived it. As soon as they had rescued the children, she would go to Svalbard with the bear and take Lord Asriel the alethiometer, and use it to help set him free; and they'd build the bridge together, and be the first across...

Sometime in the night John Faa must have carried Lyra to her bunk, because that was where she awoke. The dim sun was as high in the sky as it was going to get, only a hand's breadth above the horizon, so it must be nearly noon, she thought. Soon, when they moved further north, there would be no sun at all.

She dressed quickly and ran on deck to find nothing very much happening. All the stores had been unloaded, sledges and dog-teams had been hired and were waiting to go; everything was ready and nothing was moving. Most of the gyptians were sitting in a smoke-filled café facing the water, eating spice-cakes and drinking strong sweet coffee at the long wooden tables under the fizz and crackle of some ancient anbaric lights.

"Where's Lord Faa?" she said, sitting down with Tony Costa and his friends. "And Farder Coram? Are they getting the bear's armour for him?"

"They're a-talking to the Sysselman. That's their word for governor. You seen this bear, then, Lyra?"

"Yeah!" she said, and explained all about him. As she talked, someone else pulled a chair up and joined the group at the table.

"So you've spoken to old Iorek?" he said.

She looked at the newcomer with surprise. He was a tall, lean man with a thin black moustache and narrow blue eyes, and a perpetual expression of distant and sardonic amusement. She felt strongly about him at once, but she wasn't sure whether it was liking she felt, or dislike. His dæmon was a shabby hare as thin and tough-looking as he was.

He held out his hand and she shook it warily.

"Lee Scoresby," he said.

"The aëronaut!" she exclaimed. "Where's your balloon? Can I go up in it?"

"It's packed away right now, miss. You must be the famous Lyra. How did you get on with Iorek Byrnison?"

"You know him?"

"I fought beside him in the Tunguska campaign. Hell, I've known

194

Iorek for years. Bears are difficult critters no matter what, but he's a problem, and no mistake. Say, are any of you gentlemen in the mood for a game of hazard?"

A pack of cards had appeared from nowhere in his hand. He riffled them with a snapping noise.

"Now I've heard of the card-power of your people," Lee Scoresby was saying, cutting and folding the cards over and over with one hand and fishing a cigar out of his breast pocket with the other, "and I thought you wouldn't object to giving a simple Texan traveller the chance to joust with your skill and daring on the field of pasteboard combat. What do you say, gentlemen?"

Gyptians prided themselves on their ability with cards, and several of the men looked interested and pulled their chairs up. While they were agreeing with Lee Scoresby what to play and for what stakes, his dæmon flicked her ears at Pantalaimon, who understood and leapt lightly to her side as a squirrel.

She was speaking for Lyra's ears too, of course, and Lyra heard her say quietly, "Go straight to the bear and tell him direct. As soon as they know what's going on they'll move his armour somewhere else."

Lyra got up, taking her spice-cake with her, and no one noticed; Lee Scoresby was already dealing the cards, and every suspicious eye was on his hands.

In the dull light, fading through an endless afternoon, she found her way to the sledge depot. It was something she knew she had to do, but she felt uneasy about it, and afraid, too.

Outside the largest of the concrete sheds the great bear was working, and Lyra stood by the open gate to watch. Iorek Byrnison was dismantling a gas-engined tractor that had crashed; the metal covering of the engine was twisted and buckled and one runner bent upwards. The bear lifted the metal off as if it were cardboard, and turned it this way and that in his great hands, seeming to test it for some quality or other, before setting a rear paw on one corner and then bending the whole sheet in such a way that the dents sprang out and the shape was restored. Leaning it against the wall, he lifted the massive weight of the tractor with one paw and laid it on its side before bending to examine the crumpled runner.

As he did so, he caught sight of Lyra. She felt a bolt of cold fear strike at her, because he was so massive and so alien. She was gazing through the chain-link fence about forty yards from him, and she thought how he could clear the distance in a bound or two and sweep the wire aside like a cobweb, and she almost turned and ran away; but Pantalaimon said, "Stop! Let me go and talk to him."

He was a tern, and before she could answer he'd flown off the fence and down to the icy ground beyond it. There was an open gate a little way along, and Lyra could have followed him, but she hung back unwillingly. Pantalaimon looked at her, and then became a badger.

She knew what he was doing. Dæmons could move no more than a few yards from their humans, and if she stood by the fence and he remained a bird, he wouldn't get near the bear; so he was going to pull.

She felt angry and miserable. His badger-claws dug into the earth and he walked forward. It was such a strange tormenting feeling when your dæmon was pulling at the link between you; part physical pain deep in the chest, part intense sadness and love. And she knew it was the same for him. Everyone tested it when they were growing up: seeing how far they could pull apart, coming back with intense relief.

He tugged a little harder.

"Don't, Pan!"

But he didn't stop. The bear watched, motionless. The pain in Lyra's heart grew more and more unbearable, and a sob of longing rose in her throat.

"Pan –"

Then she was through the gate, scrambling over the icy mud towards him, and he turned into a wildcat and sprang up into her arms, and then they were clinging together tightly with little shaky sounds of unhappiness coming from them both.

"I thought you really *would* –"

"No –"

"I couldn't *believe* how much it hurt –"

And then she brushed the tears away angrily and sniffed hard. He nestled in her arms, and she knew she would rather die than let them be parted and face that sadness again; it would send her mad with grief and terror. If she died they'd still be together, like the Scholars in the crypt at Jordan.

Then girl and dæmon looked up at the solitary bear. He had no dæmon. He was alone, always alone. She felt such a stir of pity and gentleness for him that she almost reached out to touch his matted pelt, and only a sense of courtesy towards those cold ferocious eyes prevented her.

"Iorek Byrnison," she said.

"Well?"

"Lord Faa and Farder Coram have gone to try and get your armour for you."

He didn't move or speak. It was clear what he thought of their chances.

"I know where it is, though," she said, "and if I told you, maybe you could get it by yourself, I don't know."

"How do you know where it is?"

"I got a symbol-reader. I think I ought to tell you, Iorek Byrnison, seeing as they tricked you out of it in the first place. I don't think that's right. They shouldn't've done that. Lord Faa's going to argue with the Sysselman, but probably they won't let you have it whatever he says. So if I tell you, will you come with us and help rescue the kids from Bolvangar?"

"Yes."

"I…" She didn't mean to be nosy, but she couldn't help being curious. She said, "Why don't you just make some more armour out of this metal here, Iorek Byrnison?"

"Because it's worthless. Look," he said and, lifting the engine-cover with one paw, he extended a claw on the other hand and ripped right through it like a tin-opener. "My armour is made of sky-iron, made for me. A bear's armour is his soul, just as your dæmon is your soul. You might as well take *him* away –" indicating Pantalaimon – "and replace him with a doll full of sawdust. That is the difference. Now, where is my armour?"

"Listen, you got to promise not to take vengeance. They done wrong taking it, but you just got to put up with that."

"All right. No vengeance afterwards. But no holding back as I take it, either. If they fight, they die."

"It's hidden in the cellar of the priest's house," she told him. "He thinks there's a spirit in it, and he's been a-trying to conjure it out. But that's where it is."

He stood high up on his hind legs, and looked west, so that the last of the sun coloured his face a creamy brilliant yellow-white amid the gloom. She could feel the power of the great creature coming off him like waves of heat.

"I must work till sunset," he said. "I gave my word this morning to the master here. I still owe a few minutes' work."

"The sun's set where I am," she pointed out, because from her point of view it had vanished behind the rocky headland to the south-west.

He dropped to all fours.

"It's true," he said, with his face now in shadow like hers. "What's your name, child?"

"Lyra Belacqua."

"Then I owe you a debt, Lyra Belacqua," he said.

Then he turned and lurched away, padding so swiftly across the freezing ground that Lyra couldn't keep up, even running. She did run, though, and Pantalaimon flew up as a seagull to watch where the bear went and called down to tell her where to follow.

Iorek Byrnison bounded out of the depot and along the narrow street before turning into the main street of the town, past the courtyard of the Sysselman's residence where a flag hung in the still air and a sentry marched stiffly up and down, down the hill past the end of the street where the Witch-Consul lived. The sentry by this time had realized what was happening, and was trying to gather his wits, but Iorek Byrnison was already turning a corner near the harbour.

People stopped to watch or scuttled out of his careering way. The sentry fired two shots in the air, and set off down the hill after the bear, spoiling the effect by skidding on the icy slope and only regaining his balance after seizing the nearest railings. Lyra was not far behind. As she passed the Sysselman's house she was aware of a number of figures coming out into the courtyard to see what was going on, and thought she saw Farder Coram among them; but then she was past, hurtling down the street towards the corner where the sentry was already turning to follow the bear.

The priest's house was older than most, and made of costly bricks.

Three steps led up to the front door, which was now hanging in match-wood splinters, and from inside the house came screams and the crashing and tearing of more wood. The sentry hesitated outside, his rifle at the ready; but then as passers-by began to gather and people looked out of windows from across the street, he realized that he had to act, and fired a shot into the air before running in.

A moment later, the whole house seemed to shake. Glass broke in three windows and a tile slid off the roof, and then a maidservant ran out, terrified, her clucking hen of a dæmon flapping after her.

Another shot came from inside the house, and then a full-throated roar made the servant scream. As if fired from a cannon, the priest himself came hurtling out, with his pelican-dæmon in a wild flutter of feathers and injured pride. Lyra heard orders shouted, and turned to see a squad of armed policemen hurrying around the corner, some with pistols and some with rifles, and not far behind them came John Faa and the stout, fussy figure of the Sysselman.

A rending, splintering sound made them all look back at the house. A window at ground level, obviously opening on a cellar, was being wrenched apart with a crash of glass and a screech of tearing wood. The sentry who'd followed Iorek Byrnison into the house came running out and stood to face the cellar window, rifle at his shoulder; and then the window tore open completely, and out there climbed Iorek Byrnison, the bear in armour.

Without it he was formidable. With it, he was terrifying. It was rust-red, and crudely riveted together: great sheets and plates of dented discoloured metal that scraped and screeched as they rode over one another. The helmet was pointed like his muzzle, with slits for eyes, and it left the lower part of his jaw bare for tearing and biting.

The sentry fired several shots, and the policemen levelled their weapons too, but Iorek Byrnison merely shook the bullets off like rain-drops, and lunged forward in a screech and clang of metal before the sentry could escape, and knocked him to the ground. His dæmon, a husky dog, darted at the bear's throat, but Iorek Byrnison took no more notice of him than he would of a fly and, dragging the sentry to him with one vast paw, he bent and enclosed his head in his jaws. Lyra could see exactly what would happen next: he'd crush the man's skull like an egg, and there would follow a bloody fight, more deaths, and more delay; and they would never get free, with or without the bear.

Without even thinking she darted forward and put her hand on the one vulnerable spot in the bear's armour, the gap that appeared between the helmet and the great plate over his shoulders when he bent his head, where she could see the yellow-white fur dimly between the rusty edges of metal. She dug her fingers in, and Pantalaimon instantly flew to the same spot and became a wildcat, crouched to defend her; but Iorek Byrnison was still, and the riflemen held their fire.

"Iorek!" she said in a fierce undertone. "Listen! You owe me a debt, right. Well now you can repay it. Do as I ask. Don't fight these men. Just turn around and walk away with me. We *want* you, Iorek, you can't stay here. Just come down the harbour with me and don't even look back. Farder Coram and Lord Faa, let them do the talking, they'll make it all right. Leave go this man and come away with me…"

The bear slowly opened his jaws. The sentry's head, bleeding and wet and ash-pale, fell to the ground as he fainted, and his dæmon set about calming and gentling him as the bear stepped away beside Lyra.

No one else moved. They watched as the bear turned away from his victim at the bidding of the little girl with the cat-dæmon, and then they shuffled aside to make room as Iorek Byrnison padded heavily through the midst of them at Lyra's side and made for the harbour.

Her mind was all on him, and she didn't see the confusion behind her, the fear and the anger that rose up safely when he was gone. She walked with him, and Pantalaimon padded ahead of them both as if to clear the way.

When they reached the harbour, Iorek Byrnison dipped his head and unfastened the helmet with a claw, letting it clang on the frozen ground. Gyptians came out of the café, having sensed that something was going on, and watched in the gleam of the anbaric lights on the ship's deck as Iorek Byrnison shrugged off the rest of his armour and left it in a heap on the quayside. Without a word to anyone he padded to the water and slipped into it without a ripple, and vanished.

"What's happened?" said Tony Costa, hearing the indignant voices from the streets above, as the townsfolk and the police made their way to the harbour.

Lyra told him, as clearly as she could.

"But where's he gone now?" he said. "He en't just left his armour on the ground? They'll have it back, as soon's they get here!"

Lyra was afraid they might, too, for around the corner came the first policemen, and then more, and then the Sysselman and the priest and twenty or thirty onlookers, with John Faa and Farder Coram trying to keep up.

But when they saw the group on the quayside they stopped, for someone else had appeared. Sitting on the bear's armour with one ankle resting on the opposite knee was the long-limbed form of Lee Scoresby, and in his hand was the longest pistol Lyra had ever seen, casually pointing at the ample stomach of the Sysselman.

"Seems to me you ain't taken very good care of my friend's armour," he said conversationally. "Why, look at the rust! And I wouldn't be surprised to find moths in it, too. Now you just stand where you are, still and easy, and don't anybody move till the bear comes back with some lubrication. Or I guess you could all go home and read the newspaper. 'S up to you."

"There he is!" said Tony, pointing to a ramp at the far end of the quay, where Iorek Byrnison was emerging from the water, dragging something dark with him. Once he was up on the quayside he shook himself, sending great sheets of water flying in all directions, till his fur was standing up thickly again. Then he bent to take the black object in his teeth once more and dragged it along to where his armour lay. It was a dead seal.

"Iorek," said the aëronaut, standing up lazily and keeping his pistol firmly fixed on the Sysselman. "Howdy."

The bear looked up and growled briefly, before ripping the seal open with one claw. Lyra watched fascinated as he laid the skin out flat and tore off strips of blubber, which he then rubbed all over his armour, packing it carefully into the places where the plates moved over one another.

"Are you with these people?" the bear said to Lee Scoresby as he worked.

"Sure. I guess we're both hired hands, Iorek."

"Where's your balloon?" said Lyra to the Texan.

"Packed away in two sledges," he said. "Here comes the boss."

John Faa and Farder Coram, together with the Sysselman, came down the quay with four armed policemen.

"Bear!" said the Sysselman, in a high, harsh voice. "For now, you are allowed to depart in the company of these people. But let me tell you that if you appear within the town limits again, you will be treated mercilessly."

Iorek Byrnison took not the slightest notice, but continued to rub the seal-blubber all over his armour; the care and attention he was paying the task reminding Lyra of her own devotion to Pantalaimon. Just as the bear had said: the armour was his soul. The Sysselman and the policemen withdrew, and slowly the other townspeople turned and drifted away, though a few remained to watch.

John Faa put his hands to his mouth and called, "Gyptians!"

They were all ready to move. They had been itching to get under way ever since they had disembarked; the sledges were packed, the dogteams were in their traces.

John Faa said, "Time to move out, friends. We're all assembled now, and the road lies open. Mr Scoresby, you all a-loaded?"

"Ready to go, Lord Faa."

"And you, Iorek Byrnison?"

"When I am clad," said the bear.

He had finished oiling the armour. Not wanting to waste the seal-meat, he lifted the carcass in his teeth and flipped it on to the back of Lee Scoresby's larger sledge before donning the armour. It was astonishing to see how lightly he dealt with it: the sheets of metal were almost an inch thick in places, and yet he swung them round and into place as if they were silk robes. It took him less than a minute, and this time there was no harsh scream of rust.

So in less than half an hour, the expedition was on its way northwards. Under a sky peopled with millions of stars and a glaring moon, the sledges bumped and clattered over the ruts and stones until they reached clear snow at the edge of town. Then the sound changed to a quiet crunch of snow and creak of timber; and the dogs began to step out eagerly, and the motion became swift and smooth.

Lyra, wrapped up so thickly in the back of Farder Coram's sledge that only her eyes were exposed, whispered to Pantalaimon:

"Can you see Iorek?"

"He's padding along beside Lee Scoresby's sledge," the dæmon replied, looking back in his ermine-form as he clung to her wolverine-fur hood.

Ahead of them, over the mountains to the north, the pale arcs and loops of the Northern Lights began to glow and tremble. Lyra saw them through half-closed eyes, and felt a sleepy thrill of perfect happiness, to be speeding north under the Aurora. Pantalaimon struggled against her sleepiness, but it was too strong; he curled up as a mouse inside her hood. He could tell her when they woke, and it was probably a marten, or a dream, or some kind of harmless local spirit; but something was following the train of sledges, swinging lightly from branch to branch of the close-clustering pine trees, and it put him uneasily in mind of a monkey.

12

The Lost Boy

They travelled for several hours and then stopped to eat. While the men were lighting fires and melting snow for water, with Iorek Byrnison watching Lee Scoresby roast seal-meat close by, John Faa spoke to Lyra.

"Lyra, can you see that instrument to read it?" he said.

The moon itself had long set. The light from the Aurora was brighter than moonlight, but it was inconstant. However, Lyra's eyes were keen, and she fumbled inside her furs and tugged out the black velvet bag.

"Yes, I can see all right," she said. "But I know where most of the symbols are by now, anyway. What shall I ask it, Lord Faa?"

"I want to know more about how they're defending this place, Bolvangar," he said.

Without even having to think about it, she found her fingers moving the hands to point to the helmet, the griffin, and the crucible, and felt her mind settle into the right meanings like a complicated diagram in three dimensions. At once the needle began to swing round, back, round and on further, like a bee dancing its message to the hive. She watched it calmly, content not to know at first but to know that a meaning was coming, and then it began to clear. She let it dance on until it was certain.

"It's just like the witch's dæmon said, Lord Faa. There's a company of Tartars guarding the station, and they got wires all round it. They don't really expect to be attacked, that's what the symbol-reader says. But Lord Faa…"

"What, child?"

"It's a-telling me something else. In the next valley there's a village by a lake where the folk are troubled by a ghost."

John Faa shook his head impatiently, and said, "That don't matter now. There's bound to be spirits of all kinds among these forests. Tell me again about them Tartars. How many, for instance? What are they armed with?"

Lyra dutifully asked, and reported the answer:

"There's sixty men with rifles, and they got a couple of larger guns, sort of cannons. They got fire-throwers too. And … their dæmons are all wolves, that's what it says."

That caused a stir among the older gyptians, those who'd campaigned before.

"The Sibirsk regiments have wolf-dæmons," said one.

John Faa said, "I never met fiercer. We shall have to fight like tigers. And consult the bear; he's a shrewd warrior, that one."

Lyra was impatient, and said, "But Lord Faa, this ghost – I think it's the ghost of one of the kids!"

"Well, even if it is, Lyra, I don't know what anyone could do about it. Sixty Sibirsk riflemen, and fire-throwers… Mr Scoresby, step over here if you would, for a moment."

While the aëronaut came to the sledge, Lyra slipped away and spoke to the bear.

"Iorek, have you travelled this way before?"

"Once," he said in that deep flat voice.

"There's a village near, en't there?"

"Over the ridge," he said, looking up through the sparse trees.

"Is it far?"

"For you or for me?"

"For me," she said.

"Too far. Not at all far for me."

"How long would it take you to get there, then?"

"I could be there and back three times by next moonrise."

"Because Iorek, listen: I got this symbol-reader that tells me things, you see, and it's told me that there's something important I got to do over in that village, and Lord Faa won't let me go there. He just wants to get on quick, and I know that's important too. But unless I go and find out what it is, we might not know what the Gobblers are really doing."

The bear said nothing. He was sitting up like a human, his great paws folded in his lap, his dark eyes looking into hers down the length of his muzzle. He knew she wanted something.

Pantalaimon spoke: "Can you take us there and catch up with the sledges later on?"

"I could. But I have given my word to Lord Faa to obey him, not any-one else."

"If I got his permission?" said Lyra.

"Then yes."

She turned and ran back through the snow.

"Lord Faa! If Iorek Byrnison takes me over the ridge to the village, we can find out whatever it is, and then catch the sledges up further on. He knows the route," she urged. "And I wouldn't ask, except it's like what I did before, Farder Coram, you remember, with that chameleon? I didn't understand it then, but it was true, and we found out soon after. I got the same feeling now. I can't understand properly what it's saying, only I know it's important. And Iorek Byrnison knows the way, he says he could get there and back three times by next moonrise, and I couldn't be safer than I'd be with him, could I? But he won't go without he gets Lord Faa's permission."

There was a silence. Farder Coram sighed. John Faa was frowning, and his mouth inside the fur hood was set grimly.

But before he could speak, the aëronaut put in:

"Lord Faa, if Iorek Byrnison takes the little girl, she'll be as safe as if she was here with us. All bears are true, but I've known Iorek for years, and nothing under the sky will make him break his word. Give him the charge to take care of her and he'll do it, make no mistake. As for speed, he can lope for hours without tiring."

"But why should not some men go?" said John Faa.

"Well, they'd have to walk," Lyra pointed out, "because you couldn't run a sledge over that ridge. Iorek Byrnison can go faster than any man over that sort of country, and I'm light enough so's he won't be slowed down. And I promise, Lord Faa, I promise not to be any longer than I need, and not to give anything away about us, or to get in any danger."

"You're sure you need to do this? That symbol-reader en't playing the fool with you?"

"It never does, Lord Faa, and I don't think it could."

John Faa rubbed his chin.

"Well, if all comes out right, we'll have a piece more knowledge than we do now. Iorek Byrnison," he called, "are you willing to do as this child bids?"

"I do your bidding, Lord Faa. Tell me to take the child there, and I will."

"Very well. You are to take her where she wishes to go and do as she bids. Lyra, I'm a–commanding *you* now, you understand?"

"Yes, Lord Faa."

"You go and search for whatever it is, and when you've found it, you turn right round and come back. Iorek Byrnison, we'll be a-travelling on by that time, so you'll have to catch us up."

The bear nodded his great head.

"Are there any soldiers in the village?" he said to Lyra. "Will I need my armour? We shall be swifter without it."

"No," she said. "I'm certain of that, Iorek. Thank you, Lord Faa, and I promise I'll do just as you say."

Tony Costa gave her a strip of dried seal-meat to chew, and with Pantalaimon as a mouse inside her hood, Lyra clambered on to the great bear's back, gripping his fur with her mittens and his narrow muscular back between her knees. His fur was wondrously thick, and the sense of immense power she felt was overwhelming. As if she weighed nothing at all, he turned and loped away in a long swinging run up towards the ridge and into the low trees.

It took some time before she was used to the movement, and then she felt a wild exhilaration. She was riding a bear! And the Aurora was swaying above them in golden arcs and loops, and all around was the bitter Arctic cold and the immense silence of the North.

Iorek Byrnison's paws made hardly any sound as they padded forward through the snow. The trees were thin and stunted here, for they were on the edge of the tundra, but there were brambles and snagging bushes in the path. The bear ripped through them as if they were cobwebs.

They climbed the low ridge, among outcrops of black rock, and were soon out of sight of the party behind them. Lyra wanted to talk to the bear, and if he had been human she would already have been on familiar terms with him; but he was so strange and wild and cold that she was shy, almost for the first time in her life. So as he loped along, his great legs swinging tirelessly, she sat with the movement and said nothing. Perhaps he preferred that anyway, she thought; she must seem a little prattling cub, only just past babyhood, in the eyes of an armoured bear.

She had seldom considered herself before, and found the experience interesting but uncomfortable; very like riding the bear, in fact. Iorek Byrnison was pacing swiftly, moving both legs on one side of his body at the same time, and rocking from side to side in a steady powerful rhythm. She found she couldn't just sit: she had to ride actively.

They had been travelling for an hour or more, and Lyra was stiff and sore but deeply happy, when Iorek Byrnison slowed down and stopped.

"Look up," he said.

Lyra raised her eyes and had to wipe them with the inside of her wrist, for she was so cold that tears were blurring them. When she could see clearly she gasped at the sight of the sky. The Aurora had faded to a pallid trembling glimmer, but the stars were as bright as diamonds, and across the great dark diamond-scattered vault, hundreds upon hundreds of tiny black shapes were flying out of the east and south towards the north.

"Are they birds?" she said.

"They are witches," said the bear.

"Witches! What are they doing?"

"Flying to war, maybe. I have never seen so many at one time."

"Do you know any witches, Iorek?"

"I have served some. And fought some, too. This is a sight to frighten

Lord Faa. If they are flying to the aid of your enemies, you should all be afraid."

"Lord Faa wouldn't be frightened. You en't afraid, are you?"

"Not yet. When I am, I shall master the fear. But we had better tell Lord Faa about the witches, because the men might not have seen them."

He moved on more slowly, and she kept watching the sky until her eyes splintered again with tears of cold, and she saw no end to the numberless witches flying north.

Finally Iorek Byrnison stopped and said, "There is the village."

They were looking down a broken, rugged slope towards a cluster of wooden buildings beside a wide stretch of snow as flat as could be, which Lyra took to be the frozen lake. A wooden jetty showed her she was right. They were no more than five minutes from the place.

"What do you want to do?" the bear asked.

Lyra slipped off his back, and found it hard to stand. Her face was stiff with cold and her legs were shaky, but she clung to his fur and stamped until she felt stronger.

"There's a child or a ghost or something down in that village," she said, "or maybe near it, I don't know for certain. I want to go and find him and bring him back to Lord Faa and the others if I can. I thought he was a ghost, but the symbol-reader might be telling me something I can't understand."

"If he is outside," said the bear, "he had better have some shelter."

"I don't think he's dead…" said Lyra, but she was far from sure. The alethiometer had indicated something uncanny and unnatural, which was alarming; but who was she? Lord Asriel's daughter. And who was under her command? A mighty bear. How could she possibly show any fear?

"Let's just go and look," she said.

She clambered on his back again, and he set off down the broken slope, walking steadily and not pacing any more. The dogs of the village smelled or heard or sensed them coming, and began to howl frightfully; and the reindeer in their enclosure moved about nervously, their antlers clashing like dry sticks. In the still air every movement could be heard for a long way.

As they reached the first of the houses, Lyra looked to right and left, peering hard into the dimness, for the Aurora was fading and the moon still far from rising. Here and there a light flickered under a snow-thick roof, and Lyra thought she saw pale faces behind some of the window-panes, and imagined their astonishment to see a child riding a great white bear.

At the centre of the little village there was an open space next to the jetty, where boats had been drawn up, mounds under the snow. The noise of the dogs was deafening, and just as Lyra thought it must have wakened everyone, a door opened and a man came out holding a rifle. His wolverine-dæmon leapt on to the woodstack beside the door, scattering snow.

Lyra slipped down at once and stood between him and Iorek Byrnison, conscious that she had told the bear there was no need for his armour.

The man spoke in words she couldn't understand. Iorek Byrnison replied in the same language, and the man gave a little moan of fear.

"He thinks we are devils," Iorek told Lyra. "What shall I say?"

"Tell him we're not devils, but we've got friends who are. And we're looking for... Just a child. A strange child. Tell him that."

As soon as the bear had said that, the man pointed to the right, indicating some place further off, and spoke quickly.

Iorek Byrnison said, "He asks if we have come to take the child away. They are afraid of it. They have tried to drive it away, but it keeps coming back."

"Tell him we'll take it away with us, but they were very bad to treat it like that. Where is it?"

The man explained, gesticulating fearfully. Lyra was afraid he'd fire his rifle by mistake, but as soon as he'd spoken he hastened inside his house and shut the door. Lyra could see faces at every window.

"Where is the child?" she said.

"In the fish-house," the bear told her, and turned to pad down towards the jetty.

Lyra followed. She was horribly nervous. The bear was making for a narrow wooden shed, raising his head to sniff this way and that, and when he reached the door he stopped and said, "In there."

Lyra's heart was beating so fast she could hardly breathe. She raised her hand to knock at the door and then, feeling that that was ridiculous, took a deep breath to call out, but realized that she didn't know what to say. Oh, it was so dark now! She should have brought a lantern...

There was no choice, and anyway, she didn't want the bear to see her being afraid. He had spoken of mastering his fear: that was what she'd have to do. She lifted the strap of reindeer hide holding the latch in place, and tugged hard against the frost binding the door shut. It opened with a snap. She had to kick aside the snow piled against the foot of the door before she could pull it wide, and Pantalaimon was no help, running back and forth in his ermine-shape, a white shadow over the white ground, uttering little frightened sounds.

"Pan, for God's sake!" she said. "Be a bat. Go and *look* for me..."

But he wouldn't, and he wouldn't speak either. She had never seen him like this except once, when she and Roger in the crypt at Jordan had moved the dæmon-coins into the wrong skulls. He was even more frightened than she was. As for Iorek Byrnison, he was lying in the snow nearby, watching in silence.

"Come out," Lyra said as loud as she dared. "Come out!"

Not a sound came in answer. She pulled the door a little wider, and Pantalaimon leapt up into her arms, pushing and pushing at her in his cat-form, and said, "Go away! Don't stay here! Oh, Lyra, go now! Turn back!"

Trying to hold him still, she was aware of Iorek Byrnison getting to his feet, and turned to see a figure hastening down the track from the village, carrying a lantern. When he came close enough to speak, he raised the lantern and held it to show his face: an old man with a broad, lined face, and eyes nearly lost in a thousand wrinkles. His dæmon was an Arctic fox.

He spoke, and Iorek Byrnison said:

"He says that it's not the only child of that kind. He's seen others in the forest. Sometimes they die quickly, sometimes they don't die. This one is tough, he thinks. But it would be better for him if he died."

"Ask him if I can borrow his lantern," Lyra said.

The bear spoke, and the man handed it to her at once, nodding vigorously. She realized that he'd come down in order to bring it to her, and thanked him, and he nodded again and stood back, away from her and the hut and away from the bear.

Lyra thought suddenly: what if the child is Roger? And she prayed with all her force that it wouldn't be. Pantalaimon was clinging to her, an ermine again, his little claws hooked deep into her anorak.

She lifted the lantern high and took a step into the shed, and then she saw what it was that the Oblation Board was doing, and what was the nature of the sacrifice the children were having to make.

The little boy was huddled against the wood drying-rack where hung row upon row of gutted fish, all as stiff as boards. He was clutching a piece of fish to him as Lyra was clutching Pantalaimon, with both hands, hard, against her heart; but that was all he had, a piece of dried fish; because he had no dæmon at all. The Gobblers had cut it away. That was *intercision*, and this was a severed child.

13

Fencing

*H*er first impulse was to turn and run, or to be sick. A human being with no dæmon was like someone without a face, or with their ribs laid open and their heart torn out: something unnatural and uncanny that belonged to the world of night-ghasts, not the waking world of sense.

So Lyra clung to Pantalaimon and her head swam and her gorge rose, and cold as the night was, a sickly sweat moistened her flesh with something colder still.

"Ratter," said the boy. "You got my Ratter?"

Lyra was in no doubt what he meant.

"No," she said in a voice as frail and frightened as she felt. Then, "What's your name?"

"Tony Makarios," he said. "Where's Ratter?"

"I don't know..." she began, and swallowed hard to govern her nausea. "The Gobblers..." But she couldn't finish. She had to go out of the shed and sit down by herself in the snow, except that of course she wasn't by herself, she was never by herself, because Pantalaimon was always there. Oh, to be cut from him as this little boy had been parted from his

Ratter! The worst thing in the world! She found herself sobbing, and Pantalaimon was whimpering too, and in both of them there was a passionate pity and sorrow for the half-boy.

Then she got to her feet again.

"Come on," she called in a trembling voice. "Tony, come out. We're going to take you somewhere safe."

There was a stir of movement in the fish-house, and he appeared at the door, still clutching his dried fish. He was dressed in warm enough garments, a thickly padded and quilted coal-silk anorak and fur boots, but they had a second-hand look and didn't fit well. In the wider light outside that came from the faint trails of the Aurora and the snow-covered ground he looked more lost and piteous even than he had at first, crouching in the lantern-light by the fish-racks.

The villager who'd brought the lantern had retreated a few yards, and called down to them.

Iorek Byrnison interpreted: "He says you must pay for that fish."

Lyra felt like telling the bear to kill him, but she said, "We're taking the child away for them. They can afford to give one fish to pay for that."

The bear spoke. The man muttered, but didn't argue. Lyra set his lantern down in the snow and took the half-boy's hand to guide him to the bear. He came helplessly, showing no surprise and no fear at the great white beast standing so close, and when Lyra helped him to sit on Iorek's back, all he said was:

"I dunno where my Ratter is."

"No, nor do we, Tony," she said. "But we'll... We'll punish the Gobblers. We'll do that, I promise. Iorek, is that all right if I sit up there too?"

"My armour weighs far more than children," he said.

So she scrambled up behind Tony and made him cling to the long stiff fur, and Pantalaimon sat inside her hood, warm and close and full of pity. Lyra knew that Pantalaimon's impulse was to reach out and cuddle the little half-child, to lick him and gentle him and warm him as his own dæmon would have done; but the great taboo prevented that, of course.

They rode through the village and up towards the ridge, and the villagers' faces were open with horror and a kind of fearful relief at seeing that hideously mutilated creature taken away by a little girl and a great white bear.

In Lyra's heart, revulsion struggled with compassion, and compassion won. She put her arms around the skinny little form to hold him safe. The journey back to the main party was colder, and harder, and darker, but it seemed to pass more quickly for all that. Iorek Byrnison was tireless, and Lyra's riding became automatic, so that she was never in danger of falling off. The cold body in her arms was so light that in one way he was easy to manage, but he was inert; he sat stiffly without moving as the bear moved, so in another way he was difficult too.

From time to time the half-boy spoke.

"What's that you said?" asked Lyra.

"I says is she gonna know where I am?"

"Yeah, she'll know, she'll find you and we'll find her. Hold on tight now, Tony. It en't far from here…"

The bear loped onwards. Lyra had no idea how tired she was until they caught up with the gyptians. The sledges had stopped to rest the dogs, and suddenly there they all were, Farder Coram, Lord Faa, Lee Scoresby, all lunging forward to help and then falling back silent as they saw the other figure with Lyra. She was so stiff that she couldn't even loosen her arms around his body, and John Faa himself had to pull them gently open and lift her off.

"Gracious God, what is this?" he said. "Lyra, child, what have you found?"

"He's called Tony," she mumbled through frozen lips. "And they cut his dæmon away. That's what the Gobblers do."

The men held back, fearful; but the bear spoke, to Lyra's weary amazement, chiding them.

"Shame on you! Think what this child has done! You might not have more courage, but you should be ashamed to show less."

"You're right, Iorek Byrnison," said John Faa, and turned to give orders. "Build that fire up and heat some soup for the child. For both children. Farder Coram, is your shelter rigged?"

"It is, John. Bring her over and we'll get her warm…"

"And the little boy," said someone else. "He can eat and get warm, even if…"

Lyra was trying to tell John Faa about the witches, but they were all so busy, and she was so tired. After a confusing few minutes full of lantern light, woodsmoke, figures hurrying to and fro, she felt a gentle nip on her ear from Pantalaimon's ermine-teeth, and woke to find the bear's face a few inches from hers.

"The witches," Pantalaimon whispered. "I called Iorek."

"Oh yeah," she mumbled. "Iorek, thank you for taking me there and back. I might not remember to tell Lord Faa about the witches, so you better do that instead of me."

She heard the bear agree, and then she fell asleep properly.

When she woke up, it was as close to daylight as it was ever going to get. The sky was pale in the south-east, and the air was suffused with a grey mist, through which the gyptians moved like bulky ghosts, loading sledges and harnessing dogs to the traces.

She saw it all from the shelter on Farder Coram's sledge, inside which she lay under a heap of furs. Pantalaimon was fully awake before she was, trying the shape of an Arctic fox before reverting to his favourite ermine.

Iorek Byrnison was asleep in the snow nearby, his head on his great paws; but Farder Coram was up and busy, and as soon as he saw Pantalaimon emerge, he limped across to wake Lyra properly.

She saw him coming, and sat up to speak.

"Farder Coram, I know what it was that I couldn't understand! The alethiometer kept saying *bird* and *not*, and that didn't make sense, because it meant *no dæmon* and I didn't see how it could be... What is it?"

"Lyra, I'm afraid to tell you this after what you done, but that little boy died an hour ago. He couldn't settle, he couldn't stay in one place; he kept asking after his dæmon, where she was, was she a-coming soon, and all; and he kept such a tight hold on that bare old piece of fish as if... Oh, I can't speak of it, child; but he closed his eyes finally and fell still, and that was the first time he looked peaceful, for he was like any other dead person then, with their dæmon gone in the course of nature. They've been a-trying to dig a grave for him, but the earth's bound like iron. So John Faa ordered a fire built, and they're a-going to cremate him, so as not to have him despoiled by carrion-eaters.

"Child, you did a brave thing and a good thing, and I'm proud of you. Now we know what terrible wickedness those people are capable of, we can see our duty plainer than ever. What you must do is rest and eat, because you fell asleep too soon to restore yourself last night, and you have to eat in these temperatures to stop yourself getting weak..."

He was fussing around, tucking the furs into place, tightening the tension-rope across the body of the sledge, running the traces through his hands to untangle them.

"Farder Coram, where is the little boy now? Have they burned him yet?"

"No, Lyra, he's a-lying back there."

"I want to go and see him."

He couldn't refuse her that, for she'd seen worse than a dead body, and it might calm her. So with Pantalaimon as a white hare bounding delicately at her side, she trudged along the line of sledges to where some men were piling brushwood.

The boy's body lay under a checkered blanket beside the path. She knelt and lifted the blanket in her mittened hands. One man was about to stop her, but the others shook their heads.

Pantalaimon crept close as Lyra looked down on the poor wasted face. She slipped her hand out of the mitten and touched his eyes. They were marble-cold, and Farder Coram had been right; poor little Tony Makarios was no different from any other human whose dæmon had departed in death. Oh, if they took Pantalaimon from her! She swept him up and hugged him as if she meant to press him right into her heart. And all little Tony had was his pitiful piece of fish...

Where was it?

She pulled the blanket down. It was gone.

She was on her feet in a moment, and her eyes flashed fury at the men nearby.

"Where's his fish?"

They stopped, puzzled, unsure what she meant; though some of their dæmons knew, and looked at one another. One of the men began to grin uncertainly.

"Don't you *dare* laugh! I'll tear your lungs out if you laugh at him! That's all he had to cling on to, just an old dried fish, that's all he had for a dæmon to love and be kind to! Who's took it from him? Where's it gone?"

Pantalaimon was a snarling snow leopard, just like Lord Asriel's dæmon, but she didn't see that; all she saw was right and wrong.

"Easy, Lyra," said one man. "Easy, child."

"Who's took it?" she flared again, and the gyptian took a step back from her passionate fury.

"I didn't know," said another man apologetically. "I thought it was just what he'd been eating. I took it out his hand because I thought it was more respectful. That's all, Lyra."

"Then where is it?"

The man said uneasily, "Not thinking he had a need for it, I gave it to my dogs. I do beg your pardon."

"It en't my pardon you need, it's his," she said, and turned at once to kneel again, and laid her hand on the dead child's icy cheek.

Then an idea came to her, and she fumbled inside her furs. The cold air struck through as she opened her anorak, but in a few seconds she had what she wanted, and took a gold coin from her purse before wrapping herself close again.

"I want to borrow your knife," she said to the man who'd taken the fish, and when he let her have it, she said to Pantalaimon: "What was her name?"

He understood, of course, and said, "Ratter."

She held the coin tight in her left mittened hand and, holding the knife like a pencil, scratched the lost dæmon's name deeply into the gold.

"I hope that'll do, if I provide for you like a Jordan Scholar," she whispered to the dead boy, and forced his teeth apart to slip the coin into his mouth. It was hard, but she managed it, and managed to close his jaw again.

Then she gave the man back his knife and turned in the morning twilight to go back to Farder Coram.

He gave her a mug of soup straight off the fire, and she sipped it greedily.

"What we going to do about them witches, Farder Coram?" she said. "I wonder if your witch was one of them."

"*My* witch? I wouldn't presume that far, Lyra. They might be going anywhere. There's all kinds of concerns that play on the life of witches; things invisible to us; mysterious sicknesses they fall prey to, which we'd shrug off; causes of war quite beyond our understanding; joys and sorrows bound up with the flowering of tiny plants up on the tundra... But I wish I'd seen them a-flying, Lyra. I wish I'd been able to see a sight like that. Now drink up all that soup. D'you want some more? There's some pan-bread a-cooking too. Eat up, child, because we're on our way soon."

The food revived Lyra, and presently the chill at her soul began to melt. With the others, she went to watch the little half-child laid on his funeral pyre, and bowed her head and closed her eyes for John Faa's prayers; and then the men sprinkled coal-spirit and set matches to it, and it was blazing in a moment.

Once they were sure he was safely burned, they set off to travel again. It was a ghostly journey. Snow began to fall early on, and soon the world was reduced to the grey shadows of the dogs ahead, the lurching and creaking of the sledge, the biting cold, and a swirling sea of big flakes only just darker than the sky and only just lighter than the ground.

Through it all the dogs continued to run, tails high, breath puffing steam. North and further north they ran, while the pallid noontide came and went and the twilight folded itself again around the world. They stopped to eat and drink and rest in a gap in the hills, and to get their bearings, and while John Faa talked to Lee Scoresby about the way they might best use the balloon, Lyra thought of the spy-fly; and she asked Farder Coram what had happened to the smoke-leaf tin he'd trapped it in.

"I've got it tucked away tight," he said. "It's down in the bottom of that kit-bag, but there's nothing to see; I soldered it shut on board ship, like I said I would. I don't know what we're a-going to do with it, to tell you the truth; maybe we could drop it down a fire-mine, maybe that would settle it. But you needn't worry, Lyra. While I've got it, you're safe."

The first chance she had, she plunged her arm down into the stiffly-frosted canvas of the kit-bag and brought up the little tin. She could feel the buzz it was making before she touched it.

While Farder Coram was talking to the other leaders, she took the tin to Iorek Byrnison and explained her idea. It had come to her when she remembered his slicing so easily through the metal of the engine-cover.

He listened, and then took the lid of a biscuit-tin and deftly folded it into a small flat cylinder. She marvelled at the skill of his hands: unlike most bears, he and his kin had opposable thumb-claws with which they could hold things still to work on them; and he had some innate sense of the strength and flexibility of metals which meant that he only had to lift it once or twice, flex it this way and that, and he could run a claw over it in a circle to score it for folding. He did this now, folding the sides in and in until they stood in a raised rim and then making a lid to fit it. At Lyra's bidding he made two: one the same size as the original smoke-leaf tin, and another just big enough to contain the tin itself and a quantity of hairs and bits of moss and lichen all packed down tight to smother the noise. When it was closed, it was the same size and shape as the alethiometer.

When that was done, she sat next to Iorek Byrnison as he gnawed a haunch of reindeer that was frozen as hard as wood.

"Iorek," she said, "is it hard not having a dæmon? Don't you get lonely?"

"Lonely?" he said. "I don't know. They tell me this is cold. I don't know what cold is, because I don't freeze. So I don't know what lonely means either. Bears are made to be solitary."

"What about the Svalbard bears?" she said. "There's thousands of them, en't there? That's what I heard."

He said nothing, but ripped the joint in half with a sound like a splitting log.

"Beg pardon, Iorek," she said. "I hope I en't offended you. It's just that I'm curious. See, I'm extra curious about the Svalbard bears because of my father."

"Who is your father?"

"Lord Asriel. And they got him captive on Svalbard, you see. I think the Gobblers betrayed him and paid the bears to keep him in prison."

"I don't know. I am not a Svalbard bear."

"I thought you was…"

"No. I was a Svalbard bear, but I am not now. I was sent away as a punishment because I killed another bear. So I was deprived of my rank and my wealth and my armour and sent out to live at the edge of the human world and fight when I could find employment at it, or work at brutal tasks and drown my memory in raw spirits."

"Why did you kill the other bear?"

"Anger. There are ways among bears of turning away our anger with each other, but I was out of my own control. So I killed him and I was justly punished."

"And you were wealthy and high-ranking," said Lyra, marvelling. "Just like my father, Iorek! That's just the same with him after I was born. He killed someone too and they took all his wealth away. That was long before he got made a prisoner on Svalbard, though. I don't know anything about Svalbard, except it's in the farthest North… Is it all covered in ice? Can you get there over the frozen sea?"

"Not from this coast. The sea is sometimes frozen south of it, sometimes not. You would need a boat."

"Or a balloon, maybe."

"Or a balloon, yes, but then you would need the right wind."

He gnawed the reindeer haunch, and a wild notion flew into Lyra's mind as she remembered all those witches in the night sky; but she said nothing about that. Instead she asked Iorek Byrnison about Svalbard, and listened eagerly as he told her of the slow-crawling glaciers; of the rocks and ice-floes where the bright-tusked walruses lay in groups of a hundred or more, of the seas teeming with seals, of narwhals clashing their long white tusks above the icy water; of the great grim iron-bound coast, the cliffs a thousand feet and more high, where the foul cliffghasts perched and swooped; of the coal-pits and the fire-mines where the bearsmiths hammered out mighty sheets of iron and riveted them into armour…

"If they took your armour away, Iorek, where did you get this set from?"

"I made it myself in Nova Zembla from sky-metal. Until I did that I was incomplete."

"So bears can make their own souls…" she said. There was a great deal in the world to know. "Who is the King of Svalbard?" she went on. "Do bears have a King?"

"He is called Iofur Raknison."

That name shook a little bell in Lyra's mind. She'd heard it before, but where? And not in a bear's voice, either, nor in a gyptian's. The voice that had spoken it was a Scholar's, precise and pedantic and lazily arrogant, very much a Jordan College voice. She tried it again in her mind. Oh, she knew it so well!

And then she had it: the Retiring Room. The Scholars listening to Lord Asriel. It was the Palmerian Professor who had said something about Iofur Raknison. He'd used the word *panserbjørne*, which Lyra didn't know, and she hadn't known that Iofur Raknison was a bear; but what was it he'd said? The King of Svalbard was vain, and he could be flattered. There was something else, if only she could remember it, but so much had happened since then…

"If your father is a prisoner of the Svalbard bears," said Iorek Byrnison, "he will not escape. There is no wood there to make a boat. On the other hand, if he is a nobleman, he will be treated fairly. They will give him a house to live in and a servant to wait on him, and food and fuel."

"Could the bears ever be defeated, Iorek?"

"No."

"Or tricked, maybe?"

He stopped gnawing and looked at her directly. Then he said, "You will never defeat the armoured bears. You have seen my armour; now look at my weapons."

He dropped the meat and held out his paws, palm upward, for her to look at. Each black pad was covered in horny skin an inch or more thick, and each of the claws was as long as Lyra's hand at least, and as sharp as a knife. He let her run her hands over them wonderingly.

"One blow will crush a seal's skull," he said. "Or break a man's back, or tear off a limb. And I can bite. If you had not stopped me in Trollesund, I would have crushed that man's head like an egg. So much for strength; now for trickery. You cannot trick a bear. You want to see proof? Take a stick and fence with me."

Eager to try, she snapped a stick off a snow-laden bush, trimmed all the side-shoots off, and swished it from side to side like a rapier. Iorek Byrnison sat back on his haunches and waited, forepaws in his lap. When she was ready she faced him, but she didn't like to stab at him because he looked so peaceable. So she flourished it, feinting to right and left, not intending to hit him at all, and he didn't move. She did that several times, and not once did he move so much as an inch.

Finally she decided to thrust at him directly, not hard, but just to touch the stick to his stomach. Instantly his paw reached forward and flicked the stick aside.

Surprised, she tried again, with the same result. He moved far more quickly and surely than she did. She tried to hit him in earnest, wielding the stick like a fencer's foil, and not once did it land on his body. He seemed to know what she intended before she did, and when she lunged at his head, the great paw swept the stick aside harmlessly, and when she feinted, he didn't move at all.

She became exasperated, and threw herself into a furious attack, jabbing and lashing and thrusting and stabbing, and never once did she get past those paws. They moved everywhere, precisely in time to parry, precisely at the right spot to block.

Finally she was frightened, and stopped. She was sweating inside her furs, out of breath, exhausted, and the bear still sat impassive. If she had had a real sword with a murderous point, he would have been quite unharmed.

"I bet you could catch bullets," she said, and threw the stick away. "How do you *do* that?"

"By not being human," he said. "That's why you could never trick a bear. We see tricks and deceit as plain as arms and legs. We can see in a way humans have forgotten. But you know about this; you can understand the symbol-reader."

"That en't the same, is it?" she said. She was more nervous of the bear now than when she had seen his anger.

"It is the same," he said. "Adults can't read it, as I understand. As I am to human fighters, so you are to adults with the symbol-reader."

"Yes, I suppose," she said, puzzled and unwilling. "Does that mean I'll forget how to do it when I grow up?"

"Who knows? I have never seen a symbol-reader, nor anyone who could read them. Perhaps you are different from others."

He dropped to all fours again and went on gnawing his meat. Lyra had unfastened her furs, but now the cold was striking in again and she had to do them up. All in all, it was a disquieting episode. She wanted to consult the alethiometer there and then, but it was too cold, and besides, they were calling for her because it was time to move on. She took the tin boxes that Iorek Byrnison had made, put the empty one back into Farder Coram's kit-bag, and put the one with the spy-fly in it together with the alethiometer in the pouch at her waist. She was glad when they were moving again.

The leaders had agreed with Lee Scoresby that when they reached the next stopping-place, they would inflate his balloon and he would spy from the air. Naturally Lyra was eager to fly with him, and naturally it was forbidden; but she rode with him on the way there and pestered him with questions.

230

"Mr Scoresby, how would you fly to Svalbard?"

"You'd need a dirigible with a gas engine, something like a zeppelin, or else a good south wind. But hell, I wouldn't dare. Have you ever seen it? The bleakest barest most inhospitable godforsaken dead-end of nowhere."

"I was just wondering, if Iorek Byrnison wanted to go back..."

"He'd be killed. Iorek's in exile. As soon as he set foot there they'd tear him to pieces."

"How do you inflate your balloon, Mr Scoresby?"

"Two ways. I can make hydrogen by pouring sulphuric acid on to iron filings. You catch the gas it gives off and gradually fill the balloon like that. The other way is to find a ground-gas vent near a fire-mine. There's a lot of gas under the ground here, and rock-oil besides. I can make gas from rock-oil, if I need to, and from coal as well; it's not hard to make gas. But the quickest way is to use ground-gas. A good vent will fill the balloon in an hour."

"How many people can you carry?"

"Six, if I need to."

"Could you carry Iorek Byrnison in his armour?"

"I have done. I rescued him one time from the Tartars, when he was cut off and they were starving him out – that was in the Tunguska campaign; I flew in and took him off. Sounds easy, but hell, I had to calculate the weight of that old boy by guesswork. And then I had to bank on finding ground-gas under the ice-fort he'd made. But I could see what kind of ground it was from the air, and I reckoned we'd be safe in digging. See, to go down I have to let gas out of the balloon, and I can't get airborne again without more. Anyway, we made it, armour and all."

"Mr Scoresby, you know the Tartars make holes in people's heads?"

"Oh, sure. They've been doing that for thousands of years. In the

Tunguska campaign we captured five Tartars alive, and three of them had holes in their skulls. One of them had two."

"They do it to *each other*?"

"That's right. First they cut part-way around a circle of skin on the scalp, so they can lift up a flap and expose the bone. Then they cut a little circle of bone out of the skull, very carefully so they don't penetrate the brain, and then they sew the scalp back over."

"I thought they did it to their enemies!"

"Hell, no. It's a great privilege. They do it so the gods can talk to them."

"Did you ever hear of an explorer called Stanislaus Grumman?"

"Grumman? Sure. I met one of his team when I flew over the Yenisei River two years back. He was going to live among the Tartar tribes up that way. Matter of fact, I think *he* had that hole in the skull done. It was part of an initiation ceremony, but the man who told me didn't know much about it."

"So... If he was like an honorary Tartar, they wouldn't have killed him?"

"Killed him? Is he dead then?"

"Yeah. I saw his head," Lyra said proudly. "My father found it. I saw it when he showed it to the Scholars at Jordan College in Oxford. They'd scalped it, and all."

"Who'd scalped it?"

"Well, the Tartars, that's what the Scholars thought... But maybe it wasn't."

"It might not have been Grumman's head," said Lee Scoresby. "Your father might have been misleading the Scholars."

"I suppose he might," said Lyra thoughtfully. "He was asking them for money."

"And when they saw the head, they gave him the money?"

"Yeah."

"Good trick to play. People are shocked when they see a thing like that; they don't like to look too close."

"Especially Scholars," said Lyra.

"Well, you'd know better than I would. But if that was Grumman's head, I'll bet it wasn't the Tartars who scalped him. They scalp their enemies, not their own, and he was a Tartar by adoption."

Lyra turned that over in her mind as they drove on. There were wide currents full of meaning flowing fast around her: the Gobblers and their cruelty, their fear of Dust, the city in the Aurora, her father in Svalbard, her mother... And where was she? The alethiometer, the witches flying northwards. And poor little Tony Makarios; and the clockwork spy-fly; and Iorek Byrnison's uncanny fencing...

She fell asleep. And every hour they drew closer to Bolvangar.

14

Bolvangar Lights

The fact that the Gyptians had heard or seen nothing of Mrs Coulter worried Farder Coram and John Faa more than they let Lyra know; but they weren't to know that she was worried too. Lyra feared Mrs Coulter and thought about her often. And whereas Lord Asriel was now "father", Mrs Coulter was never "mother". The reason for that was Mrs Coulter's dæmon, the golden monkey, who had filled Pantalaimon with a powerful loathing and who, Lyra felt, had pried into her secrets, particularly that of the alethiometer.

And they were bound to be chasing her; it was silly to think otherwise. The spy-fly proved that, if nothing else.

But when an enemy did strike, it wasn't Mrs Coulter. The gyptians had planned to stop and rest their dogs, repair a couple of sledges, and get all their weapons into shape for the assault on Bolvangar. John Faa hoped that Lee Scoresby might find some ground-gas to fill his smaller balloon (for he had two, apparently) and go up to spy out the land. However, the aëronaut attended to the condition of the weather as closely as a sailor, and he said there was going to be a fog; and sure enough, as soon as they stopped, a thick mist descended. Lee Scoresby knew he'd see nothing from the sky, so he had to content himself with checking his equipment, though it was all in meticulous order. Then, with no warning at all, a volley of arrows flew out of the dark.

Three gyptian men went down at once, and died so silently that no one heard a thing. Only when they slumped clumsily across the dog-traces or lay unexpectedly still did the nearest men notice what was happening, and then it was already too late, because more arrows were flying at them. Some men looked up, puzzled by the fast irregular knocking sounds that came from up and down the line as arrows hurtled into wood or frozen canvas.

The first to come to his wits was John Faa, who shouted orders from the centre of the line. Cold hands and stiff limbs moved to obey as yet more arrows flew down like rain, straight rods of rain tipped with death.

Lyra was in the open, and the arrows were passing over her head. Pantalaimon heard before she did, and became a leopard and knocked her over, making her less of a target. Brushing snow out of her eyes, she rolled over to try and see what was happening, for the semi-darkness seemed to be overflowing with confusion and noise. She heard a mighty roar, and the clang and scrape of Iorek Byrnison's armour as he leapt fully clad over the sledges and into the fog, and that was followed by screams, snarling, crunching and tearing sounds, great smashing blows, cries of terror and roars of bearish fury as he laid them waste.

But who was *them*? Lyra had seen no enemy figures yet. The gyptians were swarming to defend the sledges, but that (as even Lyra could see) made them better targets; and their rifles were not easy to fire in gloves and mittens; she had only heard four or five shots, as against the cease-less knocking rain of arrows. And more and more men fell every minute.

Oh, John Faa! she thought in anguish. You didn't foresee this, and I didn't help you!

But she had no more than a second to think that, for there was a mighty snarl from Pantalaimon, and something – another dæmon – hurtled at him and knocked him down, crushing all the breath out of Lyra herself; and then hands were hauling at her, lifting her, stifling her cry with foul-smelling mittens, tossing her through the air into another's arms, and then pushing her flat down into the snow again, so that she was dizzy and breathless and hurt all at once. Her arms were hauled behind till her shoulders cracked, and someone lashed her wrists together, and then a hood was crammed over her head to muffle her screams, for scream she did, and lustily:

"Iorek! Iorek Byrnison! Help me!"

But could he hear? She couldn't tell; she was hurled this way and that, crushed on to a hard surface which then began to lurch and bump like a sledge. The sounds that reached her were wild and confused. She might have heard Iorek Byrnison's roar, but it was a long way off, and then she was jolting over rough ground, arms twisted, mouth stifled, sobbing with rage and fear. And strange voices spoke around her.

"Pan!" she gasped.

"I'm here, ssh, I'll help you breathe. Keep still…"

His mouse-paws tugged at the hood until her mouth was freer, and she gulped at the frozen air.

"Who are they?" she whispered.

"They look like Tartars. I think they hit John Faa."

"No –"

"I saw him fall. But he should have been ready for this sort of attack. We know that."

"But we should have helped him! We should have been watching the alethiometer!"

"Hush. Pretend to be unconscious."

There was a whip cracking, and the howl of racing dogs. From the way she was being jerked and bounced about, Lyra could tell how fast they were going, and though she strained to hear the sounds of battle, all she made out was a forlorn volley of shots, muffled by the distance, and then the creak and rush and soft paw-thuds in the snow were all there was to hear.

"They'll take us to the Gobblers," she whispered.

The word *severed* came to their mind. Horrible fear filled Lyra's body, and Pantalaimon nestled close against her.

"I'll fight," he said.

"So will I. I'll *kill* them."

"So will Iorek when he finds out. He'll crush them to death."

"How far are we from Bolvangar?"

He didn't know, but they thought it was less than a day's ride. After they had been driving along for such a time that her body was in torment from cramp, the pace slackened a little, and someone roughly pulled off the hood.

She looked up at a broad Asiatic face, under a wolverine hood, lit by flickering lamplight. His black eyes showed a glint of satisfaction, especially when Pantalaimon slid out of Lyra's anorak to bare his white ermine-teeth in a hiss. The man's dæmon, a big heavy wolverine, snarled back, but Pantalaimon didn't flinch.

The man hauled Lyra up to a sitting position and propped her against the side of the sledge. She kept falling sideways because her hands were still tied behind her, and so he tied her feet together instead and released her hands.

Through the snow that was falling and the thick fog, she saw how powerful this man was, and the sledge-driver too, how balanced in the sledge, how much at home in this land in a way the gyptians weren't.

The man spoke, but of course she understood nothing. He tried a different language with the same result. Then he tried English.

"You name?"

Pantalaimon bristled warningly, and she knew what he meant at once. So these men didn't know who she was! They hadn't kidnapped her because of her connection with Mrs Coulter; so perhaps they weren't in the pay of the Gobblers after all.

"Lizzie Brooks," she said.

"Lissie Broogs," he said after her. "We take you nice place. Nice peoples."

"Who are you?"

"Samoyed peoples. Hunters."

"Where are you taking me?"

"Nice place. Nice peoples. You have *panserbjørn*?"

"For protection."

"No good! Ha, ha, bear no good! We got you anyway!"

He laughed loudly. Lyra controlled herself and said nothing.

"Who those peoples?" the man asked next, pointing back the way they had come.

"Traders."

"Traders… What they trade?"

"Fur, spirits," she said. "Smoke-leaf."

"They sell smoke-leaf, buy furs?"

"Yes."

He said something to his companion, who spoke back briefly. All the time the sledge was speeding onwards, and Lyra pulled herself up more comfortably to try and see where they were heading; but the snow was falling thickly, and the sky was dark, and presently she became too cold to peer out any longer, and lay down. She and Pantalaimon could feel each other's thoughts, and tried to keep calm, but the thought of John Faa dead... And what had happened to Farder Coram? And would Iorek manage to kill the other Samoyeds? And would they ever manage to track her down?

For the first time, she began to feel a little sorry for herself.

After a long time, the man shook her by the shoulder and handed her a strip of dried reindeer-meat to chew. It was rank and tough, but she was hungry, and there was nourishment in it. After chewing it she felt a little better. She slipped her hand slowly into her furs till she was sure the alethiometer was still there, and then carefully withdrew the spy-fly tin and slipped it down into her fur boot. Pantalaimon crept in as a mouse and pushed it as far down as he could, tucking it under the bottom of her reindeer-skin legging.

When that was done she closed her eyes. Fear had made her exhausted, and soon she slipped uneasily into sleep.

She woke up when the motion of the sledge changed. It was suddenly smoother, and when she opened her eyes there were passing lights dazzling above her, so bright she had to pull the hood further over her head before peering out again. She was horribly stiff and cold, but she managed to pull herself upright enough to see that the sledge was driving swiftly between a row of high poles, each carrying a glaring anbaric light. As she got her bearings, they passed through an open metal gate at the end of the avenue of lights and into a wide open space like an empty market-place or an arena for some game or sport. It was perfectly flat and smooth and white, and about a hundred yards across. Around the edge ran a high metal fence.

At the far end of this arena the sledge halted. They were outside a low building, or a range of low buildings over which the snow lay deeply. It was hard to tell, but she had the impression that tunnels connected one part of the buildings with another, tunnels humped under the snow. At one side a stout metal mast had a familiar look, though she couldn't say what it reminded her of.

Before she could take much more in, the man in the sledge cut through the cord around her ankles, and hauled her out roughly while the driver shouted at the dogs to make them still. A door opened in the building a few yards away, and an anbaric light came on overhead, swivelling to find them, like a searchlight.

Lyra's captor thrust her forward like a trophy, without letting go, and said something. The figure in the padded coal-silk anorak answered in the same language, and Lyra saw his features: he was not a Samoyed or a Tartar. He could have been a Jordan Scholar. He looked at her, and particularly at Pantalaimon.

The Samoyed spoke again, and the man from Bolvangar said to Lyra, "You speak English?"

"Yes," she said.

"Does your dæmon always take that form?"

Of all the unexpected questions! Lyra could only gape. But Pantalaimon answered it in his own fashion by becoming a falcon, and launching himself from her shoulder at the man's dæmon, a large marmot, which struck up at Pantalaimon with a swift movement and spat as he circled past on swift wings.

"I see," said the man in a tone of satisfaction, as Pantalaimon returned to Lyra's shoulder.

The Samoyed men were looking expectant, and the man from Bolvangar nodded and took off a mitten to reach into a pocket. He took out a draw-string purse and counted out a dozen heavy coins into the hunter's hand.

The two men checked the money, and then stowed it carefully, each man taking half. Without a backward glance they got in the sledge, and the driver cracked the whip and shouted to the dogs; and they sped away across the wide white arena and into the avenue of lights, gathering speed until they vanished into the dark beyond.

The man was opening the door again.

"Come in quickly," he said. "It's warm and comfortable. Don't stand out in the cold. What is your name?"

His voice was an English one, without any accent Lyra could name. He sounded like the sort of people she had met at Mrs Coulter's: smart and educated and important.

"Lizzie Brooks," she said.

"Come in, Lizzie. We'll look after you here, don't worry."

He was colder than she was, even though she'd been outside for far longer; he was impatient to be in the warm again. She decided to play slow and dim-witted and reluctant, and dragged her feet as she stepped over the high threshold into the building.

There were two doors, with a wide space between them so that not too much warm air escaped. Once they were through the inner doorway Lyra found herself sweltering in what seemed unbearable heat, and had to pull open her furs and push back her hood.

They were in a space about eight feet square, with corridors to the right and left and in front of her the sort of reception desk you might see in a hospital. Everything was brilliantly lit, with the glint of shiny white surfaces and stainless steel. There was the smell of food in the air, familiar food, bacon and coffee, and under it a faint perpetual hospital-medical smell; and coming from the walls all around was a slight humming sound, almost too low to hear, the sort of sound you had to get used to or go mad.

Pantalaimon at her ear, a goldfinch now, whispered "Be stupid and dim. Be really slow and stupid."

Adults were looking down at her: the man who'd brought her in, another man wearing a white coat, a woman in a nurse's uniform.

"English," the first man was saying. "Traders, apparently."

"Usual hunters? Usual story?"

"Same tribe, as far as I could tell. Sister Clara, could you take little, umm, and see to her?"

"Certainly, Doctor. Come with me, dear," said the nurse, and Lyra obediently followed.

They went along a short corridor with doors on the right and a canteen on the left, from which came a clatter of knives and forks, and voices, and more cooking-smells. The nurse was about as old as Mrs Coulter, Lyra guessed, with a brisk, blank, sensible air; she would be able to stitch a wound or change a bandage, but never to tell a story. Her dæmon (and Lyra had a moment of strange chill when she noticed) was a little white trotting dog (and after a moment she had no idea why it had chilled her).

"What's your name, dear?" said the nurse, opening a heavy door.

"Lizzie."

"Just Lizzie?"

"Lizzie Brooks."

"And how old are you?"

"Eleven."

Lyra had been told that she was small for her age, whatever that meant. It had never affected her sense of her own importance, but she realized that she could use the fact now to make Lizzie shy and nervous and insignificant, and shrank a little as she went into the room.

She was half expecting questions about where she had come from and how she had arrived, and she was preparing answers; but it wasn't only imagination the nurse lacked, it was curiosity as well. Bolvangar might have been on the outskirts of London, and children might have been arriving all the time, for all the interest Sister Clara seemed to show. Her pert neat little dæmon trotted along at her heels just as brisk and blank as she was.

In the room they entered there was a couch and a table and two chairs and a filing cabinet, and a glass cupboard with medicines and bandages, and a wash-basin. As soon as they were inside, the nurse took Lyra's outer coat off and dropped it on the shiny floor.

"Off with the rest, dear," she said. "We'll have a quick little look to see you're nice and healthy, no frostbite or sniffles, and then we'll find some nice clean clothes. We'll pop you in the shower, too," she added, for Lyra had not changed or washed for days, and in the enveloping warmth, that was becoming more and more evident.

Pantalaimon fluttered in protest, but Lyra quelled him with a scowl. He settled on the couch as one by one all Lyra's clothes came off, to her resentment and shame; but she still had the presence of mind to conceal it and act dull-witted and compliant.

"And the money-belt, Lizzie," said the nurse, and untied it herself with strong fingers. She went to drop it on the pile with Lyra's other clothes, but stopped, feeling the edge of the alethiometer.

"What's this?" she said, and unbuttoned the oilcloth.

"Just a sort of toy," said Lyra. "It's mine."

"Yes, we won't take it away from you, dear," said Sister Clara, unfolding the black velvet. "That's pretty, isn't it, like a compass. Into the shower with you," she went on, putting the alethiometer down and whisking back a coal-silk curtain in the corner.

Lyra reluctantly slipped under the warm water and soaped herself while Pantalaimon perched on the curtain-rail. They were both conscious that he mustn't be too lively, for the dæmons of dull people were dull themselves. When she was washed and dry the nurse took her temperature and looked into her eyes and ears and throat, and then measured her height and put her on some scales before writing a note on a clipboard. Then she gave Lyra some pyjamas and a dressing-gown. They were clean, and of good quality, like Tony Makarios's anorak, but again there was a second-hand air about them. Lyra felt very uneasy.

"These en't mine," she said.

"No, dear. Your clothes need a good wash."

"Am I going to get my own ones back?"

"I expect so. Yes, of course."

"What is this place?"

"It's called the Experimental Station."

That wasn't an answer, and whereas Lyra would have pointed that out and asked for more information, she didn't think Lizzie Brooks would; so she assented dumbly in the dressing and said no more.

"I want my toy back," she said stubbornly when she was dressed.

"Take it, dear," said the nurse. "Wouldn't you rather have a nice woolly bear, though? Or a pretty doll?"

She opened a drawer where some soft toys lay like dead things. Lyra made herself stand and pretend to consider for several seconds before picking out a rag doll with big vacant eyes. She had never had a doll, but she knew what to do, and pressed it absently to her chest.

"What about my money-belt?" she said. "I like to keep my toy in there."

"Go on, then, dear," said Sister Clara, who was filling in a form on pink paper.

Lyra hitched up her unfamiliar pyjamas and tied the oilskin pouch around her waist.

"What about my coat and boots?" she said. "And my mittens and things?"

"We'll have them cleaned for you," said the nurse automatically.

Then a telephone buzzed, and while the nurse answered it, Lyra stooped quickly to recover the other tin, the one containing the spy-fly, and put it in the pouch with the alethiometer.

"Come along, Lizzie," said the nurse, putting the receiver down. "We'll go and find you something to eat. I expect you're hungry."

She followed Sister Clara to the canteen, where a dozen round white tables were covered in crumbs and the sticky rings where drinks had been carelessly put down. Dirty plates and cutlery were stacked on a steel trolley. There were no windows, so to give an illusion of light and space one wall was covered in a huge photogram showing a tropical beach, with bright blue sky and white sand and coconut palms.

The man who had brought her in was collecting a tray from a serving hatch.

"Eat up," he said.

There was no need to starve, so she ate the stew and mashed potatoes with relish. There was a bowl of tinned peaches and ice cream to follow. As she ate, the man and the nurse talked quietly at another table, and when she had finished, the nurse brought her a glass of warm milk and took the tray away.

The man came to sit down opposite. His dæmon, the marmot, was not blank and incurious as the nurse's dog had been, but sat politely on his shoulder watching and listening.

"Now, Lizzie," he said. "Have you eaten enough?"

"Yes, thank you."

"I'd like you to tell me where you come from. Can you do that?"

"London," she said.

"And what are you doing so far north?"

"With my father," she mumbled. She kept her eyes down, avoiding the gaze of the marmot, and trying to look as if she was on the verge of tears.

"With your father? I see. And what's he doing in this part of the world?"

"Trading. We come with a load of New Danish smoke-leaf and we was buying furs."

"And was your father by himself?"

"No. There was my uncles and all, and some other men," she said vaguely, not knowing what the Samoyed hunter had told him.

"Why did he bring you on a journey like this, Lizzie?"

"'Cause two years ago he brung my brother and he says he'll bring me next, only he never. So I kept asking him, and then he did."

"And how old are you?"

"Eleven."

"Good, good. Well, Lizzie, you're a lucky little girl. Those huntsmen who found you brought you to the best place you could be."

"They never found me," she said doubtfully. "There was a fight. There was lots of 'em and they had arrows..."

"Oh, I don't think so. I think you must have wandered away from your father's party and got lost. Those huntsmen found you on your own and brought you straight here. That's what happened, Lizzie."

"I saw a fight," she said. "They was shooting arrows and that... I want my dad," she said more loudly, and felt herself beginning to cry.

"Well, you're quite safe here until he comes," said the doctor.

"But I saw them shooting arrows!"

246

"Ah, you thought you did. That often happens in the intense cold, Lizzie. You fall asleep and have bad dreams and you can't remember what's true and what isn't. That wasn't a fight, don't worry. Your father is safe and sound and he'll be looking for you now and soon he'll come here because this is the only place for hundreds of miles, you know, and what a surprise he'll have to find you safe and sound! Now Sister Clara will take you along to the dormitory where you'll meet some other little girls and boys who got lost in the wilderness just like you. Off you go. We'll have another little talk in the morning."

Lyra stood up, clutching her doll, and Pantalaimon hopped on to her shoulder as the nurse opened the door to lead them out.

More corridors, and Lyra was tired by now, so sleepy she kept yawning and could hardly lift her feet in the woolly slippers they'd given her. Pantalaimon was drooping, and he had to change to a mouse and settle inside her dressing-gown pocket. Lyra had the impression of a row of beds, children's faces, a pillow, and then she was asleep.

Someone was shaking her. The first thing she did was to feel at her waist, and both tins were still there, still safe; so she tried to open her eyes, but oh, it was hard; she had never felt so sleepy.

"Wake up! Wake up!"

It was a whisper in more than one voice. With a huge effort, as if she were pushing a boulder up a slope, Lyra forced herself to wake up.

In the dim light from a very low-powered anbaric bulb over the doorway she saw three other girls clustered around her. It wasn't easy to see, because her eyes were slow to focus, but they seemed about her own age, and they were speaking English.

"She's awake."

"They gave her sleeping pills. Must've…"

"What's your name?"

"Lizzie," Lyra mumbled.

"Is there a load more new kids coming?" demanded one of the girls.

"Dunno. Just me."

"Where'd they get you then?"

Lyra struggled to sit up. She didn't remember taking a sleeping pill, but there might well have been something in the drink she'd had. Her head felt full of eiderdown, and there was a faint pain throbbing behind her eyes.

"Where is this place?"

"Middle of nowhere. They don't tell us."

"They usually bring more'n one kid at a time…"

"What do they do?" Lyra managed to ask, gathering her doped wits as Pantalaimon stirred into wakefulness with her.

"We dunno," said the girl who was doing most of the talking. She was a tall, red-haired girl with quick twitchy movements and a strong London accent. "They sort of measure us and do these tests and that –"

"They measure Dust," said another girl, friendly and plump and dark-haired.

"*You* don't know," said the first girl.

"They do," said the third, a subdued-looking child cuddling her rabbit-dæmon. "I heard 'em talking."

"Then they take us away one by one and that's all we know. No one comes back," said the redhead.

"There's this boy, right," said the plump girl, "he reckons –"

"Don't tell her that!" said the redhead. "Not yet."

"Is there boys here as well?" said Lyra.

"Yeah. There's lots of us. There's about thirty, I reckon."

"More'n that," said the plump girl. "More like forty."

"Except they keep taking us away," said the redhead. "They usually start off with bringing a whole bunch here, and then there's a lot of us, and one by one they all disappear."

"They're Gobblers," said the plump girl. "You know Gobblers. We was all scared of 'em till we was caught…"

Lyra was gradually coming more and more awake. The other girls' dæmons, apart from the rabbit, were close by listening at the door, and no one spoke above a whisper. Lyra asked their names. The red-haired girl was Annie, the dark plump one Bella, the thin one Martha. They didn't know the names of the boys, because the two sexes were kept apart for most of the time. They weren't treated badly.

"It's all right here," said Bella, "there's not much to do, except they give us tests and make us do exercises and then they measure us and take our temperature and stuff. It's just boring really."

"Except when Mrs Coulter comes," said Annie.

Lyra had to stop herself crying out, and Pantalaimon fluttered his wings so sharply that the other girls noticed.

"He's nervous," said Lyra, soothing him. "They must've gave us some sleeping pills, like you said, 'cause we're all dozy. Who's Mrs Coulter?"

"She's the one who trapped us, most of us, anyway," said Martha. "They all talk about her, the other kids. When she comes, you know there's going to be kids disappearing."

"She likes watching the kids, when they take us away, she likes seeing what they do to us. This boy Simon, he reckons they kill us, and Mrs Coulter watches."

"They *kill* us?" said Lyra, shuddering.

"Must do. 'Cause no one comes back."

"They're always going on about dæmons too," said Bella. "Weighing them and measuring them and all…"

"They *touch* your *dæmons?*"

"No! God! They put scales there and your dæmon has to get on them and change, and they make notes and take pictures. And they put you in this cabinet and measure Dust, all the time, they never stop measuring Dust."

"What dust?" said Lyra.

"We dunno," said Annie. "Just something from space. Not real dust. If you en't got any Dust, that's good. But everyone gets Dust in the end."

"You know what I heard Simon say?" said Bella. "He said that the Tartars make holes in their skulls to let the Dust in."

"Yeah, *he'd* know," said Annie scornfully. "I think I'll ask Mrs Coulter when she comes."

"You wouldn't dare!" said Martha admiringly.

"I would."

"When's she coming?" said Lyra.

"The day after tomorrow," said Annie.

A cold drench of terror went down Lyra's spine, and Pantalaimon crept very close. She had one day in which to find Roger and discover whatever she could about this place, and either escape or be rescued; and if all the gyptians had been killed, who would help the children stay alive in the icy wilderness?

The other girls went on talking, but Lyra and Pantalaimon nestled down deep in the bed and tried to get warm, knowing that for hundreds of miles all around her little bed there was nothing but fear.

15

The Dæmon-Cages

*I*t wasn't Lyra's way to brood; she was a sanguine and practical child, and besides, she wasn't imaginative. No one with much imagination would have thought seriously that it was possible to come all this way and rescue her friend Roger; or, having thought it, an imaginative child would immediately have come up with several ways in which it was impossible. Being a practised liar doesn't mean you have a powerful imagination. Many good liars have no imagination at all; it's that which gives their lies such wide-eyed conviction.

So now she was in the hands of the Oblation Board, Lyra didn't fret herself into terror about what had happened to the gyptians. They were all good fighters, and even though Pantalaimon said he'd seen John Faa shot, he might have been mistaken; or if he wasn't mistaken, John Faa might not have been seriously hurt. It had been bad luck that she'd fallen into the hands of the Samoyeds, but the gyptians would be along soon to rescue her, and if they couldn't manage it, nothing would stop Iorek Byrnison from getting her out; and then they'd fly to Svalbard in Lee Scoresby's balloon and rescue Lord Asriel.

In her mind, it was as easy as that.

So next morning, when she awoke in the dormitory, she was curious and ready to deal with whatever the day would bring. And eager to see Roger – in particular, eager to see him before he saw her.

She didn't have long to wait. The children in their different dormitories were woken at half-past seven by the nurses who looked after them. They washed and dressed and went with the others to the canteen for breakfast.

And there was Roger.

He was sitting with five other boys at a table just inside the door. The queue for the hatch went right past them, and she was able to pretend to drop a handkerchief and crouch to pick it up, bending low next to his chair, so that Pantalaimon could speak to Roger's dæmon Salcilia.

She was a chaffinch, and she fluttered so wildly that Pantalaimon had to be a cat and leap at her, pinning her down to whisper. Such brisk fights or scuffles between children's dæmons were common, luckily, and no one took much notice, but Roger went pale at once. Lyra had never seen anyone so white. He looked up at the blank haughty stare she gave him, and the colour flooded back into his cheeks as he brimmed over with hope, excitement, and joy; and only Pantalaimon, shaking Salcilia firmly, was able to keep Roger from shouting out and leaping up to greet his Jordan playmate.

Lyra looked away, acting as disdainfully as she could, and rolled her eyes at her new friends, leaving Pantalaimon to explain. The four girls collected their trays of cornflakes and toast and sat together, an instant gang, excluding everyone else in order to gossip about them.

You can't keep a large group of children in one place for long without giving them plenty to do, and in some ways Bolvangar was run like a school, with timetabled activities such as gymnastics and "art". Boys and girls were kept separate except for breaks and mealtimes, so it wasn't until mid-morning, after an hour and a half of sewing directed by one of the nurses, that Lyra had the chance to talk to Roger. But it had to look natural; that was the difficulty. All the children there were more or less at the same age, and it was the age when boys talk to boys and girls to girls, each making a conspicuous point of ignoring the opposite sex.

She found her chance in the canteen again, when the children came in for a drink and a biscuit. Lyra sent Pantalaimon, as a fly, to talk to Salcilia on the wall next to their table while she and Roger kept quietly in their separate groups. It was difficult to talk while your dæmon's attention was somewhere else, so Lyra pretended to look glum and rebellious as she sipped her milk with the other girls. Half her thoughts were with the tiny buzz of talk between the dæmons, and she wasn't really listening, but at one point she heard another girl with bright blonde hair say a name that made her sit up.

It was the name of Tony Makarios. As Lyra's attention snapped towards that, Pantalaimon had to slow down his whispered conversation with Roger's dæmon, and both children listened to what the girl was saying.

"No, I know why they took him," she said, as heads clustered close nearby. "It was because his dæmon didn't change. They thought he was older than he looked, or summing, and he weren't really a young kid. But really his dæmon never changed very often because Tony hisself never thought much about anything. I seen her change. She was called Ratter…"

"Why are they so interested in dæmons?" said Lyra.

"No one knows," said the blonde girl.

"I know," said one boy who'd been listening. "What they do is kill your dæmon and then see if you die."

"Well how come they do it over and over with different kids?" said someone. "They'd only need to do it once, wouldn't they?"

"I know what they do," said the first girl.

She had everyone's attention now. But because they didn't want to let the staff know what they were talking about, they had to adopt a strange, half-careless, indifferent manner, while listening with passionate curiosity.

"How?" said someone.

" 'Cause I was with him when they came for him. We was in the linen room," she said.

She was blushing hotly. If she was expecting jeers and teasing, they didn't come. All the children were subdued, and no one even smiled.

The girl went on "We was keeping quiet and then the nurse came in, the one with the soft voice. And she says, Come on, Tony, I know you're there, come on, we won't hurt you… And he says, What's going to happen? And she says, We just put you to sleep, and then we do a little operation, and then you wake up safe and sound. But Tony didn't believe her. He says –"

"The holes!" said someone. "They make a hole in your head like the Tartars! I *bet*!"

"Shut up! What else did the nurse say?" someone else put in. By this time, a dozen or more children were clustered around her table, their dæmons as urgent to know as they were, all wide-eyed and tense.

The blonde girl went on, "Tony wanted to know what they was gonna do with Ratter, see. And the nurse says, Well, she's going to sleep too, just like when you do. And Tony says, You're gonna kill her, en't yer? I know you are. We all know that's what happens. And the nurse says, No, of course not. It's just a little operation. Just a little cut. It won't even hurt, but we put you to sleep to make sure."

All the room had gone quiet now. The nurse who'd been supervising had left for a moment, and the hatch to the kitchen was shut so no one could hear from there.

"What sort of cut?" said a boy, his voice quiet and frightened. "Did she say what sort of cut?"

"She just said, It's something to make you more grown up. She said everyone had to have it, that's why grown-ups' dæmons don't change like ours do. So they have a cut to make them one shape for ever, and that's how you get grown up."

"But –"

"Does that mean –"

"What, all grown-ups've had this cut?"

"What about –"

Suddenly all the voices stopped as if they themselves had been cut, and all eyes turned to the door. Sister Clara stood there, bland and mild and matter-of-fact, and beside her was a man in a white coat whom Lyra hadn't seen before.

"Bridget McGinn," he said.

The blonde girl stood up trembling. Her squirrel-dæmon clutched her breast.

"Yes, sir?" she said, her voice hardly audible.

"Finish your drink and come with Sister Clara," he said. "The rest of you run along and go to your classes."

Obediently the children stacked their mugs on the stainless-steel trolley before leaving in silence. No one looked at Bridget McGinn except Lyra, and she saw the blonde girl's face vivid with fear.

The rest of that morning was spent in exercise. There was a small gymnasium at the Station, because it was hard to exercise outside during the long Polar night, and each group of children took turns to play in there, under the supervision of a nurse. They had to form teams and throw balls around, and at first Lyra, who had never in her life played at anything like this, was at a loss what to do. But she was quick and athletic, and a natural leader, and soon found herself enjoying it. The shouts of the children, the shrieks and hoots of the dæmons, filled the little gymnasium and soon banished fearful thoughts; which of course was exactly what the exercise was intended to do.

At lunchtime, when the children were queueing once again in the canteen, Lyra felt Pantalaimon give a chirrup of recognition, and turned to find Billy Costa standing just behind her.

"Roger told me you was here," he muttered.

"Your brother's coming, and John Faa and a whole band of gyptians," she said. "They're going to take you home."

He nearly cried aloud with joy, but subdued the cry into a cough.

"And you got to call me Lizzie," Lyra said, "*never* Lyra. And you got to tell me everything you know, right."

They sat together, with Roger close by. It was easier to do this at lunchtime, when children spent more time coming and going between the tables and the hatch and the canteen was crowded. Under the clatter of knives and forks and plates Billy and Roger both told her as much as they knew. Billy had heard from a nurse that children who had had the operation were often taken to hostels further south, which might explain how Tony Makarios came to be wandering in the wild. But Roger had something even more interesting to tell her.

"I found a hiding-place," he said.

"What? Where?"

"See that picture…" He meant the big photogram of the tropical beach. "If you look in the top right corner, you see that ceiling panel?"

The ceiling consisted of large rectangular panels set in a framework of metal strips, and the corner of the panel above the picture had lifted slightly.

"I saw that," Roger said, "and I thought the others might be like it, so I lifted 'em, and they're all loose. They just lift up. Me and this boy tried it one night in our dormitory, before they took him away. There's a space up there and you can crawl inside…"

"How far can you crawl in the ceiling?"

"I dunno. We just went in a little way. We reckoned when it was time we could hide up there, but they'd probably find us."

Lyra saw it not as a hiding-place but as a highway. It was the best thing she'd heard since she'd arrived. But before they could talk any more, a doctor banged on a table with a spoon and began to speak.

"Listen, children," he said. "Listen carefully. Every so often we have to have a fire drill. It's very important that we all get dressed properly and make our way outside without any panic. So we're going to have a practice fire drill this afternoon. When the bell rings you must stop whatever you're doing and do what the nearest grown-up says. Remember where they take you. That's the place you must go to if there's a real fire."

Well, thought Lyra, there's an idea.

During the first part of the afternoon, Lyra and four other girls were tested for Dust. The doctors didn't say that was what they were doing, but it was easy to guess. They were taken one by one to a laboratory, and of course this made them all very frightened; how cruel it would be, Lyra thought, if she perished without striking a blow at them! But they were not going to do that operation just yet, it seemed.

"We want to make some measurements," the doctor explained. It was hard to tell the difference between these people: all the men looked similar in their white coats and with their clipboards and pencils, and the women resembled one another too, the uniforms and their strange bland calm manner making them all look like sisters.

"I was measured yesterday," Lyra said.

"Ah, we're making different measurements today. Stand on the metal plate – oh, slip your shoes off first. Hold your dæmon, if you like. Look forward, that's it, stare at the little green light. Good girl…"

Something flashed. The doctor made her face the other way and then to left and right, and each time something clicked and flashed.

"That's fine. Now come over to this machine and put your hand into the tube. Nothing to harm you, I promise. Straighten your fingers. That's it."

"What *are* you measuring?" she said. "Is it Dust?"

"Who told you about Dust?"

"One of the other girls, I don't know her name. She said we was all over Dust. I en't dusty, at least I don't think I am. I had a shower yesterday."

"Ah, it's a different sort of dust. You can't see it with your ordinary eyesight. It's a special dust. Now clench your fist – that's right. Good. Now if you feel around in there you'll find a sort of handle thing – got that? Take hold of that, there's a good girl. Now can you put your other hand over this way – rest it on this brass globe. Good. Fine. Now you'll feel a slight tingling, nothing to worry about, it's just a slight anbaric current…"

Pantalaimon, in his most tense and wary wildcat-form, prowled with lightning-eyed suspicion around the apparatus, continually returning to rub himself against Lyra.

She was sure by now that they weren't going to perform the operation on her yet, and sure too that her disguise as Lizzie Brooks was secure; so she risked a question.

"Why do you cut people's dæmons away?"

"What? Who's been talking to you about that?"

"This girl, I dunno her name. She said you cut people's dæmons away."

"Nonsense…"

He was agitated, though. She went on:

"'Cause you take people out one by one and they never come back. And some people reckon you just kill 'em, and other people say different, and this girl told me you cut –"

"It's not true at all. When we take children out, it's because it's time for them to move on to another place. They're growing up. I'm afraid your friend is alarming herself. Nothing of the sort! Don't even think about it. Who is your friend?"

"I only come here yesterday, I don't know anyone's name."

"What does she look like?"

"I forget. I think she had sort of brown hair … light brown, maybe … I dunno."

The doctor went to speak quietly to the nurse. As the two of them conferred, Lyra watched their dæmons. This nurse's was a pretty bird, just as neat and incurious as Sister Clara's dog, and the doctor's was a large heavy moth. Neither moved. They were awake, for the bird's eyes were bright and the moth's feelers waved languidly, but they weren't animated, as she would have expected them to be. Perhaps they weren't really anxious or curious at all.

Presently the doctor came back and they went on with the examination, weighing her and Pantalaimon separately, looking at her from behind a special screen, measuring her heartbeat, placing her under a little nozzle that hissed and gave off a smell like fresh air.

In the middle of one of the tests, a loud bell began to ring and kept ringing.

"The fire alarm," said the doctor, sighing. "Very well. Lizzie, follow Sister Betty."

"But all their outdoor clothes are down in the dormitory building, Doctor. She can't go outside like this. Should we go there first, do you think?"

He was annoyed at having his experiments interrupted, and snapped his fingers in irritation.

"I suppose this is just the sort of thing the practice is meant to show up," he said. "What a nuisance."

"When I came yesterday," Lyra said helpfully, "Sister Clara put my other clothes in a cupboard in that first room where she looked at me. The one next door. I could wear them."

"Good idea!" said the nurse. "Quick, then."

With a secret glee, Lyra hurried there behind the nurse and retrieved her proper furs and leggings and boots, and pulled them on quickly while the nurse dressed herself in coal-silk.

Then they hurried out. In the wide arena in front of the main group of buildings, a hundred or so people, adults and children, were milling about: some in excitement, some in irritation, many just bewildered.

"See?" one adult was saying. "It's worth doing this to find out what chaos we'd be in with a real fire."

Someone was blowing a whistle and waving their arms, but no one was taking much notice. Lyra saw Roger and beckoned. Roger tugged Billy Costa's arm and soon all three of them were together in a maelstrom of running children.

"No one'll notice if we take a look around," said Lyra. "It'll take 'em ages to count everyone, and we can say we just followed someone else and got lost."

They waited till most of the grown-ups were looking the other way, and then Lyra scooped up some snow and rammed it into a loose powdery snowball, and hurled it at random into the crowd. In a moment all the children were doing it, and the air was full of flying snow. Screams of laughter covered completely the shouts of the adults trying to regain control, and then the three children were around the corner and out of sight.

The snow was so thick that they couldn't move quickly, but it didn't seem to matter; no one was following. Lyra and the others scrambled over the curved roof of one of the tunnels, and found themselves in a strange moonscape of regular hummocks and hollows, all swathed in white under the black sky and lit by reflections from the lights around the arena.

"What we looking for?" said Billy.

"Dunno. Just looking," said Lyra, and led the way to a squat, square building a little apart from the rest, with a low-powered anbaric light at the corner.

The hubbub from behind was as loud as ever, but more distant. Clearly the children were making the most of their freedom, and Lyra hoped they'd keep it up for as long as they could. She moved around the edge of the square building, looking for a window. The roof was only seven feet or so off the ground, and unlike the other buildings, it had no roofed tunnel to connect it with the rest of the Station.

There was no window, but there was a door. A notice above it said ENTRY STRICTLY FORBIDDEN in red letters.

Lyra set her hand on it to try, but before she could turn the handle, Roger said:

"Look! A bird! Or –"

His *or* was an exclamation of doubt, because the creature swooping down from the black sky was no bird at all: it was someone Lyra had seen before.

"The witch's dæmon!"

The goose beat his great wings, raising a flurry of snow as he landed.

"Greetings, Lyra," he said. "I followed you here, though you didn't see me. I have been waiting for you to come out into the open. What is happening?"

She told him quickly.

"Where are the gyptians?" she said. "Is John Faa safe? Did they fight off the Samoyeds?"

"Most of them are safe. John Faa is wounded, though not severely. The men who took you were hunters and raiders who often prey on parties of travellers, and alone they can travel more quickly than a large party. The gyptians are still a day's journey away."

The two boys were staring in fear at the goose-dæmon and at Lyra's familiar manner with him, because of course they'd never seen a dæmon without his human before, and they knew little about witches.

Lyra said to them, "Listen, you better go and keep watch, right. Billy, you go that way, and Roger, watch out the way we just come. We en't got long."

They ran off to do as she said, and then Lyra turned back to the door.

"Why are you trying to get in there?" said the goose-dæmon.

"Because of what they do here. They cut –" she lowered her voice – "they cut people's dæmons away. Children's. And I think maybe they do it in here. At least, there's *something* here, and I was going to look. But it's locked…"

"I can open it," said the goose, and beat his wings once or twice, throwing snow up against the door; and as he did, Lyra heard something turn in the lock.

"Go in carefully," said the dæmon.

Lyra pulled opened the door against the snow and slipped inside. The goose-dæmon came with her. Pantalaimon was agitated and fearful, but he didn't want the witch's dæmon to see his fear, so he had flown to Lyra's breast and taken sanctuary inside her furs.

As soon as her eyes had adjusted to the light, Lyra saw why.

In a series of glass cases on shelves around the walls were all the dæmons of the severed children: ghost-like forms of cats, or birds, or rats, or other creatures, each bewildered and frightened and as pale as smoke.

The witch's dæmon gave a cry of anger, and Lyra clutched Pantalaimon to her and said, "Don't look! Don't look!"

"Where are the children of these dæmons?" said the goose-dæmon, shaking with rage.

Lyra explained fearfully about her encounter with little Tony Makarios, and looked over her shoulder at the poor caged dæmons, who were clustering forwards pressing their pale faces to the glass. Lyra could hear faint cries of pain and misery. In the dim light from a low-powered anbaric bulb she could see a name on a card at the front of each case, and yes, there was an empty one with *Tony Makarios* on it. There were four or five other empty ones with names on, too.

"I want to let these poor things go!" she said fiercely. "I'm going to smash the glass and let 'em out —"

And she looked around for something to do it with, but the place was bare. The goose-dæmon said, "Wait."

He was a witch's dæmon, and much older than she was, and stronger.

She had to do as he said.

"We must make these people think someone forgot to lock the place and shut the cages," he explained. "If they see broken glass and footprints in the snow, how long do you think your disguise will last? And it must hold out till the gyptians come. Now do exactly as I say: take a handful of snow, and when I tell you, blow a little of it against each cage in turn."

She ran outside. Roger and Billy were still on guard, and there was still a noise of shrieking and laughter from the arena, because only a minute or so had gone by.

She grabbed a big double handful of the light powdery snow, and then came back to do as the goose-dæmon said. As she blew a little snow on each cage, the goose made a clicking sound in his throat, and the catch at the front of the cage came open.

When she had unlocked them all, she lifted the front of the first one, and the pale form of a sparrow fluttered out, but fell to the ground before she could fly. The goose tenderly bent and nudged her upright with his beak, and the sparrow became a mouse, staggering and confused. Pantalaimon leapt down to comfort her.

Lyra worked quickly, and within a few minutes every dæmon was free. Some were trying to speak, and they clustered around her feet and even tried to pluck at her leggings, though the taboo held them back. She could tell why, poor things; they missed the heavy solid warmth of their humans' bodies; just as Pantalaimon would have done, they longed to press themselves against a heartbeat.

"Now, quick," said the goose. "Lyra, you must run back and mingle with the other children. Be brave, child. The gyptians are coming as fast as they can. I must help these poor dæmons to find their people…" He came closer and said quietly, "But they'll never be one again.

They're sundered for ever. This is the most wicked thing I have ever seen... Leave the footprints you've made; I'll cover them up. Hurry now..."

"Oh, please! Before you go! Witches... They do fly, don't they? I wasn't dreaming when I saw them flying the other night?"

"Yes, child; why?"

"Could they pull a balloon?"

"Undoubtedly, but –"

"Will Serafina Pekkala be coming?"

"There isn't time to explain the politics of witch-nations. There are vast powers involved here, and Serafina Pekkala must guard the interests of her clan. But it may be that what's happening here is part of all that's happening elsewhere. Lyra, you're needed inside. Run, run!"

She ran, and Roger, who was watching wide-eyed as the pale dæmons drifted out of the building, waded towards her through the thick snow.

"They're – it's like the crypt in Jordan – they're dæmons!"

"Yes, hush. Don't tell Billy, though. Don't tell anyone yet. Come on back."

Behind them, the goose was beating his wings powerfully, throwing snow over the tracks they'd made; and near him, the lost dæmons were clustering or drifting away, crying little bleak cries of loss and longing. When the footprints were covered, the goose turned to herd the pale dæmons together. He spoke, and one by one they changed, though you could see the effort it cost them, until they were all birds; and like fledglings they followed the witch's dæmon, fluttering and falling and running through the snow after him, and finally, with great difficulty, taking off. They rose in a ragged line, pale and spectral against the deep black sky, slowly gaining height, feeble and erratic though some of them

265

were, and though others lost their will and fluttered downwards; but the great grey goose wheeled round and nudged them back, herding them gently on until they were lost against the profound dark.

Roger was tugging at Lyra's arm.

"Quick," he said, "they're nearly ready."

They stumbled away to join Billy, who was beckoning from the corner of the main building. The children were tired now, or else the adults had regained some authority, because people were lining up raggedly by the main door, with much jostling and pushing. Lyra and the other two slipped out from the corner and mingled with them, but before they did, Lyra said:

"Pass the word around among all the kids – they got to be ready to escape. They got to know where the outdoor clothes are and be ready to get them and run out as soon as we give the signal. And they got to keep this a deadly secret, understand?"

Billy nodded, and Roger said, "What's the signal?"

"The fire bell," said Lyra. "When the time comes, I'll set it off."

They waited to be counted off. If anyone in the Oblation Board had had anything to do with a school, they would have arranged this better: because they had no regular group to go to, each child had to be ticked off against the complete list, and of course they weren't in alphabetical order; and none of the adults was used to keeping control. So there was a good deal of confusion, despite the fact that no one was running around any more.

Lyra watched and noticed. They weren't very good at this at all. They were slack in a lot of ways, these people; they grumbled about fire drills, they didn't know where the outdoor clothes should be kept, they couldn't get children to stand in line properly; and their slackness might be to her advantage.

They had almost finished when there came another distraction, though, and from Lyra's point of view, it was the worst possible.

She heard the sound as everyone else did. Heads began to turn and scan the dark sky for the zeppelin, whose gas-engine was throbbing clearly in the still air.

The one lucky thing was that it was coming from the direction opposite to the one in which the grey goose had flown. But that was the only comfort. Very soon it was visible, and a murmur of excitement went around the crowd. Its fat sleek silver form drifted over the avenue of lights, and its own lights blazed downwards from the nose and the cabin slung beneath the body.

The pilot cut the speed and began the complex business of adjusting the height. Lyra realized what the stout mast was for: of course, it was a mooring mast. As the adults ushered the children inside, with everyone staring back and pointing, the ground crew clambered up the ladders in the mast and prepared to attach the mooring cables. The engines were roaring, and snow was swirling up from the ground, and the faces of passengers showed in the cabin windows.

Lyra looked, and there was no mistake. Pantalaimon clutched at her, became a wildcat, hissed in hatred, because looking out with curiosity was the beautiful dark-haired head of Mrs Coulter, with her golden dæmon in her lap.

16

The Silver Guillotine

*L*yra ducked her head at once under the shelter of her wolverine hood, and shuffled in through the double doors with the other children. Time enough later to worry about what she'd say when they came face to face: she had another problem to deal with first, and that was how to hide her furs where she could get at them without asking permission.

But luckily, there was such disorder inside, with the adults trying to hurry the children through so as to clear the way for the passengers from the zeppelin, that no one was watching very carefully. Lyra slipped out of the anorak, the leggings and the boots and bundled them up as small as she could before shoving through the crowded corridors to her dormitory.

Quickly she dragged a locker to the corner, stood on it, and pushed at the ceiling. The panel lifted, just as Roger had said, and into the space beyond she thrust the boots and leggings. As an afterthought, she took the alethiometer from her pouch and hid it in the inmost pocket of the anorak before shoving that through too.

She jumped down, pushed back the locker, and whispered to

Pantalaimon, "We must just pretend to be stupid till she sees us, and then say we were kidnapped. And nothing about the gyptians or Iorek Byrnison especially."

Because Lyra now realized, if she hadn't done so before, that all the fear in her nature was drawn to Mrs Coulter as a compass needle is drawn to the Pole. All the other things she'd seen, and even the hideous cruelty of the intercision, she could cope with; she was strong enough; but the thought of that sweet face and gentle voice, the image of that golden playful monkey, was enough to melt her stomach and make her pale and nauseous.

But the gyptians were coming. Think of that. Think of Iorek Byrnison. And don't give yourself away, she said, and drifted back towards the canteen, where a lot of noise was coming from.

Children were lining up to get hot drinks, some of them still in their coal-silk anoraks. Their talk was all of the zeppelin and its passenger.

"It was *her* – with the monkey-dæmon –"

"Did she get you, too?"

"She said she'd write to my mum and dad and I bet she never..."

"She never told us about kids getting killed. She never said nothing about that."

"That monkey, he's the *worst* – he caught my Karossa and nearly killed her – I could feel all weak..."

They were as frightened as Lyra was. She found Annie and the others, and sat down.

"Listen," she said, "can you keep a secret?"

"Yeah!"

The three faces turned to her, vivid with expectation.

"There's a plan to escape," Lyra said quietly. "There's some people coming to take us away, right, and they'll be here in about a day. Maybe sooner. What we all got to do is be ready as soon as the signal goes and get our cold-weather clothes at once and run out. No waiting about. You just got to run. Only if you don't get your anoraks and boots and stuff you'll die of cold."

"What signal?" Annie demanded.

"The fire bell, like this afternoon. It's all organized. All the kids're going to know and none of the grown-ups. Especially not *her*."

Their eyes were gleaming with hope and excitement. And all through the canteen the message was being passed around. Lyra could tell that the atmosphere had changed. Outside, the children had been energetic and eager for play; then when they had seen Mrs Coulter they were bubbling with a suppressed hysterical fear; but now there was a control and purpose to their talkativeness. Lyra marvelled at the effect hope could have.

She watched through the open doorway, but carefully, ready to duck her head, because there were adult voices coming, and then Mrs Coulter herself was briefly visible, looking in and smiling at the happy children, with their hot drinks and their cake, so warm and well-fed. A little shiver ran almost instantaneously through the whole canteen, and every child was still and silent, staring at her.

Mrs Coulter smiled and passed on without a word. Little by little the talk started again.

Lyra said, "Where do they go to talk?"

"Probably the conference room," said Annie. "They took us there once," she added, meaning her and her dæmon. "There was about twenty grown-ups there and one of 'em was giving a lecture and I had to stand there and do what he told me, like seeing how far my Kyrillion could go away from me, and then he hypnotized me and did some other things… It's a big room with a lot of chairs and tables and a little platform. It's behind the front office. Hey, I bet *they're* going to pretend the fire drill went off all right. I bet they're scared of her, same as we are…"

For the rest of the day, Lyra stayed close to the other girls, watching, saying little, remaining inconspicuous. There was exercise, there was sewing, there was supper, there was playtime in the lounge: a big shabby room with board games and a few tattered books and a table-tennis table. At some point Lyra and the others became aware that there was some kind of subdued emergency going on, because the adults were hurrying to and fro or standing in anxious groups talking urgently. Lyra guessed they'd discovered the dæmons' escape, and were wondering how it had happened.

But she didn't see Mrs Coulter, which was a relief. When it was time for bed, she knew she had to let the other girls into her confidence.

"Listen," she said, "do they ever come round and see if we're asleep?"

"They just look in once," said Bella. "They just flash a lantern round, they don't really look."

"Good. 'Cause I'm going to go and look round. There's a way through the ceiling that this boy showed me…"

She explained, and before she'd even finished, Annie said, "I'll come with you!"

"No, you better not, 'cause it'll be easier if there's just one person missing. You can all say you fell asleep and you don't know where I've gone."

"But if I came with you –"

"More likely to get caught," said Lyra.

Their two dæmons were staring at each other, Pantalaimon as a wild-cat, Annie's Kyrillion as a fox. They were quivering. Pantalaimon uttered the lowest, softest hiss and bared his teeth, and Kyrillion turned aside and began to groom himself unconcernedly.

"All right then," said Annie, resigned.

It was quite common for struggles between children to be settled by their dæmons in this way, with one accepting the dominance of the other. Their humans accepted the outcome without resentment, on the whole, so Lyra knew that Annie would do as she asked.

They all contributed items of clothing to bulk out Lyra's bed and make it look as if she was still there, and swore to say they knew nothing about it. Then Lyra listened at the door to make sure no one was coming, jumped up on the locker, pushed up the panel and hauled herself through.

"Just don't say anything," she whispered down to the three faces watching.

Then she dropped the panel gently back into place and looked around.

She was crouching in a narrow metal channel supported in a framework of girders and struts. The panels of the ceilings were slightly translucent, so some light came up from below, and in the faint gleam Lyra could see this narrow space (only two feet or so in height) extending in all directions around her. It was crowded with metal ducts and pipes, and it would be easy to get lost in, but provided she kept to the metal and avoided putting any weight on the panels, and as long as she made no noise, she should be able to go from one end of the Station to the other.

"It's just like back in Jordan, Pan," she whispered, "looking in the Retiring Room."

"If you hadn't done that, none of this would have happened," he whispered back.

"Then it's up to me to undo it, isn't it?"

She got her bearings, working out approximately which direction the conference room was in, and then set off. It was a far from easy journey. She had to move on hands and knees, because the space was too low to crouch in, and every so often she had to squeeze under a big square duct or lift herself over some heating pipes. The metal channels she crawled in followed the tops of internal walls, as far as she could tell, and as long as she stayed in them she felt a comforting solidity below her; but they were very narrow, and had sharp edges, so sharp that she cut her knuckles and her knee on them, and before long she was sore all over, and cramped, and dusty.

But she knew roughly where she was, and she could see the dark bulk of her furs crammed in above the dormitory to guide her back. She could tell where a room was empty because the panels were dark, and from time to time she heard voices from below, and stopped to listen, but it was only the cooks in the kitchen, or the nurses in what Lyra, in her Jordan way, thought of as their common room. They were saying nothing interesting, so she moved on.

At last she came to the area where the conference room should be, according to her calculations; and sure enough, there was an area free of any pipework, where air-conditioning and heating ducts led down at one end, and where all the panels in a wide rectangular space were lit evenly. She placed her ear to the panel, and heard a murmur of male adult voices, so she knew she had found the right place.

She listened carefully, and then inched her way along till she was as close as she could get to the speakers. Then she lay full-length in the metal channel and leaned her head sideways to hear as well as she could.

There was the occasional clink of cutlery, or the sound of glass on glass as drink was poured, so they were having dinner as they talked. There were four voices, she thought, including Mrs Coulter's. The other three were men. They seemed to be discussing the escaped dæmons.

"But who is in charge of supervising that section?" said Mrs Coulter's gentle musical voice.

"A research student called McKay," said one of the men. "But there are automatic mechanisms to prevent this sort of thing happening –"

"They didn't work," she said.

"With respect, they did, Mrs Coulter. McKay assures us that he locked all the cages when he left the building at eleven hundred hours today. The outer door of course would not have been open in any case, because he entered and left by the inner door, as he normally did. There's a code that has to be entered in the ordinator controlling the locks, and there's a record in its memory of his doing so. Unless that's done, an alarm goes off."

"But the alarm didn't go off," she said.

"It did. Unfortunately, it rang when everyone was outside, taking part in the fire drill."

"But when you went back inside –"

"Unfortunately both alarms are on the same circuit; that's a design fault that will have to be rectified. What it meant was that when the fire bell was turned off after the practice, the laboratory alarm was turned off as well. Even then it would still have been picked up, because of the normal checks that would have taken place after every disruption of routine; but by that time, Mrs Coulter, you had arrived unexpectedly, and if you recall, you asked specifically to meet the laboratory staff there and then, in your room. Consequently, no one returned to the laboratory until some time later."

"I see," said Mrs Coulter coldly. "In that case, the dæmons must have been released during the fire drill itself. And that widens the list of suspects to include every adult in the Station. Had you considered that?"

"Had you considered that it might have been done by a child?" said someone else.

She was silent, and the second man went on:

"Every adult had a task to do, and every task would have taken their full attention, and every task was done. There is no possibility that any of the staff here could have opened the door. None. So either someone came from outside altogether with the intention of doing that, or one of the children managed to find his way there, open the door and the cages, and return to the front of the main building."

"And what are you doing to investigate?" she said. "No; on second thoughts, don't tell me. Please understand, Dr Cooper, I'm not criticizing out of malice. We have to be quite extraordinarily careful. It was an atrocious lapse to have allowed both alarms to be on the same circuit. That must be corrected at once. Possibly the Tartar officer in charge of the guard could help your investigation? I merely mention that as a possibility. Where were the Tartars during the fire drill, by the way? I suppose you have considered that?"

"Yes, we have," said the man wearily. "The guard was fully occupied on patrol, every man. They keep meticulous records."

"I'm sure you're doing your very best," she said. "Well, there we are. A great pity. But enough of that for now. Tell me about the new separator."

Lyra felt a thrill of fear. There was only one thing this could mean.

"Ah," said the doctor, relieved to find the conversation turning to another subject, "there's a real advance. With the first model we could never entirely overcome the risk of the patient dying of shock, but we've improved that no end."

"The Skraelings did it better by hand," said a man who hadn't spoken yet.

"Centuries of practice," said the other man.

"But simply *tearing* was the only option for some time," said the main speaker, "however distressing that was to the adult operators. If you remember, we had to discharge quite a number for reasons of stress-related anxiety. But the first big breakthrough was the use of anaesthesia combined with the Maystadt anbaric scalpel. We were able to reduce death from operative shock to below five per cent."

"And the new instrument?" said Mrs Coulter.

Lyra was trembling. The blood was pounding in her ears, and Pantalaimon was pressing his ermine-form against her side, and whispering, "Hush, Lyra, they won't do it – we won't let them do it –"

"Yes, it was a curious discovery by Lord Asriel himself that gave us the key to the new method. He discovered that an alloy of manganese and titanium has the property of insulating body from dæmon. By the way, what is happening with Lord Asriel?"

"Perhaps you haven't heard," said Mrs Coulter. "Lord Asriel is under suspended sentence of death. One of the conditions of his exile in Svalbard was that he gave up his philosophical work entirely. Unfortunately, he managed to obtain books and materials, and he's pushed his heretical investigations to the point where it's positively dangerous to let him live. At any rate, it seems that the Consistorial Court of Discipline has begun to debate the question of the sentence of death, and the probability is that it'll be carried out. But your new instrument, Doctor. How does it work?"

"Ah – yes – sentence of death, you say? Gracious God … I'm sorry. The new instrument. We're investigating what happens when the intercision is made with the patient in a conscious state, and of course that couldn't be done with the Maystadt Process. So we've developed a kind of guillotine, I suppose you could say. The blade is made of manganese and titanium alloy, and the child is placed in a compartment – like a small cabin – of alloy mesh, with the dæmon in a similar compartment connecting with it. While there is a connection, of course, the link remains. Then the blade is brought down between them, severing the link at once. They are then separate entities."

"I should like to see it," she said. "Soon, I hope. But I'm tired now. I think I'll go to bed. I want to see all the children tomorrow. We shall find out who opened that door."

There was the sound of chairs being pushed back, polite expressions, a door closing. Then Lyra heard the others sit down again, and go on talking, but more quietly.

"What is Lord Asriel up to?"

"I think he's got an entirely different idea of the nature of Dust. That's the point. It's profoundly heretical, you see, and the Consistorial Court of Discipline can't allow any other interpretation than the authorized one. And besides, he wants to experiment –"

"To experiment? With Dust?"

"Hush! Not so loud…"

"Do you think she'll make an unfavourable report?"

"No, no. I think you dealt with her very well."

"Her *attitude* worries me…"

"Not philosophical, you mean?"

"Exactly. A *personal* interest. I don't like to use the word, but it's almost ghoulish."

"That's a bit strong."

"But do you remember the first experiments, when she was so keen to see them pulled apart –"

Lyra couldn't help it: a little cry escaped her, and at the same time she tensed and shivered, and her foot knocked against a stanchion.

"What was that?"

"In the ceiling –"

"Quick!"

The sound of chairs being thrown aside, feet running, a table pulled across the floor. Lyra tried to scramble away, but there was so little space, and before she could move more than a few yards the ceiling panel beside her was thrust up suddenly, and she was looking into the startled face of a man. She was close enough to see every hair in his moustache. He was as startled as she was, but with more freedom to move, he was able to thrust a hand into the gap and seize her arm.

"A child!"

"Don't let her go –"

Lyra sank her teeth into his large freckled hand. He cried out, but didn't let go, even when she drew blood. Pantalaimon was snarling and spitting, but it was no good, the man was much stronger than she was, and he pulled and pulled until her other hand, desperately clinging to the stanchion, had to loosen, and she half-fell through into the room.

Still she didn't utter a sound. She hooked her legs over the sharp edge of the metal above, and struggled upside down, scratching, biting, punching, spitting in passionate fury. The men were gasping and grunting with pain or exertion, but they pulled and pulled.

And suddenly all the strength went out of her.

It was as if an alien hand had reached right inside where no hand had a right to be, and wrenched at something deep and precious.

She felt faint, dizzy, sick, disgusted, limp with shock.

One of the men was *holding* Pantalaimon.

He had seized Lyra's dæmon in his human hands, and poor Pan was shaking, nearly out of his mind with horror and disgust. His wildcat shape, his fur now dull with weakness, now sparking glints of anbaric alarm... He curved towards his Lyra as she reached with both hands for him...

They fell still. They were captured.

She *felt* those hands... It wasn't *allowed*... Not *supposed* to touch... *Wrong*...

"Was she on her own?"

A man was peering into the ceiling space.

"Seems to be on her own..."

"Who is she?"

"The new child."

"The one the Samoyed hunters..."

"Yes."

"You don't suppose *she* ... the dæmons..."

"Could well be. But not on her own, surely?"

"Should we tell –"

"I think that would put the seal on things, don't you?"

"I agree. Better she doesn't hear at all."

"But what can we do about this?"

"She can't go back with the other children."

"Impossible!"

"There's only one thing we *can* do, it seems to me."

"Now?"

"Have to. Can't leave it till the morning. She wants to watch."

"We could do it ourselves. No need to involve anyone else."

The man who seemed to be in charge, the man who wasn't holding either Lyra or Pantalaimon, tapped his teeth with a thumbnail. His eyes were never still; they flicked and slid and darted this way and that. Finally he nodded.

"Now. Do it now," he said. "Otherwise she'll talk. The shock will prevent that, at least. She won't remember who she is, what she saw, what she heard... Come on."

Lyra couldn't speak. She could hardly breathe. She had to let herself be carried through the Station, along white empty corridors, past rooms humming with anbaric power, past the dormitories where children slept with their dæmons on the pillow beside them, sharing their dreams; and every second of the way she watched Pantalaimon, and he reached for her, and their eyes never left each other.

Then a door which opened by means of a large wheel; a hiss of air; and a brilliantly-lit chamber with dazzling white tiles and stainless steel. The fear she felt was almost a physical pain; it was a physical pain, as they pulled her and Pantalaimon over towards a large cage of pale silver mesh, above which a great pale silver blade hung poised to separate them for ever and ever.

She found a voice at last, and screamed. The sound echoed loudly off the shiny surfaces, but the heavy door had hissed shut; she could scream and scream for ever, and not a sound would escape.

But Pantalaimon, in answer, had twisted free of those hateful hands – he was a lion, an eagle; he tore at them with vicious talons, great wings beat wildly, and then he was a wolf, a bear, a polecat – darting, snarling, slashing, a succession of transformations too quick to register, and all the time leaping, flying, dodging from one spot to another as their clumsy hands flailed and snatched at the empty air.

But they had dæmons too, of course. It wasn't two against three, it was two against six. A badger, an owl and a baboon were all just as intent to pin Pantalaimon down, and Lyra was crying to them, "Why? Why are *you* doing this? Help us! You shouldn't be helping them!"

And she kicked and bit more passionately than ever, until the man holding her gasped and let go for a moment – and she was free, and Pantalaimon sprang towards her like a spark of lightning, and she clutched him to her fierce breast, and he dug his wildcat-claws into her flesh, and every stab of pain was dear to her.

"Never! Never! Never!" she cried, and backed against the wall to defend him to their death.

But they fell on her again, three big brutal men, and she was only a child, shocked and terrified; and they tore Pantalaimon away, and threw her into one side of the cage of mesh and carried him, struggling still, around to the other. There was a mesh barrier between them, but he was still part of her, they were still joined. For a second or so more, he was still her own dear soul.

Above the panting of the men, above her own sobs, above the high wild howl of her dæmon, Lyra heard a humming sound, and saw one man (bleeding from the nose) operate a bank of switches. The other two looked up, and her eyes followed theirs. The great pale silver blade was rising slowly, catching the brilliant light. The last moment in her complete life was going to be the worst by far.

"What is going on here?"

A light, musical voice: her voice. Everything stopped.

"What are you doing? And who is this child –"

She didn't complete the word *child*, because in that instant she recognized Lyra. Through tear-blurred eyes Lyra saw her totter and clutch at a bench; her face, so beautiful and composed, grew in a moment haggard and horror-struck.

"Lyra –" she whispered.

The golden monkey darted from her side in a flash, and tugged

Pantalaimon out from the mesh cage as Lyra fell out herself. Pantalaimon pulled free of the monkey's solicitous paws and stumbled to Lyra's arms.

"Never, never," she breathed into his fur, and he pressed his beating heart to hers.

They clung together like survivors of a shipwreck, shivering on a desolate coast. Dimly she heard Mrs Coulter speaking to the men, but she couldn't even interpret her tone of voice. And then they were leaving that hateful room, and Mrs Coulter was half-carrying, half-supporting her along a corridor, and then there was a door, a bedroom, scent in the air, soft light.

Mrs Coulter laid her gently on the bed. Lyra's arm was so tight around Pantalaimon that she was trembling with the force of it. A tender hand stroked her head.

"My dear, dear child," said that sweet voice. "However did you come to be here?"

17

The Witches

*L*yra moaned and trembled uncontrollably, just as if she had been pulled out of water so cold that her heart had nearly frozen. Pantalaimon simply lay against her bare skin, inside her clothes, loving her back to herself, but aware all the time of Mrs Coulter, busy preparing a drink of something, and most of all of the golden monkey, whose hard little fingers had run swiftly over Lyra's body when only Pantalaimon could have noticed; and who had felt, around her waist, the oilskin pouch with its contents.

"Sit up, dear, and drink this," said Mrs Coulter, and her gentle arm slipped around Lyra's back and lifted her.

Lyra clenched herself, but relaxed almost at once as Pantalaimon thought to her: We're only safe as long as we pretend. She opened her eyes and found that they'd been containing tears, and to her surprise and shame she sobbed and sobbed.

Mrs Coulter made sympathetic sounds and put the drink into the monkey's hands while she mopped Lyra's eyes with a scented handkerchief.

"Cry as much as you need to, darling," said that soft voice, and Lyra determined to stop as soon as she possibly could. She struggled to hold back the tears, she pressed her lips together, she choked down the sobs that still shook her chest.

Pantalaimon played the same game: fool them, fool them. He became a mouse and crept away from Lyra's hand to sniff timidly at the drink in the monkey's clutch. It was innocuous: an infusion of camomile, nothing more. He crept back to Lyra's shoulder and whispered, "Drink it."

She sat up and took the hot cup in both hands, alternately sipping and blowing to cool it. She kept her eyes down. She must pretend harder than she'd ever done in her life.

"Lyra, darling," Mrs Coulter murmured, stroking her hair. "I thought we'd lost you for ever! What happened? Did you get lost? Did someone take you out of the flat?"

"Yeah," Lyra whispered.

"Who was it, dear?"

"A man and a woman."

"Guests at the party?"

"I think so. They said you needed something that was downstairs and I went to get it and they grabbed hold of me and took me in a car somewhere. But when they stopped I ran out quick and dodged away and they never caught me. But I didn't know where I was…"

Another sob shook her briefly, but they were weaker now, and she could pretend this one was caused by her story.

"And I just wandered about trying to find my way back, only these Gobblers caught me… And they put me in a van with some other kids and took me somewhere, a big building, I dunno where it was."

With every second that went past, with every sentence she spoke, she felt a little strength flowing back. And now that she was doing something difficult and familiar and never quite predictable, namely lying, she felt a sort of mastery again, the same sense of complexity and control that the alethiometer gave her. She had to be careful not to say anything obviously impossible; she had to be vague in some places and invent plausible details in others; she had to be an artist, in short.

"How long did they keep you in this building?" said Mrs Coulter.

Lyra's journey along the canals and her time with the gyptians had taken weeks: she'd have to account for that time. She invented a voyage with the Gobblers to Trollesund, and then an escape, lavish with details from her observation of the town; and a time as maid-of-all-work at Einarsson's Bar, and then a spell working for a family of farmers inland, and then being caught by the Samoyeds and brought to Bolvangar.

"And they were going to – going to cut –"

"Hush, dear, hush. I'm going to find out what's been going on."

"But why were they going to do that? I never done anything wrong! All the kids are afraid of what happens in there, and no one knows. But it's horrible. It's worse than anything… Why are they doing that, Mrs Coulter? Why are they so cruel?"

"There, there… You're safe, my dear. They won't ever do it to you. Now I know you're here, and you're safe, you'll never be in danger again. No one's going to harm you, Lyra darling; no one's ever going to hurt you…"

"But they do it to other children! Why?"

"Ah, my love –"

"It's Dust, isn't it?"

"Did they tell you that? Did the doctors say that?"

"The kids know it. All the kids talk about it, but no one knows! And they nearly done it to me – you got to tell me! You got no right to keep it secret, not any more!"

"Lyra … Lyra, Lyra. Darling, these are big difficult ideas, Dust and so on. It's not something for children to worry about. But the doctors do it for the children's own good, my love. Dust is something bad, something wrong, something evil and wicked. Grown-ups and their dæmons are infected with Dust so deeply that it's too late for them. They can't be helped… But a quick operation on children means they're safe from it. Dust just won't stick to them ever again. They're safe and happy and –"

Lyra thought of little Tony Makarios. She leaned forward suddenly and retched. Mrs Coulter moved back and let go.

"Are you all right, dear? Go to the bathroom –"

Lyra swallowed hard and brushed her eyes.

"You don't have to do that to us," she said. "You could just leave us. I bet Lord Asriel wouldn't let anyone do that if he knew what was going on. If he's got Dust and you've got Dust, and the Master of Jordan and every other grown-up's got Dust, it must be all right. When I get out I'm going to tell all the kids in the world about this. Anyway, if it was so good, why'd you stop them doing it to me? If it was good you should've let them do it. You should have been glad."

Mrs Coulter was shaking her head and smiling a sad wise smile.

"Darling," she said, "some of what's good has to hurt us a little, and naturally it's upsetting for others if *you're* upset… But it doesn't mean your dæmon is taken away from you. He's still there! Goodness me, a lot of the grown-ups here have had the operation. The nurses seem happy enough, don't they?"

Lyra blinked. Suddenly she understood their strange blank incuriosity, the way their little trotting dæmons seemed to be sleepwalking.

Say nothing, she thought, and shut her mouth hard.

"Darling, no one would ever dream of performing an operation on a child without testing it first. And no one in a thousand years would take a child's dæmon away altogether! All that happens is a little cut, and then everything's peaceful. For ever! You see, your dæmon's a wonderful friend and companion when you're young, but at the age we call puberty, the age you're coming to very soon, darling, dæmons bring all sort of troublesome thoughts and feelings, and that's what lets Dust in. A quick little operation before that, and you're never troubled again. And your dæmon stays with you, only ... just not connected. Like a ... like a wonderful pet, if you like. The best pet in the world! Wouldn't you like that?"

Oh, the wicked liar, oh, the shameless untruths she was telling! And even if Lyra hadn't known them to be lies (Tony Makarios; those caged dæmons) she would have hated it with a furious passion. Her dear soul, the darling companion of her heart, to be cut away and reduced to a little trotting *pet*? Lyra nearly blazed with hatred, and Pantalaimon in her arms became a polecat, the most ugly and vicious of all his forms, and snarled.

But they said nothing. Lyra held Pantalaimon tight and let Mrs Coulter stroke her hair.

"Drink up your camomile," said Mrs Coulter softly. "We'll have them make up a bed for you in here. There's no need to go back and share a dormitory with other girls, not now I've got my little assistant back. My favourite! The best assistant in the world. D'you know, we searched all over London for you, darling? We had the police searching every town in the land. Oh, I missed you so much! I can't tell you how happy I am to find you again..."

All the time, the golden monkey was prowling about restlessly, one minute perching on the table swinging his tail, the next clinging to Mrs Coulter and chittering softly in her ear, the next pacing the floor with tail erect. He was betraying Mrs Coulter's impatience, of course, and finally she couldn't hold it in.

"Lyra, dear," she said, "I think that the Master of Jordan gave you something before you left. Isn't that right? He gave you an alethiometer. The trouble is, it wasn't his to give. It was left in his care. It's really too valuable to be carried about – d'you know, it's one of only two or three in the world! I think the Master gave it to you in the hope that it would fall into Lord Asriel's hands. He told you not to tell me about it, didn't he?"

Lyra twisted her mouth.

"Yes, I can see. Well, never mind, darling, because you *didn't* tell me, did you? So you haven't broken any promises. But listen, dear, it really ought to be properly looked after. I'm afraid it's so rare and delicate that we can't let it be at risk any longer."

"Why shouldn't Lord Asriel have it?" Lyra said, not moving.

"Because of what he's doing. You know he's been sent away to exile, because he's got something dangerous and wicked in mind. He needs the alethiometer to finish his plan, but believe me, dear, the last thing anyone should do is let him have it. The Master of Jordan was sadly mistaken. But now that you know, it really would be better to let me have it, wouldn't it? It would save you the trouble of carrying it around, and all the worry of looking after it – and really it must have been such a puzzle, wondering what a silly old thing like that was any good for…"

Lyra wondered how she had ever, ever, ever found this woman to be so fascinating and clever.

"So if you've got it now, dear, you'd really better let me have it to look after. It's in that belt around your waist, isn't it? Yes, that was a clever thing to do, putting it away like this…"

Her hands were at Lyra's skirt, and then she was unfastening the stiff oilcloth. Lyra tensed herself. The golden monkey was crouching at the end of the bed, trembling with anticipation, little black hands to his mouth. Mrs Coulter pulled the belt away from Lyra's waist and unbuttoned the pouch. She was breathing fast. She took out the black velvet cloth and unfolded it, finding the tin box Iorek Byrnison had made.

Pantalaimon was a cat again, tensed to spring. Lyra drew her legs up away from Mrs Coulter, and swung them down to the floor so that she too could run when the time came.

"What's this?" said Mrs Coulter, as if amused. "What a funny old tin! Did you put it in here to keep it safe, dear? All this moss... You have been careful, haven't you? Another tin, inside the first one! And soldered! Who did this, dear?"

She was too intent on opening it to wait for an answer. She had a knife in her handbag with a lot of different attachments, and she pulled out a blade and dug it under the lid.

At once a furious buzzing filled the room.

Lyra and Pantalaimon held themselves still. Mrs Coulter, puzzled, curious, pulled at the lid, and the golden monkey bent close to look.

Then in a dazzling moment the black form of the spy-fly hurtled out of the tin and crashed hard into the monkey's face.

He screamed and flung himself backwards; and of course it was hurting Mrs Coulter too, and she cried out in pain and fright with the monkey, and then the little clockwork devil swarmed upwards at her, up her breast and throat towards her face.

Lyra didn't hesitate. Pantalaimon sprang for the door and she was after him at once, and she tore it open and raced away faster than she had ever run in her life.

"Fire alarm!" Pantalaimon shrieked, as he flew ahead of her.

She saw a button on the next corner, and smashed the glass with her desperate fist. She ran on, heading towards the dormitories, smashed another alarm and another, and then people began to come out into the corridor, looking up and down for the fire.

By this time she was near the kitchen, and Pantalaimon flashed a thought into her mind, and she darted in. A moment later she had turned on all the gas taps and flung a match at the nearest burner. Then she dragged a bag of flour from a shelf and hurled it at the edge of a table so it burst and filled the air with white, because she had heard that flour will explode if it's treated like that near a flame.

Then she ran out and on as fast as she could towards her own dormitory. The corridors were full now: children running this way and that, vivid with excitement, for the word *escape* had got around. The oldest were making for the store-rooms where the clothing was kept, and herding the younger ones with them. Adults were trying to control it all, and none of them knew what was happening. Shouting, pushing, crying, jostling people were everywhere.

Through it all Lyra and Pantalaimon darted like fish, making always for the dormitory, and just as they reached it, there was a dull explosion from behind that shook the building.

The other girls had fled: the room was empty. Lyra dragged the locker to the corner, jumped up, hauled the furs out of the ceiling, felt for the alethiometer. It was still there. She tugged the furs on quickly, pulling the hood forward, and then Pantalaimon, a sparrow at the door, called:

"Now!"

She ran out. By luck a group of children who'd already found some cold-weather clothing were racing down the corridor towards the main entrance, and she joined them, sweating, her heart thumping, knowing that she had to escape or die.

The way was blocked. The fire in the kitchen had taken quickly, and whether it was the flour or the gas, something had brought down part of the roof. People were clambering over twisted struts and girders to get up to the bitter cold air. The smell of gas was strong. Then came another explosion, louder than the first and closer. The blast knocked several people over, and cries of fear and pain filled the air.

Lyra struggled up, and with Pantalaimon calling, "This way! This way!" among the other dæmon-cries and flutterings, she hauled herself over the rubble. The air she was breathing was frozen, and she hoped that the children had managed to find their outdoor clothing; it would be a fine thing to escape from the Station only to die of cold.

There really was a blaze now. When she got out on to the roof under the night sky she could see flames licking at the edges of a great hole in the side of the building. There was a throng of children and adults by the main entrance, but this time the adults were more agitated and the children more fearful: much more fearful.

"Roger! Roger!" Lyra called, and Pantalaimon, keen-eyed as an owl, hooted that he'd seen him.

A moment later they found each other.

"Tell 'em all to come with me!" Lyra shouted into his ear.

"They won't – they're all panicky –"

"Tell 'em what they do to the kids that vanish! They cut their dæmons off with a big knife! Tell 'em what you saw this afternoon – all them dæmons we let out! Tell 'em that's going to happen to them too unless they get away!"

Roger gaped, horrified, but then collected his wits and ran to the nearest group of hesitating children. Lyra did the same, and as the message passed along, some children cried out and clutched their dæmons in fear.

"Come with me!" Lyra shouted. "There's a rescue a-coming! We got to get out the compound! Come on, run!"

The children heard her and followed, streaming across the enclosure towards the avenue of lights, their boots pattering and creaking in the hard-packed snow.

Behind them adults were shouting, and there was a rumble and crash as another part of the building fell in. Sparks gushed into the air, and flames billowed out with a sound like tearing cloth; but cutting through this came another sound, dreadfully close and violent. Lyra had never heard it before, but she knew it at once: it was the howl of the Tartar guards' wolf-dæmons. She felt weak from head to foot, and many children turned in fear and stumbled to a stop, for there running at a low swift tireless lope came the first of the Tartar guards, rifle at the ready, with the mighty leaping greyness of his dæmon beside him.

Then came another, and another. They were all in padded mail, and they had no eyes – or at least you couldn't see any eyes behind the snow-slits of their helmets. The only eyes you could see were the round black ends of the rifle-barrels and the blazing yellow eyes of the wolf-dæmons above the slaver dripping from their jaws.

Lyra faltered. She hadn't dreamed of how frightening those wolves were. And now that she knew how casually people at Bolvangar broke the great taboo, she shrank from the thought of those dripping teeth…

The Tartars ran to stand in a line across the entrance to the avenue of lights, their dæmons beside them as disciplined and drilled as they were. In another minute there'd be a second line, because more were coming, and more behind them. Lyra thought with despair: children can't fight soldiers. It wasn't like the battles in the Oxford Claybeds, hurling lumps of mud at the brick-burners' children.

Or perhaps it was! She remembered hurling a handful of clay in the broad face of a brick-burner boy bearing down on her. He'd stopped to claw the stuff out of his eyes, and then the townies leapt on him.

She'd been standing in the mud. She was standing in the snow.

Just as she'd done that afternoon, but in deadly earnest now, she scooped a handful together and hurled it at the nearest soldier.

"Get 'em in the eyes!" she yelled, and threw another.

Other children joined in, and then someone's dæmon had the notion of flying as a swift beside the snowball and nudging it directly at the eye-slits of the target – and then they all joined in, and in a few moments the Tartars were stumbling about spitting and cursing and trying to brush the packed snow out of the narrow gap in front of their eyes.

"Come on!" Lyra screamed, and flung herself at the gate into the avenue of lights.

The children streamed after her, every one, dodging the snapping jaws of the wolves and racing as hard as they could down the avenue towards the beckoning open dark beyond.

A harsh scream came from behind as an officer shouted an order, and then a score of rifle bolts worked at once, and then there was another scream and a tense silence, with only the fleeing children's pounding feet and gasping breath to be heard.

They were taking aim. They wouldn't miss.

But before they could fire, a choking gasp came from one of the Tartars, and a cry of surprise from another.

Lyra stopped and turned to see a man lying on the snow, with a grey-feathered arrow in his back. He was writhing and twitching and coughing out blood, and the other soldiers were looking around to left and right for whoever had fired it, but the archer was nowhere to be seen.

And then an arrow came flying straight down from the sky, and struck another man behind the head. He fell at once. A shout from the officer, and everyone looked up at the dark sky.

"Witches!" said Pantalaimon.

And so they were: ragged elegant black shapes sweeping past high above, with a hiss and swish of air through the needles of the cloud-pine branches they flew on. As Lyra watched, one swooped low and loosed an arrow: another man fell.

And then all the Tartars turned their rifles up and blazed into the dark, firing at nothing, at shadows, at clouds, and more and more arrows rained down on them.

But the officer in charge, seeing the children almost away, ordered a squad to race after them. Some children screamed. And then more screamed, and they weren't moving forward any more, they were turning back in confusion, terrified by the monstrous shape hurtling towards them from the dark beyond the avenue of lights.

"Iorek Byrnison!" cried Lyra, her chest nearly bursting with joy.

The armoured bear at the charge seemed to be conscious of no weight except what gave him momentum. He bounded past Lyra almost in a blur and crashed into the Tartars, scattering soldiers, dæmons, rifles to all sides. Then he stopped and whirled round, with a lithe athletic power, and struck two massive blows, one to each side, at the guards closest to him.

A wolf-dæmon leapt at him: he slashed at her in mid-air, and bright fire spilled out of her as she fell to the snow, where she hissed and howled before vanishing. Her human died at once.

The Tartar officer, faced with this double attack, didn't hesitate. A long high scream of orders, and the force divided itself into two: one to keep off the witches, the bigger part to overcome the bear. His troops were magnificently brave. They dropped to one knee in groups of four and fired their rifles as if they were on the practice range, not budging an inch as Iorek's mighty bulk hurtled towards them. A moment later they were dead.

Iorek struck again, twisting to one side, slashing, snarling, crushing, while bullets flew about him like wasps or flies, doing no harm at all. Lyra urged the children on and out into the darkness beyond the lights. They must get away, because dangerous as the Tartars were, far more dangerous were the adults of Bolvangar.

So she called and beckoned and pushed to get the children moving. As the lights behind them threw long shadows on the snow, Lyra found her heart moving out towards the deep dark of the Arctic night and the clean coldness, leaping forward to love it as Pantalaimon was doing, a hare now delighting in his own propulsion.

"Where we going?" someone said.

"There's nothing out here but snow!"

"There's a rescue party coming," Lyra told them. "There's fifty gyptians or more. I bet there's some relations of yours, too. All the gyptian families that lost a kid, they all sent someone."

"I en't a gyptian," a boy said.

"Don't matter. They'll take you anyway."

"Where?" someone said querulously.

"Home," said Lyra. "That's what I come here for, to rescue you, and I brung the gyptians here to take you home again. We just got to go on a bit further and then we'll find 'em. The bear was with 'em, so they can't be far off."

"D'you see that bear!" one boy was saying. "When he slashed open that dæmon – the man died as if someone whipped his heart out, just like that!"

"I never knew dæmons could be killed," someone else said.

They were all talking now; the excitement and relief had loosened everyone's tongue. As long as they kept moving, it didn't matter if they talked.

"Is that true," said a girl, "about what they do back there?"

"Yeah," Lyra said. "I never thought I'd ever see anyone without their dæmon. But on the way here, we found this boy on his own without any dæmon. He kept asking for her, where she was, would she ever find him. He was called Tony Makarios."

"I know him!" said someone, and others joined in: "Yeah, they took him away about a week back…"

"Well, they cut his dæmon away," said Lyra, knowing how it would affect them. "And a little bit after we found him, he died. And all the dæmons they cut away, they kept them in cages in a square building back there."

"It's true," said Roger. "And Lyra let 'em out during the fire drill."

"Yeah, I seen 'em!" said Billy Costa. "I didn't know what they was at first, but I seen 'em fly away with that goose."

"But why do they do it?" demanded one boy. "Why do they cut people's dæmons away? That's torture! Why do they do it?"

"Dust," suggested someone doubtfully.

But the boy laughed in scorn. "Dust!" he said. "There en't no such thing! They just made that up! I don't believe in it."

"Here," said someone else, "look what's happening to the zeppelin!"

They all looked back. Beyond the dazzle of lights, where the fight was still continuing, the great length of the airship was not floating freely at the mooring mast any longer; the free end was drooping downwards, and beyond it was rising a globe of –

"Lee Scoresby's balloon!" Lyra cried, and clapped her mittened hands with delight.

The other children were baffled. Lyra herded them onwards, wondering how the aëronaut had got his balloon that far. It was clear what he was doing, and what a good idea, to fill his balloon with the gas out of theirs, to escape by the same means that crippled their pursuit!

"Come on, keep moving, else you'll freeze," she said, for some of the children were shivering and moaning from the cold, and their dæmons were crying too in high thin voices.

Pantalaimon found this irritating, and as a wolverine he snapped at one girl's squirrel-dæmon who was just lying across her shoulder whimpering faintly.

"Get in her coat! Make yourself big and warm her up!" he snarled, and the girl's dæmon, frightened, crept inside her coal-silk anorak at once.

The trouble was that coal-silk wasn't as warm as proper fur, no matter how much it was padded out with hollow coal-silk fibres. Some of the children looked like walking puffballs, they were so bulky, but their gear had been made in factories and laboratories far away from the cold, and it couldn't really cope. Lyra's furs looked ragged and they stank, but they kept the warmth in.

"If we don't find the gyptians soon they en't going to last," she whispered to Pantalaimon.

"Keep 'em moving, then," he whispered back. "If they lie down they're finished. You know what Farder Coram said…"

Farder Coram had told her many tales of his own journeys in the North, and so had Mrs Coulter – always supposing that hers were true. But they were both quite clear about one point, which was that you must keep going.

"How far we gotta go?" said a little boy.

"She's just making us walk out here to kill us," said a girl.

"Rather be out here than back there," someone said.

"I wouldn't! It's warm back in the Station. There's food and hot drinks and everything."

"But it's all on fire!"

"What we going to do out here? I bet we starve to death…"

Lyra's mind was full of dark questions that flew around like witches, swift and untouchable, and somewhere, just beyond where she could reach, there was a glory and a thrill which she didn't understand at all.

But it gave her a surge of strength, and she hauled one girl up out of a snowdrift, and shoved at a boy who was dawdling, and called to them all: "Keep going! Follow the bear's tracks! He come up with the gyptians, so the track'll lead us to where they are! Just keep walking!"

Big flakes of snow were beginning to fall. Soon it would have covered Iorek Byrnison's tracks altogether. Now that they were out of sight of the lights of Bolvangar, and the blaze of the fire was only a faint glow, the only light came from the faint radiance of the snow-covered ground. Thick clouds obscured the sky, so there was neither moon nor Northern Lights; but by peering closely, the children could make out the deep trail Iorek Byrnison had ploughed in the snow. Lyra encouraged, bullied, hit, half-carried, swore at, pushed, dragged, lifted tenderly, wherever it was needed, and Pantalaimon (by the state of each child's dæmon) told her what was needed in each case.

I'll get 'em there, she kept saying to herself. I come here to get 'em and I'll bloody get 'em.

Roger was following her example, and Billy Costa was leading the way, being sharper-eyed than most. Soon the snow was falling so thickly that they had to cling on to one another to keep from getting lost, and Lyra thought, perhaps if we all lie close and keep warm like that… Dig holes in the snow…

She was hearing things. There was the snarl of an engine somewhere, not the heavy thump of a zeppelin but something higher like the drone of a hornet. It drifted in and out of hearing.

And howling... Dogs? Sledge dogs? That too was distant and hard to be sure of, blanketed by millions of snowflakes and blown this way and that by little puffing gusts of wind. It might have been the gyptians' sledge dogs, or it might have been wild spirits of the tundra, or even those freed dæmons crying for their lost children.

She was seeing things... There weren't any lights in the snow, were there? They must be ghosts as well... Unless they'd come round in a circle, and were stumbling back into Bolvangar.

But these were little yellow lantern-beams, not the white glare of anbaric lights. And they were moving, and the howling was nearer, and before she knew for certain whether she'd fallen asleep, Lyra was wandering among familiar figures, and men in furs were holding her up: John Faa's mighty arm lifted her clear of the ground, and Farder Coram was laughing with pleasure; and as far through the blizzard as she could see, gyptians were lifting children into sledges, covering them with furs, giving them seal-meat to chew. And Tony Costa was there, hugging Billy and then punching him softly only to hug him again and shake him for joy. And Roger...

"Roger's coming with us," she said to Farder Coram. "It was him I meant to get in the first place. We'll go back to Jordan in the end. What's that noise –"

It was that snarl again, that engine, like a crazed spy-fly ten thousand times the size.

Suddenly there came a blow that sent her sprawling, and Pantalaimon couldn't defend her, because the golden monkey –

Mrs Coulter –

The golden monkey was wrestling, biting, scratching at Pantalaimon, who was flickering through so many changes of form it was hard to see him, and fighting back: stinging, lashing, tearing. Mrs Coulter, meanwhile, her face in its furs a frozen glare of intense feeling, was dragging Lyra to the back of a motorized sledge, and Lyra struggled as hard as her dæmon. The snow was so thick that they seemed to be isolated in a little blizzard of their own, and the anbaric headlights of the sledge only showed up the thick swirling flakes a few inches ahead.

"Help!" Lyra cried, to the gyptians who were just *there* in the blinding snow and who could see nothing. "Help me! Farder Coram! Lord Faa! Oh God, help!"

Mrs Coulter shrieked a high command in the language of the northern Tartars. The snow swirled open, and there they were, a squad of them, armed with rifles, and the wolf-dæmons snarled beside them. The chief saw Mrs Coulter struggling, and picked up Lyra with one hand as if she were a doll and threw her into the sledge, where she lay stunned and dazed.

A rifle banged, and then another, as the gyptians realized what was happening. But firing at targets you can't see is dangerous when you can't see your own side either. The Tartars, in a tight group now around the sledge, were able to blaze at will into the snow, but the gyptians dared not shoot back for fear of hitting Lyra.

Oh, the bitterness she felt! The tiredness!

Still dazed, with her head ringing, she hauled herself up to find Pantalaimon desperately fighting the monkey still, with wolverine-jaws fastened tight in a golden arm, changing no more but grimly hanging on. And who was that?

Not Roger?

Yes, Roger, battering at Mrs Coulter with fists and feet, hurtling his

300

head against hers, only to be struck down by a Tartar who swiped at him like someone brushing away a fly. It was all a phantasmagoria now: white, black, a swift green flutter across her vision, ragged shadows, racing light –

A great swirl lifted curtains of snow aside, and into the cleared area leapt Iorek Byrnison, with a clang and screech of iron on iron. A moment later and those great jaws snapped left, right, a paw ripped open a mailed chest, white teeth, black iron, red wet fur –

Then something was pulling her *up* powerfully, *up*, and she seized Roger too, tearing him out of the hands of Mrs Coulter and clinging tight, each child's dæmon a shrill bird fluttering in amazement as a greater fluttering swept all around them, and then Lyra saw in the air beside her a witch, one of those elegant ragged black shadows from the high air, but close enough to touch; and there was a bow in the witch's bare hands, and she exerted her bare pale arms (in this freezing air!) to pull the string and then loose an arrow into the eye-slit of a mailed and louring Tartar hood only three feet away –

And the arrow sped in and halfway out at the back, and the man's wolf-dæmon vanished in mid-leap even before he hit the ground.

Up! Into mid-air Lyra and Roger were caught and swept, and found themselves clinging with weakening fingers to a cloud-pine branch, where the young witch was sitting tense with balanced grace, and then she leant down and to the left and something huge was looming and there was the ground.

They tumbled into the snow beside the basket of Lee Scoresby's balloon.

"Skip inside," called the Texan, "and bring your friend, by all means. Have ye seen that bear?"

Lyra saw that three witches were holding a rope looped around a rock, anchoring the great buoyancy of the gas-bag to the earth.

"Get in!" she cried to Roger, and scrambled over the leather-bound rim of the basket to fall in a snowy heap inside. A moment later Roger fell on top of her, and then a mighty noise halfway between a roar and a growl made the very ground shake.

"C'mon, Iorek! On board, old feller!" yelled Lee Scoresby, and over the side came the bear in a hideous creak of wicker and bending wood.

Then a swirl of lighter air lifted the mist and snow aside for a moment, and in the sudden clearance Lyra saw everything that was happening around them. She saw a party of gyptian raiders under John Faa harrying the Tartar rearguard and sweeping them back towards the blazing ruins of Bolvangar; she saw the other gyptians helping child after child safe aboard their sledges, tucking them warmly down under the furs; she saw Farder Coram casting around anxiously, leaning on his stick, his autumn-coloured dæmon leaping through the snow and looking this way and that.

"Farder Coram!" Lyra cried. "Over here!"

The old man heard, and turned to look in amazement at the balloon straining against the rope and the witches holding it down, at Lyra waving frantically from the basket.

"Lyra!" he cried. "You're safe, gal? You're safe?"

"As safe as I ever was!" she shouted back. "Goodbye, Farder Coram! Goodbye! Take all the kids back home!"

"We'll do that, sure as I live! Go well, my child – go well – go well, my dear –"

And at the same moment the aëronaut lowered his arm in a signal, and the witches let go of the rope.

The balloon lifted immediately and surged upwards into the snow-thick air at a rate Lyra could scarcely believe. After a moment the ground disappeared in the mist, and up they went, faster and faster, so that she thought no rocket could have left the earth more swiftly. She lay holding on to Roger on the floor of the basket, pressed down by the acceleration.

Lee Scoresby was cheering and laughing and uttering wild Texan yells of delight; Iorek Byrnison was calmly unfastening his armour, hooking a deft claw into all the linkages and undoing them with a twist before packing the separate pieces in a pile. Somewhere outside, the flap and swish of air through cloud-pine needles and witch-garments told that the witches were keeping them company into the upper airs.

Little by little Lyra recovered her breath, her balance and her heartbeat. She sat up and looked around.

The basket was much bigger than she'd thought. Ranged around the edges were racks of philosophical instruments, and there were piles of furs, and bottled air, and a variety of other things too small or confusing to make out in the thick mist they were ascending through.

"Is this a cloud?" she said.

"Sure is. Wrap your friend in some furs before he turns into an icicle. It's cold here but it's gonna get colder."

"How did you find us?"

"Witches. There's one witch-lady who wants to talk to you. When we get clear of the cloud we'll get our bearings and then we can sit and have a yarn."

"Iorek," said Lyra, "thank you for coming."

The bear grunted, and settled down to lick the blood off his fur. His weight meant that the basket was tilted to one side, but that didn't matter. Roger was wary, but Iorek Byrnison took no more notice of him than of a flake of snow. Lyra contented herself with clinging to the rim of the basket, just under her chin when she was standing, and peering wide-eyed into the swirling cloud.

Only a few seconds later the balloon passed out of the cloud altogether and, still rising rapidly, soared on into the heavens.

What a sight!

Directly above them the balloon swelled out in a huge curve. Above and ahead of them the Aurora was blazing, with more brilliance and grandeur than she had ever seen. It was all around, or nearly, and they were nearly part of it. Great swathes of incandescence trembled and parted like angels' wings beating; cascades of luminescent glory tumbled down invisible crags to lie in swirling pools or hang like vast waterfalls.

So Lyra gasped at that, and then she looked below, and saw a sight almost more wondrous.

As far as the eye could see, to the very horizon in all directions, a tumbled sea of white extended without a break. Soft peaks and vaporous chasms rose or opened here and there, but mostly it looked like a solid mass of ice.

And rising through it in ones and twos and larger groups as well came small black shadows, those ragged figures of such elegance, witches on their branches of cloud-pine.

They flew swiftly, without any effort, up and towards the balloon, leaning to one side or another to steer. And one of them, the archer who'd saved Lyra from Mrs Coulter, flew directly alongside the basket, and Lyra saw her clearly for the first time.

She was young – younger than Mrs Coulter; and fair, with bright green eyes; and clad like all the witches in strips of black silk, but wearing no furs, no hood or mittens. She seemed to feel no cold at all. Around her brow was a simple chain of little red flowers. She sat her cloud-pine branch as if it were a steed, and seemed to rein it in a yard from Lyra's wondering gaze.

"Lyra?"

"Yes! And are you Serafina Pekkala?"

"I am."

Lyra could see why Farder Coram loved her, and why it was breaking his heart, though she had known neither of those things a moment before. He was growing old; he was an old broken man; and she would be young for generations.

"Have you got the symbol-reader?" said the witch, in a voice so like the high wild singing of the Aurora itself that Lyra could hardly hear the sense for the sweet sound of it.

"Yes. I got it in my pocket, safe."

Great wing-beats told of another arrival, and then he was gliding beside her: the grey goose-dæmon. He spoke briefly and then wheeled away to glide in a wide circle around the balloon as it continued to rise.

"The gyptians have laid waste to Bolvangar," said Serafina Pekkala. "They have killed twenty-two guards and nine of the staff, and they've set light to every part of the buildings that still stood. They are going to destroy it completely."

"What about Mrs Coulter?"

"No sign of her."

She cried out in a wild yell, and other witches circled and flew in towards the balloon.

"Mr Scoresby," she said. "The rope, if you please."

"Ma'am, I'm very grateful. We're still rising. I guess we'll go on up a while yet. How many of you will it take to pull us north?"

"We are strong," was all she said.

Lee Scoresby was attaching a coil of stout rope to the leather-covered iron ring that gathered the ropes running over the gas-bag, and from which the basket itself was suspended. When it was securely fixed, he threw the free end out, and at once six witches darted towards it, caught hold, and began to pull, urging the cloud-pine branches towards the Polar Star.

As the balloon began to move in that direction, Pantalaimon came to perch on the edge of the basket as a tern. Roger's dæmon came out to look, but crept back again soon, for Roger was fast asleep, as was Iorek Byrnison. Only Lee Scoresby was awake, calmly chewing a thin cigar and watching his instruments.

"So, Lyra," said Serafina Pekkala. "Do you know why you're going to Lord Asriel?"

Lyra was astonished. "To take him the alethiometer, of course!" she said.

She had never considered the question; it was obvious. Then she recalled her first motive, from so long ago that she'd almost forgotten it.

"Or… To help him escape. That's it. We're going to help him get away."

But as she said that, it sounded absurd. Escape from Svalbard? Impossible!

"Try, anyway," she added stoutly. "Why?"

"I think there are things I need to tell you," said Serafina Pekkala.

"About Dust?"

It was the first thing Lyra wanted to know.

"Yes, among other things. But you are tired now, and it will be a long flight. We'll talk when you wake up."

Lyra yawned. It was a jaw-cracking, lung-bursting yawn that lasted almost a minute, or felt like it, and for all that Lyra struggled, she couldn't resist the onrush of sleep. Serafina Pekkala reached a hand over the rim of the basket and touched her eyes, and as Lyra sank to the floor, Pantalaimon fluttered down, changed to an ermine, and crawled to his sleeping-place by her neck.

The witch settled her branch into a steady speed beside the basket as they moved north towards Svalbard.

Part Three
Svalbard

18

Fog and Ice

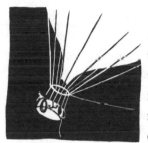

*L*ee Scoresby arranged some furs over Lyra. She curled up close to Roger and they lay together asleep as the balloon swept on towards the Pole. The aëronaut checked his instruments from time to time, chewed on the cigar he would never light with the inflammable hydrogen so close, and huddled deeper into his own furs.

"This little girl's pretty important, huh?" he said after several minutes.

"More than she will know," Serafina Pekkala said.

"Does that mean there's gonna be much in the way of armed pursuit? You understand, I'm speaking as a practical man with a living to earn. I can't afford to get busted up or shot to pieces without some kind of compensation agreed in advance. I ain't trying to lower the tone of this expedition, believe me, ma'am. But John Faa and the gyptians paid me a fee that's enough to cover my time and skill and the normal wear and tear on the balloon, and that's all. It didn't include acts-of-war insurance. And let me tell you, ma'am, when we land Iorek Byrnison on Svalbard, that will count as an act of war."

He spat a piece of smoke-leaf delicately overboard.

"So I'd like to know what we can expect in the way of mayhem and ructions," he finished.

"There may be fighting," said Serafina Pekkala. "But you have fought before."

"Sure, when I'm paid. But the fact is, I thought this was a straightforward transportation contract, and I charged according. And I'm a-wondering now, after that little dust-up down there, I'm a-wondering how far my transportation responsibility extends. Whether I'm bound to risk my life and my equipment in a war among the bears, for example. Or whether this little child has enemies on Svalbard as hottempered as the ones back at Bolvangar. I merely mention all this by way of making conversation."

"Mr Scoresby," said the witch, "I wish I could answer your question. All I can say is that all of us, humans, witches, bears, are engaged in a war already, although not all of us know it. Whether you find danger on Svalbard or whether you fly off unharmed, you are a recruit, under arms, a soldier."

"Well, that seems kinda precipitate. Seems to me a man should have a choice whether to take up arms or not."

"We have no more choice in that than in whether or not to be born."

"Oh, I like choice, though," he said. "I like choosing the jobs I take and the places I go and the food I eat and the companions I sit and yarn with. Don't you wish for a choice once in a while?"

Serafina Pekkala considered, and then said, "Perhaps we don't mean the same thing by *choice*, Mr Scoresby. Witches own nothing, so we're not interested in preserving value or making profits, and as for the choice between one thing and another, when you live for many hundreds of years you know that every opportunity will come again. We have different needs. You have to repair your balloon and keep it in good condition, and that takes time and trouble, I see that; but for us to fly, all we have to do is tear off a branch of cloud-pine; any will do, and there are plenty more. We don't feel cold, so we need no warm clothes. We have no means of exchange apart from mutual aid. If a witch needs something, another witch will give it to her. If there is a war to be fought, we don't consider cost one of the factors in deciding whether or not it is right to fight. Nor do we have any notion of honour, as bears do, for instance. An insult to a bear is a deadly thing. To us … inconceivable. How could you insult a witch? What would it matter if you did?"

"Well, I'm kinda with you on that. Sticks and stones, I'll break yer bones, but names ain't worth a quarrel. But ma'am, you see my dilemma, I hope. I'm a simple aëronaut, and I'd like to end my days in comfort. Buy a little farm, a few head of cattle, some horses… Nothing grand, you notice. No palace or slaves or heaps of gold. Just the evening wind over the sage, and a ceegar, and a glass of bourbon whiskey. Now the trouble is, that costs money. So I do my flying in exchange for cash, and after every job I send some gold back to the Wells Fargo Bank, and when I've got enough, ma'am, I'm gonna sell this balloon and book me a passage on a steamer to Port Galveston, and I'll never leave the ground again."

"There's another difference between us, Mr Scoresby. A witch would no sooner give up flying than give up breathing. To fly is to be perfectly ourselves."

"I see that, ma'am, and I envy you; but I ain't got your sources of satisfaction. Flying is just a job to me, and I'm just a technician. I might as well be adjusting valves in a gas-engine or wiring up anbaric circuits. But I chose it, you see. It was my own free choice. Which is why I find this notion of a war I ain't been told nothing about, kinda troubling."

"Iorek Byrnison's quarrel with his king is part of it too," said the witch. "This child is destined to play a part in that."

"You speak of destiny," he said, "as if it was fixed. And I ain't sure I like that any more than a war I'm enlisted in without knowing about it. Where's my free will, if you please? And this child seems to me to have more free will than anyone I ever met. Are you telling me that she's just some kind of clockwork toy wound up and set going on a course she can't change?"

"We are all subject to the fates. But we must all act as if we are not," said the witch, "or die of despair. There is a curious prophecy about this child: she is destined to bring about the end of destiny. But she must do so without knowing what she is doing, as if it were her nature and not her destiny to do it. If she's told what she must do, it will all fail; death will sweep through all the worlds; it will be the triumph of despair, for ever. The universes will all become nothing more than interlocking machines, blind and empty of thought, feeling, life…"

They looked down at Lyra, whose sleeping face (what little they could see inside her hood) wore a stubborn little frown.

"I guess part of her knows that," said the aëronaut. "Looks prepared for it, anyways. How about the little boy? You know she came all this way to save him from those fiends back there? They were playmates, back in Oxford or somewhere. Did you know that?"

"Yes, I did know that. Lyra is carrying something of immense value, and it seems that the fates are using her as a messenger to take it to her father. So she came all this way to find her friend, not knowing that her friend was brought to the North by the fates, in order that she might follow and bring something to her father."

"That's how you read it, huh?"

For the first time the witch seemed unsure.

"That is how it seems... But we can't read the darkness, Mr Scoresby. It is more than possible that I might be wrong."

"And what brought *you* into all this, if I can ask?"

"Whatever they were doing at Bolvangar, we felt it was wrong with all our hearts. Lyra is their enemy; so we are her friends. We don't see more clearly than that. But also there is my clan's friendship for the gyptian people, which goes back to the time when Farder Coram saved my life. We are doing this at their bidding. And they have ties of obligation with Lord Asriel."

"I see. So you're towing the balloon to Svalbard for the gyptians' sake. And does that friendship extend to towing us back again? Or will I have to wait for a kindly wind, and depend on the indulgence of the bears in the meantime? Once again, ma'am, I'm asking merely in a spirit of friendly enquiry."

"If we can help you back to Trollesund, Mr Scoresby, we shall do so. But we don't know what we shall meet on Svalbard. The bears' new king has made many changes; the old ways are out of favour; it might be a difficult landing. And I don't know how Lyra will find her way to her father. Nor do I know what Iorek Byrnison has it in mind to do, except that his fate is involved with hers."

"I don't know either, ma'am. I think he's attached himself to the little girl as a kind of protector. She helped him get his armour back, you see. Who knows what bears feel? But if a bear ever loved a human being, he loves her. As for landing on Svalbard, it's never been easy. Still, if I can call on you for a tug in the right direction, I'll feel kinda easier in my mind; and if there's anything I can do for you in return, you only have to say. But just so as I know, would you mind telling me whose side I'm on in this invisible war?"

"We are both on Lyra's side."

"Oh, no doubt about that."

They flew on. Because of the clouds below there was no way of telling how fast they were going. Normally, of course, a balloon remained still with respect to the wind, floating at whatever speed the air itself was moving; but now, pulled by the witches, the balloon was moving through the air instead of with it, and resisting the movement, too, because the unwieldy gas-bag had none of the streamlined smoothness of a zeppelin. As a result, the basket swung this way and that, rocking and bumping much more than on a normal flight.

Lee Scoresby wasn't concerned for his comfort so much as for his instruments, and he spent some time making sure they were securely lashed to the main struts. According to the altimeter, they were nearly ten thousand feet up. The temperature was minus twenty degrees. He had been colder than this, but not much, and he didn't want to get any colder now; so he unrolled the canvas sheet he used as an emergency bivouac, and spread it in front of the sleeping children to keep off the wind, before lying down back to back with his old comrade in arms, Iorek Byrnison, and falling asleep.

When Lyra woke up, the moon was high in the sky, and everything in sight was silver-plated, from the rolling surface of the clouds below to the frost-spears and icicles on the rigging of the balloon.

Roger was sleeping, and so were Lee Scoresby and the bear. Beside the basket, however, the witch-queen was flying steadily.

"How far are we from Svalbard?" Lyra said.

"If we meet no winds, we shall be over Svalbard in twelve hours or so."

"Where are we going to land?"

"It depends on the weather. We'll try to avoid the cliffs, though.

There are creatures living there who prey on anything that moves. If we can, we'll set you down in the interior, away from Iofur Raknison's palace."

"What's going to happen when I find Lord Asriel? Will he want to come back to Oxford, or what? I don't know if I ought to tell him I know he's my father, neither. He might want to pretend he's still my uncle. I don't hardly know him at all."

"He won't want to go back to Oxford, Lyra. It seems that there is something to be done in another world, and Lord Asriel is the only one who can bridge the gulf between that world and this. But he needs something to help him."

"The alethiometer!" Lyra said. "The Master of Jordan gave it to me and I thought there was something he wanted to say about Lord Asriel, except he never had the chance. I knew he didn't *really* want to poison him. Is he going to read it and see how to make the bridge? I bet I could help him. I can probably read it as good as anyone now."

"I don't know," said Serafina Pekkala. "How he'll do it, and what his task will be, we can't tell. There are powers who speak to us, and there are powers above them; and there are secrets even from the most high."

"The alethiometer would tell me! I could read it now…"

But it was too cold; she would never have managed to hold it. She bundled herself up and pulled the hood tight against the chill of the wind, leaving only a slit to look through. Far ahead, and a little below, the long rope extended from the suspension-ring of the balloon, pulled by six or seven witches sitting on their cloud-pine branches. The stars shone as bright and cold and hard as diamonds.

"Why en't you cold, Serafina Pekkala?"

"We feel cold, but we don't mind it, because we will not come to harm. And if we wrapped up against the cold, we wouldn't feel other things, like the bright tingle of the stars, or the music of the Aurora, or best of all the silky feeling of moonlight on our skin. It's worth being cold for that."

"Could I feel them?"

"No. You would die if you took your furs off. Stay wrapped up."

"How long do witches live, Serafina Pekkala? Farder Coram says hundreds of years. But you don't look old at all."

"I am three hundred years or more. Our oldest witch-mother is nearly a thousand. One day, Yambe-Akka will come for her. One day she'll come for me. She is the goddess of the dead. She comes to you smiling and kindly, and you know it is time to die."

"Are there men witches? Or only women?"

"There are men who serve us, like the Consul at Trollesund. And there are men we take for lovers or husbands. You are so young, Lyra, too young to understand this, but I shall tell you anyway and you'll under-stand it later: men pass in front of our eyes like butterflies, creatures of a brief season. We love them; they are brave, proud, beautiful, clever; and they die almost at once. They die so soon that our hearts are contin-ually racked with pain. We bear their children, who are witches if they are female, human if not; and then in the blink of an eye they are gone, felled, slain, lost. Our sons, too. When a little boy is growing, he thinks he is immortal. His mother knows he isn't. Each time becomes more painful, until finally your heart is broken. Perhaps that is when Yambe-Akka comes for you. She is older than the tundra. Perhaps, for her, witches' lives are as brief as men's are to us."

"Did you love Farder Coram?"

"Yes. Does he know that?"

"I don't know, but I know he loves you."

"When he rescued me he was young and strong and full of pride and beauty. I loved him at once. I would have changed my nature, I would have forsaken the star-tingle and the music of the Aurora; I would never have flown again – I would have given all that up in a moment, without a thought, to be a gyptian boat-wife and cook for him and share his bed and bear his children. But you cannot change what you are, only what you do. I am a witch. He is a human. I stayed with him for long enough to bear him a child…"

"He never said! Was it a girl? A witch?"

"No. A boy, and he died in the great epidemic of forty years ago, the sickness that came out of the East. Poor little child; he flickered into life and out of it like a mayfly. And it tore pieces out of my heart, as it always does. It broke Coram's. And then the call came for me to return to my own people, because Yambe-Akka had taken my mother, and I was clan-queen. So I left, as I had to."

"Did you never see Farder Coram again?"

"Never. I heard of his deeds; I heard how he was wounded by the Skraelings, with a poisoned arrow, and I sent herbs and spells to help him recover, but I wasn't strong enough to see him. I heard how broken he was after that, and how his wisdom grew, how much he studied and read, and I was proud of him and his goodness. But I stayed away, for they were dangerous times for my clan, and witch-wars were threatening, and besides, I thought he would forget me and find a human wife…"

"He never would," said Lyra stoutly. "You oughter go and see him. He still loves you, I know he does."

"But he would be ashamed of his own age, and I wouldn't want to make him feel that."

"Perhaps he would. But you ought to send a message to him, at least. That's what I think."

Serafina Pekkala said nothing for a long time. Pantalaimon became a tern and flew to her branch for a second, to acknowledge that perhaps they had been insolent.

Then Lyra said, "Why do people have dæmons, Serafina Pekkala?"

"Everyone asks that, and no one knows the answer. As long as there have been human beings, there have been dæmons. It's what makes us different from animals."

"Yeah! We're different from them all right... Like bears. They're strange, en't they, bears? You think they're like a person, and then suddenly they do something so strange or ferocious you think you'll never understand them... But you know what Iorek said to me, he said that his armour for him was like what a dæmon is for a person. It's his soul, he said. But that's where they're different again, because he *made* this armour hisself. They took his first armour away when they sent him into exile, and he found some sky-iron and made some new armour, like making a new soul. We can't make our dæmons. Then the people at Trollesund, they got him drunk on spirits and stole it away, and I found out where it was and he got it back... But what I wonder is, why's he coming to Svalbard? They'll fight him. They might kill him... I love Iorek. I love him so much I wish he wasn't coming."

"Has he told you who he is?"

"Only his name. And it was the Consul at Trollesund who told us that."

"He is high-born. He is a prince. In fact, if he had not committed a great crime, he would be the king of the bears by now."

"He told me their king was called Iofur Raknison."

"Iofur Raknison became king when Iorek Byrnison was exiled. Iofur is a prince, of course, or he wouldn't be allowed to rule; but he is clever in a human way; he makes alliances and treaties; he lives not as bears do, in ice-forts, but in a new-built palace; he talks of exchanging ambassadors with human nations and developing the fire-mines with the help of human engineers... He is very skilful and subtle. Some say that he provoked Iorek into the deed for which he was exiled, and others say that even if he didn't, he encourages them to think he did, because it adds to his reputation for craft and subtlety."

"What *did* Iorek do? See, one reason I love Iorek, it's because of my father doing what *he* did and being punished. Seems to me they're like each other. Iorek told me he'd killed another bear, but he never said how it came about."

"The fight was over a she-bear. The male whom Iorek killed would not display the usual signals of surrender when it was clear that Iorek was stronger. For all their pride, bears never fail to recognize superior force in another bear and surrender to it, but for some reason this bear didn't do it. Some say that Iofur Raknison worked on his mind, or gave him confusing herbs to eat. At any rate, the young bear persisted, and Iorek Byrnison allowed his temper to master him. The case was not hard to judge; he should have wounded, not killed."

"So otherwise he'd be king," Lyra said. "And I heard something about Iofur Raknison from the Palmerian Professor at Jordan, 'cause he'd been to the North and met him. He said ... I wish I could remember what it was ... I think he'd tricked his way on to the throne or something... But you know, Iorek said to me once that bears couldn't be tricked, and showed me that I couldn't trick him. It sounds as if they was *both* tricked, him and the other bear. Maybe only bears can trick bears, maybe people can't. Except... The people at Trollesund, they tricked him, didn't they? When they got him drunk and stole his armour?"

"When bears act like people, perhaps they can be tricked," said

Serafina Pekkala. "When bears act like bears, perhaps they can't. No bear would normally drink spirits. Iorek Byrnison drank to forget the shame of exile, and it was only that which let the Trollesund people trick him."

"Ah, yes," said Lyra, nodding. She was satisfied with that idea. She admired Iorek almost without limit, and she was glad to find confirmation of his nobility. "That's clever of you," she said. "I wouldn't have known that if you hadn't told me. I think you're probably cleverer than Mrs Coulter."

They flew on. Lyra chewed some of the seal-meat she found in her pocket.

"Serafina Pekkala," she said after some time, "what's Dust? 'Cause it seems to me that all this trouble's about Dust, only no one's told me what it is."

"I don't know," Serafina Pekkala told her. "Witches have never worried about Dust. All I can tell you is that where there are priests, there is fear of Dust. Mrs Coulter is not a priest, of course, but she is a powerful agent of the Magisterium, and it was she who set up the Oblation Board and persuaded the Church to pay for Bolvangar, because of her interest in Dust. We can't understand her feelings about it. But there are many things we have never understood. We see the Tartars making holes in their skulls, and we can only wonder at the strangeness of it. So Dust may be strange, and we wonder at it, but we don't fret and tear things apart to examine it. Leave that to the Church."

"The Church?" said Lyra. Something had come back to her: she remembered talking with Pantalaimon, in the Fens, about what it might be that was moving the needle of the alethiometer, and they had thought of the photo-mill on the high altar at Gabriel College, and how elementary particles pushed the little vanes around. The Intercessor there was clear about the link between elementary particles and religion. "Could be," she said, nodding. "Most Church things, they keep secret, after all. But most Church things are old, and Dust en't old, as far as I know. I wonder if Lord Asriel might tell me..."

She yawned again.

"I better lie down," she said to Serafina Pekkala, "else I'll probably freeze. I been cold down on the ground, but I never been this cold. I think I might die if I get any colder."

"Then lie down and wrap yourself in the furs."

"Yeah, I will. If I was going to die, I'd rather die up here than down there, any day. I thought when they put us under that blade thing, I thought that was it... We both did. Oh, that was cruel. But we'll lie down now. Wake us up when we get there," she said, and got down on the pile of furs, clumsy and aching in every part of her with the profound intensity of the cold, and lay as close as she could to the sleeping Roger.

And so the four travellers sailed on, sleeping in the ice-encrusted balloon, towards the rocks and glaciers, the fire-mines and the ice-forts of Svalbard.

Serafina Pekkala called to the aëronaut, and he woke at once, groggy with cold, but aware from the movement of the basket that something was wrong. It was swinging wildly as strong winds buffeted the gas-bag, and the witches pulling the rope were barely managing to hold it. If they let go, the balloon would be swept off course at once, and to judge by his glance at the compass, would be swept towards Nova Zembla at nearly a hundred miles an hour.

"Where are we?" Lyra heard him call. She was half-waking herself, uneasy because of the motion, and so cold that every part of her body was numb.

She couldn't hear the witch's reply, but through her half-closed hood she saw, in the light of an anbaric lantern, Lee Scoresby hold on to a strut and pull at a rope leading up into the gas-bag itself. He gave a sharp tug as if against some obstruction, and looked up into the buffeting dark before looping the rope around a cleat on the suspension-ring.

"I'm letting out some gas," he shouted to Serafina Pekkala. "We'll go down. We're way too high."

The witch called something in return, but again Lyra couldn't hear it. Roger was waking too; the creaking of the basket was enough to wake the deepest sleeper, never mind the rocking and bumping. Roger's dæmon and Pantalaimon clung together like marmosets, and Lyra concentrated on lying still and not leaping up in fear.

"'S all right," Roger said, sounding much more cheerful than she was. "Soon's we get down we can make a fire and get warm. I got some matches in me pocket. I pinched 'em out of the kitchen at Bolvangar."

The balloon was certainly descending, because they were enveloped a second later in the thick freezing cloud. Scraps and wisps of it flew through the basket, and then everything was obscured, all at once. It was like the thickest fog Lyra had ever known. After a moment or two there came another cry from Serafina Pekkala, and the aëronaut unlooped the rope from the cleat and let go. It sprang upwards through his hands, and even over the creak and the buffeting and the howl of the wind through the rigging, Lyra heard or felt a mighty thump from somewhere far above.

Lee Scoresby saw her wide eyes.

"That's the gas-valve," he shouted. "It works on a spring to hold the gas in. When I pull it down, some gas escapes outa the top, and we lose buoyancy and go down."

"Are we nearly —"

She didn't finish, because something hideous happened. A creature half the size of a man, with leathery wings and hooked claws, was crawling over the side of the basket towards Lee Scoresby. It had a flat head, with bulging eyes and a wide frog-mouth, and from it came wafts of abominable stink. Lyra had no time to scream, even, before Iorek Byrnison reached up and cuffed it away. It fell out of the basket and vanished with a shriek.

"Cliff-ghast," said Iorek briefly.

The next moment Serafina Pekkala appeared, and clung to the side of the basket, speaking urgently.

"The cliff-ghasts are attacking. We'll bring the balloon to the ground, and then we must defend ourselves. They're –"

But Lyra didn't hear the rest of what was said, because there was a rending, ripping sound, and everything tilted sideways. Then a terrific blow hurled the three humans against the side of the balloon where Iorek Byrnison's armour was stacked. Iorek put out a great paw to hold them in, because the basket was jolting so violently. Serafina Pekkala had vanished. The noise was appalling: over every other sound there came the shrieking of the cliff-ghasts, and Lyra saw them hurtling past, and smelt their foul stench.

Then there came another jerk, so sudden that it threw them all to the floor again, and the basket began to sink with frightening speed, spinning all the while. It felt as if they had torn loose from the balloon, and were dropping unchecked by anything; and then came another series of jerks and crashes, the basket being tossed rapidly from side to side as if they were bouncing between rock walls.

The last thing Lyra saw was Lee Scoresby firing his long-barrelled pistol directly in the face of a cliff-ghast; and then she shut her eyes tight, and clung to Iorek Byrnison's fur with passionate fear. Howls, shrieks, the lash and whistle of the wind, the creak of the basket like a tormented animal, all filled the wild air with hideous noise.

Then came the biggest jolt of all, and she found herself hurled out altogether. Her grip was torn loose, and all the breath was knocked out of her lungs as she landed in such a tangle that she couldn't tell which way was up; and her face in the tight-pulled hood was full of powder, dry, cold, crystals –

It was snow; she had landed in a snow-drift. She was so battered that she could hardly think. She lay quite still for several seconds before feebly spitting out the snow in her mouth, and then she blew just as feebly until there was a little space to breathe in.

Nothing seemed to be *hurting* in particular; she just felt utterly breathless. Cautiously she tried to move hands, feet, arms, legs, and to raise her head.

She could see very little, because her hood was still filled with snow. With an effort, as if her hands weighed a ton each, she brushed it off and peered out. She saw a world of grey, of pale greys and dark greys and blacks, where fog-drifts wandered like wraiths.

The only sounds she could hear were the distant cries of the cliff-ghasts, high above, and the crash of waves on rocks, some way off.

"Iorek!" she cried. Her voice was faint and shaky, and she tried again, but no one answered. "Roger!" she called, with the same result.

She might have been alone in the world, but of course she never was, and Pantalaimon crept out of her anorak as a mouse to keep her company.

"I've checked the alethiometer," he said, "and it's all right. Nothing's broken."

"We're lost, Pan!" she said. "Did you see those cliff-ghasts? And Mr Scoresby shooting 'em? God help us if they come down here…"

"We better try and find the basket," he said, "maybe."

"We better not call out," she said. "I did just now, but maybe I better not in case they hear us. I wish I knew where we were."

"We might not like it if we did," he pointed out. "We might be at the bottom of a cliff with no way up, and the cliff-ghasts at the top to see us when the fog clears."

She felt around, once she had rested a few more minutes, and found that she had landed in a gap between two ice-covered rocks. Freezing fog covered everything; to one side there was the crash of waves about fifty yards off, by the sound of it, and from high above there still came the shrieking of the cliff-ghasts, though that seemed to be abating a little. She could see no more than two or three yards in the murk, and even Pantalaimon's owl-eyes were helpless.

She made her way painfully, slipping and sliding on the rough rocks, away from the waves and up the beach a little, and found nothing but rocks and snow, and no sign of the balloon or any of the occupants.

"They *can't* have all just vanished," she whispered.

Pantalaimon prowled cat-formed a little further afield, and came across four heavy sand-bags broken open, with the scattered sand already freezing hard.

"Ballast," Lyra said. "He must've slung 'em off to fly up again..."

She swallowed hard to subdue the lump in her throat, or the fear in her breast, or both.

"Oh, God, I'm frightened," she said. "I hope they're safe."

He came to her arms and then, mouse-formed, crept into her hood where he couldn't be seen. She heard a noise, something scraping on rock, and turned to see what it was.

"Iorek!"

But she choked the word back unfinished, for it wasn't Iorek

Byrnison at all. It was a strange bear, clad in polished armour with the dew on it frozen into frost, and with a plume in his helmet.

He stood still, about six feet away, and she thought she really was finished.

The bear opened his mouth and roared. An echo came back from the cliffs and stirred more shrieking from far above. Out of the fog came another bear, and another. Lyra stood still, clenching her little human fists.

The bears didn't move until the first one said, "Your name?"

"Lyra."

"Where have you come from?"

"The sky."

"In a balloon?"

"Yes."

"Come with us. You are a prisoner. Move, now. Quickly."

Weary and scared, Lyra began to stumble over the harsh and slippery rocks, following the bear, wondering how she could talk her way out of this.

19

Captivity

 he bears took Lyra up a gully in the cliffs, where the fog lay even more thickly than on the shore. The cries of the cliff-ghasts and the crash of the waves grew fainter as they climbed, and presently the only sound was the ceaseless crying of seabirds. They clambered in silence over rocks and snowdrifts, and although Lyra peered wide-eyed into the enfolding greyness, and strained her ears for the sound of her friends, she might have been the only human on Svalbard; and Iorek might have been dead.

The bear-sergeant said nothing to her until they were on level ground. There they stopped. From the sound of the waves, Lyra judged them to have reached the top of the cliffs, and she dared not run away in case she fell over the edge.

"Look up," said the bear, as a waft of breeze moved aside the heavy curtain of the fog.

There was little daylight in any case, but Lyra did look, and found herself standing in front of a vast building of stone. It was as tall at least as the highest part of Jordan College, but much more massive, and carved all over with representations of warfare, showing bears victorious and Skraelings surrendering, showing Tartars chained and slaving in the fire-mines, showing zeppelins flying from all parts of the world bearing gifts and tributes to the king of the bears, Iofur Raknison.

At least, that was what the bear-sergeant told her the carvings showed. She had to take his word for it, because every projection and ledge on the deeply sculpted façade was occupied by gannets and skuas, which cawed and shrieked and wheeled constantly around overhead, and whose droppings had coated every part of the building with thick smears of dirty white.

The bears seemed not to see the mess, however, and they led the way in through the huge arch, over the icy ground that was filthy with the spatter of the birds. There was a courtyard, and high steps, and gate-ways, and at every point bears in armour challenged the incomers and were given a password. Their armour was polished and gleaming, and they all wore plumes in their helmets. Lyra couldn't help comparing every bear she saw with Iorek Byrnison, and always to his advantage; he was more powerful, more graceful, and his armour was real armour, rust-coloured, blood-stained, dented with combat, not elegant, enam-elled and decorative like most of what she saw around her now.

As they went further in, the temperature rose, and so did something else. The smell in Iofur's palace was repulsive: rancid seal-fat, dung, blood, refuse of every sort. Lyra pushed back her hood to be cooler, but she couldn't help wrinkling her nose. She hoped bears couldn't read human expressions. There were iron brackets every few yards, holding blubber-lamps, and in their flaring shadows it wasn't always easy to see where she was treading, either.

Finally they stopped outside a heavy door of iron. A guard-bear pulled back a massive bolt, and the sergeant suddenly swung his head at Lyra, knocking her head over heels through the doorway. Before she could scramble up, she heard the door being bolted behind her.

It was profoundly dark, but Pantalaimon became a firefly, and shed a tiny glow around them. They were in a narrow cell where the walls dripped with damp, and there was one stone bench for furniture. In the furthest corner there was a heap of rags she took for bedding, and that was all she could see.

Lyra sat down, with Pantalaimon on her shoulder, and felt in her clothes for the alethiometer.

"It's certainly had a lot of banging about, Pan," she whispered. "I hope it still works."

Pantalaimon flew down to her wrist and sat there glowing, while Lyra composed her mind. With a part of her, she found it remarkable that she could sit here in terrible danger and yet sink into the calm she needed to read the alethiometer; and yet it was so much a part of her now that the most complicated questions sorted themselves out into their constituent symbols as naturally as her muscles moved her limbs: she hardly had to think about them.

She turned the hands and thought the question: "Where is Iorek?"

The answer came at once: "A day's journey away, carried there by the balloon after your crash; but hurrying this way."

"And Roger?"

"With Iorek."

"What will Iorek do?"

"He intends to break into the palace and rescue you, in the face of all the difficulties."

She put the alethiometer away, even more anxious than before.

"They won't let him, will they?" she said. "There's too many of 'em. I wish I was a witch, Pan, then you could go off and find him and take messages and all, and we could make a proper plan..."

Then she had the fright of her life.

A man's voice spoke in the darkness a few feet away, and said, "Who are you?"

She leapt up with a cry of alarm. Pantalaimon became a bat at once, shrieking, and flew around her head as she backed against the wall.

"Eh? Eh?" said the man again. "Who is that? Speak up! Speak up!"

"Be a firefly again, Pan," she said shakily. "But don't go too close."

The little wavering point of light danced through the air and fluttered around the head of the speaker. And it hadn't been a heap of rags after all: it was a grey-bearded man chained to the wall, whose eyes glittered in Pantalaimon's luminance, and whose tattered hair hung over his shoulders. His dæmon, a weary-looking serpent, lay in his lap, flicking out her tongue occasionally as Pantalaimon flew near.

"What's your name?" she said.

"Jotham Santelia," he replied. "I am the Regius Professor of Cosmology at the University of Gloucester. Who are you?"

"Lyra Belacqua. What have they locked you up for?"

"Malice and jealousy... Where do you come from? Eh?"

"From Jordan College," she said.

"What? Oxford?"

"Yes."

"Is that scoundrel Trelawney still there? Eh?"

"The Palmerian Professor? Yes," she said.

"Is he, by God! Eh? They should have forced his resignation long ago. Duplicitous plagiarist! Coxcomb!"

Lyra made a neutral sound.

"Has he published his paper on gamma-ray photons yet?" the Professor said, thrusting his face up towards Lyra's.

She moved back.

"I don't know," she said and then, making it up out of pure habit, "no," she went on. "I remember now. He said he still needed to check some figures. And ... he said he was going to write about Dust as well. That's it."

"Scoundrel! Thief! Blackguard! Rogue!" shouted the old man, and he shook so violently that Lyra was afraid he'd have a fit. His dæmon slithered lethargically off his lap as the Professor beat his fists against his shanks. Drops of saliva flew out of his mouth.

"Yeah," said Lyra, "I always thought he was a thief. And a rogue and all that."

If it was unlikely for a scruffy little girl to turn up in his cell knowing the very man who figured in his obsessions, the Regius Professor didn't notice. He *was* mad, and no wonder, poor old man; but he might have some scraps of information that Lyra could use.

She sat carefully near him, not near enough for him to touch, but near enough for Pantalaimon's tiny light to show him clearly.

"One thing Professor Trelawney used to boast about," she said, "was how well he knew the king of the bears –"

"Boast! Eh? Eh? I should say he boasts! He's nothing but a popinjay! And a pirate! Not a scrap of original research to his name! Everything filched from better men!"

"Yeah, that's right," said Lyra earnestly. "And when he does do something of his own, he gets it wrong."

"Yes! Yes! Absolutely! No talent, no imagination, a fraud from top to bottom!"

"I mean, for example," said Lyra, "I bet you know more about the bears than he does, for a start."

"Bears," said the old man, "ha! I could write a treatise on them! That's why they shut me away, you know."

"Why's that?"

"I know too much about them, and they daren't kill me. They daren't do it, much as they'd like to. I know, you see. I have friends. Yes! Powerful friends."

"Yeah," said Lyra. "And I bet you'd be a wonderful teacher," she went on. "Being as you got so much knowledge and experience."

Even in the depths of his madness a little common sense still flickered, and he looked at her sharply, almost as if he suspected her of sarcasm. But she had been dealing with suspicious and cranky scholars all her life, and she gazed back with such bland admiration that he was soothed.

"Teacher," he said, "teacher... Yes, I could teach. Give me the right pupil, and I will light a fire in his mind!"

"Because your knowledge ought not to just vanish," Lyra said encouragingly. "It ought to be passed on so people remember you."

"Yes," he said, nodding seriously. "That's very perceptive of you, child. What is your name?"

"Lyra," she told him again. "Could you teach me about the bears?"

"The bears..." he said doubtfully.

"I'd really like to know about cosmology and Dust and all, but I'm not clever enough for that. You need really clever students for that. But I could learn about the bears. You could teach me about them all right. And we could sort of practise on that and work up to Dust, maybe."

He nodded again.

"Yes," he said, "yes, I believe you're right. There is a correspondence between the microcosm and the macrocosm! The stars are alive, child. Did you know that? Everything out there is alive, and there are grand purposes abroad! The universe is full of *intentions*, you know. Everything happens for a purpose. Your purpose is to remind me of that. Good, good – in my despair I had forgotten. Good! Excellent, my child!"

"So, have you seen the king? Iofur Raknison?"

"Yes. Oh, yes. I came here at his invitation, you know. He intended to set up a university. He was going to make me Vice-Chancellor. That would be one in the eye for the Royal Arctic Society, eh! Eh? And that scoundrel Trelawney! Ha!"

"What happened?"

"I was betrayed by lesser men. Trelawney among them, of course. He was here, you know. On Svalbard. Spread lies and calumny about my qualifications. Calumny! Slander! Who was it discovered the final proof of the Barnard-Stokes hypothesis, eh? Eh? Yes, Santelia, that's who. Trelawney couldn't take it. Lied through his teeth. Iofur Raknison had me thrown in here. I'll be out one day, you'll see. I'll be Vice-Chancellor, oh yes. Let Trelawney come to me then begging for mercy! Let the Publications Committee of the Royal Arctic Society spurn my contributions then! Ha! I'll expose them all!"

"I expect Iorek Byrnison will believe you, when he comes back," Lyra said.

"Iorek Byrnison? No good waiting for that. *He'll* never come back."

"He's on his way now."

"Then they'll kill him. He's not a bear, you see. He's an outcast. Like me. Degraded, you see. Not entitled to any of the privileges of a bear."

"Supposing Iorek Byrnison did come back, though," Lyra said. "Supposing he challenged Iofur Raknison to a fight..."

"Oh, they wouldn't allow it," said the Professor decisively. "Iofur would never lower himself to acknowledge Iorek Byrnison's right to fight him. Hasn't *got* a right. Iorek might as well be a seal now, or a walrus, not a bear. Or worse: Tartar or Skraeling. They wouldn't fight him honourably like a bear; they'd kill him with fire-hurlers before he got near. Not a hope. No mercy."

"Oh," said Lyra, with a heavy despair in her breast. "And what about the bears' other prisoners? Do you know where they keep them?"

"Other prisoners?"

"Like … Lord Asriel."

Suddenly the Professor's manner changed altogether. He cringed and shrank back against the wall, and shook his head warningly.

"Sssh! Quiet! They'll hear you!" he whispered.

"Why mustn't we mention Lord Asriel?"

"Forbidden! Very dangerous! Iofur Raknison will not allow him to be mentioned!"

"Why?" Lyra said, coming closer and whispering herself so as not to alarm him.

"Keeping Lord Asriel prisoner is a special charge laid on Iofur by the Oblation Board," the old man whispered back. "Mrs Coulter herself came here to see Iofur and offered him all kinds of rewards to keep Lord Asriel out of the way. I know about it, you see, because at the time I was in Iofur's favour myself. I met Mrs Coulter! Yes. Had a long conversation with her. Iofur was besotted with her. Couldn't stop talking about her. Would do anything for her. If she wants Lord Asriel kept a hundred miles away, that's what will happen. Anything for Mrs Coulter, anything. He's going to name his capital city after her, did you know that?"

"So he wouldn't let anyone go and see Lord Asriel?"

"No! Never! But he's afraid of Lord Asriel too, you know. Iofur's playing a difficult game. But he's clever. He's done what they both want. He's kept Lord Asriel isolated, to please Mrs Coulter; and he's let Lord Asriel have all the equipment he wants, to please *him*. Can't last, this equilibrium. Unstable. Pleasing both sides. Eh? The wave function of this situation is going to collapse quite soon. I have it on good authority."

"Really?" said Lyra, her mind elsewhere, furiously thinking about what he'd just said.

"Yes. My dæmon's tongue can taste probability, you know."

"Yeah. Mine too. When do they feed us, Professor?"

"Feed us?"

"They must put some food in sometime, else we'd starve. And there's bones on the floor. I expect they're seal bones, aren't they?"

"Seal ... I don't know. It might be."

Lyra got up and felt her way to the door. There was no handle, naturally, and no keyhole, and it fitted so closely at top and bottom that no light showed. She pressed her ear to it, but heard nothing. Behind her the old man was muttering to himself. She heard his chain rattle as he turned over wearily and lay the other way, and presently he began to snore.

She felt her way back to the bench. Pantalaimon, tired of putting out light, had become a bat, which was all very well for him; he fluttered around squeaking quietly while Lyra sat and chewed a fingernail.

Quite suddenly, with no warning at all, she remembered what it was that she'd heard the Palmerian Professor saying in the Retiring Room all that time ago. Something had been nagging at her ever since Iorek Byrnison had first mentioned Iofur's name, and now it came back: what Iofur Raknison wanted more than anything else, Professor Trelawney had said, was a dæmon.

Of course, she hadn't understood what he meant; he'd spoken of *panserbjørne* instead of using the English word, so she didn't know he was talking about bears, and she had no idea that Iofur Raknison wasn't a man. And a man would have had a dæmon anyway, so it hadn't made sense.

But now it was plain. Everything she'd heard about the bear-king added up: the mighty Iofur Raknison wanted nothing more than to be a human being, with a dæmon of his own.

And as she thought that, a plan came to her: a way of making Iofur Raknison do what he would normally never have done; a way of restoring Iorek Byrnison to his rightful throne; a way, finally, of getting to the place where they had put Lord Asriel, and taking him the alethiometer.

The idea hovered and shimmered delicately, like a soap bubble, and she dared not even look at it directly in case it burst. But she was familiar with the way of ideas, and she let it shimmer, looking away, thinking about something else.

She was nearly asleep when the bolts clattered and the door opened. Light spilled in, and she was on her feet at once, with Pantalaimon hidden swiftly in her pocket.

As soon as the bear-guard bent his head to lift the haunch of seal-meat and throw it in, she was at his side, saying:

"Take me to Iofur Raknison. You'll be in trouble if you don't. It's very urgent."

He dropped the meat from his jaws and looked up. It wasn't easy to read bears' expressions, but he looked angry.

"It's about Iorek Byrnison," she said quickly. "I know something about him, and the king needs to know."

"Tell me what it is, and I'll pass the message on," said the bear.

"That wouldn't be right, not for someone else to know before the king does," she said. "I'm sorry, I don't mean to be rude, but you see, it's the rule that the king has to know things first."

Perhaps he was slow-witted. At any rate, he paused, and then threw the meat into the cell before saying, "Very well. You come with me."

He led her out into the open air, for which she was grateful. The fog had lifted and there were stars glittering above the high-walled courtyard. The guard conferred with another bear, who came to speak to her.

"You cannot see Iofur Raknison when you please," he said. "You have to wait till he wants to see you."

"But this is urgent, what I've got to tell him," she said. "It's about Iorek Byrnison. I'm sure His Majesty would want to know it, but all the same I can't tell it to anyone else, don't you see? It wouldn't be polite. He'd be ever so cross if he knew we hadn't been polite."

That seemed to carry some weight, or else to mystify the bear sufficiently to make him pause. Lyra was sure her interpretation of things was right: Iofur Raknison was introducing so many new ways that none of the bears was certain yet how to behave, and she could exploit this uncertainty in order to get to Iofur.

So that bear retreated to consult the bear above him, and before long Lyra was ushered inside the Palace again, but into the State quarters this time. It was no cleaner here, and in fact the air was even harder to breathe than in the cell, because all the natural stinks had been overlaid by a heavy layer of cloying perfume. She was made to wait in the corridor, then in an ante-room, then outside a large door, while bears discussed and argued and scurried back and forth, and she had time to look around at the preposterous decoration: the walls were rich with gilt plasterwork, some of which was already peeling off or crumbling with damp, and the florid carpets were trodden with filth.

Finally the large door was opened from the inside. A blaze of light from half a dozen chandeliers, a crimson carpet, and more of that thick perfume hanging in the air; and the faces of a dozen or more bears, all gazing at her, none in armour but each with some kind of decoration: a golden necklace, a head-dress of purple feathers, a crimson sash.

Curiously, the room was also occupied by birds; terns and skuas perched on the plaster cornice, and swooped low to snatch at bits of fish that had fallen out of one another's nests in the chandeliers.

And on a dais at the far end of the room, a mighty throne reared up high. It was made of granite for strength and massiveness, but like so many other things in Iofur's palace, it was decorated with over-elaborate swags and festoons of gilt that looked like tinsel on a mountainside.

Sitting on the throne was the biggest bear she had ever seen. Iofur Raknison was even taller and bulkier than Iorek, and his face was much more mobile and expressive, with a kind of humanness in it which she had never seen in Iorek's. When Iofur looked at her she seemed to see a man looking out of his eyes, the sort of man she had met at Mrs Coulter's, a subtle politician used to power. He was wearing a heavy gold chain around his neck, with a gaudy jewel hanging from it, and his claws – a good six inches long – were each covered in gold leaf. The effect was one of enormous strength and energy and craft; he was quite big enough to carry the absurd over-decoration; on him it didn't look preposterous, it looked barbaric and magnificent.

She quailed. Suddenly her idea seemed too feeble for words.

But she moved a little closer, because she had to, and then she saw that Iofur was holding something on his knee, as a human might let a cat sit there – or a dæmon.

It was a big stuffed doll, a manikin with a vacant stupid human face. It was dressed as Mrs Coulter would dress, and it had a sort of rough resemblance to her. He was pretending he had a dæmon. Then she knew she was safe.

She moved up close to the throne and bowed very low, with Pantalaimon keeping quiet and still in her pocket.

"Our greetings to you, great King," she said quietly. "Or I mean *my* greetings, not his."

"Not whose?" he said, and his voice was lighter than she had thought it would be, but full of expressive tones and subtleties. When he spoke, he waved a paw in front of his mouth to dislodge the flies that clustered there.

"Iorek Byrnison's, Your Majesty," she said. "I've got something very important and secret to tell you, and I think I ought to tell you in private, really."

"Something about Iorek Byrnison?"

She came close to him, stepping carefully over the bird-spattered floor, and brushed away the flies buzzing at her face.

"Something about dæmons," she said, so that only he could hear.

His expression changed. She couldn't read what it was saying, but there was no doubt that he was powerfully interested. Suddenly he lumbered forward off the throne, making her skip aside, and roared an order to the other bears. They all bowed their heads and backed out towards the door. The birds, which had risen in a flurry at his roar, squawked and swooped around overhead before settling again on their nests.

When the throne room was empty but for Iofur Raknison and Lyra, he turned to her eagerly.

"Well?" he said. "Tell me who you are. What is this about dæmons?"

"I *am* a dæmon, Your Majesty," she said.

He stopped still.

"Whose?" he said.

"Iorek Byrnison's," was her answer.

It was the most dangerous thing she had ever said. She could see quite clearly that only his astonishment prevented him from killing her on the spot. She went on at once:

"Please, Your Majesty, let me tell you all about it first before you harm me. I've come here at my own risk, as you can see, and there's nothing I've got that could hurt you. In fact I want to help you, that's why I've come. Iorek Byrnison was the first bear to get a dæmon, but it should have been you. I would much rather be your dæmon than his, that's why I came."

"How?" he said, breathlessly. "How has a bear got a dæmon? And why him? And how are you so far from him?"

The flies left his mouth like tiny words.

"That's easy. I can go far from him because I'm like a witch's dæmon. You know how they can go hundreds of miles from their humans? It's like that. And as for how he got me, it was at Bolvangar. You've heard of Bolvangar, because Mrs Coulter must have told you about it, but she probably didn't tell you everything they were doing there."

"Cutting…" he said.

"Yes, cutting, that's part of it, intercision. But they're doing all kinds of other things too, like making artificial dæmons. And experimenting on animals. When Iorek Byrnison heard about it he offered himself for an experiment to see if they could make a dæmon for him, and they did. It was me. My name is Lyra. Just like when people have dæmons, they're animal-formed, so when a bear has a dæmon, it'll be human. And I'm his dæmon. I can see into his mind and know exactly what he's doing and where he is and –"

"Where is he now?"

"On Svalbard. He's coming this way as fast as he can."

"Why? What does he want? He must be mad! We'll tear him to pieces!"

"He wants me. He's coming to get me back. But I don't want to be his dæmon, Iofur Raknison, I want to be yours. Because once they saw how powerful a bear was with a dæmon, the people at Bolvangar decided not to do that experiment ever again. Iorek Byrnison was going to be the only bear who ever had a dæmon. And with me helping him, he could lead all the bears against you. That's what he's come to Svalbard for."

The bear-king roared his anger. He roared so loudly that the crystal in the chandeliers tinkled, and every bird in the great room shrieked, and Lyra's ears rang.

But she was equal to it.

"That's why I love you best," she said to Iofur Raknison, "because you're passionate and strong as well as clever. And I just had to leave him and come and tell you, because I don't want him ruling the bears. It ought to be you. And there *is* a way of taking me away from him and making me your dæmon, but you wouldn't know what it was unless I told you, and you might do the usual thing about fighting bears like him that've been outcast; I mean, not fight him properly, but kill him with fire-hurlers or something. And if you did that, I'd just go out like a light and die with him."

"But you – how can –"

"I *can* become your dæmon," she said, "but only if you defeat Iorek Byrnison in single combat. Then his strength will flow into you, and my mind will flow into yours, and we'll be like one person, thinking each other's thoughts; and you can send me miles away to spy for you, or keep me here by your side, whichever you like. And I'd help you lead the bears to capture Bolvangar, if you like, and make them create more dæmons for your favourite bears; or if you'd rather be the only bear with a dæmon, we could destroy Bolvangar for ever. We could do anything, Iofur Raknison, you and me together!"

All the time she was holding Pantalaimon in her pocket with a trembling hand, and he was keeping as still as he could, in the smallest mouse-form he had ever assumed.

Iofur Raknison was pacing up and down with an air of explosive excitement.

"Single combat?" he was saying. "Me? I must fight Iorek Byrnison? Impossible! He is outcast! How can that be? How can I fight him? Is that the only way?"

"It's the only way," said Lyra, wishing it were not, because Iofur Raknison seemed bigger and more fierce every minute. Dearly as she loved Iorek, and strong as her faith was in him, she couldn't really believe that he would ever beat this giant among giant bears. But it was the only hope they had. Being mown down from a distance by fire-hurlers was no hope at all.

Suddenly Iofur Raknison turned.

"Prove it!" he said. "Prove that you are a dæmon!"

"All right," she said. "I can do that, easy. I can find out anything that you know and no one else does, something that only a dæmon would be able to find out."

"Then tell me what was the first creature I killed."

"I'll have to go into a room by myself to do this," she said. "When I'm your dæmon you'll be able to see how I do it, but until then it's got to be private."

"There is an ante-room behind this one. Go into that, and come out when you know the answer."

Lyra opened the door and found herself in a room lit by one torch, and empty but for a cabinet of mahogany containing some tarnished silver ornaments. She took out the alethiometer and asked: "Where is Iorek now?"

"Four hours away, and hurrying ever faster."

"How can I tell him what I've done?"

"You must trust him."

She thought anxiously of how tired he would be. But then she reflected that she was not doing what the alethiomcter had just told her to do: she wasn't trusting him.

She put that thought aside and asked the question Iofur Raknison wanted. What was the first creature he had killed?

The answer came: Iofur's own father.

She asked further, and learned that Iofur had been alone on the ice as a young bear, on his first hunting expedition, and had come across a solitary bear. They had argued and fought, and Iofur had killed him. When he learned later that it was his own father (for bears were brought up by their mothers, and seldom saw their fathers) he concealed the truth of what he had done. No one knew about it but Iofur himself.

She put the alcthiometer away, and wondered how to tell him about it.

"Flatter him!" whispered Pantalaimon. "That's all he wants."

So Lyra opened the door and found Iofur Raknison waiting for her, with an expression of triumph, slyness, apprehension, and greed.

"Well?"

She knelt down in front of him and bowed her head to touch his left forepaw, the stronger, for bears were left-handed.

"I beg your pardon, Iofur Raknison!" she said. "I didn't know you were so strong and great!"

"What's this? Answer my question!"

"The first creature you killed was your own father. I think you're a new god, Iofur Raknison. That's what you must be. Only a god would have the strength to do that."

"You know! You can see!"

"Yes, because I *am* a dæmon, like I said."

"Tell me one thing more. What did the Lady Coulter promise me when she was here?"

Once again Lyra went into the empty room and consulted the alethiometer before returning with the answer.

"She promised you that she'd get the Magisterium in Geneva to agree that you could be baptised as a Christian, even though you hadn't got a dæmon then. Well, I'm afraid that she hasn't done that, Iofur Raknison, and quite honestly I don't think they'd ever agree to that if you didn't have a dæmon. I think she knew that, and she wasn't telling you the truth. But in any case when you've got me as your dæmon you *could* be baptised if you wanted to, because no one could argue then. You could demand it and they wouldn't be able to turn you down."

"Yes... True. That's what she said. True, every word. And she has deceived me? I trusted her, and she deceived me?"

"Yes, she did. But she doesn't matter any more. Excuse me, Iofur Raknison. I hope you won't mind me telling you, but Iorek Byrnison's only four hours away now, and maybe you better tell your guard bears not to attack him as they normally would. If you're going to fight him for me he'll have to be allowed to come to the Palace."

"Yes..."

"And maybe when he comes I better pretend I still belong to him, and say I got lost or something. He won't know. I'll pretend. Are you going to tell the other bears about me being Iorek's dæmon and then belonging to you when you beat him?"

"I don't know... What should I do?"

"I don't think you better mention it yet. Once we're together, you and me, we can think what's best to do and decide then. What you need to do now is explain to all the other bears why you're going to let Iorek fight you like a proper bear, even though he's an outcast. Because they won't understand, and we got to find a reason for that. I mean, they'll do what you tell them anyway, but if they see the reason for it, they'll admire you even more."

"Yes. What should we tell them?"

"Tell them... Tell them that to make your kingdom completely secure, you've called Iorek Byrnison here yourself to fight him, and the winner will rule over the bears for ever. See, if you make it look like *your* idea that he's coming, and not his, they'll be really impressed. They'll think you're able to call him here from far away. They'll think you can do anything."

"Yes..."

The great bear was helpless. Lyra found her power over him almost intoxicating, and if Pantalaimon hadn't nipped her hand sharply to remind her of the danger they were all in, she might have lost all her sense of proportion.

But she came to herself and stepped modestly back to watch and wait as the bears, under Iofur's excited direction, prepared the combat-ground for Iorek Byrnison; and meanwhile Iorek, knowing nothing about it, was hurrying ever closer towards what she wished she could tell him was a fight for his life.

20

À Outrance

 ights between bears were common, and the subject of much ritual. For a bear to kill another was rare, though, and when that happened it was usually by accident, or when one bear mistook the signals from another, as in the case of Iorek Byrnison. Cases of straightforward murder, like Iofur's killing of his own father, were rarer still.

But occasionally there came circumstances in which the only way of settling a dispute was a fight to the death. And for that, a whole ceremonial was prescribed.

As soon as Iofur announced that Iorek Byrnison was on his way, and a combat would take place, the combat-ground was swept and smoothed, and armourers came up from the fire-mines to check Iofur's armour. Every rivet was examined, every link tested, and the plates were burnished with the finest sand. Just as much attention was paid to his claws. The gold leaf was rubbed off, and each separate six-inch hook was sharpened and filed to a deadly point. Lyra watched with a growing sickness in the pit of her stomach, for Iorek Byrnison wouldn't be having this attention; he had been marching over the ice for nearly twenty-four hours already without rest or food; he might have been injured in the crash. And she had let him in for this fight without his knowledge. At one point, after Iofur Raknison had tested the sharpness of his claws on a fresh-killed walrus, slicing its skin open like paper, and the power of his crashing blows on the walrus's skull (two blows, and it was cracked like an egg), Lyra had to make an excuse to Iofur and go away by herself to weep with fear.

Even Pantalaimon, who could normally cheer her up, had little to say that was hopeful. All she could do was consult the alethiometer: he is an hour away, it told her, and again, she must trust him; and (this was harder to read) she even thought it was rebuking her for asking the same question twice.

By this time, word had spread among the bears, and every part of the combat ground was crowded. Bears of high rank had the best places, and there was a special enclosure for the she-bears, including of course Iofur's wives. Lyra was profoundly curious about she-bears, because she knew so little about them, but this was no time to wander about asking questions. Instead she stayed close to Iofur Raknison and watched the courtiers around him assert their rank over the common bears from outside, and tried to guess the meaning of the various plumes and badges and tokens they all seemed to wear. Some of the highest-ranking, she saw, carried little manikins like Iofur's rag-doll dæmon, trying to curry favour, perhaps, by imitating the fashion he'd begun. She was sardonically pleased to notice that when they saw that Iofur had discarded his, they didn't know what to do with theirs. Should they throw them away? Were they out of favour now? How should they behave?

Because that was the prevailing mood in his court, she was beginning to see. They weren't sure what they were. They weren't like Iorek Byrnison, pure and certain and absolute; there was a constant pall of uncertainty hanging over them, as they watched one another and watched Iofur.

And they watched her, with open curiosity. She remained modestly close to Iofur and said nothing, lowering her eyes whenever a bear looked at her.

The fog had lifted by this time, and the air was clear; and as chance would have it, the brief lifting of darkness towards noon coincided with the time Lyra thought Iorek was going to arrive. As she stood shivering on a little rise of dense-packed snow at the edge of the combat-ground, she looked up towards the faint lightness in the sky, and longed with all her heart to see a flight of ragged elegant black shapes descending to bear her away; or to see the Aurora's hidden city, where she would be able to walk safely along those broad boulevards in the sunlight; or to see Ma Costa's broad arms, to smell the friendly smells of flesh and cooking that enfolded you in her presence...

She found herself crying, with tears which froze almost as soon as they formed, and which she had to brush away painfully. She was so frightened. Bears, who didn't cry, couldn't understand what was happening to her; it was some human process, meaningless. And of course Pantalaimon couldn't comfort her as he normally would, though she kept her hand in her pocket firmly around his warm little mouse-form, and he nuzzled at her fingers.

Beside her, the smiths were making the final adjustments to Iofur Raknison's armour. He reared like a great metal tower, shining in polished steel, the smooth plates inlaid with wires of gold; his helmet enclosed the upper part of his head in a glistening carapace of silver-grey, with deep eye-slits; and the underside of his body was protected by a close-fitting sark of chain-mail. It was when she saw this that Lyra realized that she had betrayed Iorek Byrnison, for Iorek had nothing like it. His armour protected only his back and sides. She looked at Iofur Raknison, so sleek and powerful, and felt a deep sickness in her, like guilt and fear combined.

She said, "Excuse me, Your Majesty, if you remember what I said to you before…"

Her shaking voice felt thin and weak in the air. Iofur Raknison turned his mighty head, distracted from the target three bears were holding up in front for him to slash at with his perfect claws.

"Yes? Yes?"

"Remember, I said I'd better go and speak to Iorek Byrnison first, and pretend –"

But before she could even finish her sentence, there was a roar from the bears on the watch-tower. The others all knew what it meant and took it up with a triumphant excitement. They had seen Iorek.

"Please?" Lyra said urgently. "I'll fool him, you'll see."

"Yes. Yes. Go now. Go and *encourage* him!"

Iofur Raknison was hardly able to speak for rage and excitement.

Lyra left his side and walked across the combat-ground, bare and clear as it was, leaving her little footprints in the snow, and the bears on the far side parted to let her through. As their great bodies lumbered aside, the horizon opened, gloomy in the pallor of the light. Where was Iorek Byrnison? She could see nothing; but then, the watch-tower was high, and they could see what was still hidden from her. All she could do was walk forward in the snow.

He saw her before she saw him. There was a bounding and a heavy clank of metal, and in a flurry of snow Iorek Byrnison stood beside her.

"Oh, Iorek! I've done a terrible thing! My dear, you're going to have to fight Iofur Raknison, and you en't ready – you're tired and hungry, and your armour's –"

"What terrible thing?"

"I told him you was coming, because I read it on the symbol-reader; and he's desperate to be like a person and have a dæmon, just desperate. So I tricked him into thinking that I was your dæmon, and I was going to desert you and be his instead, but he had to fight you to make it happen. Because otherwise, Iorek, dear, they'd never let you fight, they were going to just burn you up before you got close –"

"You tricked Iofur Raknison?"

"Yes. I made him agree that he'd fight you instead of just killing you straight off like an outcast, and the winner would be king of the bears. I had to do that, because –"

"Belacqua? No. You are Lyra Silvertongue," he said. "To fight him is all I want. Come, little dæmon."

She looked at Iorek Byrnison in his battered armour, lean and ferocious, and felt as if her heart would burst with pride.

They walked together towards the massive hulk of Iofur's palace, where the combat-ground lay flat and open at the foot of the walls. Bears clustered at the battlements, white faces filled every window, and their heavy forms stood like a dense wall of misty white ahead, marked with the black dots of eyes and noses. The nearest ones moved aside, making two lines for Iorek Byrnison and his dæmon to walk between. Every bear's eyes were fixed on them.

Iorek halted across the combat-ground from Iofur Raknison. The king came down from the rise of trodden snow, and the two bears faced each other several yards apart.

Lyra was so close to Iorek that she could feel a trembling in him like a great dynamo, generating mighty anbaric forces. She touched him briefly on the neck at the edge of his helmet and said "Fight well, Iorek, my dear. You're the real king, and he en't. He's nothing."

Then she stood back.

"Bears!" Iorek Byrnison roared. An echo rang back from the palace walls, and startled birds out of their nests. He went on, "The terms of this combat are these. If Iofur Raknison kills me, then he will be king for ever, safe from challenge or dispute. If I kill Iofur Raknison, I shall be your king. My first order to you all will be to tear down that palace, that perfumed house of mockery and tinsel, and hurl the gold and marble into the sea. Iron is bear-metal. Gold is not. Iofur Raknison has polluted Svalbard. I have come to cleanse it. Iofur Raknison, I challenge you."

Then Iofur bounded forward a step or two, as if he could hardly hold himself back.

"Bears!" he roared in his turn. "Iorek Byrnison has come back at my invitation. I drew him here. It is for me to make the terms of this combat, and they are these: if I kill Iorek Byrnison, his flesh shall be torn apart and scattered to the cliff-ghasts. His head shall be displayed above my palace. His memory shall be obliterated. It shall be a capital crime to speak his name..."

He continued, and then each bear spoke again. It was a formula, a ritual faithfully followed. Lyra looked at the two of them, so utterly different: Iofur so glossy and powerful, immense in his strength and health, splendidly armoured, proud and kinglike; and Iorek smaller, though she had never thought he would look small, and poorly equipped, his armour rusty and dented. But his armour was his soul. He had made it and it fitted him. They were one. Iofur was not content with his armour; he wanted another soul as well. He was restless while Iorek was still.

And she was aware that all the other bears were making the comparison too. But Iorek and Iofur were more than just two bears. There were two kinds of beardom opposed here, two futures, two destinies. Iofur had begun to take them in one direction, and Iorek would take them in another, and in the same moment, one future would close for ever as the other began to unfold.

As their ritual combat moved towards the second phase, the two bears began to prowl restlessly on the snow, edging forward, swinging their heads. There was not a flicker of movement from the spectators, but all eyes followed them.

Finally the warriors were still and silent, watching each other face to face across the width of the combat-ground.

Then with a roar and a blur of snow both bears moved at the same moment. Like two great masses of rock balanced on adjoining peaks and shaken loose by an earthquake, that bound down the mountainsides gathering speed, leaping over crevasses and knocking trees into splinters, until they crash into each other so hard that both are smashed to powder and flying chips of stone: that was how the two bears came together. The crash as they met resounded in the still air and echoed back from the Palace wall. But they weren't destroyed, as rock would have been. They both fell aside, and the first to rise was Iorek. He twisted up in a lithe spring and grappled with Iofur, whose armour had been damaged by the collision and who couldn't easily raise his head. Iorek made at once for the vulnerable gap at his neck. He raked the white fur, and then hooked his claws beneath the edge of Iofur's helmet and wrenched it forward.

Sensing the danger, Iofur snarled and shook himself as Lyra had seen Iorek shake himself at the water's edge, sending sheets of water flying high into the air. And Iorek fell away, dislodged, and with a screech of twisting metal Iofur stood up tall, straightening the steel of his backplates by sheer strength. Then like an avalanche he hurled himself down on Iorek, who was still trying to rise.

Lyra felt her own breath knocked out of her by the force of that crashing fall. Certainly the very ground shook beneath her. How could Iorek survive that? He was struggling to twist himself and gain a purchase on the ground, but his feet were uppermost, and Iofur had fixed his teeth somewhere near Iorek's throat. Drops of hot blood were flying through the air: one landed on Lyra's fur, and she pressed her hand to it like a token of love.

Then Iorek's rear claws dug into the links of Iofur's chain-mail sark and ripped downwards. The whole front came away, and Iofur lurched sideways to look at the damage, leaving Iorek to scramble upright again.

For a moment the two bears stood apart, getting their breath back. Iofur was hampered now by that chain-mail, because from a protection it had changed all at once into a hindrance: it was still fastened at the bottom, and trailed around his rear legs. However, Iorek was worse off. He was bleeding freely from a wound at his neck, and panting heavily.

But he leapt at Iofur before the king could disentangle himself from the clinging chain-mail, and knocked him head over heels, following up with a lunge at the bare part of Iofur's neck, where the edge of the helmet was bent. Iofur threw him off, and then the two bears were at each other again, throwing up fountains of snow that sprayed in all directions and sometimes made it hard to see who had the advantage.

Lyra watched, hardly daring to breathe, and squeezing her hands together so tight it hurt. She thought she saw Iofur tearing at a wound in Iorek's belly, but that couldn't be right, because a moment later, after another convulsive explosion of snow, both bears were standing upright like boxers, and Iorek was slashing with mighty claws at Iofur's face, with Iofur hitting back just as savagely.

Lyra trembled at the weight of those blows. As if a giant were swinging a sledgehammer, and that hammer were armed with five steel spikes...

Iron clanged on iron, teeth crashed on teeth, breath roared harshly, feet thundered on the hard-packed ground. The snow around was splashed with red and trodden down for yards into a crimson mud.

Iofur's armour was in a pitiful state by this time, the plates torn and distorted, the gold inlay torn out or smeared thickly with blood, and his helmet gone altogether. Iorek's was in much better condition, for all its ugliness: dented, but intact, standing up far better to the great sledgehammer-blows of the bear-king, and turning aside those brutal six-inch claws.

But against that, Iofur was bigger and stronger than Iorek, and Iorek was weary and hungry, and had lost more blood. He was wounded in the belly, on both arms, and at the neck, whereas Iofur was bleeding only from his lower jaw. Lyra longed to help her dear friend, but what could she do?

And it was going badly for Iorek now. He was limping; every time he put his left forepaw on the ground, they could see that it hardly bore his weight. He never used it to strike with, and the blows from his right hand were feebler, too, almost little pats compared with the mighty crushing buffets he'd delivered only a few minutes before.

Iofur had noticed. He began to taunt Iorek, calling him broken-hand, whimpering cub, rust-eaten, soon-to-die, and other names, all the while swinging blows at him from right and left which Iorek could no longer parry. Iorek had to move backwards, a step at a time, and to crouch low under the rain of blows from the jeering bear-king.

Lyra was in tears. Her dear, her brave one, her fearless defender, was going to die, and she would not do him the treachery of looking away, for if he looked at her he must see her shining eyes and their love and belief, not a face hidden in cowardice or a shoulder fearfully turned away.

So she looked, but her tears kept her from seeing what was really happening, and perhaps it would not have been visible to her anyway. It certainly was not seen by Iofur.

Because Iorek was moving backwards only to find clean dry footing and a firm rock to leap up from, and the useless left arm was really fresh and strong. You could not trick a bear, but, as Lyra had showed him, Iofur did not want to be a bear, he wanted to be a man; and Iorek was tricking him.

At last he found what he wanted: a firm rock deep-anchored in the permafrost. He backed against it, tensing his legs and choosing his moment.

It came when Iofur reared high above, bellowing his triumph, and turning his head tauntingly towards Iorek's apparently weak left side.

That was when Iorek moved. Like a wave that has been building its strength over a thousand miles of ocean, and which makes little stir in the deep water, but which when it reaches the shallows rears itself up high into the sky, terrifying the shore-dwellers, before crashing down on the land with irresistible power – so Iorek Byrnison rose up against Iofur, exploding upwards from his firm footing on the dry rock and slashing with a ferocious left hand at the exposed jaw of Iofur Raknison.

It was a horrifying blow. It tore the lower part of his jaw clean off, so that it flew through the air scattering blood-drops in the snow many yards away.

Iofur's red tongue lolled down dripping over his open throat. The bear-king was suddenly voiceless, biteless, helpless. Iorek needed nothing more. He lunged, and then his teeth were in Iofur's throat, and he shook and shook this way, that way, lifting the huge body off the ground and battering it down as if Iofur were no more than a seal at the water's edge.

Then he ripped upwards, and Iofur Raknison's life came away in his teeth.

There was one ritual yet to perform. Iorek sliced open the dead king's unprotected chest, peeling the fur back to expose the narrow white and red ribs like the timbers of an upturned boat. Into the ribcage Iorek reached, and he plucked out Iofur's heart, red and steaming, and ate it there in front of Iofur's subjects.

Then there was acclamation, pandemonium, a crush of bears surging forward to pay homage to Iofur's conqueror.

Iorek Byrnison's voice rose above the clamour.

"Bears! Who is your king?"

And the cry came back, in a roar like that of all the shingle in the world in an ocean-battering storm:

"Iorek Byrnison!"

The bears knew what they must do. Every single badge and sash and coronet was thrown off at once and trampled contemptuously underfoot, to be forgotten in a moment. They were Iorek's bears now, and true bears, not uncertain semi-humans, conscious only of a torturing inferiority. They swarmed to the Palace and began to hurl great blocks of marble from the topmost towers, rocking the battlemented walls in their mighty fists until the stones came loose and then hurling them over the cliffs to crash on the jetty hundreds of feet below.

Iorek ignored them and unhooked his armour to attend to his wounds, but before he could begin, Lyra was beside him, stamping her foot on the frozen scarlet snow and shouting to the bears to stop smashing the Palace, because there were prisoners inside. They didn't hear, but Iorek did, and when he roared they stopped at once.

358

"Human prisoners?" Iorek said.

"Yes – Iofur Raknison put them in the dungeons – they ought to come out first and get shelter somewhere, else they'll be killed with all the falling rocks –"

Iorek gave swift orders, and some bears hurried into the Palace to release the prisoners. Lyra turned to Iorek.

"Let me help you – I want to make sure you en't too badly hurt, Iorek dear – oh, I wish there was some bandages or something! That's an awful cut on your belly –"

A bear laid a mouthful of some stiff green stuff, thickly frosted, on the ground at Iorek's feet.

"Bloodmoss," said Iorek. "Press it in the wounds for me, Lyra. Fold the flesh over it and then hold some snow there till it freezes."

He wouldn't let any bears attend to him, despite their eagerness. Besides, Lyra's hands were deft, and she was desperate to help; so the little child bent over the great bear-king, packing in the bloodmoss and freezing the raw flesh till it stopped bleeding. When she had finished, her mittens were sodden with Iorek's blood, but his wounds were staunched.

And by that time the prisoners – a dozen or so men, shivering and blinking and huddling together – had come out. There was no point in talking to the Professor, Lyra decided, because the poor man was mad; and she would have liked to know who the other men were, but there were many other urgent things to do. And she didn't want to distract Iorek, who was giving rapid orders and sending bears scurrying this way and that, but she was anxious about Roger, and about Lee Scoresby and the witches, and she was hungry and tired… She thought the best thing she could do just then was to keep out of the way.

So she curled up in a quiet corner of the combat-ground with

Pantalaimon as a wolverine to keep her warm, and piled snow over herself as a bear would do, and went to sleep.

Something nudged her foot, and a strange bear voice said, "Lyra Silvertongue, the king wants you."

She woke up nearly dead with cold, and couldn't open her eyes, for they had frozen shut; but Pantalaimon licked them to melt the ice on her eyelashes, and soon she was able to see the young bear speaking to her in the moonlight.

She tried to stand, but fell over twice.

The bear said, "Ride on me," and crouched to offer his broad back, and half-clinging, half-falling, she managed to stay on while he took her to a steep hollow, where many bears were assembled.

And among them was a small figure who ran towards her, and whose dæmon leapt up to greet Pantalaimon.

"Roger!" she said.

"Iorek Byrnison made me stay out there in the snow while he came to fetch you away – we fell out the balloon, Lyra! After you fell out we got carried miles and miles, and then Mr Scoresby let some more gas out and we crashed into a mountain, and we fell down such a slope like you never seen! And I don't know where Mr Scoresby is now, nor the witches. There was just me and Iorek Byrnison. He come straight back this way to look for you. And they told me about his fight..."

Lyra looked around. Under the direction of an older bear, the human prisoners were building a shelter out of driftwood and scraps of canvas. They seemed pleased to have some work to do. One of them was striking a flint to light a fire.

"There is food," said the young bear who had woken Lyra.

A fresh seal lay on the snow. The bear sliced it open with a claw and showed Lyra where to find the kidneys. She ate one raw: it was warm and soft and delicious beyond imagining.

"Eat the blubber too," said the bear, and tore off a piece for her. It tasted of cream flavoured with hazelnuts. Roger hesitated, but followed her example. They ate greedily, and within a very few minutes Lyra was fully awake and beginning to be warm.

Wiping her mouth, she looked around, but Iorek was not in sight.

"Iorek Byrnison is speaking with his counsellors," said the young bear. "He wants to see you when you have eaten. Follow me."

He led them over a rise in the snow to a spot where bears were beginning to build a wall of ice-blocks. Iorek sat at the centre of a group of older bears, and he rose to greet her.

"Lyra Silvertongue," he said. "Come and hear what I am being told."

He didn't explain her presence to the other bears, or perhaps they had learned about her already; but they made room for her and treated her with immense courtesy, as if she were a queen. She felt proud beyond measure to sit beside her friend Iorek Byrnison under the Aurora as it flickered gracefully in the polar sky, and join the conversation of the bears.

It turned out that Iofur Raknison's dominance over them had been like a spell. Some of them put it down to the influence of Mrs Coulter, who had visited him before Iorek's exile, though Iorek had not known about it, and given Iofur various presents.

"She gave him a drug," said one bear, "which he fed secretly to Hjalmur Hjalmurson, and made him forget himself."

Hjalmur Hjalmurson, Lyra gathered, was the bear whom Iorek had killed, and whose death had brought about his exile. So Mrs Coulter was behind that! And there was more.

"There are human laws that prevent certain things that she was planning to do, but human laws don't apply on Svalbard. She wanted to set up another station here like Bolvangar, only worse, and Iofur was going to allow her to do it, against all the custom of the bears; because humans have visited, or been imprisoned, but never lived and worked here. Little by little she was going to increase her power over Iofur Raknison, and his over us, until we were her creatures running back and forth at her bidding, and our only duty to guard the abomination she was going to create…"

That was an old bear speaking. His name was Søren Eisarson, and he was a counsellor, one who had suffered under Iofur Raknison.

"What is she doing now, Lyra?" said Iorek Byrnison. "Once she hears of Iofur's death, what will her plans be?"

Lyra took out the alethiometer. There was not much light to see it by, and Iorek commanded that a torch be brought.

"What happened to Mr Scoresby?" Lyra said while they were waiting. "And the witches?"

"The witches were attacked by another witch-clan. I don't know if the others were allied to the child-cutters, but they were patrolling our skies in vast numbers, and they attacked in the storm. I didn't see what happened to Serafina Pekkala. As for Lee Scoresby, the balloon soared up again after I fell out with the boy, taking him with it. But your symbol-reader will tell you what their fate is."

A bear pulled up a sledge on which a cauldron of charcoal was smouldering, and thrust a resinous branch into the heart of it. The branch caught at once, and in its glare Lyra turned the hands of the alethiometer and asked about Lee Scoresby.

It turned out that he was still aloft, borne by the winds towards Nova Zembla, and that he had been unharmed by the cliff-ghasts and had fought off the other witch-clan.

Lyra told Iorek, and he nodded, satisfied.

"If he is in the air, he will be safe," he said. "What of Mrs Coulter?"

The answer was complicated, with the needle swinging from symbol to symbol in a sequence that made Lyra puzzle for a long time. The bears were curious, but restrained by their respect for Iorek Byrnison, and his for Lyra, and she put them out of her mind and sank again into the alethiometric trance.

The play of symbols, once she had discovered the pattern of it, was dismaying.

"It says she's… She's heard about us flying this way, and she's got a transport zeppelin that's armed with machine-guns – I think that's it – and they're a-flying to Svalbard right now. She don't know yet about Iofur Raknison being beaten, of course, but she will soon because… Oh yes, because some witches will tell her, and they'll learn it from the cliff-ghasts. So I reckon there are spies in the air all around, Iorek. She was a-coming to … to pretend to help Iofur Raknison, but really she was going to take over power from him, with a regiment of Tartars that's a-coming by sea, and they'll be here in a couple of days.

"And as soon as she can she's a-going to where Lord Asriel is kept prisoner, and she's going to have him killed. Because… It's coming clear now: something I never understood before, Iorek! It's why she wants to kill Lord Asriel: it's because she knows what he's going to do, and she fears it, and she wants to do it herself and gain control before he does… It must be the city in the sky, it must be! She's trying to get to it first! And now it's telling me something else…"

She bent over the instrument, concentrating furiously as the needle darted this way and that. It moved almost too fast to follow: Roger, looking over her shoulder, couldn't even see it stop, and was conscious only of a swift flickering dialogue between Lyra's fingers turning the hands and the needle answering, as bewilderingly unlike language as the Aurora was.

"Yes," she said finally, putting the instrument down in her lap and blinking and sighing as she woke out of her profound concentration. "Yes, I see what it says. She's after me again. She wants something I've got, because Lord Asriel wants it too. They need it for this... For this experiment, whatever it is..."

She stopped there, to take a deep breath. Something was troubling her, and she didn't know what it was. She was sure that this *something* that was so important was the alethiometer itself, because after all, Mrs Coulter *had* wanted it, and what else could it be? And yet it wasn't, because the alethiometer had a different way of referring to itself, and this wasn't it.

"I suppose it's the alethiometer," she said unhappily. "It's what I thought all along. I've got to take it to Lord Asriel before she gets it. If *she* gets it, we'll all die."

As she said that, she felt so tired, so bone-deep weary and sad that to die would have been a relief. But the example of Iorek kept her from admitting it. She put the alethiometer away and sat up straight.

"How far away is she?" said Iorek.

"Just a few hours. I suppose I ought to take the alethiometer to Lord Asriel as soon as I can."

"I will go with you," said Iorek.

She didn't argue. While Iorek gave commands and organized an armed squad to accompany them on the final part of their journey north, Lyra sat still, conserving her energy. She felt that something had gone out of her during that last reading. She closed her eyes and slept, and presently they woke her and set off.

21

Lord Asriel's Welcome

*L*yra rode a strong young bear, and Roger rode another, while Iorek paced tirelessly ahead and a squad armed with a fire-hurler followed, guarding the rear.

The way was long and hard. The interior of Svalbard was mountainous, with jumbled peaks and sharp ridges deeply cut by ravines and steep-sided valleys, and the cold was intense. Lyra thought back to the smooth-running sledges of the gyptians on the way to Bolvangar; how swift and comfortable that progress now seemed to have been! The air here was more penetratingly chill than any she had experienced before; or it might have been that the bear she was riding wasn't as light-footed as Iorek; or it might have been that she was tired to her very soul. At all events, it was desperately hard going.

She knew little of where they were bound, or how far it was. All she knew was what the older bear Søren Eisarson had told her while they were preparing the fire-hurler. He had been involved in negotiating with Lord Asriel about the terms of his imprisonment, and he remembered it well.

At first, he'd said, the Svalbard bears regarded Lord Asriel as being no different from any of the other politicians, kings, or trouble-makers who had been exiled to their bleak island. The prisoners were important, or they would have been killed outright by their own people; they might be valuable to the bears one day, if their political fortunes changed and they returned to rule in their own countries; so it might pay the bears not to treat them with cruelty or disrespect.

So Lord Asriel had found conditions on Svalbard no better and no worse than hundreds of other exiles had done. But certain things had made his jailers more wary of him than of other prisoners they'd had. There was the air of mystery and spiritual peril surrounding anything that had to do with Dust; there was the clear panic on the part of those who'd brought him there; and there were Mrs Coulter's private communications with Iofur Raknison.

Besides, the bears had never met anything quite like Lord Asriel's own haughty and imperious nature. He dominated even Iofur Raknison, arguing forcefully and eloquently, and persuaded the bear-king to let him choose his own dwelling-place.

The first one he was allotted was too low down, he said. He needed a high spot, above the smoke and stir of the fire-mines and the smithies. He gave the bears a design of the accommodation he wanted, and told them where it should be; and he bribed them with gold, and he flattered and bullied Iofur Raknison, and with a bemused willingness the bears set to work. Before long a house had arisen on a headland facing north: a wide and solid place with fireplaces that burned great blocks of coal mined and hauled by bears, and with large windows of real glass. There he dwelt, a prisoner acting like a king.

And then he set about assembling the materials for a laboratory.

With furious concentration he sent for books, instruments, chemicals, all manner of tools and equipment. And somehow it had come, from this source or that; some openly, some smuggled in by the visitors he insisted he was entitled to have. By land, sea and air, Lord Asriel assembled his materials, and within six months of his committal, he had all the equipment he wanted.

And so he worked, thinking and planning and calculating, waiting for the one thing he needed to complete the task that so terrified the Oblation Board. It was drawing closer every minute.

Lyra's first glimpse of her father's prison came when Iorek Byrnison stopped at the foot of a ridge for the children to move and stretch themselves, because they had been getting dangerously cold and stiff.

"Look up there," he said.

A wide broken slope of tumbled rocks and ice, where a track had been laboriously cleared, led up to a crag outlined against the sky. There was no Aurora, but the stars were brilliant. The crag stood black and gaunt, but at its summit was a spacious building from which light spilled lavishly in all directions: not the smoky inconstant gleam of blubber-lamps, nor the harsh white of anbaric spotlights, but the warm creamy glow of naphtha.

The windows from which the light emerged also showed Lord Asriel's formidable power. Glass was expensive, and large sheets of it were prodigal of heat in these fierce latitudes; so to see them here was evidence of wealth and influence far greater than Iofur Raknison's vulgar palace.

They mounted their bears for the last time, and Iorek led the way up the slope towards the house. There was a courtyard that lay deep under snow, surrounded by a low wall, and as Iorek pushed open the gate they heard a bell ring somewhere in the building.

Lyra got down. She could hardly stand. She helped Roger down too and, supporting each other, the children stumbled through the thigh-deep snow towards the steps up to the door.

Oh, the warmth there would be inside that house! Oh, the peaceful rest!

She reached for the handle of the bell, but before she could reach it, the door opened. There was a small dimly-lit vestibule to keep the warm air in, and standing under the lamp was a figure she recognized: Lord Asriel's manservant Thorold, with his pinscher-dæmon Anfang.

Lyra wearily pushed back her hood.

"Who..." Thorold began, and then saw who it was, and went on, "Not Lyra? Little Lyra? Am I dreaming?"

He reached behind him to open the inner door.

A hall, with a coal fire blazing in a stone grate; warm naphtha light glowing on carpets, leather chairs, polished wood... It was like nothing Lyra had seen since leaving Jordan College, and it brought a choking gasp to her throat.

Lord Asriel's snow-leopard dæmon growled.

Lyra's father stood there, his powerful dark-eyed face at first fierce, triumphant, and eager; and then the colour faded from it; his eyes widened, in horror, as he recognized his daughter.

"No! No!"

He staggered back and clutched at the mantelpiece. Lyra couldn't move.

"Get out!" Lord Asriel cried. "Turn round, get out, go! *I did not send for you!*"

She couldn't speak. She opened her mouth twice, three times, and then managed to say:

"No, no, I came because –"

He seemed appalled; he kept shaking his head, he held up his hands as if to ward her off; she couldn't believe his distress.

She moved a step closer to reassure him, and Roger came to stand with her, anxious. Their dæmons fluttered out into the warmth, and after a moment Lord Asriel passed a hand across his brow and recovered slightly. The colour began to return to his cheeks as he looked down at the two children.

"Lyra," he said. "That is Lyra?"

"Yes, Uncle Asriel," she said, thinking that this wasn't the time to go into their true relationship. "I came to bring you the alethiometer from the Master of Jordan."

"Yes, of course you did," he said. "Who is this?"

"It's Roger Parslow," she said. "He's the Kitchen boy from Jordan College. But –"

"How did you get here?"

"I was just going to say, there's Iorek Byrnison outside, he's brought us here. He came with me all the way from Trollesund, and we tricked Iofur –"

"Who's Iorek Byrnison?"

"An armoured bear. He brought us here."

"Thorold," he called, "run a hot bath for these children, and prepare them some food. Then they will need to sleep. Their clothes are filthy; find them something to wear. Do it now, while I talk to this bear."

Lyra felt her head swim. Perhaps it was the heat, or perhaps it was relief. She watched the servant bow and leave the hall, and Lord Asriel go into the vestibule and close the door behind, and then she half-fell into the nearest chair.

Only a moment later, it seemed, Thorold was speaking to her.

"Follow me, miss," he was saying, and she hauled herself up and went with Roger to a warm bathroom, where soft towels hung on a heated rail, and where a tub of water steamed in the naphtha light.

"You go first," said Lyra. "I'll sit outside and we'll talk."

So Roger, wincing and gasping at the heat, got in and washed. They had swum naked together often enough, frolicking in the Isis or the Cherwell with other children, but this was different.

"I'm afraid of your uncle," said Roger through the open door. "I mean your father."

"Better keep calling him my uncle. I'm afraid of him too, sometimes."

"When we first come in he never saw me at all. He only saw you. And he was horrified, till he saw me. Then he calmed down all at once."

"He was just shocked," said Lyra. "Anyone would be, to see someone they didn't expect. He last saw me after that time in the Retiring Room. It's bound to be a shock."

"No," said Roger, "it's more than that. He was looking at me like a wolf, or summing."

"You're imagining it."

"I en't. I'm more scared of him than I was of Mrs Coulter, and that's the truth."

He splashed himself. Lyra took out the alethiometer.

"D'you want me to ask the symbol-reader about it?" Lyra said.

"Well, I dunno. There's things I'd rather not know. Seems to me everything I heard of since the Gobblers come to Oxford, everything's been bad. There en't been nothing good more than about five minutes ahead. Like I can see now, this bath's nice, and there's a nice warm towel there, about five minutes away. And once I'm dry maybe I'll think of summing nice to eat, but no further ahead than that. And when I've eaten maybe I'll look forward to a kip in a comfortable bed. But after that, I dunno, Lyra. There's been terrible things we seen, en't there?

And more a-coming, more'n likely. So I think I'd rather not know what's in the future. I'll stick to the present."

"Yeah," said Lyra wearily. "There's times I feel like that too."

So although she held the alethiometer in her hands for a little longer, it was only for comfort; she didn't turn the wheels, and the swinging of the needle passed her by. Pantalaimon watched it in silence.

After they'd both washed, and eaten some bread and cheese and drunk some wine and hot water, the servant Thorold said, "The boy is to go to bed. I'll show him where to go. His Lordship asks if you'd join him in the Library, Miss Lyra."

Lyra found Lord Asriel in a room whose wide windows overlooked the frozen sea far below. There was a coal fire under a wide chimney-piece, and a naphtha lamp turned down low, so there was little in the way of distracting reflections between the occupants of the room and the bleak starlit panorama outside. Lord Asriel, reclining in a large arm-chair on one side of the fire, beckoned her to come and sit in the other chair facing him.

"Your friend Iorek Byrnison is resting outside," he said. "He prefers the cold."

"Did he tell you about his fight with Iofur Raknison?"

"Not in detail. But I understand that he is now the king of Svalbard. Is that true?"

"Of course it's true. Iorek never lies."

"He seems to have appointed himself your guardian."

"No. John Faa told him to look after me, and he's doing it because of that. He's following John Faa's orders."

"How does John Faa come into this?"

"I'll tell you if you tell me something," she said. "You're my father, en't you?"

"Yes. So what?"

"So you should have told me before, that's what. You shouldn't hide things like that from people, because they feel stupid when they find out, and that's cruel. What difference would it make if I knew I was your daughter? You could have said it years ago. You could've told me and asked me to keep it secret, and I would, no matter how young I was, I'd have done that if you asked me. I'd have been so proud nothing would've torn it out of me, if you asked me to keep it secret. But you never. You let other people know, but you never told me."

"Who did tell you?"

"John Faa."

"Did he tell you about your mother?"

"Yes."

"Then there's not much left for me to tell. I don't think I want to be interrogated and condemned by an insolent child. I want to hear what you've seen and done on the way here."

"I brought you the bloody alethiometer, didn't I?" Lyra burst out. She was very near to tears. "I looked after it all the way from Jordan, I hid it and I treasured it, all through what's happened to us, and I learned about using it, and I carried it all this bloody way when I could've just given up and been safe, and you en't even said thank you, nor showed any sign that you're glad to see me. I don't know why I ever done it. But I did, and I kept on going, even in Iofur Raknison's stinking palace with all them bears around me I kept on going, all on me own, and I tricked him into fighting with Iorek so's I could come on here for your sake… And when you *did* see me you like to fainted, as if I was some horrible thing you never wanted to see again. You en't human, Lord Asriel. You en't my *father*. My *father* wouldn't treat me like that. Fathers are supposed to love their daughters, en't they? You don't love me, and I don't love you, and that's a fact. I love Farder Coram, and I love Iorek Byrnison; I love an armoured bear more'n I love my father. And I bet Iorck Byrnison loves me more'n you do."

"You told me yourself he's only following John Faa's orders. If you're going to be sentimental I shan't waste time talking to you."

"Take your bloody alethiometer, then, and I'm going back with Iorek."

"Where?"

"Back to the palace. He can fight with Mrs Coulter and the Oblation Board, when they turn up. If he loses then I'll die too, I don't care. If he wins we'll send for Lee Scoresby and I'll sail away in his balloon and –"

"Who's Lee Scoresby?"

"An aëronaut. He brought us here and then we crashed. Here you are, here's the alethiometer. It's all in good order."

He made no move to take it, and she laid it on the brass fender around the hearth.

"And I suppose I ought to tell you that Mrs Coulter's on her way to Svalbard, and as soon as she hears what's happened to Iofur Raknison, she'll be on her way here. In a zeppelin, with a whole lot of soldiers, and they're a–going to kill us all, by order of the Magisterium."

"They'll never reach us," he said calmly.

He was so quiet and relaxed that some of her ferocity dwindled.

"You don't know," she said uncertainly.

"Yes I do."

"Have you got another alethiometer, then?"

"I don't need an alethiometer for that. Now I want to hear about your journey here, Lyra. Start from the beginning. Tell me everything."

So she did. She began with her hiding in the Retiring Room, and went on to the Gobblers' taking Roger, and her time with Mrs Coulter, and everything else that had happened.

It was a long tale, and when she finished it she said, "So there's one thing I want to know, and I reckon I've got the right to know it, like I had the right to know who I really was. And if you didn't tell me that, you've got to tell me this, in recompense. So: what's Dust? And why's everyone so afraid of it?"

He looked at her as if trying to guess whether she would understand what he was about to say. He had never looked at her seriously before, she thought; until now he had always been like an adult indulging a child in a pretty trick. But he seemed to think she was ready.

"Dust is what makes the alethiometer work," he said.

"Ah … I thought it might! But what else? How did they find out about it?"

"In one way the Church has always been aware of it. They've been preaching about Dust for centuries, only they didn't call it by that name.

"But some years ago a Muscovite called Boris Mikhailovitch Rusakov discovered a new kind of elementary particle. You've heard of electrons, photons, neutrinos and the rest? They're called elementary particles because you can't break them down any further: there's nothing inside them but themselves. Well, this new kind of particle was elementary all right, but it was very hard to measure because it didn't react in any of the usual ways. The hardest thing for Rusakov to understand was why the new particle seemed to cluster where human beings were, as if it were attracted to us. And especially to adults. Children too, but not nearly so much until their dæmons have taken a fixed form. During the years of puberty they begin to attract Dust more strongly, and it settles on them as it settles on adults.

"Now all discoveries of this sort, because they have a bearing on the doctrines of the Church, have to be announced through the Magisterium in Geneva. And this discovery of Rusakov's was so unlikely and strange that the Inspector from the Consistorial Court of Discipline suspected Rusakov of diabolic possession. He performed an exorcism in the laboratory, he interrogated Rusakov under the rules of the Inquisition, but finally they had to accept the fact that Rusakov wasn't lying or deceiving them: Dust really existed.

"That left them with the problem of deciding what it was. And given the Church's nature, there was only one thing they could have chosen. The Magisterium decided that Dust was the physical evidence for original sin. Do you know what original sin is?"

She twisted her lips. It was like being back at Jordan, being quizzed on something she'd been half-taught. "Sort of," she said.

"No, you don't. Go to the shelf beside the desk and bring me the Bible."

Lyra did so, and handed the big black book to her father.

"You do remember the story of Adam and Eve?"

"Course," she said. "She wasn't supposed to eat the fruit and the serpent tempted her, and she did."

"And what happened then?"

"Umm... They were thrown out. God threw them out of the garden."

"God had told them not to eat the fruit, because they would die. Remember, they were naked in the garden, they were like children, their dæmons took on any form they desired. But this is what happened."

He turned to Chapter Three of Genesis, and read:

"And the woman said unto the serpent, We may eat of the fruit of the trees of the garden:

"But of the fruit of the tree which is in the midst of the garden, God hath said, Ye shall not eat of it, neither shall ye touch it, lest ye die.

"And the serpent said unto the woman, Ye shall not surely die:

"For God doth know that in the day ye eat thereof, then your eyes shall be opened, and your dæmons shall assume their true forms, and ye shall be as gods, knowing good and evil.

"And when the woman saw that the tree was good for food, and that it was pleasant to the eyes, and a tree to be desired to reveal the true form of one's dæmon, she took of the fruit thereof, and did eat, and gave also unto her husband with her; and he did eat.

"And the eyes of them both were opened, and they saw the true form of their dæmons, and spoke with them.

"But when the man and the woman knew their own dæmons, they knew that a great change had come upon them, for until that moment it had seemed that they were at one with all the creatures of the earth and the air, and there was no difference between them:

"And they saw the difference, and they knew good and evil; and they were ashamed, and they sewed fig leaves together to cover their naked-ness..."

He closed the book.

"And that was how sin came into the world," he said, "sin and shame and death. It came the moment their dæmons became fixed."

"But..." Lyra struggled to find the words she wanted: "but it en't *true*, is it? Not true like chemistry or engineering, not that kind of true? There wasn't *really* an Adam and Eve? The Cassington Scholar told me it was just a kind of fairy-tale."

"The Cassington Scholarship is traditionally given to a free-thinker; it's his function to challenge the faith of the Scholars. Naturally he'd say that. But think of Adam and Eve like an imaginary number, like the square root of minus one: you can never see any concrete proof that it exists, but if you include it in your equations, you can calculate all manner of things that couldn't be imagined without it.

"Anyway, it's what the Church has taught for thousands of years. And when Rusakov discovered Dust, at last there was a physical proof that something happened when innocence changed into experience.

"Incidentally, the Bible gave us the name Dust as well. At first they were called Rusakov Particles, but soon someone pointed out a curious verse toward the end of the Third Chapter of Genesis, where God's cursing Adam for eating the fruit."

He opened the Bible again and pointed it out to Lyra. She read:

"In the sweat of thy face shalt thou eat bread, till thou return unto the ground; for out of it wast thou taken: for dust thou art, and unto dust shalt thou return..."

Lord Asriel said, "Church scholars have always puzzled over the translation of that verse. Some say it should read not 'unto dust shalt thou return' but 'thou shalt be subject to dust', and others say the whole verse is a kind of pun on the words 'ground' and 'dust', and it really means that God's admitting his own nature to be partly sinful. No one agrees. No one can, because the text is corrupt. But it was too good a word to waste, and that's why the particles became known as Dust."

"And what about the Gobblers?" Lyra said.

"The General Oblation Board... Your mother's gang. Clever of her to spot the chance of setting up her own power base, but she's a clever woman, as I dare say you've noticed. It suits the Magisterium to allow all kinds of different agencies to flourish. They can play them off against one another; if one succeeds, they can pretend to have been sup-porting it all along, and if it fails, they can pretend it was a renegade outfit which had never been properly licensed.

"You see, your mother's always been ambitious for power. At first she tried to get it in the normal way, through marriage, but that didn't work, as I think you've heard. So she had to turn to the Church. Naturally she couldn't take the route a man could have taken – priesthood and so on – it had to be unorthodox; she had to set up her own order, her own channels of influence, and work through that. It was a good move to specialize in Dust. Everyone was frightened of it; no one knew what to do; and when she offered to direct an investigation, the Magisterium was so relieved that they backed her with money and resources of all kinds."

"But they were *cutting* –" Lyra couldn't bring herself to say it; the words choked in her mouth. "You know what they were doing! Why did the Church let them do anything like that?"

"There was a precedent. Something like it had happened before. Do you know what the word *castration* means? It means removing the sex-ual organs of a boy so that he never develops the characteristics of a man. A *castrato* keeps his high treble voice all his life, which is why the Church allowed it: so useful in Church music. Some *castrati* became great singers, wonderful artists. Many just became fat spoiled half-men. Some died from the effects of the operation. But the Church wouldn't flinch at the idea of a little *cut*, you see. There was a precedent. And this would be so much more *hygienic* than the old methods, when they did-n't have anaesthetics or sterile bandages or proper nursing care. It would be gentle by comparison."

"It isn't!" Lyra said fiercely. "It isn't!"

"No. Of course not. That's why they had to hide away in the far

North, in darkness and obscurity. And why the Church was glad to have someone like your mother in charge. Who could doubt someone so charming, so well-connected, so sweet and reasonable? But because it was an obscure and unofficial kind of operation, she was someone the Magisterium could deny if they needed to, as well."

"But whose idea was it to do that *cutting* in the first place?"

"It was hers. She guessed that the two things that happen at adolescence might be connected: the change in one's dæmon and the fact that Dust began to settle. Perhaps if the dæmon were separated from the body, we might never be subject to Dust – to original sin. The question was whether it was possible to separate dæmon and body without killing the person. But she's travelled in many places, and seen all kinds of things. She's travelled in Africa, for instance. The Africans have a way of making a slave called a *zombi*. It has no will of its own; it will work day and night without ever running away or complaining. It looks like a corpse…"

"It's a person without their dæmon!"

"Exactly. So she found out that it was possible to separate them."

"And … Tony Costa told me about the horrible phantoms they have in the Northern forests. I suppose they might be the same kind of thing."

"That's right. Anyway, the General Oblation Board grew out of ideas like that, and out of the Church's obsession with original sin."

Lord Asriel's dæmon twitched her ears, and he laid his hand on her beautiful head.

"There was something else that happened when they made the cut," he went on. "And they didn't see it. The energy that links body and dæmon is immensely powerful. When the cut is made, all that energy dissipates in a fraction of a second. They didn't notice, because they mistook it for shock, or disgust, or moral outrage, and they trained themselves to feel numb towards it. So they missed what it could do, and they never thought of harnessing it…"

Lyra couldn't sit still. She got up and walked to the window, and stared over the wide bleak darkness with unseeing eyes. They were too cruel. No matter how important it was to find out about original sin, it was too cruel to do what they'd done to Tony Makarios and all the others. Nothing justified that.

"And what were *you* doing?" she said. "Did you do any of that cutting?"

"I'm interested in something quite different. I don't think the Oblation Board goes far enough. I want to go to the source of Dust itself."

"The source? Where's it come from, then?"

"From the other universe we can see through the Aurora."

Lyra turned around again. Her father was lying back in his chair, lazy and powerful, his eyes as fierce as his dæmon's. She didn't love him, she couldn't trust him, but she had to admire him, and the extravagant luxury he'd assembled in this desolate wasteland, and the power of his ambition.

"What is that other universe?" she said.

"One of uncountable billions of parallel worlds. The witches have known about them for centuries, but the first theologians to prove their existence mathematically were excommunicated fifty or more years ago. However, it's true; there's no possible way of denying it.

"But no one thought it would ever be possible to cross from one universe to another. That would violate fundamental laws, we thought. Well, we were wrong; we learned to see the world up there. If light can cross, so can we. And we had to *learn* to see it, Lyra, just as you learned to use the alethiometer.

"Now that world, and every other universe, came about as a result of possibility. Take the example of tossing a coin: it can come down heads or tails, and we don't know before it lands which way it's going to fall. If it comes down heads, that means that the possibility of its coming down tails has collapsed. Until that moment the two possibilities were equal.

"But on another world, it does come down tails. And when that happens, the two worlds split apart. I'm using the example of tossing a coin to make it clearer. In fact, these possibility-collapses happen at the level of elementary particles, but they happen in just the same way: one moment several things are possible, the next moment only one happens, and the rest don't exist. Except that other worlds have sprung into being, on which they *did* happen.

"And I'm going to that world beyond the Aurora," he said, "because I think that's where all the Dust in this universe comes from. You saw those slides I showed the Scholars in the Retiring Room. You saw Dust pouring into this world from the Aurora. You've seen that city yourself. If light can cross the barrier between the universes, if Dust can, if we can see that city, then we can build a bridge and cross. It needs a phenomenal burst of energy. But I can do it. Somewhere out there is the origin of all the Dust, all the death, the sin, the misery, the destructiveness in the world. Human beings can't see anything without wanting to destroy it, Lyra. *That's* original sin. And I'm going to destroy it. Death is going to die."

"Is that why they put you here?"

"Yes. They are terrified. And with good reason."

He stood up, and so did his dæmon, proud and beautiful and deadly. Lyra sat still. She was afraid of her father, and she admired him profoundly, and she thought he was stark mad; but who was she to judge?

"Go to bed," he said. "Thorold will show you where to sleep."

He turned to go.

"You've left the alethiometer," she said.

"Ah, yes; I don't actually need that now," he said. "It would be no use to me without the books, anyway. D'you know, I think the Master of Jordan was giving it to *you*. Did he actually ask you to bring it to me?"

"Well, yes!" she said. But then she thought again, and realized that in fact the Master never had asked her to do that; she had assumed it all the time, because why else would he have given it to her? "No," she said. "I don't know. I thought –"

"Well, I don't want it. It's yours, Lyra."

"But –"

"Good night, child."

Speechless, too bewildered by this to voice any of the dozen urgent questions that pressed at her mind, she took up the alethiometer and wrapped it in its black velvet. Then she sat by the fire and watched him leave the room.

22

Betrayal

She woke to find a stranger shaking her arm, and then as Pantalaimon sprang awake and growled, she recognized Thorold. He was holding a naphtha lamp, and his hand was trembling.

"Miss – miss – get up quickly. I don't know what to do. He's left no orders. I think he's mad, miss."

"What? What's happening?"

"Lord Asriel, miss. He's been almost in a delirium since you went to bed. I've never seen him so wild. He packed a lot of instruments and batteries in a sledge and he harnessed up the dogs and left. But he's got the boy, miss!"

"Roger? He's taken Roger?"

"He told me to wake him and dress him, and I didn't think to argue – I never have – the boy kept on asking for you, miss – but Lord Asriel wanted him alone – you know when you first came to the door, miss? And he saw you and couldn't believe his eyes, and wanted you gone?"

Lyra's head was in such a whirl of weariness and fear that she could hardly think but, "Yes? Yes?" she said.

"It was because he needed a child to finish his experiment, miss! And

Lord Asriel has a way special to himself of bringing about what he wants, he just has to call for something and –"

Now Lyra's head was full of a roar, as if she were trying to stifle some knowledge from her own consciousness.

She had got out of bed, and was reaching for her clothes, and then she suddenly collapsed, and a fierce cry of despair enveloped her. She was uttering it, but it was bigger than she was; it felt as if the despair were uttering her. For she remembered his words: *the energy that links body and dæmon is immensely powerful*; and to bridge the gap between worlds needed *a phenomenal burst of energy...*

She had just realized what she'd done.

She had struggled all this way to bring something to Lord Asriel, thinking she knew what he wanted; and it wasn't the alethiometer at all. What he wanted was a child.

She had brought him Roger.

That was why he'd cried out, "I did not send for you!" when he saw her; he had sent for a child, and the fates had brought him his own daughter. Or so he'd thought, until she'd stepped aside and shown him Roger.

Oh, the bitter anguish! She had thought she was *saving* Roger, and all the time she'd been diligently working to betray him...

Lyra shook and sobbed in a frenzy of emotion. It couldn't be true.

Thorold tried to comfort her, but he didn't know the reason for her extremity of grief, and could only pat her shoulder nervously.

"Iorek –" she sobbed, pushing the servant aside. "Where's Iorek Byrnison? The bear? Is he still outside?"

The old man shrugged helplessly.

"Help me!" she said, trembling all over with weakness and fear. "Help me dress. I got to go. *Now!* Do it *quick!*"

He put the lamp down and did as she told him. When she commanded, in that imperious way, she was very like her father, for all that her face was wet with tears and her lips trembling. While Pantalaimon paced the floor lashing his tail, his fur almost sparking, Thorold hastened to bring her stiff, reeking furs and help her into them. As soon as all the buttons were done up and all the flaps secured, she made for the door, and felt the cold strike her throat like a sword and freeze the tears at once on her cheeks.

"Iorek!" she called. "Iorek Byrnison! Come, because I need you!"

There was a shake of snow, a clank of metal, and the bear was there. He had been sleeping calmly under the falling snow. In the light spilling from the lamp Thorold was holding at the window, Lyra saw the long faceless head, the dark eye holes, the gleam of white fur below red-black metal, and wanted to embrace him and seek some comfort from his iron helmet, his ice-tipped fur.

"Well?" he said.

"We got to catch Lord Asriel. He's taken Roger and he's a-going to – I daren't think – oh, Iorek, I beg you, go quick, my dear!"

"Come then," he said, and she leapt on his back.

There was no need to ask which way to go: the tracks of the sledge led straight out from the courtyard and over the plain, and Iorek leapt forward to follow them. His motion was now so much a part of Lyra's being that to sit balanced was entirely automatic. He ran over the thick snowy mantle on the rocky ground faster than he'd ever done, and the armour-plates shifted under her in a regular swinging rhythm.

Behind them, the other bears paced easily, pulling the fire-hurler with them. The way was clear, for the moon was high and the light it cast over the snowbound world was as bright as it had been in the balloon: a world of bright silver and profound black. The tracks of Lord

Asriel's sledge ran straight towards a range of jagged hills, strange stark pointed shapes jutting up into a sky as black as the alethiometer's velvet cloth. There was no sign of the sledge itself – or was there a feather-touch of movement on the flank of the highest peak? Lyra peered ahead, straining her eyes, and Pantalaimon flew as high as he could and looked with an owl's clear vision.

"Yes," he said, on her wrist a moment later; "it's Lord Asriel, and he's lashing his dogs on furiously, and there's a child in the back…"

Lyra felt Iorek Byrnison change pace. Something had caught his attention. He was slowing and lifting his head to cast left and right.

"What is it?" Lyra said.

He didn't say. He was listening intently, but she could hear nothing. Then she did hear something: a mysterious, vastly distant rustling and crackling. It was a sound she had heard before: the sound of the Aurora. Out of nowhere a veil of radiance had fallen to hang shimmering in the northern sky. All those unseen billions and trillions of charged particles and possibly, she thought, of Dust, conjured a radiating glow out of the upper atmosphere. This was going to be a display more brilliant and extraordinary than any Lyra had yet seen, as if the Aurora knew the drama that was taking place below, and wanted to light it with the most awe-inspiring effects.

But none of the bears were looking up: their attention was all on the earth. It wasn't the Aurora, after all, that had caught Iorek's attention. He was standing stock still now, and Lyra slipped off his back, knowing that his senses needed to cast around freely. Something was troubling him.

Lyra looked around, back across the vast open plain leading to Lord Asriel's house, back towards the tumbled mountains they'd crossed earlier, and saw nothing. The Aurora grew more intense. The first veils trembled and raced to one side, and jagged curtains folded and unfolded above, increasing in size and brilliance every minute; arcs and loops swirled across from horizon to horizon, and touched the very zenith with bows of radiance. She could hear more clearly than ever the immense singing hiss and swish of vast intangible forces.

"Witches!" came a cry in a bear-voice, and Lyra turned in joy and relief.

But a heavy muzzle knocked her forward, and with no breath left to gasp she could only pant and shudder, for there in the place where she had been standing was the plume of a green-feathered arrow. The head and the shaft were buried in the snow.

Impossible! she thought weakly, but it was true, for another arrow clattered off the armour of Iorek, standing above her. These were not Serafina Pekkala's witches; they were from another clan. They circled above, a dozen of them or more, swooping down to shoot and soaring up again, and Lyra swore with every word she knew.

Iorek Byrnison gave swift orders. It was clear that the bears were practised at witch-fighting, for they had moved at once into a defensive formation, and the witches moved just as smoothly into attack. They could only shoot accurately from close range, and in order not to waste arrows they would swoop down, fire at the lowest part of their dive, and turn upwards at once. But when they reached the lowest point, and their hands were busy with bow and arrow, they were vulnerable, and the bears would explode upwards with raking paws to drag them down. More than one fell, and was quickly dispatched.

Lyra crouched low beside a rock, watching for a witch-dive. A few shot at her, but the arrows fell wide; and then Lyra, looking up at the sky, saw the greater part of the witch-flight peel off and turn back.

If she was relieved by that, her relief didn't last more than a few moments. Because from the direction in which they'd flown, she saw many others coming to join them; and in mid-air with them there was a group of gleaming lights; and across the broad expanse of the Svalbard plain, under the radiance of the Aurora, she heard a sound she dreaded. It was the harsh throb of a gas-engine. The zeppelin, with Mrs Coulter and her troops on board, was catching up.

Iorek growled an order and the bears moved at once into another formation. In the lurid flicker from the sky Lyra watched as they swiftly unloaded their fire-hurler. The advance-guard of the witch-flight had seen them too, and began to swoop downwards and rain arrows on them, but for the most part the bears trusted to their armour and worked swiftly to erect the apparatus: a long arm extending upwards at an angle, a cup or bowl a yard across; and a great iron tank wreathed in smoke and steam.

As she watched, a bright flame gushed out, and a team of bears swung into practised action. Two of them hauled the long arm of the fire-thrower down, another scooped shovelfuls of fire into the bowl, and at an order they released it, to hurl the flaming sulphur high into the dark sky.

The witches were swooping so thickly above them that three fell in flames at the first shot alone, but it was soon clear that the real target was the zeppelin. The pilot either had never seen a fire-hurler before, or was underestimating its power, for he flew straight on towards the bears without climbing or turning a fraction to either side.

Then it became clear that they had a powerful weapon in the zeppelin too: a machine-rifle mounted on the nose of the gondola. Lyra saw sparks flying up from some of the bears' armour, and saw them huddle over under its protection, before she heard the rattle of the bullets. She cried out in fear.

"They're safe," said Iorek Byrnison. "Can't pierce armour with little bullets."

The fire-thrower worked again: this time a mass of blazing sulphur hurtled directly upwards to strike the gondola and burst in a cascade of flaming fragments on all sides. The zeppelin banked to the left, and roared away in a wide arc before making again for the group of bears working swiftly beside the apparatus. As it neared, the arm of the fire-thrower creaked downwards; the machine-rifle coughed and spat, and two bears fell, to a low growl from Iorek Byrnison; and when the aircraft was nearly overhead, a bear shouted an order, and the spring-loaded arm shot upwards again.

This time the sulphur hurtled against the envelope of the zeppelin's gas-bag. The rigid frame held a skin of oiled silk in place to contain the hydrogen, and although this was tough enough to withstand minor scratches, a hundredweight of blazing rock was too much for it. The silk ripped straight through, and sulphur and hydrogen leapt to meet each other in a catastrophe of flame.

At once the silk became transparent; the entire skeleton of the zeppelin was visible, dark against an inferno of orange and red and yellow, hanging in the air for what seemed like an impossibly long time before drifting to the ground almost reluctantly. Little figures black against the snow and the fire came tottering or running from it, and witches flew down to help drag them away from the flames. Within a minute of the zeppelin's hitting the ground it was a mass of twisted metal, a pall of smoke, and a few scraps of fluttering fire.

But the soldiers on board, and the others too (though Lyra was too far away by now to spot Mrs Coulter, she knew she was there) wasted no time. With the help of the witches they dragged the machine-gun out and set it up, and began to fight in earnest on the ground.

"On," said Iorek. "They will hold out for a long time."

He roared, and a group of bears peeled away from the main group and attacked the Tartars' right flank. Lyra could feel his desire to be there among them, but all the time her nerves were screaming: On! On! and her mind was filled with pictures of Roger and Lord Asriel; and Iorek Byrnison knew, and turned up the mountain and away from the fight, leaving his bears to hold back the Tartars.

On they climbed. Lyra strained her eyes to look ahead, but not even Pantalaimon's owl-eyes could see any movement on the flank of the mountain they were climbing. Lord Asriel's sledge-tracks were clear, however, and Iorek followed them swiftly, loping through the snow and kicking it high behind them as he ran. Whatever happened behind now was simply that: behind. Lyra had left it. She felt she was leaving the world altogether, so remote and intent she was, so high they were climbing, so strange and uncanny was the light that bathed them.

"Iorek," she said, "will you find Lee Scoresby?"

"Alive or dead, I will find him."

"And if you see Serafina Pekkala…"

"I will tell her what you did."

"Thank you, Iorek," she said.

They spoke no more for some time. Lyra felt herself moving into a kind of trance beyond sleep and waking: a state of conscious dreaming, almost, in which she was dreaming that she was being carried by bears to a city in the stars.

She was going to say something about it to Iorek Byrnison, when he slowed down and came to a halt.

"The tracks go on," said Iorek Byrnison. "But I cannot."

Lyra jumped down and stood beside him to look. He was standing at the edge of a chasm. Whether it was a crevasse in the ice or a fissure in the rock was hard to say, and made little difference in any case; all that mattered was that it plunged downwards into unfathomable gloom.

And the tracks of Lord Asriel's sledge ran to the brink ... and on, across a bridge of compacted snow.

This bridge had clearly felt the strain of the sledge's weight, for a crack ran across it close to the other edge of the chasm, and the surface on the near side of the crack had settled down a foot or so. It might support the weight of a child: it would certainly not stand under the weight of an armoured bear.

And Lord Asriel's tracks ran on beyond the bridge and further up the mountain. If she went on, it would have to be by herself.

Lyra turned to Iorek Byrnison.

"I got to go across," she said. "Thank you for all you done. I don't know what's going to happen when I get to him. We might all die, whether I get to him or not. But if I come back I'll come and see you to thank you properly, King Iorek Byrnison."

She laid a hand on his head. He let it lie there and nodded gently.

"Goodbye, Lyra Silvertongue," he said.

Her heart thumping painfully with love, she turned away and set her foot on the bridge. The snow creaked under her, and Pantalaimon flew up and over the bridge, to settle in the snow on the far side and encourage her onwards. Step after step she took, and wondered with every step whether it would be better to run swiftly and leap for the other side, or go slowly as she was doing and tread as lightly as possible. Halfway across there came another loud creak from the snow; a piece fell off near her feet and tumbled into the abyss, and the bridge settled down another few inches against the crack.

She stood perfectly still. Pantalaimon was crouched leopard-formed ready to leap down and reach for her.

The bridge held. She took another step, then another, and then she felt something settling down below her feet and leapt for the far side with all her strength. She landed belly-down in the snow as the entire length of the bridge fell into the crevasse with a soft *whoosh* behind her.

Pantalaimon's claws were in her furs, holding tight.

After a minute she opened her eyes and crawled up away from the edge. There was no way back. She stood and raised her hand to the watching bear. Iorek Byrnison stood on his hind legs to acknowledge her, and then turned and made off down the mountain in a swift run to help his subjects in the battle with Mrs Coulter and the soldiers from the zeppelin.

Lyra was alone.

23

The Bridge to the Stars

*O*nce Iorek Byrnison was out of sight, Lyra felt a great weakness coming over her, and she turned blindly and felt for Pantalaimon.

"Oh, Pan, dear, I can't go on! I'm so frightened – and so tired – all this way, and I'm scared to death! I wish it was someone else instead of me, I do honestly!"

Her dæmon nuzzled at her neck in his cat-form, warm and comforting.

"I just don't know what we got to do," Lyra sobbed. "It's too much for us, Pan, we can't..."

She clung to him blindly, rocking back and forth and letting the sobs cry out wildly over the bare snow.

"And even if – if Mrs Coulter got to Roger first there'd be no saving him, because she'd take him back to Bolvangar, or worse, and they'd kill me out of vengeance... Why *do* they do these things to children, Pan? Do they all hate children so much, that they want to tear them apart like this? Why *do* they do it?"

But Pantalaimon had no answer; all he could do was hug her close.

Little by little, as the storm of fear subsided, she came to a sense of herself again. She was Lyra, cold and frightened by all means, but herself.

"I wish…" she said, and stopped. There was nothing that could be gained by wishing for it. A final deep shaky breath, and she was ready to go on.

The moon had set by now, and the sky to the south was profoundly dark, though the billions of stars lay on it like diamonds on velvet. They were outshone, though, by the Aurora, outshone a hundred times. Never had Lyra seen it so brilliant and dramatic; with every twitch and shiver, new miracles of light danced across the sky. And behind the ever-changing gauze of light that other world, that sunlit city, was clear and solid.

The higher they climbed, the more the bleak land spread out below them. To the north lay the frozen sea, compacted here and there into ridges where two sheets of ice had pressed together, but otherwise flat and white and endless, reaching to the Pole itself and far beyond, featureless, lifeless, colourless, and bleak beyond Lyra's imagination. To the east and west were more mountains, great jagged peaks thrusting sharply upwards, their scarps piled high with snow and raked by the wind into blade-like edges as sharp as scimitars. To the south lay the way they had come, and Lyra looked most longingly back, to see if she could spy her dear friend Iorek Byrnison and his troops; but nothing stirred on the wide plain. She was not even sure if she could see the burned wreckage of the zeppelin, or the crimson-stained snow around the corpses of the warriors.

Pantalaimon flew high, and swooped back to her wrist in his owl-form.

"They're just beyond the peak!" he said. "Lord Asriel's laid out all his instruments, and Roger can't move away –"

And as he said that, the Aurora flickered and dimmed, like an anbaric bulb at the end of its life, and then *went out* altogether. In the gloom, though, Lyra sensed the presence of the Dust, for the air seemed to be full of dark intentions, like the forms of thoughts not yet born.

In the enfolding dark she heard a child's cry:

"Lyra! Lyra!"

"I'm a-coming!" she cried back, and stumbled upwards, clambering, sprawling, struggling, at the end of her strength; but hauling herself on and further on through the ghostly-gleaming snow.

"Lyra! Lyra!"

"I'm nearly there," she gasped. "Nearly there, Roger!"

Pantalaimon was changing rapidly, in his agitation: lion, ermine, eagle, wildcat, hare, salamander, owl, leopard, every form he'd ever taken, a kaleidoscope of forms among the Dust –

"Lyra!"

Then she reached the summit, and saw what was happening.

Fifty yards away in the starlight Lord Asriel was twisting together two wires that led to his upturned sledge, on which stood a row of batteries and jars and pieces of apparatus, already frosted with crystals of cold. He was dressed in heavy furs, his face illuminated by the flame of a naphtha lamp. Crouching like the Sphinx beside him was his dæmon, her beautiful spotted coat glossy with power, her tail moving lazily in the snow.

In her mouth she held Roger's dæmon.

The little creature was struggling, flapping, fighting, one moment a bird, the next a dog, then a cat, a rat, a bird again, and calling every moment to Roger himself, who was a few yards off, straining, trying to pull away against the heart-deep tug, and crying out with the pain and the cold. He was calling his dæmon's name, and calling Lyra; he ran to

Lord Asriel and plucked his arm, and Lord Asriel brushed him aside. He tried again, crying and pleading, begging, sobbing, and Lord Asriel took no notice except to knock him to the ground.

They were on the edge of a cliff. Beyond them was nothing but a huge illimitable dark. They were a thousand feet or more above the frozen sea.

All this Lyra saw by starlight alone; but then, as Lord Asriel connected his wires, the Aurora blazed all of a sudden into brilliant life. Like the long finger of blinding power that plays between two terminals, except that this was a thousand miles high and ten thousand miles long: dipping, soaring, undulating, glowing, a cataract of glory.

He was *controlling* it...

Or leading power down from it; for there was a wire running off a huge reel on the sledge, a wire that ran directly upwards to the sky. Down from the dark swooped a raven, and Lyra knew it for a witch-dæmon. A witch was helping Lord Asriel, and she had flown that wire into the heights.

And the Aurora was blazing again.

He was nearly ready.

He turned to Roger and beckoned, and Roger helplessly came, shaking his head, begging, crying, but helplessly going forward.

"No! Run!" Lyra cried, and hurled herself down the slope at him.

Pantalaimon leapt at the snow leopard and snatched Roger's dæmon from her jaws. In a moment the snow leopard had leapt after him, and Pantalaimon let the other dæmon go, and both young dæmons, changing flick-flick-flick, turned and battled with the great spotted beast.

She slashed left-right with needle-filled paws, and her snarling roar drowned even Lyra's cries. Both children were fighting her, too; or fighting the forms in the turbid air, those dark intentions, that came thick and crowding down the streams of Dust –

And the Aurora swayed above, its continual surging flicker picking out now this building, now that lake, now that row of palm trees, so close you'd think that you could step from this world to that.

Lyra leapt up and seized Roger's hand.

She pulled hard, and then they tore away from Lord Asriel and ran, hand in hand, but Roger cried and twisted, because the leopard had his dæmon again; and Lyra knew that heart-convulsing pain and tried to stop –

But they couldn't stop.

The cliff was sliding away beneath them.

An entire shelf of snow, sliding inexorably down –

The frozen sea, a thousand feet below –

"LYRA!"

Heart-beats –

Tight-clutching hands –

And high above, the greatest wonder.

The vault of heaven, star-studded, profound, was suddenly pierced as if by a spear.

A jet of light, a jet of pure energy released like an arrow from a great bow, shot upwards. The sheets of light and colour that were the Aurora tore apart; a great rending, grinding, crunching, tearing sound reached from one end of the universe to the other; there was dry land in the sky –

Sunlight!

Sunlight shining on the fur of a golden monkey...

For the fall of the snow-shelf had halted; perhaps an unseen ledge had broken its fall; and Lyra could see, over the trampled snow of the summit, the golden monkey spring out of the air to the side of the leopard, and she saw the two dæmons bristle, wary and powerful. The monkey's tail was erect, the snow leopard's swept powerfully from side to side. Then the monkey reached out a tentative paw, the leopard lowered her head with a graceful sensual acknowledgement, they touched –

And when Lyra looked up from them, Mrs Coulter herself stood there, clasped in Lord Asriel's arms. Light played around them like sparks and beams of intense anbaric power. Lyra, helpless, could only imagine what had happened: somehow Mrs Coulter must have crossed that chasm, and followed her up here…

Her own parents, together!

And embracing so passionately: an undreamt-of thing.

Her eyes were wide. Roger's body lay dead in her arms, still, quiet, at rest. She heard her parents talking:

Her mother said, "They'll never allow it –"

Her father said, "Allow it? We've gone beyond being *allowed*, as if we were children. I've made it possible for anyone to cross, if they wish."

"They'll forbid it! They'll seal it off and excommunicate anyone who tries!"

"Too many people will want to. They won't be able to prevent them. This will mean the end of the Church, Marisa, the end of the Magisterium, the end of all those centuries of darkness! Look at that light up there: that's the sun of another world! Feel the warmth of it on your skin, now!"

"They are stronger than anyone, Asriel! You don't know –"

"I don't know? I? No one in the world knows better than I how strong the Church is! But it isn't strong enough for this. The Dust will change everything, anyway. There's no stopping it now."

"Is that what you wanted? To choke us and kill us all with sin and darkness?"

"I wanted to break out, Marisa! And I have done. Look, look at the palm trees waving on the shore! Can you feel that wind? A wind from another world! Feel it on your hair, on your face..."

Lord Asriel pushed back Mrs Coulter's hood and turned her head to the sky, running his hands through her hair. Lyra watched breathless, not daring to move a muscle.

The woman clung to Lord Asriel as if she were dizzy, and shook her head, distressed.

"No – no – they're coming, Asriel – they know where I've gone –"

"Then come with me, away and out of this world!"

"I daren't –"

"You? *Dare* not? Your child would come. Your child would dare anything, and shame her mother."

"Then take her and welcome. She's more yours than mine, Asriel."

"Not so. You took her in; you tried to mould her. You wanted her then."

"She was too coarse, too stubborn. I'd left it too late... But where is she now? I followed her footsteps up..."

"You want her, still? Twice you've tried to hold her, and twice she's got away. If I were her I'd run, and keep on running, sooner than give you a third chance."

His hands, still clasping her head, tensed suddenly and drew her towards him in a passionate kiss. Lyra thought it seemed more like cruelty than love, and looked at their dæmons, to see a strange sight: the snow leopard tense, crouching with her claws just pressing in the golden monkey's flesh, and the monkey relaxed, blissful, swooning on the snow.

Mrs Coulter pulled fiercely back from the kiss and said, "No, Asriel – my place is in this world, not that –"

"Come with me!" he said, urgent, powerful. "Come and work with me!"

"We couldn't work together, you and I."

"No? You and I could take the universe to pieces and put it together again, Marisa! We could find the source of Dust and stifle it for ever! And you'd like to be part of that great work; don't lie to me about it. Lie about everything else, lie about the Oblation Board, lie about your lovers – yes, I know about Boreal, and I care nothing – lie about the Church, lie about the child, even, but don't lie about what you truly want…"

And their mouths were fastened together with a powerful greed. Their dæmons were playing fiercely; the snow leopard rolled over on her back, and the monkey raked his claws in the soft fur of her neck, and she growled a deep rumble of pleasure.

"If I don't come, you'll try and destroy me," said Mrs Coulter, breaking away.

"Why should I want to destroy you?" he said, laughing, with the light of the other world shining around his head. "Come with me, work with me, and I'll care whether you live or die. Stay here, and you lose my interest at once. Don't flatter yourself that I'd give you a second's thought. Now stay and work your mischief in this world, or come with me."

Mrs Coulter hesitated; her eyes closed, she seemed to sway as if she were fainting; but she kept her balance and opened her eyes again, with an infinite beautiful sadness in them.

"No," she said. "No."

Their dæmons were apart again. Lord Asriel reached down and curled his strong fingers into the snow leopard's fur. Then he turned his back and walked up and away without another word. The golden monkey leapt into Mrs Coulter's arms, making little sounds of distress, reaching out to the snow leopard as she paced away, and Mrs Coulter's face was a mask of tears. Lyra could see them glinting; they were real.

Then her mother turned, shaking with silent sobs, and moved down the mountain and out of Lyra's sight.

Lyra watched her coldly, and then looked up towards the sky.

Such a vault of wonders she had never seen.

The city hanging there so empty and silent looked new-made, waiting to be occupied; or asleep, waiting to be woken. The sun of that world was shining into this, making Lyra's hands golden, melting the ice on Roger's wolfskin hood, making his pale cheeks transparent, glistening in his open sightless eyes.

She felt wrenched apart with unhappiness. And with anger, too; she could have killed her father: if she could have torn out his heart, she would have done so there and then, for what he'd done to Roger. And to her: tricking her – how *dare* he?

She was still holding Roger's body. Pantalaimon was saying something, but her mind was ablaze, and she didn't hear until he pressed his wildcat-claws into the back of her hand to make her. She blinked.

"What? What?"

"Dust!" he said.

"What are you talking about?"

"Dust. He's going to find the source of Dust and destroy it, isn't he?"

"That's what he said."

"And the Oblation Board and the Church and Bolvangar and Mrs Coulter and all, they want to destroy it too, don't they?"

"Yeah... Or stop it affecting people... Why?"

"Because if *they* all think Dust is bad, it must be good."

She didn't speak. A little hiccup of excitement leapt in her chest. Pantalaimon went on:

"We've heard them all talk about Dust, and they're so afraid of it, and you know what? We believed them, even though we could see that what they were doing was wicked and evil and wrong... We thought Dust must be bad too, because they were grown-up and they said so. But what if it isn't? What if it's –"

She said breathlessly, "Yeah! What if it's really *good*..."

She looked at him and saw his green wildcat-eyes ablaze with her own excitement. She felt dizzy, as if the whole world were turning beneath her.

If Dust were a *good* thing... If it were to be sought and welcomed and cherished...

"We could look for it too, Pan!" she said.

That was what he wanted to hear.

"We could get to it before he does," he went on, "and..."

The enormity of the task silenced them. Lyra looked up at the blazing sky. She was aware of how small they were, she and her dæmon, in comparison with the majesty and vastness of the universe; and of how little they knew, in comparison with the profound mysteries above them.

"We *could*," Pantalaimon insisted. "We came all this way, didn't we? We *could* do it."

"We'd be alone. Iorek Byrnison couldn't follow us and help. Nor could Farder Coram or Serafina Pekkala, or Lee Scoresby or no one."

"Just us, then. Don't matter. We're not alone, anyway; not like..."

She knew he meant *not like Tony Makarios; not like those poor lost dæmons at Bolvangar; we're still one being; both of us are one.*

"And we've got the alethiometer," she said. "Yeah. I reckon we've got to do it, Pan. We'll go up there and we'll search for Dust, and when we've found it we'll know what to do."

Roger's body lay still in her arms. She let him down gently.

"And we'll do it," she said.

She turned away. Behind them lay pain and death and fear; ahead of them lay doubt, and danger, and fathomless mysteries. But they weren't alone.

So Lyra and her dæmon turned away from the world they were born in, and looked towards the sun, and walked into the sky.

LANTERN SLIDES

Sometimes it becomes possible for an author to revisit a story and play with it, not to adapt it into another medium (it's not always a good idea for the original author to do that), nor to revise or 'improve' it (tempting though that is, it's too late: you should have done that before it was published, and your business now is with new books, not old ones). But simply to play.

And in every narrative there are gaps: places where, although things happened and the characters spoke and acted and lived their lives, the story says nothing about them. It was fun to visit a few of these gaps and speculate a little on what I might see there.

As for why I call these little pieces 'lantern slides', it's because I remember the wooden boxes my grandfather used to have, each one packed neatly with painted glass slides showing scenes from Bible stories or fairy tales or ghost stories or comic little plays with absurd-looking figures. From time to time he would get out the heavy old magic lantern and project some of these pictures on to a screen, and we would sit in the darkened room with the smell of hot metal and watch one scene succeeding another, trying to make sense of the narrative and wondering what St Paul was doing in the story of Little Red Riding Hood; because they never came out of the box in quite the right order.

I think it was my grandfather's magic lantern that Lord Asriel used in the second chapter of *Northern Lights*. Here are some lantern slides, and it doesn't matter what order they come in.

Philip Pullman
Oxford
February 2007

JORDAN COLLEGE, like a great clockwork mechanism with every part connected ultimately to every other, and all slowly and heavily ticking despite the fur of dust on every cog, the curtains of cobweb draped in every corner, the mouse-dirt, the insect-husks, the leaf-skeletons blown in every time the wind was in the east... Rituals and habits whose origins no one could remember, but which no one wanted to disturb. The great wheels and the small, the pins and the levers all performing their functions despite the wheezing and the creaking and the groaning of ancient timber. Sometimes the individual parts (a servant or a Scholar) forgot precisely what their function was in relation to the whole, but never that the whole had a function; and it was enough to do again what you had done yesterday, and every day before that, and trust to custom.

Lyra hanging about the Castle Mill boatyard. Each gyptian family had their particular patterns for decorating their boats, based on simple floral designs but becoming more and more complex and fanciful. Lyra watching old Piet van Poppel touching up his boat one day and laboriously copying the rose-and-lily pattern he was using, and then back in her room trying to paint it on her second-best dress before realizing that it would be better embroidered. And very soon after, having pricked her fingers countless times and snapped the threads and lost all patience with the task, throwing it away in disgust, and having to explain its absence to Mrs Lonsdale.

LEE SCORESBY, attracted north by the money being made in the gold rush and making none, but acquiring a balloon by chance in a card game. He was the lover of a witch from the Karelia region, briefly, but she was killed in battle – "She spoiled me for women younger'n three hundred"; but he had plenty of lovers all the same.

ASRIEL among the bears: "Iofur Raknison, I'm going to be entirely frank with you," followed by a string of confident and overbearing lies – had he noticed the bear-king's doll-dæmon, the clue that he was unbearlike enough to be tricked? Or was it just luck? – but he knew the bears well enough. He was very like his daughter.

MRS COULTER selected her lovers for their power and influence, but it did no harm if they were good-looking. Did she ever become fond of a lover? Not once. She could not keep her servants, either.

Lyra had a crush on Dick Orchard, the older boy who could spit further than anyone else. She would hang about the Covered Market gazing at him hopelessly, and cover her pillow with clumsy kisses, just to see what it felt like.

EVERY YEAR the Domestic Bursar at Jordan would send for Lyra – or have her tracked down and caught – and have a photogram taken. Lyra submitted indifferently, and scowled at the camera; it was just one of the things that happened. It didn't occur to her to ask where the pictures went. As a matter of fact they all went to Lord Asriel, but he would never have let her know.

BENNY the pastry cook at Jordan, whose dæmon was male, sitting in the warm cabin with his cousins the Costa family and listening to the story of how Lyra hijacked their boat, and their demand that someone discipline the brat. Their indignation was too much to bear without laughing. In return he told them about how she rescued a starling from the Kitchen cat, only for it to die anyway, and of how she plucked and gutted it clumsily and smuggled it into the great ovens, hoping to retrieve it when it was cooked. But the chef sent her packing, and in the bustle the starling was sent to table with the rest of the Feast, and was eaten with relish by the Master. The truth came out when the doctor had to be summoned to deal with the poor man's suffering. Lyra was unrepentant. "It wasn't for him," she said. "He's obviously got a delicate stomach. I could have eaten it." She was banned from the Kitchens for a term. "Seems to me we got off lightly," said Tony Costa.

SERAFINA PEKKALA on her cloud-pine would find a still field of air at night and listen to the silence. Like the air itself, which was never quite still, the silence was full of little currents and turbulence, of patches of density and pockets of attenuation, all shot through with darts and drifts of whispering that were made of silence themselves. It was as different from the silence of a closed room as fresh spring water is from stale. Later, Serafina realized that she was listening to Dust.